PRAI… ... S
BESTSELLING REAPERS MOTORCYCLE CLUB SERIES

"F… 1 and riveting characters, I fell in love from page one!"
— Evans, *New York Times* bestselling author of *Manwhore*

"S… isters the imagination, resulting in a thrill ride as raw
as … written." —*Publishers Weekly*

"J… le has a great voice in this genre . . . This is such a
we… torcycle club book." —*USA Today*

"I… book. It's raw, gritty, and incredibly sexy . . . Very real
an… ngerous, and I couldn't stop reading. The sexual ten-
sio… the charts . . . Prepare to get seriously hot under the
col… y, dark, realistic, and yet romantic." —*SeattlePI*

"V… akes no prisoners as she tempts readers back into [this]
da… volatile world . . . A potent mixture of love, anger, lust,
an… ption . . . Wylde's powerful voice and dynamic charac-
ter… his series fresh, addictive, and pure, unadulterated fun."
—*RT Book Reviews* (4 ½ Stars, 2014 Erotic Romance Winner)

"S… hot! . . . I continue to recommend this series as a real
pee… different kind of life." —Red Hot Books

"T… t balance of badass alpha hero, feisty kickass heroine,
sup… ot erotic sex scenes, real genuine emotions, and love
an… Dychood." —*Sinfully . . . Addicted to All Male Romance*
Pl…

"R… ntensely erotic." —The Book Pushers

REAPER'S FIRE

JOANNA WYLDE

B

BERKLEY BOOKS, NEW YORK

BERKLEY

An imprint of Penguin Random House LLC
375 Hudson Street, New York, New York 10014

This book is an original publication of Penguin Random House LLC.

Library of Congress Cataloging-in-Publication Data

Names: Wylde, Joanna, author.
Title: Reaper's fire / Joanna Wylde.
Description: Berkley trade paperback edition. | New York : Berkley Books,
2016. | Series: Reapers Motorcycle Club ; 5
Identifiers: LCCN 2016017627 (print) | LCCN 2016023013 (ebook) | ISBN
9781101988961 (softcover) | ISBN 9781101988978 ()
Subjects: LCSH: Motorcyclists—Fiction. | Motorcycle clubs—Fiction. |
Man-woman relationships—Fiction. | BISAC: FICTION / Romance /
Contemporary. | FICTION / Romance / General. | FICTION / Action &
Adventure. | GSAFD: Romantic suspense fiction. | Love stories.
Classification: LCC PS3623.Y544 R425 2016 (print) | LCC PS3623.Y544 (ebook) |
DDC 813/.6—dc23
LC record available at https://lccn.loc.gov/2016017627

PUBLISHING HISTORY
Berkley trade paperback edition / August 2016

PRINTED IN THE UNITED STATES OF AMERICA

10 9 8 7 6 5 4 3 2 1

Interior text design by Kristin del Rosario.

Penguin
Random
House

In loving memory of Allie Baker.

ACKNOWLEDGMENTS

Thank you very much to my editor, Cindy Hwang, and my agent, Amy Tannenbaum, for making this book possible.

Thanks also to all the people who helped with beta reading and editing, including Cara Carnes, Kylie Scott, Jen Frederick, Margarita, Danielle, and Kandace (please forgive me if I've left a name off—I always live in fear that I'll do that, but it doesn't mean you aren't appreciated!). Love to my Boozer Babes and Reanelle, Jessica, Suz, and Lori, and a special thanks to the Joanna Wylde Junkies reader group, who always brighten my day.

Finally, thank you to my family, especially my husband and kids, who have given so much to make my writing career possible.

I'd like to give a final shout-out to my Nana, who taught me that it's okay to have a picnic with paper plates and sterling silver, because why not?

PROLOGUE

TINKER

My stomach cramped again, and I shuddered. There was blood in the toilet. Not a lot of blood, but not a little bit, either. Big, stringy clots and bright red drips and . . . squeezing my eyes tight, I forced myself to ignore the pain, focusing on the phone in my hand instead.

"I'm sorry, Tinker, but Mr. Graham can't leave court right now."

Craig's always-smooth, professional voice cracked as he said the words, because we both knew what he was really saying: Mr. Graham *wouldn't* leave court, because winning his case was more important than his wife's health. Even Brandon's own paralegal was ashamed of him.

"Craig, I think I'm losing the baby. I need my husband. Did you tell him that?"

Silence.

"Tinker, he's not coming. I . . . I don't know what to say. You should probably get to a hospital. Do you have someone who can drive you?"

I looked down between my legs, watching as another drip of blood plopped into the bowl, creating a slightly darker spot in the pinkish water. It wasn't easy to see past my stomach—my once-flat belly was long gone. God, how had this happened?

"Yeah, I can call my friend Margarita," I said slowly. "Let Brandon know I'm going to the ER."

"All right," Craig said. "And, Tinker?"

"Yes?"

"I'm sorry."

My daughter, Tricia, was born still at eleven thirty a.m. She weighed just over two pounds and I named her for my mother.

The sun had gone down when someone knocked faintly on my hospital room door. I stared at the ceiling, ignoring the knock, wondering what I'd done wrong. I'd failed her . . . She was this tiny, precious thing, and I'd had one job—to carry her to term safely. What kind of woman couldn't even protect her own baby?

The knock came again, and Margarita stirred in the chair next to me.

Maybe it was Brandon.

He'd texted an hour ago, saying that he'd be down just as soon as he could. I didn't care. All that mattered was my baby girl. I'd wanted her so badly, even if Brandon didn't, and now she was dead. *Dead*. What a terrible, ugly word.

The door opened a crack, and a man peeked through.

"Can I come in?" Craig asked hesitantly. I nodded at Margarita, who waved him in. From the hallway I could hear a baby's cry— fucking sadists put me on the maternity ward, because apparently that was the best place for me medically. The sounds of other women's happiness twisted the knife in my empty stomach.

Tricia.

My heart had exploded with love when I'd seen the positive pregnancy test, and then exploded again the first time I'd felt her kick. Every day was a miracle, and I'd followed her development on the maternity calendar religiously.

I'd held her for two hours before they took her away.

"Tinker, I'm so sorry for your loss," Craig said, stepping inside. He carried a bundle of flowers. I stared at him blankly, wondering how the hell my husband's assistant could make it to the fucking hospital when Brandon couldn't. She'd been his daughter, too.

I hated him.

"Let me take those," Margarita said, and while her words were perfectly polite, her tone was just this side of menacing. Fair enough. Craig worked for Brandon and Brandon was the enemy. She despised him. Always had. Most of my friends from before our marriage did, something I really should've paid more attention to when he proposed. My dad always called me stubborn, said I had to figure things out the hard way, even as a little girl.

Guess he was right.

"Brandon—"

"Unless you're going to say Brandon isn't here because he was in a fatal car crash, don't bother," Margarita snapped. Craig looked between us, then his head dropped, shaking slowly.

"I'm so sorry," he repeated. "He was closing down his computer when I left."

We stared at him, the silence growing more uncomfortable, because what could you say? Craig flushed, and I took pity on him.

"It's not your fault," I said. "Do you want to sit down?"

"No," he replied, shuffling his feet. "I should get home. Mr. Graham has court first thing in the morning, and I need to go in early to finish prepping. Take care, Tinker. If there's any way we can help—I mean, the staff at the prosecutor's office—let me know. We're all thinking of you."

To hell with that. If they thought of me at all, it was because they pitied me. Fair enough, because I was pretty fucking pitiable. There was another knock at the door, then Brandon opened it, stepping into the room.

"Tinker?" he asked softly. He carried two dozen red roses, which meant he at least had the presence of mind to feel guilty. One dozen for romance, two for forgiveness. That time he'd cheated on me, I'd gotten diamond earrings.

I hated diamonds. Always had. Seemed like a husband should know that about his wife.

"Little late, aren't you?" Margarita asked, her voice like ice. Brandon stared her down.

"I'd like some time alone with Tinker."

"No fucking way—"

"It's all right," I told her, twisting my wedding set around on my finger. The engagement ring alone totaled nearly four carats, encrusted and bright. It wasn't the original, of course. Brandon liked to upgrade it every few years, because God knew his wife couldn't wear something simple. His family came from money—supposedly a lot of it, based on the prenup I'd signed—but I'd always thought it was tacky as hell. Margarita glanced toward me, and I read her look. *Are you sure you want him here?*

"It's fine," I told her. "Why don't you take Craig to find some coffee or something? He's probably had a long day."

"Coffee would be perfect," Craig blurted out, more rattled than I'd ever seen him. I had to give him credit—coming to the hospital couldn't have been easy. The flowers he'd brought probably cost ten bucks down at Pike Place, but I liked them better than Brandon's overpriced roses.

They were sincere.

Margarita and Craig walked out, leaving me alone with my husband.

"So," he said, setting the bouquet on the small table next to me, nearly knocking over my cup of water in the process. "How are you doing? I'm so sorry I couldn't come down. It was the motorcycle gang case, and you know how big a deal it is. Today we were scheduled to cross-examine a key witness, and I didn't feel comfortable letting anyone else take over. I would've come if I could."

Brandon gave me his politician's smile, the same smile he used to schmooze future donors for his campaign. He hadn't announced anything yet, but I'd known for a while that he planned to run for King County Prosecuting Attorney when the position opened up in two years. The current prosecutor would be retiring, and as head of the criminal division, Brandon was the logical successor.

"Sit down next to the bed," I said quietly. "We need to talk."

"Of course," he replied, all concern. The portrait of a loving husband. Too bad there wasn't a camera to capture the moment. Might make a good campaign poster, so long as they Photoshopped some color onto my cheeks.

"She was a little girl," I told him. I hadn't known ahead of time—I'd wanted it to be a surprise. "They don't know why she died. They said that sometimes late-term miscarriages are caused by genetic abnormalities."

He sighed heavily, then looked down, shaking his head. God, but the man was a good actor. Guess that was my consolation—I wasn't the only one who'd fallen for his shit. There was a reason he always won with juries.

People *wanted* to believe him.

"It's probably for the best," he said slowly. "She wouldn't have been healthy, and you have so much to handle already. Once the campaign starts—"

I studied the man I'd slept with for ten years, ignoring the drone of his voice. There was just the hint of a bald spot on the top of his head. Nothing serious, but I knew he'd met with a doctor to discuss hair plugs. Dreamily, I pictured taking my big chef's knife and chopping it down through his skull. Bone was hard, but I kept my knives very, very sharp.

God, but I was a fucked-up excuse for a human being.

"It's over," I said shortly, sliding my rings off my finger. Brandon's head jerked up, and he stared at me, his expression genuine for once.

"What?"

I held the sparkling jewelry out toward him, but he didn't take it.

"It's over," I repeated. "This whole marriage was a mistake and I'd like you to leave now. My lawyer will be in touch—I'll ask Smith for a referral. I think the faster we finalize things, the better."

"Baby, I'm so sorry," he said, and while the words were apologetic, I could see the little vein in his forehead starting to pulse. Brandon was angry. Good.

I was angry, too.

"Get out of my room," I added, my voice low but fierce, my free hand rubbing across my empty stomach.

"Tinker, they've obviously given you drugs for the pain—you're not thinking right. We need to talk this through. You'll see—"

"Oh, I *see* already. Your wife was in the hospital, your child was dying, and you cared more about your conviction rate than our survival. I think you've made your priorities clear."

For once—maybe for the first time ever—Brandon didn't know what to say. He just sat there, staring at me like a big, dumb slug. Satisfying as that was, it wasn't enough. He needed to go away and never come back. Yup, that was the solution . . . The marriage was over. I should have felt liberated, but I couldn't feel anything at all. Probably for the best. Grief yawned ahead of me, a black pit I wasn't sure I'd ever manage to escape. Wasn't sure I wanted to.

"Get out."

"What?"

"Get. Out," I snarled, sudden anger uncurling and exploding through me. Guess I *could* still feel something after all. "And take your fucking rings with you. If I have to look at your smug, disgusting face for another second I'm going to kick your ass."

"Tinker, you need to settle down," he said firmly, frowning like a stern father. But I already had a dad, and he was better than this man would ever be. Brandon reached for the call button. "Let's talk to the nurse. You obviously need a sedative or—*oww!* What the fuck, Tinker?"

It took two hands to raise his massive, overpriced bundle of roses high enough to hit him again, this time across his picture-perfect, spray-tanned face.

"Get out!" I shrieked. Brandon ducked, backing away. I managed to get in one more whack before he got out of range.

"Tinker, you have to settle down!" he shouted. I heard running footsteps in the hall. "Tinker, please—you aren't thinking straight."

"I'm thinking straighter than I have in years!" I shouted back, throwing the bundle of flowers after him. "Get the fuck out of my room and get the fuck out of my life! And take your fucking piece of shit diamonds with you, too, asshole!"

Digging through the covers, I found the rings, pitching them toward my future ex as hard as I could.

"Owww!" he shouted, clutching at his face. A few drops of blood hit the floor. "Jesus Christ, Tinker. What's wrong with you?"

"What's going on?" the nurse asked, pushing the door open. She stared at us, wide-eyed. "Security!"

Things moved fast after that.

As the guards came, I struggled out of the bed, screaming at Brandon like a banshee the entire time. He seemed stunned, completely unable to comprehend what'd just happened, which I thought was fucking hysterical. Brandon's ego had always operated on the too-big-to-fail theory.

Margarita rushed in, catching my arm and pulling me back toward the bed.

"Calm down or they'll shoot you full of happy drugs," she whispered in my ear. My chest heaved as I glared at Brandon, showing him every bit of my utter hate and anguish.

"I don't want to calm down," I hissed, wondering if I could launch myself forward and scratch his eyes out before they caught me.

"Yes, you do," she said. "Because otherwise he'll think he's the victim here. Don't give him that. Knowing your luck, he'll press charges."

A snort of laughter burst out of me, because wouldn't that be just like Brandon? Not that he would . . . Not really. That would be far too embarrassing. Couldn't risk scuffing up that precious image of his, now, could we?

I looked up to find the guards escorting him out of the room. The nurse was pushing me toward the bed and I did what she said, because everything else aside, I really didn't want to get sedated or whatever. She helped me sit down, her face firm but compassionate.

"I know this has been a terrible day—probably the worst of your life," she said. "But you can't physically attack people or we'll have to restrain you. Would you like me to call a counselor?"

"I'm sorry," I told her, which was a damned lie. "And no, I don't want a counselor. Not right now, at least."

"That was her husband," Margarita said. "He couldn't be bothered to leave work earlier when she was losing the baby."

The nurse's eyes widened, and she glanced back toward Brandon. "Seriously?"

"Seriously," Margarita confirmed, her face fierce. The nurse shook her head and looked at me again.

"Well, whatever he did, we can't have people fighting in the rooms," she said. "Is this going to be a problem?"

I shook my head. "No, no more problems."

The nurse nodded, then gave me another sharp look.

"So you're done with him? For real?"

I didn't have to think twice before answering.

"Yeah, I'm definitely done with him."

"Good for you, sweetie. You deserve better."

Damn straight I do. A lot better.

CHAPTER ONE

EIGHTEEN MONTHS LATER
HALLIES FALLS, WASHINGTON STATE
GAGE

*Handyman needed for family-owned building—free rent in
exchange for work. Call Tinker Garrett or inquire inside
Tinker's Teahouse, Antiques & Fine Chocolates for more
information.*

I ripped off one of the little paper tabs with a phone number on
it, glancing in the shop window. No signs of life, but the sign said
"Open."

Pulling a worn bandanna out of my back pocket, I wiped my forehead, cursing the fucking heat. Hottest summer on record, and Hallies
Falls was even worse than back home in Coeur d'Alene. Couldn't even
sleep at night because the piece of shit AC couldn't keep up in my
craptastic hotel room. Glancing at the sign again, I figured I might as
well go for the job. It'd get me out of the damned hotel and provide
good cover at the same time. Anything was a step up at this point.

A string of bells jingled as I opened the shop door. Very old-
school, which I guess made sense because the whole shop was like
stepping through a time warp to the eighteen hundreds. There were

fancy little shelves holding fancy little teacups. Each of the windows held a fully set table with cloth napkins, shiny silver, and a hundred more tiny, breakable things that would probably shatter if I looked at them too hard. The battered wooden floor had been scattered with old-fashioned floor rugs to create separate display areas, along with strategically placed side tables and even a couple of old dressers. It was clever, although how the hell it made enough money to keep the doors open was beyond me—couldn't be much market for specialty tea shit in a town like Hallies Falls.

Across the back of the shop was a glassed-in case full of chocolates, along with an old-fashioned cash register straight out of *Little House on the Prairie*. I walked over to it.

"Anyone here?" I asked, frowning. There was a door behind the counter that opened into what looked like a small kitchen in the back. I heard a strange, shuffling sound and reached for my gun automatically, then jerked my hand away. *Fuck.* I'd been jumpy as hell ever since I pulled into this stupid town. Those instincts might keep me alive, but they'd also sink me if I gave away too much.

"Be with you in a sec," said a sexy, drawling voice from behind the counter. A voice that oozed smoke and heat and warm darkness, putting my cock on high alert. "I was just checking the temperature in the candy case."

Long, slender fingers tipped with bright red polish reached up to grip the countertop for support as the hottest, most fuckable woman I'd ever met in my life stood up and smiled at me. Yeah, this had been a bad idea. I'd seen Tinker Garrett in the distance once already—my club brother, Painter, and I had checked her while she was unloading the trunk of a sweet, cherry-red Mustang convertible a couple days earlier. I'd known then she was exactly my type, but now that I'd looked at her up close? Fuckin' hell . . . I'd managed a goddamned strip club for two years, but this bitch put all those girls to shame and she hadn't even taken off her clothes yet. An image of her naked and sprawled across one of those prissy little tables filled my mind. I had to hold back a shudder.

Walk out—this isn't going to end well.

"Hi, I'm Tinker," she said, reaching up to wipe the sweat off her forehead. That set her tits in motion, and for an instant I blanked out entirely, wondering if her nipples were pink or brown. Pink, I decided. Her skin was super pale and white, like creamy . . . Fuck, I didn't know. Like something creamy and lickable.

She had black hair with bangs, and she wore this tight little top that somehow managed to look prim and seductive at the same time. Didn't hurt that her boobs were absolutely perfect. High and pointed and big enough to overflow in my hands while I held them.

Throw in a pair of puffy red lips designed to suck cock and wide, green eyes with thick black lashes?

Yeah, I'd hit that. Early and often.

"Can I help you?" she asked, and I reached across the counter, wiping away a small smudge of dirt on her cheek. She flinched, and I caught hold of myself. *Great, scare the shit out of her, why don't you?*

"Sorry," I said. "You've got dirt on your face."

She gave a bright laugh. "I've probably got dirt all over. It's one of those grubby, sticky kind of days, you know?"

Sticky? In her mouth it was a dirty word, and I wanted to make her stickier. My eyes crawled across her body, watching as a bead of sweat rolled down her neck and into her cleavage. I licked my lips. Tinker cleared her throat, gently reminding me that we were in the middle of a conversation.

"You don't exactly look like one of my regular customers, so I'm assuming you're here about the job?" she asked, smiling at me. By then I'd half forgotten why I'd walked into the store—she was that fuckable. Tiny and pretty, but still round in all the right places. Despite the mess, she radiated class—I wanted to drag her down into the dark with me.

Swallowing, I managed not to reach down and give my dick the adjusting it seriously needed, which took real willpower.

"Yeah, according to the sign, you've got an apartment available in exchange for work. Still open?"

"Yes," she said, and I swear her eyes dimmed a little. "But I need to get these chocolates into the basement before they melt.

The AC wasn't working when I came in this morning. The temperature's rising"—*not the only thing*—"and I can't afford to lose product. Can you come back in an hour or so?"

"You call anyone about the AC yet?" I asked, realizing this could be the perfect in. She frowned, those gorgeous lips pouting as I considered sucking them into my mouth. Maybe chewing on them for a while. My dick surged—apparently we were in agreement.

"No," she told me. "I mean, I tried. But the closest repair place is in Omak, and the guy isn't available for another week at least. Not much around here, you know?"

No shit.

"Let me take a look at it," I suggested. This really was a perfect opportunity to get in with her, build up my cover . . . Great, now I was thinking about getting *into* her. Thank fuck for the counter between us, because my cock was rock hard. "I'm Cooper, by the way. Cooper Romero."

"Tinker Garrett," she replied, offering her hand across the glass. Her fingers were delicate and tiny, but not fragile. I felt the strength in her grip, and she wasn't afraid to look me in the eye. "Nice to meet you. Have you done maintenance work before?"

I considered the question, deciding not to lie more than was necessary—it's always the extra lies that cause trouble. Keep it simple and don't volunteer information.

"Not formally, no," I admitted. "But I've done a bit of everything over the years. Generally pretty good at figuring things out, if I've got enough time, and it sounds like this isn't an hourly job anyway. Not so much a cash operation?"

She flushed. I should get the hell out of here—I already had a job to do, and it didn't involve banging Tinker Garrett. She tugged her hand free and reached up, catching her black hair and pulling it back into a ponytail, jiggling her boobs in the process.

So much for doing the right thing.

She caught my look and blushed, looking uncomfortable for the first time since I'd walked in. "Stupid hair—it's hot in here, and I couldn't stand it on my neck for another minute. You're right—the job is off the books. I know that's—"

"No worries," I said, offering her a sly smile. She flushed harder, and I felt a surge of triumph because I wasn't the only one feeling it. "I'm just a guy lookin' for a place to sleep. How many hours a week do you need me to work?"

"Um, twenty?" she asked, turning it into a question. That was perfect—enough work to make me look busy and explain my presence, but not enough to get in the way of my real job. "But I haven't even had you fill out an application yet, and I need to put away the chocolate."

"Show me the AC," I replied, figuring I might as well take charge. "I'll look it over and see if I can fix it while you do that. Sound good?"

She glanced around, and I had to bite back a snort of laughter. She obviously didn't feel comfortable giving me free rein of the place, but at the same time she wanted that AC fixed. Bad. Couldn't blame her, either. Shop felt like it was a hundred and ten in there, and the day wasn't over yet.

"It's up on the roof," she said finally. "Come on through the back. I'll show you where the stairs are."

Excellent, although as I followed her up the stairs—eyes glued to her ass—I couldn't help but think she was a little too trusting for her own good. Any other guy might take advantage of the situation. I sure as hell wanted to.

Focus, I reminded myself. *She's not the target.*

Fucking shame.

An hour later my dick had calmed down, leaving me alone with a piece of shit air conditioner that should've been put out of its misery ten years ago. The old building was three stories tall, with a fake facade and a black tar roof that had to be at least a thousand degrees, maybe more. Either way, it was so hot that melted tar had coated my knees, ruining my favorite pair of jeans.

Christ, but I was a moron.

Yes, I needed cover to stay in Hallies Falls, and the thought of working for Tinker Garrett appealed greatly. But there were less complicated covers that didn't involve broiling myself alive on a roof that screamed "structurally unsound." Fucking AC unit wasn't much better. Damned thing was held together with duct tape—okay, that wasn't entirely fair . . . some of it was electrical tape—and I couldn't figure out how it'd kept running this long. My best theory was animal sacrifice. I'd found five dead squirrels inside. Little fuckers had chewed through the wiring, probably in some kind of satanic ritual.

Now their fluffy little corpses had bloated in the sun—just waiting to explode all over me—because kneeling in hot tar wasn't shitty enough. I needed to cut my losses and the get the fuck out of there. Life was too damned short.

"Hey there."

I turned to find Tinker stepping out onto the roof from the raised stairwell. She walked toward me, hips swaying in her cropped jeans with the cuffs rolled up. She'd tied a red bandanna around her head, and with her fitted shirt and generous curves she looked just like a Harley pinup girl.

A pinup girl carrying a tall glass of iced tea.

"Thought you could use a drink," she said, raising a hand to shade her eyes from the sun. I took the glass, chugging down half of it in one swallow, then considered pouring the rest of it over her boobs, because God made those tits to be seen and appreciated.

Instead I thanked her.

"So how's the AC looking?" she asked, catching her bottom lip and chewing on it mournfully.

"Squirrels ate your wiring," I said bluntly. "I can probably get it running again, but it needs to be replaced."

"It's August already," she replied, sighing heavily. A better man would've made sympathetic noises, but I didn't give a shit about her AC. I was too busy imagining her tongue licking my cock, because what can I say? I've always been a simple man with simple needs.

"You think you can keep it running for another couple weeks? That'll give me enough time to figure out what to do."

Christ I wanted to fuck her. Seriously, it was like the bitch had been made for me, all perfect and put together but just a little dirty. Sweaty.

Small enough I could control her every move if I wanted to, but lush and soft and—

Opt out, asshole. You don't want a complication like this. Tell her you changed your mind about the job.

"I'll need to get some parts in Omak," I said instead. "I already called to check. Trip should take an hour and a half, maybe a little longer, which means I'll still have plenty of daylight to finish the repair. Assuming I've got the job, that is."

She looked up me, green eyes wide with relief, although she was trying not to show it. I had the job, and we both knew it. Too easy.

"Cooper Romero . . . How long have you been in town?"

"Less than a week."

"And how long are you planning to stick around?"

"For a while," I said, which was a damned lie. I had a mission to accomplish—then it was home to Coeur d'Alene, because fuck this little shithole of a town. "My old lady and I decided to end things. I needed to get away for a while, and wanted to be somewhere I wouldn't run into her but close enough to still see my kids."

Her eyes caught mine.

"Boys or girls?"

"Boys," I said slowly, knowing I had her. "One's ten and the other's twelve."

"You must miss them," she said softly. Um, yeah. I'd totally miss them if they existed. *You're a fucking asshole, lying to her like that.*

Hell, at least I was consistent.

"Every day. If you want me to get that part, I'd better leave soon."

She glanced back down at the ancient unit and nodded her head.

"That'd be great. How much cash do you think you'll need?"

"Shouldn't be too much—it's more labor than anything. I'll bring you a receipt."

• • •

Fixing the AC took longer than I'd expected. It was nearly seven that night before I screwed the access panel back on, packed up my tools, and started down the stairs to the shop, reeking of sweat and tar. My jeans were ruined, but I'd stripped off my shirt early on, so it was okay. It'd still been hot as fuck up there, but at least I'd been able to catch the occasional breeze on the roof. I felt tired in a good way—not so much that I wouldn't be able to make my assigned "date" that night, but enough that I felt like I'd accomplished something. Sheer boredom had been the hardest part of the last couple days. You can only sit in a hotel room for so long before losing your fucking mind.

The stairs landed in a narrow hallway outside the main shop. There was a small bathroom in the back—shared with the storefront next door—although it looked to me like nobody had used the space in a long time. I stepped inside to clean myself up. Pointless. I'd have to pick up some Orange GOOP on the way home, otherwise I'd never get this shit off.

Of course, I had a feeling my real target was into dirty hands. Not that I knew Talia Jackson all that well, but I'd seen enough of her in action over the past week to get a feel for her. She was young, stupid, and had a crazy sense of entitlement, all because her brother—Marsh—was the president of the local motorcycle club. Talia was everything I hated in a woman, but the little bitch was my ticket into the Nighthawk Raiders.

None of this should've been necessary. They were nothing more than a support club, and they owed a percentage of everything they earned to the Reapers MC—a percentage that had fallen by more than half in the last three months.

Fucking traitors.

Marsh was up to something. It was my job to catch the bastard, which meant that tonight—instead of bending Tinker Garrett over her prissy little counter and banging her until she forgot her own name—I was stuck meeting Talia and her girl posse at a bar.

Christ, I might even have to dance.

The irony wasn't lost on me—how many dancers had I hired over the years? So many I couldn't remember. Now I'd be the one performing for a woman, only I wouldn't be getting paid. I washed as best I could, scrubbing my face and using my shirt as a towel. Then I tucked it into my back pocket and pushed through the door into Tinker's little kitchen. No sign of her, but I heard music playing softly in the main shop. Where the hell had she gone?

I pushed through the kitchen door and looked down. Ah shit. Tinker was on her back on the tile behind the counter, one leg resting flat, the other propped up and bent at the knee. Her arm was over her eyes and I couldn't quite tell if she was asleep.

It would take all of thirty seconds to get her shorts off and shove my dick deep inside—she'd never know what hit her. Just like that, I was rock hard and ready for action. Whipping my shirt out of my back pocket, I let it dangle across the front of my jeans. Otherwise I'd give her an eyeful.

Jesus Christ, but I was a masochist, because despite how complicated this was starting to feel, I couldn't regret answering her ad.

Not even a little bit.

TINKER

It was almost seven that evening when I felt the AC kick back on. I'd been lying on my back on the (relatively) cool tile floor behind the counter, staring up at the pressed-tin ceiling and trying to remember why I hadn't already moved back to Seattle.

In Seattle it rained.

Cool breezes blew off the bay and the lush greenery covered everything with its shaded canopy. People didn't really need air-conditioning, but if they happened to have it and it broke, there were lots of repairmen available.

Of course, Seattle also had Brandon. Not only that, my dad didn't want to move, and I'd come to realize I couldn't leave him here alone. It wasn't safe for him, not since Mom died.

Ugh.

At least the AC was working again, blowing down from the ceiling vent across my sweaty body, reminding me that while the world might not be crawling with perfect men, at least there were still a few useful ones running around. Cooper Romero was a keeper, and it had nothing to do with how sexy he was . . . although the fact that he was sex on a stick—make that sex *with* a stick—didn't exactly diminish his appeal.

When I'd dragged him up to the black tar roof to show him the ancient AC, I'd expected him to make a run for it. Any sensible man would. Instead, he'd spent the whole afternoon busting his ass to save my chocolates—*Oh God, I wish that were code for something more exciting*—officially qualifying him as a superhero in my book.

As for me, there wasn't much I could do once I got all the sweets safely downstairs into the basement. There weren't any customers walking in off the street, and seeing as I couldn't make or ship candy in a 102-degree shop, I'd alternated between attempting to read a book, looking over orders I couldn't fulfill on my laptop, and bringing Cooper glasses of iced tea. I'd been nervous around him at first, but you can only stay nervous for so long when you're sweating like a pig—there's a certain freedom in knowing you look like hell and there's no saving your hair. I'd thrown my arm across my eyes in a pathetic attempt to block out reality toward the end.

When cold air started flowing into the room, I could've cried with relief. He'd never had a chance to fill out the application form, and I'd long since decided it didn't matter. Unless he was an ax murderer, I'd give him the apartment and the job.

Might give it to him even if he was, to be honest.

"It's working again," Cooper announced, and I jerked, startled. Shit, had I fallen asleep? Opening my eyes, I looked up to find him standing over me. Dear God in heaven—that was one hell of a bare chest.

Holy. Shit.

I'd taken note of his build when he first walked in the shop, but everything under his shirt had been theoretical. Now there was six-foot-plus of raw sex appeal right there, all sweaty and sculpted and . . . well, let's just say I'd be stopping off on the way home to pick up some fresh batteries.

That's when the situation hit me—Cooper Romero was the hottest man I'd met in forever, and he'd just found me lying on the floor in my own sweat and filth like a dog. Typical luck. I pretended I wasn't totally embarrassed (I was) and was not in the least bit freaked out by how unspeakably attractive this guy was. Okay, "attractive" wasn't quite the right word, because it implied a certain level of polish and class that just didn't fit Cooper at all.

Brandon was *attractive*.

Cooper?

I'd lick him all over and massage his butt if he asked. He stared down at me, his eyes carefully blank, making it very clear he wasn't asking. *Story of my fucking life.* Sitting up, I pushed myself to my feet without bothering to dust off. Lost cause at this point.

"Not sure how much life the AC has left," he said slowly. "I managed to get it going, but fixing it right would cost more than it's worth and then some."

Of course it would.

"I just need to get through the summer," I told him, wiping a finger under my eye. My perfectly applied, vintage-style makeup had melted, leaving me with a clown face. Fortunately I'd (mostly) given up on caring three hours ago, right around the time I'd discovered the floor tiles were cooler than the rest of the room. "After that, I'll worry about the furnace and by next summer I might not even be here anymore."

"Really?" he asked, cocking a brow. "You selling out?"

"Not sure," I told him. "I'm not thinking that far ahead right now. Things are very iffy with my dad . . . I think he's got some—"

No. I couldn't say it. Saying it out loud made it too real, plus the last thing I needed were a bunch of rumors flying around town. So far we'd kept Dad's situation mostly to family and friends.

"Tinker?"

Shaking myself, I smiled at him. "Thank you so much for fixing that. I'm not even sure what I would've done—I can't afford to miss a week's worth of orders. Not only would it put me behind, it would burn my customers."

He nodded, studying me thoughtfully. God, he really was beautiful . . . Nothing like Brandon's polished sophistication. No, Cooper gave off more of a warrior-tossing-you-over-his-fearless-steed kind of vibe. Yeah, like that would end well, because my track record with men was so fucking perfect, right?

Pull your head out of the gutter. He probably has a girlfriend.

At least I could finally lock up this hellhole of a shop and get a shower.

"Thank you so much—you have no idea how much I appreciate it."

"No, but the whole throwing yourself at my feet thing was a subtle hint," he said, and I realized he was teasing me. Was he flirting? I couldn't decide if that kicked ass or scared the shit out of me.

"Anyway, it's getting late," I told him, feeling suddenly awkward. "I'm going to grab some dinner down the street, and then I could take you over and show you the apartment."

A small, knowing smile crossed his face, and I realized he thought I was hitting on him.

"No," I said quickly, mortified. "I wasn't asking you out. Omigod, this is weird."

"What, you aren't turned on by a man who smells like old socks?" he asked lightly, raising his arm and giving a sniff. He was joking, but the sweat wasn't a turnoff. Nope. Not even a little bit. "If that's not enough for you, the roof tar on my ass should be a big attraction."

Closing my eyes, I bit back a groan. He started laughing. Not in a cruel way, but companionably, which I guess made sense because both of us were disgusting as hell. Of course, now I wanted to check out his ass, but I managed to keep my eyes on target (mostly) when I answered him.

"Well, it's sexy but I'll manage to control myself somehow. I do want to grab dinner, though, and we need to figure out the apartment details."

"I'll take the place, doesn't matter what it is," he replied. "I'm in a hotel and it's getting old. I'd love to move in on Sunday, but I can't go look at it right now—gotta get my ass cleaned up. Meeting up with someone later."

Of course he was, because men who looked like Cooper didn't spend Friday nights alone.

"Sounds great," I told him, refusing to show any disappointment. "Just text me when you're ready, and I'll get you the key."

He opened his mouth to say something, but a sudden pounding against the locked shop door caught us both off guard. I spun around to find Talia Jackson glaring at me through the glass. Talia and three of her skankier friends, including Sadie Baxter, a girl I used to babysit when I was in college.

A girl who was now twenty.

Damn.

"Cooper!" Talia shouted. "What the fuck are you doing?"

I glanced at my new handyman, startled. Talia Jackson and her brother, Marsh, were two of the nastiest people I'd ever met. Marsh was president of the local motorcycle gang, a group called the Nighthawk Raiders. The club had been around most of my life, but it was only in recent years that they'd turned really bad. I mean, they were never the kinder, gentler sort of bikers, but I'd never been actively afraid when I'd heard a motorcycle, either.

Now? Let's just say we'd all gotten a little edgy.

"That's my girl," Cooper said, and something deep down inside of me died a little. Of course he'd go for someone like Talia. She might have the heart of a deranged circus clown—you know, the kind that survives by eating the souls of innocent children—but she was hot.

Really hot.

Not only that, she was slutty, and while I wasn't into the whole slut-shaming thing (like I had room to judge after the bachelorette party debacle . . . ugh), I wasn't naive enough to think he was attracted to her personality. Cooper Romero might have a sweet smile, and he'd fixed my AC, but now I had proof positive that he'd never be into a girl like me.

Specifically, a grown-up with curves.

All righty, then. Probably for the best anyway.

"Just a sec!" I called to her, determined to take the high road, then I grabbed my keys so I could open the door. She pushed inside with her posse, and I do mean *pushed*. Little bitch shoved me so hard I nearly knocked over the display of antique Russian teacups my mother had lovingly collected. (So far as I knew, she'd never sold a single one of them, but it'd made her happy.)

"Careful," I warned, and Talia turned on me.

"What did you just say to me?"

"Babe, let's talk," Cooper said, catching her arm and pulling her into his body. She squealed, going from aggressive to flirty in an instant.

"You're all sweaty. It's *sooo* disgusting."

I noted she wasn't trying to get away. Cooper smiled down at her, a hint of something feral in his eyes. Yeah, okay—whatever smile he'd been giving me, it hadn't held any of that kind of intensity.

Yours truly was officially chopped liver.

"I was just about to head out and grab a shower," he told her. "Wanna come with me?"

She pouted. "I can't. The girls and I need to get fixed up. I'll see you at the bar, though, right?"

He looked down at her, offering a sexy, indulgent smile. "Can't wait."

"Perfect," she said, reaching around to grab his ass for a quick squeeze. Then she turned and strutted back out without a word to me, her gaggle of girls following like well-trained geese. Sadie gave a little finger wave on the way. The door closed behind them with a cheerful little jingle, and I wondered why the hell I even bothered with Hallies Falls.

I missed Seattle.

So what if it had Brandon? I could drown him in Lake Washington. Problem solved.

"Sorry about that—Talia is a little high-strung," Cooper said.

"Oh, I know all about her," I replied, hoping I didn't sound as catty as I felt. Cooper didn't seem to notice.

"I'm new to town, but she's been showing me around," Cooper continued, stepping over to stand in front of me, hands shoved deep in his front pockets. "I should get going."

"Of course—don't let me keep you. What time do you think you'll be in touch tomorrow?"

"Afternoon work?"

"No problem. Looking forward to hearing from you."

He nodded and pushed through the door, walking down the street without a second look back. I locked up behind him, wondering why all the hottest guys were douchebags. Not that Cooper had acted like a douche, but he had to be my age or older—late thirties—and Talia was the same age as Sadie. She was also a raging bitch. There was only one reason a man like him would date a girl like that, and it had nothing to do with personality or character.

Cooper Romero might be beautiful, but obviously he was shallow. Suppose it was too much to hope for a man who could fix an air conditioner and have a soul at the same time.

Pity.

CHAPTER TWO

GAGE

"Gonna be a long night," I told Reese "Picnic" Hayes through the phone. I'd been checking in with my club's president at least once a day, on the theory that if I didn't call, he might send someone to save me. Now I was leaning against the side of the diner where I'd parked my bike before going in for lunch. I'd walked over to check out Tinker's store afterward on a whim. Now I had a job and a cover. Make that a job, a cover, and balls bluer than a Smurf in the dead of winter. "Talia ambushed me with her girlfriends, crawled all over me. Been working all day and I smell like dead squirrel, so I guess that means we've hooked her. No other reason I can see a woman comin' near me right now."

Picnic laughed. "That was the goal, right?"

"Yeah," I replied sourly. "You owe me a shitload of beer when I get back, brother. Gonna have to triple-wrap my dick before sticking it in a snatch like that."

"What's the problem?" he asked. "I saw her picture—she's hot, even if she *is* a bitch. Since when do you care about their personalities?"

Frowning, I glared at my bike. It looked weird without my Reapers whips hanging off the handlebars. I'd stripped off anything that might identify me as a club member. It felt wrong. Everything about this operation was wrong on some level, starting with the fact that I'd been stupid enough to volunteer.

Yes, I'd been sick of managing the Reapers MC's strip club and I'd wanted a change of pace. But I'd also wanted to leave the crazy bitch-drama behind. Instead it looked like I'd walked right into the queen bitch's nest.

"Getting laid is great," I replied slowly. "But this one is nasty. Too young for me, and boring. Never heard someone talk so much without saying a goddamn thing."

"Thought you liked the young ones," Pic commented dryly.

He was right, but a few minutes talking to Tinker had reminded me how nice it was to hang with a more mature woman for once. She'd been into me, but she'd been all business, too—no bullshit games . . . just amazing curves combined with hard work and a brain.

I'd taken a few minutes to stalk her on my phone in between clearing out squirrel corpses.

Impressive woman. The tea shop portion of her business was obviously just a storefront, with the bulk of her operation centered on gourmet chocolates she made herself. They were sold in shops all over Seattle, Tacoma, and Portland. So far as I could tell, business was booming.

Talia, on the other hand, didn't do any real work at all. Not only that, the little twat was skinny and skanky and had a mouth on her that made *me* flinch, which was sayin' a lot.

"Talia isn't just young," I said. "The bitch never shuts up, and all she does is whine. Everyone's out to get her, nobody understands her, and her shit doesn't stink. She'd last maybe five minutes out at the Armory before her ass got banned permanently. I cannot fucking believe that the Nighthawk brothers have put up with her this long."

"Well, take her out tonight and see if you can get an intro to one of them. Better yet, get an invite to their clubhouse and see for yourself what's really happening out there. They're bringing in new brothers like crazy right now—standards are probably low enough to let someone like you through the door."

"Usually I'd take that as an insult," I replied, snorting. "But I probably deserve it right now. You'll never guess what I spent my day doing."

"Knitting," he said flatly. "I think we all know you have a secret love of the womanly arts. I'm assuming you're working on a nice motorcycle cozy for my Christmas present? You know, something to go with the embroidered Reapers pillow you gave me last year?"

I closed my eyes, counting to ten. *Don't engage. That'll just make him happy. The dick.*

"I spent the day on a roof repairing an air conditioner. It was a thousand degrees up there—fucking tar melted all over everything."

"Why the hell would you do that?"

"Because I've got a new job. Maintenance for one Tinker Garrett. She owns an apartment building, and in exchange for doing some work around the place, I'll have a place to stay, park my truck, all that good shit."

"Sounds like a great cover," Picnic said. "Gives you a reason to stick around town, not to mention saving some cash."

"Yup. She bought my story about the divorce. I thought convincing Talia might be a problem, but she hasn't even bothered to ask why an independent trucker would suddenly move to a town in the middle of nowhere. Too busy talking about herself."

"You really don't like her, do you?"

"What gave it away?"

Picnic snorted again.

"Anyway, I think we're on track. Only one complication. Well, aside from the fact that they'll probably kill me if they figure out I'm a Reaper."

"What's that?"

"Talia Jackson may be a total cunt, but Tinker Garrett is looking damned fuckable. It's distracting."

"You've got the hots for the landlady?" Picnic asked, and I could practically see the shit-eating grin on his face. "That's fuckin' hysterical. Club's worst player is cock-blocked by duty to his brothers . . . Brings a tear to my eye, Gage. Really does. I'll be sure to tell everyone, make sure they understand the depths of your dick's sacrifice."

"This is why nobody likes you," I said, reaching up to scratch the back of my neck as the asshole laughed. I caught a whiff under my arm in the process and flinched. "Jesus Christ, but I stink. Gonna head back to the hotel and get cleaned up before I have to see Her Bitchness tonight."

"Have fun with that," Picnic replied. "And save your receipts. Club'll cover the cost of your condoms."

"You're a giver, boss. Inspiration to us all."

"You love me and you know it."

"Let's just say I have strong feelings and leave it at that."

Fucker was still laughing when I hung up on him.

It was nearly ten that night before I showed my face at the bar. I'd arranged to meet Talia there, and while I definitely wanted her thinking I was into her, I didn't want to make it too easy. It was like fishing—always a mistake to try reeling them in the first time they nibble the bait. It's better to let them get a good taste and then set the hook.

Jack's Roadhouse was like every other small-town dive I'd ever been in—populated almost entirely by locals, ranging in age from the newly minted twenty-one-year-olds (or at least those who'd managed to get fake IDs, although in a town this small it was more about plausible deniability than anything else) to a few old men who had to be in their seventies. The music was classic rock, the beer was strictly domestic, and the battered tables had seen better days. Wasn't a half-bad place, though—people seemed to be enjoying themselves, and there were some girls on the dance floor strutting their stuff.

Talia and her posse had staked out a table about halfway back, near the dance floor. The table was littered with empty shot glasses and several untouched glasses of water—guess they weren't into pacing themselves. I recognized a couple of the women from earlier in the week. Talia spent a lot of time in the bar, which made my job that much easier. Totally natural for a man who's new to town to visit the local watering hole, and even more natural to home in on a woman who looked like Talia Jackson. On paper she was a perfect ten.

In the flesh? Not so much.

The girl had no curves, for one thing. She was also hard—aged beyond her years with a nasty, calculating air in everything she did. Fucking her would be like fucking a strip of jerky. I watched as the girls raised their glasses, polishing off another round of shots before slamming them back down on the table with a crash. Talia looked up, catching a glimpse of me.

"Cooper!" she shrieked, jumping up and running over toward me. My arms rose to catch her, and then her legs were wrapped around my waist, clutching me tightly. Her mouth covered mine for a kiss that burned with alcohol and the lingering taste of buffalo wings.

You're doing this for the Reapers, I reminded myself. *No different than one of our club whores fucking a guy to get information.* Somehow I managed to kiss her back, hands gripping her ass. My hungry dick responded, which was something of a blessing. Maybe having Tinker around would be a good thing after all—I could just think of her anytime I had to touch Talia.

After what felt like a thousand years, Marsh's sister pulled away, catching my face with both hands.

"I have great news!"

"What's that?" I asked, wondering how drunk she was.

"My brother wants to meet you," she slurred, blinking owlishly.

Fucking hell, that *was* good news. The sooner I got in with Marsh Jackson and figured out what was going on, the sooner I'd be able to get the hell out of this shithole.

Of course, then I'd never get my chance with Tinker. In that instant I remembered why I didn't like women my own age—they complicated things.

They were interesting instead of interchangeable.

"That's great," I told Talia, making sure I didn't sound too enthusiastic. Just 'cause this was her turf didn't mean I had to give her full custody of my balls. "He's a biker, right?"

Talia rolled her eyes, sliding down my body until her feet touched the floor. Then she reached up, straightening my hair.

Like a pet.

"No, he's *the* biker," she corrected. "He's the president of the Nighthawk Raiders—that means he owns this fucking town. If you plan to stick around—even as an independent—you don't want him pissed off at you."

"Really?" I asked, raising a brow. "And what happens if he gets pissed at me?"

She shrugged, the gesture playful. "Not sure. You'd have to ask my last boyfriend."

I laughed. "And let me guess—nobody knows what happened to him?"

Her eyes sparkled.

"How'd you figure it out?" she asked, a hint of steel in her voice. "It's a bit of a mystery. One night he cheated on me, and the next he was just gone. It was a real shame, because he had a kid and everything."

I smiled adoringly at the sociopathic little bitch. At least there wasn't any danger of feeling guilty about using her to infiltrate the club—cunt had a gift for killing off even the slightest hint of empathy.

"Sounds like a loser," I replied. "You're better off without him."

Talia giggled, fluttering her lashes.

"I know."

We spent the next two hours playing bullshit games. It went a little something like this:

Talia would drop hints that she and her girls were thirsty.

I'd buy a round for the table.

I'd dance with her for a song.

Repeat.

Necessary groundwork, no getting around that. Didn't mean I enjoyed it. The girl was a fucking mess—raging bitch one minute, insecure little princess the next. At one point she dragged me into the alley behind the bar for a blow job, which I guess was okay, but the entire time all I could think about was how much I wanted it to be over.

Then the Nighthawk Raiders showed up, and everything changed.

I clocked sixteen of them, not counting whatever prospects they might've left outside with the bikes. They strolled into the bar around midnight, talking and laughing loudly, instantly dominating the room. Marsh was a big guy, and I'd seen him around town a couple times. Built like a bull, with long, dark blond hair in a ratty ponytail. The Nighthawks made their way to the back, followed by two waitresses loaded down with pitchers of beer.

Clearly they were regulars.

"C'mon," Talia said, catching my hand and dragging me across the room. "Marsh wants to meet you."

I felt them sizing me up as I approached. This was strange—usually I was the one men approached, not the other way around. The Reapers owned Washington State, even if Marsh seemed to have forgotten that. Hell, he'd have recognized me if he'd done his part and paid his respects at the Armory like every other club president living in our territory.

Cockwad.

"Marsh, this is Cooper," Talia said. "You remember I told you about him? He's new to town. I met him and his cousin earlier this week."

Marsh leaned back in his chair, crossing his arms as he looked me over. I saw him take in my POW/MIA belt buckle, Harley T-shirt, and hair tied back.

"I hear you're a biker," he said flatly. I nodded, meeting his gaze.

"Yup, independent," I replied. "New to town."

"Where'd you come from?"

"No one place. My ex and the kids are down in Ellensburg. Needed somewhere to land that was close enough to see them, but far enough I don't have to see them too much. Pulling my shit together after the divorce."

"Cooper's a long-haul trucker," Talia said, giving her brother a sweet smile. "He's staying at the hotel for now, but he's looking for a place. I was wondering if any of the trailers out by the clubhouse were empty."

Yeah, no fucking way I wanted that—we needed me to get close, but not too close. One mistake and I'd find my throat slit.

"I found a place," I told her. "Tinker Garrett hired me today— I'm her new handyman. It comes with an apartment."

Talia sneered. "That old bitch has a stick up her ass."

One of the guys laughed, and I glanced at his colors for a name. Cord.

"Sounds like someone's jealous," he said to me, nodding toward Talia. "Tinker's prime snatch. Let us know what you think if you get a taste. I saw this—"

"Shut the fuck up," Talia snarled. "That cunt is nothing. *Nothing.*"

"Not what I hear," Cord replied, eyes hardening. "You see that ass of hers? I'd tap that. Sounds like someone's jealous."

"Shut up," Marsh growled, echoing his sister. Cord stared him down without blinking, and I realized not all the Nighthawks were happy with the current situation. Good to know. Their little standoff lasted for almost a minute, and I felt the tension growing.

Then Marsh burst out laughing.

"We need a drink," he announced. "Talia, go get us a round of shots. On me."

She looked between us for a minute, obviously frustrated, then caught my hand.

"C'mon," she muttered. "Fucking assholes."

Her brother roared with laughter again, and the rest of them copied like a bunch of hyenas. Not all of them, though. Cord and a couple others weren't laughing at all.

So.

Now I'd met all my targets, and maybe found some future allies. I could work with this.

CHAPTER THREE

TINKER

Cooper didn't have time to move that weekend after all, so I ended up dropping off a set of keys for him at his hotel on Saturday afternoon. Coincidentally, I happened to be dressed in my finest because I'd made plans to meet Margarita for dinner in Ellensburg that night. (She'd driven over for a conference presentation earlier in the day at Central Washington University.) Not that my looks mattered— I knew Cooper was interested in Talia. Still, a woman's got her pride, and I hadn't exactly been at my best when he'd seen me yesterday.

I'd texted him to let him know I was on the way, and he met me out in the hotel parking lot, looking sexy as ever.

It wasn't fair, I decided as he swaggered over to my car. If I was smart, I'd have handed him the keys and pulled out of the parking lot, but instead I stepped out of my Mustang in a way that couldn't help but draw attention to the fact that my skirt was very, very short. Oh, and it was a total coincidence that I'd opted for a push-up bra, I reminded myself, even as I savored the way his eyes went straight to my chest.

Curves, baby. Yeah. I got 'em.

"You look good," he said, and I bit back a smile.

"Well, it *is* Saturday night," I said, deciding he didn't need to know my hot date was with a very married girlfriend. "I have the keys to your place here. It's unit 2A. You can let yourself in anytime, but it might be good if we meet later in the week so I can show you around. Any idea what time might work for you?"

He frowned, "Probably not until Monday or Tuesday. I've got some loose ends to tie up first."

I took a minute to imagine what it'd feel like to be tied up by a guy like Cooper. Then the roar of a motorcycle pulling into the lot caught my attention, and I watched as another man rolled to a stop next to us. He swung a leg over his bike, pulling off his helmet to reveal messy blond hair. He was younger than me—probably in his early twenties—and he was hot as hell.

God, what is it with you and perving on the barely legal ones?

"Hey there," the new arrival said, openly checking me out. (Nice shot in the ego, that.) "Aren't you going to introduce me, Coop?"

Something passed between the two men, some hint of warning or danger or . . . I couldn't tell, but I got the distinct sense that Cooper was annoyed with his friend.

"You got here earlier than I expected," Cooper said. "This is Tinker—looks like I'll be renting from her. I need a place and she's got one, so it works out perfect. Tinker, this is Levi, my cousin."

Cousin? Must've been an interesting family tree, because while Cooper had darker skin and thick black hair, Levi was pale and blond. He was also young, but that didn't stop me from noticing that he and his older cousin had one thing in common.

Both of them were beautiful.

So unfair.

"Nice to meet you, Levi," I said, offering him a friendly smile. "I'm looking forward to you moving in, Cooper. I need to get going, though—I'm headed down to Ellensburg for the night. Later!"

Their eyes followed me as I climbed into my car, and I'm not ashamed to admit that I took care to show even more leg this time.

The engine started with a powerful rumble—all raw power and muscle—and I held back a laugh as I reversed out, then thrust it into first and drove off with a spray of gravel.

So what if my new handyman had a hot, skanky little girlfriend waiting for him?

I'd bet my last dollar that girl couldn't handle a stick half as well as me.

I didn't see Cooper Romero again until Tuesday night, when he pulled up to the Garrett apartment building in a semi truck. Behind it was a flatbed trailer with his bike on it. I'd watched, wide-eyed, from the kitchen window, wondering what the hell I'd been thinking, hiring a man I knew so little about that I didn't even realize he was a trucker.

Oopsie.

Cooper swung down out of the cab, giving the trailer a quick once-over before heading toward the house. Brushing off my clothes, I gave my hair a quick check in the hall tree and opened the front door.

"Hey there," I said, hoping my voice sounded calmer and more sophisticated than I felt. Cooper was so beautiful he unnerved me. I'd sort of hoped that maybe I'd been wrong about how sexy he was—that I'd exaggerated it in my mind or something, out of sheer desperation.

Not so much.

The man was still tall and built, and today his hair was hanging loose around his shoulders. I swear, he looked like a male model, or he would've if he'd bothered to shave anytime in the last couple days. He didn't quite have a beard, but there was definitely more than scruff on his cheeks. It would feel all rough and prickly against my cheek if—*stop it right now. What are you, a teenager in heat?*

"Wow, that's a big truck," I said. Cooper cocked a brow and smirked.

"I get that a lot."

Rolling my eyes, I bit back a laugh. "That came out wrong. All

I meant was that I didn't realize you drove a semi. I don't think we have room in the parking lot for it. You could park the cab in the back, but there's not enough room for the trailer."

"No worries," he replied. "I just borrowed it from a friend to carry my bike to town. I'll be taking it back to him tomorrow."

"I guess I didn't realize you were a trucker," I said, considering the big rig, wondering how he'd be able to do repairs if he was traveling all the time. *Should've had him fill out an application, dumbass . . .* "I guess you're on the road a lot?"

"I'm taking some time off," he said. "I've been doing long-haul routes for years. Came home a few weeks ago to find my wife had moved on, so now I'm working on a divorce. She lives down in Ellensburg, but I wanted a fresh start. Somewhere far enough away to have my own space, but close enough to see my kids more than twice a year."

"How did you pick Hallies Falls, of all places? I mean, I can think of a lot of towns that might be better."

All of them. All of them would be better, in my experience.

Cooper shrugged, offering me a grin that made my stomach clench.

"I passed through here a few years back with a friend, thought it looked pretty. When I needed a place to land it came to mind—simple as that."

"So you're only going to be here short term?" I asked, although I really didn't have any room to criticize. Sure, I'd hired him to do work around the building, but it wasn't like we had a contract or anything. I'd probably sell the place and go back to Seattle if Dad . . . Nope, wasn't ready to think about that. Denial. Denial had served the women of my family well for generations. No reason to change that now.

"I haven't decided yet," he replied. "Depends on whether I find a reason to stick around, I guess."

Whatever I might've said in reply died as a battered old Jeep Wrangler pulled up, parking along the street in front of the building. The door flew open and out climbed Talia Jackson. Her eyes snapped toward us, narrowing.

"Hey, baby!" she called, walking over to stand pointedly between me and Cooper. I watched as she wrapped herself around him for a deep kiss. Part of me hoped he'd tell her to fuck off. Instead he kissed her back, digging his hands into her flat ass. Then Talia broke free, turning to smirk at me.

Message received.

"Nice to see you, Talia," I said, thinking of Princess Diana. Calm, cool, graceful Diana. Now I just needed to channel *her*, instead of going all Kardashian on Talia's tacky ass like I wanted to. "I was just about to show Cooper his new place. Would you like to join us?"

She looked over at the building.

"I can't understand why you'd want to live here," she declared loudly at Cooper. "They're a bunch of old people, and I'm sure they'll bitch at you all the time just because you have a life."

Dear God, were we really going here?

Inhale pink, exhale blue. You can do this.

"I'll show you the apartment, and then you can get settled," I announced, ignoring her. "Second floor, right behind the main house. That's a good one, because it has its own separate entrance off the parking lot. Gives you more privacy."

Cooper nodded, following me as I stepped off the wide porch and around the side of the house to the attached apartment building. There wasn't much of a stoop on the stairwell, but it had a nice awning over the entry. Handy in the winter.

"It's just one bedroom," I said, unlocking the door. I pushed it open, and Cooper and Talia followed me into the living room. The apartment stretched across the width of the building, so there was light coming in from both sides. Across from the door was a dining area with a kitchenette.

"It's all natural-gas heat," I told him. "That keeps the utilities under control. The bedroom and bathroom are just through here."

They followed me through the living room into the bedroom, Talia looking around eagerly. Apparently her disgust didn't run quite as deep as she'd let on. Fair enough—it was a nice building, built by my grandpa and lovingly maintained by my dad. They'd always taken their work very seriously.

"Do you have a bed?" Talia asked Cooper. "When are we breaking this place in?"

And just like that I was done.

"So, that's everything," I announced. "There's a paper with all the garbage and utilities information in the kitchen, along with my contact information. It's taped inside the cabinet next to the sink. Call me if you need anything, otherwise I'll just let you get settled."

I started toward the door, wondering if it would be okay to declare he wasn't allowed overnight guests. Specifically, that he wasn't allowed *female* overnight guests.

Hmmm . . . probably not. Pisser.

I'd just reached the door when Cooper's hand caught my arm, scaring the crap out of me.

"Sorry," he said as I spun on him with a definitively unsexy squawk. "I just wanted to thank you. The place looks great."

"Wonderful," I snapped, glaring down at his hand. I could smell him all around me, feel the strength in his fingers. If a super hot guy was going to answer my ad, why did it have to be one who already had a girlfriend? That was flat out unfair.

"So, maybe we should talk in the morning," he said. "If you put together a list of everything that needs doing, I can get started tomorrow. Looks like there's a few projects here and there that could use some work."

I barely noticed his words—I was too busy watching his lips move. They were really, really pretty. Perfect. Exactly right for sucking on. Something twinged between my legs and I felt my nipples tighten. His hand squeezed my arm again, feeling strangely intimate, and his eyes pierced mine.

"So, tomorrow?"

"Um, sure," I said quickly, realizing I needed to get the hell out of there before I embarrassed myself. "I'll see you later."

Wouldn't want to get in the way of them "breaking in" the bedroom.

This wasn't going to end well.

Maybe I should fire him.

I was climbing the steps back to my house and giving the idea serious consideration when my foot caught on a rotten board that'd been on my to-fix list since last spring. I tried pulling it free, but it stuck. Then I kicked at it, and suddenly the damned thing gave way, sending my foot plunging through.

Well, crap.

Firing him wasn't really an option . . . I'd been advertising for a handyman for nearly a month, and during that whole time I'd only gotten two calls. One was a prank and the other was Steve Gribble, whose wife had kicked him out (again) for getting drunk and losing his job (again).

I'd just have to suck it up and deal with Cooper and his stupid, evil, gorgeous girlfriends. Yup, that'd work. All I needed to do was think of him as convenient eye candy, like the guys in those sexy firefighter calendars. Fun to look at, impossible to touch, and not quite real.

I could handle this.

SUNDAY AFTERNOON, TWO WEEKS LATER

"Bring more wine," I hissed into the phone. "He's taking off his shirt and I'm starting to overheat."

"Does he have tattoos?" my best friend, Carrie, asked in a harsh whisper. "I keep imagining tattoos swirling all over that chest of his, and . . . Oh God. I think I need to change my panties."

"No tats that I can see. But he's getting sweaty."

"Do you think two bottles will be enough?"

Shaking my head slowly, I sighed as Cooper stopped the lawn mower long enough to take a deep drink of water. God, the way his throat moved when he swallowed . . . and those muscles bunching in his back. Damn.

"Three. Better be safe. It's a big yard."

• • •

Generally speaking, I'm not the kind of girl who drinks during the day. I mean, I will. Sometimes. You know, like at a Fourth of July BBQ where people start cracking beers around one in the afternoon? But this was a Sunday and I had four hundred caramels—a full week's orders—to package for the courier first thing the next morning. A hangover wasn't on the agenda.

Seriously, though.

He'd taken off his shirt.

Why the hell was I putting myself through this? And more importantly, why had I moved him into the apartment that shared a wall with my own childhood bedroom like some total creeper? There was another vacant unit around the back side of the building.

Lust.

Yup. I was woman enough to own it. Tinker Garrett, aged thirty-six, was in lust with Cooper Romero. The man was so damned easy on the eyes that it caused me physical pain. Okay, not pain. Warm tinglies. And he was exactly what I needed, too. According to the rental application that I'd belatedly asked him to fill out, he was two years older than me. Should've been perfect, right? Too bad he was into twenty-year-old nutjobs with small boobs and tight asses.

Speaking of Talia, I'd already heard far more than I wanted to from her since he'd moved in.

Specifically, I heard her screaming during sex. Screaming about how good he was, screaming how much she wanted him, screaming instructions with a sense of sexual entitlement I pretended to despise but secretly made me feel jealous.

Fucking bitch.

Gah. I forced myself away from the window, looking around the faded living room of my family home. I'd been born upstairs in the same bedroom I slept in now. Somehow, despite the fact that I had a college degree, thriving business, and one failed marriage behind me, I'd landed right where I started.

Of course, I loved the building in my own weird way. Grandpa had built it back in 1922, and he'd built it to last. Unfortunately, even good construction needs maintenance, and after Mom died eight months back, I'd realized that Dad could barely manage getting to the kitchen without getting lost. He'd obviously been letting things slide for several years now, but I'd been too busy living my life in Seattle to notice. The place was in worse shape than I'd ever seen it.

That's why I couldn't evict Cooper for having a girlfriend who wasn't me. Well, that and the law and the general sense of decency and fair play my parents raised me with, but I swear—if it weren't for all that, he'd be out on his ass. I took another deep swig of the wine, hoping Carrie didn't fuck around on her way over.

Jerk.

Sexy, beautiful jerk . . .

Grabbing my glass of wine, I peered through the window so I could see him better.

"Tricia?" my dad called, his voice wavering. "Is that you in the living room? Did they deliver my package?"

"It's me, Dad," I replied, tearing my eyes away from Cooper. "And it's Tinker, remember?"

I watched as my big, strong father—my childhood hero—stared at me, confusion written all over his face.

"I'm waiting for the parts," he said slowly. "Want to rebuild the carburetor on Tricia's T-bird, but I don't have the parts I need. Did you take them?"

"Dad, Mom isn't with us anymore," I reminded him softly. "And you sold the T-bird years ago."

He stared at me blankly.

"I guess I forgot," he finally admitted. "Sometimes I do that . . ."

No shit.

"Don't worry about it," I said, walking over to give him a hug. "Hey, my friend Carrie is coming over in a little while. We're going to have some girl time—just a heads-up, okay?"

He patted my back absently, then kissed the side of my head.

"That sounds nice. You kids have fun, but not too much TV, okay? Rots your brains."

Smiling, I squeezed him tight, because despite his failing memory, he was still my daddy. Somewhere deep down inside, his love for me burned bright, even if he couldn't quite express it the normal way any longer.

The lawn mower roared as Cooper pushed it across the yard, working his way carefully around Mom's rosebushes. I caught another glimpse of him through the window and pulled away from Dad quickly—no way I wanted to be hugging my father while I perved on the guy outside.

Too creepy, even for a creeper like myself.

"Do you still have that open apartment?" Carrie asked half an hour later, leaning back to prop her feet up on the porch railing. I refilled my glass of wine, settling deeper into the same swing we'd played on during a thousand childhood sleepovers. It needed a coat of paint.

"Yeah, but I've got someone interested. Why do you ask?"

"Because I'm thinking of moving in," she said seriously. I raised my brows.

"You own a house," I reminded her gently.

"But I don't have *him*," she said, eyes darting toward Cooper, who was using the Weedwacker to edge the sidewalks. He caught me looking, giving a knowing quirk of his lips. An hour earlier this would've embarrassed the hell out of me, but Carrie and I'd nearly put the second bottle to bed. Reality had fuzzed out nicely.

"Well, we'll see how it plays out," I reminded her, not wanting to jinx it. "Just because he does a good job today doesn't mean he'll be trustworthy in the long run. He hangs out with the motorcycle club, you know. Not only that, he's dating Talia Jackson. I'm not his type."

The words fell between us, and Carrie gave an exaggerated shiver.

"That girl is such a heinous little bitch."

"Thanks for pointing that out. I hadn't noticed. Hell, I'd planned on inviting her over for drinks with us next Sunday."

She smacked me, and the whole swing swayed.

"Careful! You nearly knocked over my wine," I accused.

"I brought over three bottles," she pointed out. "The only reason you aren't sitting here drinking water is me, so be nice."

We glared at each other, and for a good thirty seconds I managed to hold my angry face. Carrie broke first, and then we were both giggling, just like in high school.

"Cheers," she said, lifting her glass.

"Cheers," I replied. "I missed this. When I was living in Seattle, I mean. I had lots of friends there, but no one like you."

Carrie threw her arm over my shoulder, giving me a hug. Then she reached down and lifted the bottle, emptying the last few drops into my glass.

"I'm glad you're home," she said. "I know things haven't gone like you planned, but I still think you belong here in Hallies Falls."

I rolled my eyes.

Whatever.

Then I chugged the rest of my glass, because it really wasn't very good wine—not like what Brandon and I used to drink together. Cooper passed in front of us, flashing me a quick smile.

"I'm in heat," Carrie moaned.

"You're married."

"Oh, get over yourself—it's not like he's real."

I frowned at her, confused. "Of course he's real. He just pushed the lawn mower right by us."

Carrie rolled her eyes.

"No, I mean nothing will happen with him," she said. "I'm married, and you aren't his type. That makes him safe fantasy material."

"I could be his type," I insisted.

"You're beautiful," she said. "You've got that sexy, curvy body and retro style from hell, which kicks ass. But if Cooper's into Talia Jackson, he's not gonna be into you. Even without the age thing, this guy likes girls without curves. Talia's like a wire hanger with breasts. Really little ones. She's a tacky street racer and you're a classic muscle car. Just two different things, you know?"

Sighing, I slumped back in the swing, realizing she was right.

I'd known it already, but somehow after the third glass of wine I'd been feeling more optimistic. But for better or worse, Carrie and I shared more than our love of fast cars. We had a deal—forged in the pain and humiliation of junior high—to always tell each other the truth, no matter how hard.

"Hey, it's not a bad thing," she said, nudging my shoulder. "Not like the guy's a serious prospect anyway. Doesn't seem to have a real job, mows lawns for his rent, and hangs out with a motorcycle gang. You can't tell me you were picking out china patterns in your head, were you?"

"No, but I wouldn't mind getting laid."

"So let's hit a club in Ellensburg this weekend," she said. "Two can play this game, you know—pick up some cute college boy, teach him a thing or two. I swear, his future wife will thank you."

I groaned.

"One time . . ."

Carrie burst out laughing. "Nothing ever dies in this town, babe. You're a cougar on the prowl and we all know it! Why just the other day I warned a young man to get off the street before you caught him."

Pushing off the swing I stood up, pointing my glass at her accusingly.

"It never would've happened if it wasn't for you and Margarita."

"I realize this. You don't have to keep thanking me."

The front door opened, and my dad looked out.

"Do you know where your mother is?" he asked. "I'm getting hungry. She should be fixing dinner by now."

Carrie and I shared a look.

"I'll get it going soon, Dad," I told him. "But Mom's not with us anymore, remember?"

Confusion crossed his face, followed by embarrassment as my heart clenched.

"Sorry, I wasn't thinking."

"I'll get some chicken started—how does that sound?"

He didn't answer, turning and shuffling back through the door.

"You're going to have to do something before too much longer," Carrie said softly. "It's not safe for him to be here alone at the house."

"Nothing's happened," I pointed out. "He gets confused, but it's not like he sets fires or something."

She just stared at me, and in that instant I regretted the zero-bullshit clause in our friendship.

"I'm gonna go light the grill," I told her, sighing. "Are you staying for dinner?"

"No, but I'll hang around for a while longer," she said. "Darren doesn't get off work for another hour."

"You guys can eat with us if you like. It's just grilled chicken and rice, but we've got plenty."

"Let me text him and see," she said, brightening. "I'm not in the mood to cook and the girls won't be home until later. They grow up too damned fast, babe."

I managed to hide my flinch, nodding and smiling. Darren had knocked Carrie up our senior year of high school, which wasn't normally a good thing. It seemed to have worked out for them all right, though. The twins were a handful, but they were good kids.

Couldn't believe they'd be eighteen in another year.

My little Tricia would still be a toddler. I grabbed my glass and chugged, willing away the thought. I'd cried enough for a lifetime already.

"Sounds good. Let's go fire up the grill."

Half an hour later I was in my happy place again, by sheer force of will. Force of will and wine, that was . . . Now I stood over the grill, basting chicken breasts and sipping my drink.

Back when I was a freshman, me and Dad built a covered porch off the kitchen so we could barbecue out there year-round. Mom was all about cooking outside because she hated scrubbing pans. I'd missed the freedom to cook outside in Seattle—Brandon thought a grill would make the deck look tacky. Just another reason to celebrate ditching his ass.

Back in the kitchen, I had Carrie putting finishing touches on the salad, and the rice was bubbling away—it wasn't fancy, but it'd be good. Things should be ready right about the time Darren arrived. We'd even set the picnic table in the courtyard gazebo with a pretty blue-checkered cloth.

"Smells good."

I looked up to find Cooper on the steps, leaning against the railing. He looked so pretty. I smiled big and nearly told him so, then remembered I was drunk and bit my tongue. (Literally bit it, which hurt like hell and made my eyes water. I'm sure he thought I was crazy. Fair enough.)

"Great job on the yard," I told him after a few seconds of agonizing pain. "It's a relief to have you helping out. How's the apartment?"

"Hell of a lot better than the hotel," he said. "Although I'm not much of a cook."

He glanced at the grill, taking in the chicken. A small part of me wanted to ask if Talia was a good cook. The words were halfway to my mouth, but the single, tiny little chunk of my brain that was still sober managed to tackle them and wrestle them back to the ground before I made an ass of myself.

"I worked as a private chef for several years," I told him. *Suck it, brain. I can work my skills into a conversation without being obvious.* "Then I started making the chocolates, and the business took off. Pretty soon I couldn't keep up with both, so I cut my clients loose."

"Impressive," Cooper said.

"You want to join us?" I asked.

"Yes."

I burst out laughing, because he said the word so fast and so fervently that there could be no question—Cooper wanted some of that chicken. Was this a bad idea? *No reason you can't be friendly with the guy,* Miss Sober Brain informed me primly. *You've got plenty of chaperones.*

Nice.

"Okay. We'll be serving up in about half an hour. Carrie's hubby will be off work around six, then he's heading over."

"Carrie the one you were talkin' with on the porch?"

"Yup," I said, popping the "p" on the end. Then I took another deep swig of my wine. "She's been my best friend since we were kids. My dad is here, too, so it'll be five of us."

"Sure you have enough to spare?" he asked. "I don't want to impose."

"No worries," I said blithely. "It'll be fine."

"I'll go grab a shower, then."

"See you in a bit."

I thought I played it off pretty well, although I'll own up to scoping out his ass as he walked away. His shirt hung loose from a back pocket, the muscles in his back rippling.

"Goddamn," Carrie said, and I jumped.

"You startled me," I accused, spinning to find her in the kitchen door, eyes wide. "You better be careful—Darren will catch you watching him."

She shrugged.

"Darren and I have an agreement," she said. "We can look, we just don't touch. We've been married a long time, you know. He doesn't get jealous."

This was bullshit and we both knew it. I considered invoking the sacred clause, then decided that if I was going to perv on my handyman, it'd be nice to have company.

"Paper plates tonight," I announced, and Carrie grinned. "I'm not in the mood to wash dishes."

GAGE

Fuck, but that woman was sexy, especially when she was a little drunk . . . made her all cute and bubbly.

I stepped into my tiny bathroom, wondering for the thousandth time why I'd volunteered for this gig. I'd had a good thing going back in Coeur d'Alene. Sure, the dancers at The Line were nonstop drama, but when I saw an ass I wanted to tap, it was usually available. Not so much with Tinker Garrett.

The biggest obstacle was the Talia situation, of course. But over the past two weeks, I'd realized something unsettling—I sort of liked Tinker as a person. I mean, not that we'd spent much time together, but I saw how she went out of her way to do the right thing. A good girl all around, and the fact that she'd moved home to take care of her dad after her mother died proved the point.

Then there were those curves. Fucking hell, I thought about her tits and ass all the time. I'd always been a sucker for curves, although back home it was more about big, fake boobs and mouths like vacuum cleaners. Tinker made fancy chocolates and had a store full of teacups.

Not. My. Type.

Too bad my cock hadn't gotten the memo on that.

My phone buzzed, and I grabbed it, finding a text from my president.

PICNIC: Status update?

Reaching into the shower stall I flipped it on, figuring I'd let it run for a few minutes while I called him back. The building was old, and I'd already learned that it took a while before the water got hot. Dialing his number, I waited for him to answer.

"Yeah?" he asked.

"You texted me, boss."

"Wanted to see how things were going," Pic said.

"Not much to report. I mean, not much beyond what we already suspected. Marsh is running the club into the ground and there's definitely bullshit in the air. He's reporting lost shipments to Bellingham, but you don't hear anyone bitching about product getting jacked at the clubhouse. The newer guys aren't smart enough to keep their mouths shut, and they've all got plenty of cash in their pockets. The older ones have all pulled away. He's double-dealing us."

"You figure out how he managed to take over yet?"

"So far as I can tell, he got a couple friends in and then turned one or two of the others," I said. "They called for a vote right after that big bust last year, and elected him while the old guard were all locked up. Painter's sources in prison were right on all the details. Now Marsh is holding power because he has the numbers and he's adding soldiers every day. What I can't figure out is why the original members who are still left haven't bailed. Not that they'd open up to me—if they notice me at all, it's because I'm Talia's bitch."

"Loyalty," Picnic said, sounding frustrated. "Same thing that holds every club together. They probably haven't lost hope yet."

"I'd say they're pretty damned close," I told him grimly. "I can see a situation where we have a second, unofficial club starting in town."

Picnic gave a low whistle. "That'd be unfortunate."

"Ya think?"

"Well, that's why we sent you—best to stop it before it gets any worse. How's the new living situation?" he asked, changing the subject. I glanced around the small apartment. I'd stayed in worse, but over the years I'd gotten used to something a lot better.

"It's working," I said.

"And your landlady? You still horny for her?"

I considered my answer carefully—I wanted to be honest with him, but if I admitted too much, I'd never hear the end of it.

"She's nice," I finally said, compromising. "Invited me for dinner tonight."

"Be careful. Talia's your ticket, not this Tinker bitch, no matter how much you want to fuck her. Don't forget that."

"I know my job, boss," I replied. "It's about the club—I get it."

It was always about the club.

"Let us know if you need anything, then. You still doin' okay on money?"

"Yeah, I'll call you if it's an issue," I said. "We good?"

"We're good."

"Talk to you later."

Dropping the phone on the counter, I stripped off my dirty jeans and stepped into the shower. I gave my hair a quick wash, then dropped a soapy hand to my dick and let myself think about Tinker Garrett. She and her friend sat out on that porch all afternoon, laughing and drinking, looking so fuckin' cute that it took every last bit of my self-control not to drag her off to my place by her hair.

That hair . . . always had a thing for dark hair.

Tinker wasn't like other women. Part of it was that whole look she had going for her, sort of like one of those girls they used to paint on the side of airplanes during World War II. Bangs cut straight across her forehead, retro halter top, and tight jeans rolled up above her ankles. I'd caught a tantalizing hint of a tattoo across her back, but I hadn't been able to see much of it. If she'd walked into The Line, I'd have hired her in an instant.

An image of her riding a pole slid through my mind, and I shuddered.

Grabbing some more soap, I jerked my dick harder, wondering what she'd look like naked. Maybe once this was all over, I'd stick around an extra day or two and find out. First thing, I'd rip off that halter of hers and check out those boobs. They weren't stripper huge, but they were plenty big and all natural. Round, just like the rest of her. All curves and dips, narrowing to a tiny waist before smoothing back out into hips a man could dig his fingers into.

I imagined doing just that, holding on tight while I fucked her from behind. Ass or cunt? Both. Definitely. Those tits would swing around while I did her, and she'd give little breathy moans with every thrust. Gorgeous.

Leaning back against the wall, I kept pumping. Wouldn't take much more to push me over the edge—I'd been primed all afternoon, especially when I'd caught her watching me. She was hot for it, too. I saw it in her eyes and the way she licked her lips . . . They'd look real sweet wrapped around my cock. Would she swallow? My balls tightened, pressure burning deep inside. I decided that for the purposes of this fantasy, Tinker definitely liked to swallow. She'd drink my come and smile the whole time, reaching down between her legs and—

I came in a series of hard spurts, spraying the shower wall the way I wanted to spray her ass.

Fuck me, but that was good.

I rinsed myself and turned off the water, reaching for a towel. Nice to take the edge off, otherwise I wasn't sure I'd make it through dinner. Any other time, any other place, she'd be under me already, but I knew my job.

Reapers forever, forever Reapers.

Sometimes loyalty sucks.

CHAPTER FOUR

TINKER

Cooper still had drops of water dripping off his freshly washed hair when he came back out to the courtyard. Combined with the week's worth of scruff on his face, it gave him a rough-and-ready look that left me feeling almost woozy—the man was raw sex.

"How's it coming?" he asked, offering a slow smile that made my knees shake.

"Just about done," I replied, wishing I'd had slightly less wine. I wasn't totally drunk, but I'd indulged enough that the edges of my world had fuzzed out nicely. In some ways this was good, because I felt less nervous around him. On the other hand, I'd be far more likely to do something stupid . . . Say, grab his butt or lean over and lick that little trickle of water rolling down the side of his neck.

"Anything I can do to help?"

I reached down with my tongs, picking up a piece of chicken so I could check the internal temperature. Perfect.

"You can hold the kitchen door open for me—everything else is inside," I said, turning off the gas before setting the chicken breasts on the platter. "We'll be ready to eat in a few minutes. I just need to grab the rest of the food and take it over to the picnic table."

Cooper held the door for me as I walked past him. It opened onto a mudroom that would've been a porch if the house didn't merge into the apartment building. We passed through to the kitchen, where I found Carrie and Darren exchanging a rather heated kiss.

"Get a room," I announced loudly. "Otherwise I'm turning the hose on you."

"Fuck off," Darren said, pulling away from her. "If you're still making out when you've been married for eighteen years, then you get a vote."

Carrie and I laughed as Cooper joined us.

"Don't think we've met," Darren said, scoping him out carefully. Cooper held out his hand and they shook. I got a when-alpha-males-meet vibe, and Carrie rolled her eyes.

"Cooper Romero. I'm Tinker's new handyman."

"Yeah, I heard about you. Why'd you move to Hallies Falls?"

"Darren, don't be rude," Carrie scolded, pulling away from him. Darren ignored her as Cooper gave an easy laugh, stepping back to lean against the counter, big arms crossed over his chest.

"I'm in the middle of a divorce. My ex is in Ellensburg with our boys. I was looking for somewhere close enough to visit, but far enough that I won't run into her on a regular basis."

"What do you do? Besides working for Tinker, I mean."

"Darren!" Carrie said, swatting his arm.

"I'm protective of Tinker," Darren replied lightly, but his eyes were serious. "I saw you with the Nighthawk Raiders MC the other day. You a member?"

"Nope," Cooper said. "Just dating a girl connected to the club, that's all. I like to ride my bike and mind my own business. And to answer your question, I'm a trucker. That's my rig parked out back. I'm taking a bit of a break for now—just need to sort out the legal stuff first."

Darren nodded, seeming satisfied but still not overly friendly.

"Sorry, Cooper—Darren needs to learn to pretend he's civilized in front of company," Carrie said, rolling her eyes. "Let's take the food out to the picnic table."

She picked up the little caddy that held paper plates, napkins, and some silverware, grabbing the salad in her other hand. Darren unplugged the small rice cooker on the counter and followed her out the door, leaving me alone with Cooper.

"I'm sorry about that," I told him. "I'd love to say that it's not typical, but Darren has always been super protective of Carrie and I, even when we were kids. He's like my big brother."

Cooper gave me a slow, beautiful smile and shook his head. "Don't worry about it. Having people who give a shit is a good thing."

I smiled back at him, wondering why the hell he couldn't fall down at my feet and declare his undying love. Of course, then I'd have stepkids . . . I'd never considered stepchildren. A stab of pain shot through me, and I shoved down my thoughts before they started down the dark path.

"Anything else I can do to help?" he asked, stepping closer to me. I could smell him—fresh and clean and male. My nipples hardened, and I shot up a swift prayer of thanks up that the halter had a little padding built in for the sake of discretion. Obviously the designer wasn't a fan of nipping out any more than I was. Cooper reached over and touched my cheek softly. My heart stuttered.

"You had an eyelash," he said, holding up his finger. Then he stepped back and picked up the platter of chicken. "Should I take this outside?"

Deflating, I admitted for the first time to myself that Carrie might just be right—maybe I really did need to get laid. I'd thought he was flirting with me, which was stupid. *The man has a girlfriend. Get your mind out of your panties.*

"Great," I told him, refusing to blush. "I'll go find my dad. Oh, there's drinks in the fridge and wine on the counter. Grab whatever you want."

GAGE

I carried the platter out through the kitchen door and into the courtyard, wondering how a town beautiful enough to hold a place like this could have fallen into the hands of someone like Marsh Jackson. The summer had been hot and dry, but Tinker's courtyard remained a lush oasis of green, even in the heat.

The building itself was arranged like a big C with the Garrett house attached to one end of it. In the center of the C was a courtyard with a cedar gazebo, which was where we were eating. It looked like something out of a movie about England—you know, the kind where there are bricks on the bottom and dark beams crossing white walls above? It stood two stories tall, and there were flowers and hanging baskets everywhere. Like something out of a storybook.

"Have a seat," Carrie said, her cheeks flushed. Darren wrapped an arm around her, giving her a squeeze. They were a good-looking couple—reminded me of Bam Bam and Dancer back in Coeur d'Alene—with the air of people who'd been together for a long time. I wondered what that'd be like. I'd never been with the same woman longer than a year, and never particularly regretted it. Either I wasn't the kind of man who needed an old lady or I'd never met the right one.

Across from Darren sat Tinker's dad, Tom. He was a good guy, although it'd taken only a couple days to figure out he wasn't firing on all cylinders. One of the tenants—Mary Webbly, who was probably about ten years older than Tom—had told me that he'd gone downhill in a big way since his wife had died earlier in the year. Up to that point, Tinker had lived in Seattle.

Interesting family dynamics there.

I sat down across from Darren, who was obviously still scoping me out, trying to decide if I was a threat to his girls or not. He smelled something off about the situation, I'd bet a thousand bucks on it. Fair enough. Tinker sat down next to me, and then she was handing out paper plates and what looked like surprisingly fancy, real silverware.

"So, when do you plan to start driving your truck again?" Darren asked me, reaching for his beer. "You changing careers, or just taking a breather?"

"Short break, that's all," I told him, scooping out a generous serving of rice. "Like I said, just need to figure shit out with my ex. Don't want her screwing me on the divorce paperwork while I'm out of town."

Darren nodded. "Always good to get that finalized as quickly as possible."

Tinker coughed, shifting in her seat. I glanced at her, surprised to see her cheeks had flushed.

"You know, not every conversation needs to be about finalizing divorces," she said, draining her wineglass. Carrie reached for the bottle, deftly refilling it, and I had to bite back a grin. The girls had been packing it away—there were going to be headaches in the morning, no question.

"You know what? You should divorce that husband of yours," her dad declared, smiling at her. "I've never liked him."

She had a husband? First I'd heard of it. Fuck. I didn't like the thought of her married, not one little bit. And where the hell was the asshole, anyway? Only a moron would leave a woman like Tinker alone.

I'd never met the man, but I wanted to kick his ass already.

"I *am* getting a divorce, Dad," she replied, rolling her eyes. "Remember? It's just taking a while because of the property and all Brandon's family stuff. The situation is complicated."

"Lawyers," Tom muttered. "Can't trust 'em. None of 'em. Never liked that boy."

Carrie coughed, her eyes dancing. "I think we all know how you feel about lawyers, Tom."

Tinker snorted. "Oh God. Do you remember the first time Dad learned that Brandon was a deputy prosecutor? I thought he'd have a heart attack."

"I'm healthier than a horse," Tom declared, but my mind was stuck on the news that Tinker's *husband*—Christ, that word left a sour taste in my mouth—was a prosecutor. I fucking hated prose-cutors. At least she was ending it.

"I know, Dad," she said, reaching past me to catch his hand, giving it a squeeze. It forced her to lean close, and I caught a whiff of her hair. Peaches. She smelled like peaches, and I'd bet my bike that round ass of her would look just like one.

Shoot me in the fucking head already and put me out of my misery.

Tinker's hand brushed my chest again as she pulled it back, and she and her girl were laughing about something else. I looked up to find Darren watching me, his eyes speculative. Catching his gaze, I nodded at him and he nodded back.

Yeah, I'd have to watch out for that one. He saw me for what I was—a predator. He'd be a problem, no question. Still, I was glad that Tinker had someone like that in her life.

"Darren, you look like a hippie with that beard," Tom said suddenly. "All the young guys look like hippies these days. Like the town ran out of razors or something."

"Dad! You can't say things like that!"

"Sure I can," he replied, eyes twinkling. "I just did. And I didn't say that being a hippie was a bad thing. Your mom was a hippie, did you know that?"

Tinker put down her glass.

"Seriously?"

"Yup. The summer I met Tricia, she ran around wearing long skirts the whole time, and that hair of hers . . . It was so pretty. I hardly knew what to think. Never thought I could fall in love so fast. We were crazy, too. Her dad hated me, but that didn't stop us from driving down to San Francisco in her car—a little orange Volkswagen—and spending part of the summer there. We dropped acid and danced in the park, then camped in a flophouse with a bunch of friends. It was a real good time."

Tinker choked, staring at him wide-eyed. Couldn't blame her, either—the man looked like an old farmer who'd never traveled more than fifty miles from his hometown. Tom scooped up another serving of rice, oblivious to her shock.

"Wow," Carrie said. "I can't wrap my head around that. Tricia never even let Tinker stay out past ten on the weekends."

Tom smirked. "Yeah, the wild ones always turn into the most protective parents. It's because we know how many different ways there are to find trouble. We had a shotgun wedding, did I ever tell you that? I swear, your grandpa was all ready to kill me until he found out she was knocked up."

"Stop!" Tinker said, holding up a hand. "I can't hear things like that. Just leave me in peaceful ignorance, okay?"

Tom laughed, looking pleased with himself. His mind might wander at times, but right now he was obviously with us and enjoying every minute. Must've been a hell of a guy in his prime.

"You want another beer?" Darren asked me, lifting up his empty.

"Sure," I said, reaching for mine and polishing it off.

"We really need to change the subject now," Tinker announced. "Dad, you aren't allowed to talk unless it's about something safe and neutral."

Tom laughed, then nodded his head. "Sure thing, Stinker."

She groaned, and Carrie burst out laughing. "Remember how we used to call you Stinker Bell?"

Tinker flipped her off, then turned to me with a big, fake smile. "So tell me, Cooper, how do you feel about friends who don't know when to keep their mouths shut? I was considering hitting her over the head with a shovel, but I hear drowning works, too."

Grinning at her, I shook my head. "Slippery slope, Tinker. In the end, those are the kind of friends you can really count on. If you kill them off, you got nobody to help you bury the bodies."

Carrie burst out laughing. "See? I'm right and you're wrong. Again."

"I hate both of you," Tinker declared, but she was giggling. "Now I'm not going to share any of my caramels."

"Oh, fuck off," Carrie replied. "You know damned well you can't say no to me."

"She's a force of nature," Darren agreed, dropping down into the seat next to her. He handed me another bottle. "You put the two of them together and things can get scary."

"Be nice or I'll tell about that time you got stuck up in the tree house."

"I was six years old, Stink."

"Yeah, but you cried like you were two," Tinker said, waggling her eyebrows. "I'll never forget it. He kept whining about wanting his mommy, and Dad had to climb up and get him."

"Do you really want to play this game, Stink?" Darren asked, arching a brow. "Because if you want to play chicken, I'm game. So Cooper, when Tinker and Carrie—"

"Shut your mouth!" Tinker hissed as Carrie smacked him on the shoulder.

"Don't you dare, you horrible man!"

"Hey, I wasn't going *there*," Darren insisted, holding up his hands. "I planned to tell him about when you went swimming at the quarry and your suit came off."

An image of her naked and slippery in the water sprung to life in my mind. I coughed, shifting uncomfortably. That brought our legs into contact, which wasn't exactly helpful.

"Shut your mouth, Darren," Tinker repeated, but she looked relieved. Interesting—there must be a hell of a story behind that little exchange. I wanted to hear it.

"Truce?" Darren asked.

"Truce," Tinker agreed.

"Jesus, Darren. You suck," Carrie said, poking his side.

"She started it."

Tom nudged my shoulder. "I understand that they're adults, but sometimes all I can see are little kids."

"You love us and you know it," Carrie reminded him. Tom grunted, but he came around and gave Tinker a kiss on the top of the head when he stood to go. We watched him walk inside, then Carrie turned to Tinker.

"Do you really think they did all that crazy shit? I can't picture your dad on acid." She shuddered.

"Not sure I want to know," Tinker replied. "And I definitely don't want to picture it."

Darren snorted. "The old man's been around. Up at elk camp he told some great stories."

"You're supposed to share things like that," Carrie said.

"It's just guys blowing smoke," he replied mildly. "Never gave it much thought. You about done, babe? We should probably get going."

"Yeah, I'm done," she said, narrowing her eyes at him. "What else aren't you telling me?"

"I'm a man of many secrets," Darren said, poking her nose. "You'll have to torture them out of me."

Carrie laughed. "That can be arranged."

"Take your disgusting married love and get out of here," Tinker said, flapping a hand at them. "I meant what I said about the hose earlier—I'll turn it on you if you start making out."

"Don't you want some help cleaning up first?" Carrie asked.

"I'll take care of it," Tinker replied. "Just throw your plates in the garbage and put the silverware in the sink."

"You sure?"

"I can help," I volunteered, because apparently my balls weren't blue enough already. Tinker gave me a beautiful smile.

"Thanks," she said, her voice low and mellow.

Did I say blue balls? Make that purple.

Fuck.

TINKER

Five minutes later, Carrie and Darren had said their good-byes, leaving me and Cooper alone. Well, sort of alone. I mean, we *were* in a gazebo in a courtyard surrounded by apartments. I had no doubt that Mrs. Webbly was watching at this very minute. She'd lived in the ground floor apartment facing the street—across the lawn from my own house—since before I was born, and considered herself something of a guardian for the community.

"So you obviously grew up here," Cooper commented. God, he

was pretty. I'd spent the whole meal refusing to look at him so I wouldn't make an ass of myself. *He has a girlfriend, remember?* "But your husband didn't?"

"Brandon started out as a junior deputy prosecutor in Seattle, but now he's worked his way up to director of the King County criminal division. I worked as a private chef when he first started, and then I expanded into the chocolate business a few years later. We split up about eighteen months ago. We're still dealing with paperwork, and I'm trying to decide if I should buy him out of the house."

Cooper eyed me, as if waiting for me to say more but I wasn't going there. What'd happened between me and Brandon wasn't public, and that's the way I wanted it. Cooper seemed to figure this out, because he changed the subject.

"So how long have you been back in Hallies Falls?"

"About six months," I replied. "I came home when my mom passed. Dad wasn't doing too well, and the more I saw, the more I realized he couldn't manage on his own. It's getting to a point where I'll have to make some tough decisions. My real life is in Seattle, and everyone there thinks I should just move him. Put him in a home, and either sell the apartment building or find a property manager. Can't quite wrap my head around that, though. This place has been a part of me my entire life."

Cooper nodded, his face thoughtful.

"Loyalty is a good thing," he pointed out. "Gotta respect that."

I found myself smiling at him in surprise.

"Thanks. Not everyone sees it that way."

"Yeah, well opinions are like assholes, remember?" he said. "Sometimes you just need to tune out the static for a while."

"Exactly—and that's what I'm doing. Sooner or later I'll have to make the decision, because I can't keep up running the business forever without a real commercial kitchen. I could build one in the basement of the house, but it'd be a big commitment, because it'll take at least five years before I recoup all the costs. Thankfully,

Mom and Dad transferred title on the place to me years ago, so I
don't need to worry about liquidating, even if Dad needs long-term
care."

"That's good news," he said, and I fell into his eyes a little. They
were dark and rich, and then he licked his lips and heat rushed
through me. I wanted to kiss him so bad, then drag him back to my
room and—

"Tinker?"

"Yes?" I asked breathlessly.

"Where should I put the food?"

So much for dragging him back to my room. Ugh.

"Just take it into the kitchen and set it on the counter," I said,
looking around to see if there was anything I could discreetly stab
myself with—maybe that would pull my head out of the gutter. At
least there wasn't much leftover food to deal with, so I loaded the
dishwasher while he carried everything inside. Then he leaned
against the counter next to me, watching as I washed the silverware
by hand.

"Why don't you put it in the machine?" he asked.

"It's my grandma's sterling," I said. "I don't want the dishwasher
to damage it."

Cooper raised a brow.

"You always use sterling silver for a picnic with paper plates?"

I laughed.

"Grandma always did," I said. "And she let me use her good
china for tea parties, too. Using the silverware makes me happy—
brings back memories. When I use the plates all I can think about
is the fact that I'm creating more work for myself. Can you dry?"

"Sure," he said, catching the towel I tossed toward him. It only
took about ten minutes to wash everything up, but he stood next
to me the whole time. Every minute or two our bodies would bump,
and I swear, I felt his presence in the air itself. My breasts were
tight, and I kept catching myself shifting my hips as flickers of
awareness and arousal ran through me.

We finished way too soon for my taste, or maybe it wasn't soon enough. I had this vivid daydream that he'd sweep me up with a kiss, maybe haul me back to my bedroom and ravish me. You know, like in an old romance novel, where men were men and women stayed home and waited to be ravished in elaborately decorated country manor houses . . . Our apartment building was Tudor revival. That should count, right?

Now we stood staring at each other. His eyes were intense, and if it'd been anyone else on earth, I'd have sworn he was into me. Then his phone rang. Cooper pulled it out and frowned.

"What's up, Talia?" he asked, dumping cold water all over my fantasies. So much for my impending ravishment—stupid Tudors, giving me hope. I turned away, pretending to be fascinated by something in my spice cabinet. Yup, there was the dill. You can never have too much dill. "No, not really doing anything. How soon? Okay, I'll head right over."

He hung up as I reached for the little bottle, which was on the top shelf. I ignored him, determined not to react to his talk with the girlfriend, because how pathetic would that be?

"Let me get that for you," he said, right in my ear. It startled me so much that I jumped back, right into his body. One strong arm came around my waist to steady me while the other reached for the bottle. My entire body seemed to melt into his strength, and my boobs made a serious bid for escape from my halter top when the hard muscles of his chest touched my back. I felt him bulging a little against my butt. Not like he had a full boner, but the package was definitely there, and it wasn't soft.

Goose bumps broke out all over my body.

"I really enjoyed dinner," he said, the words a low whisper in my ear. "But I need to get going now—I'm meeting up with Talia. Here's your dill."

Cooper handed me the little bottle, then let me go before walking out of the kitchen.

What. The. Fuck.

Through the kitchen window, I watched as he threw a leg over his motorcycle. Then he was kicking it to life, pulling away from the curb with a spray of gravel. Every nerve in my body tingled, my nipples were like rocks, and my panties were soaked. Nobody had made me feel this way in forever, and yet instead of staying here to finish the job, he'd left to go see his girlfriend.

Hateful bitch.

My fingers hurt, and I looked down to realize I'd been squeezing the bottle so hard they'd turned white. I scowled, tossing it in the garbage, because who the fuck likes dill, anyway?

CHAPTER FIVE

GAGE

For once, I was thankful that I had a date with Talia. Yes, she was a controlling bitch and I hated dealing with her . . . But it reminded me why I wasn't free to go after Tinker. I couldn't afford an entanglement with another woman. Not if I wanted to stay loyal to my club.

My dick disagreed.

It thought we should just bang Tinker on the kitchen counter, because fuck loyalty. Gotta admit, it was damned tempting. I had this recurring fantasy of ripping off her pants, smacking her ass a couple times for color, and then splitting her wide open while she screamed at me. She'd be hot and tight and warm . . .

Fuck.

It actually hurt to climb on my bike—that's how much she'd worked me up. At least the ride out to the Nighthawks' clubhouse gave me the time to pull my shit together. I turned into the parking lot, nodding to the prospect standing watch outside. He looked like he was fifteen years old, and I couldn't see him weighing much over a hundred and twenty-five pounds. Marsh was obviously scraping bottom at this point.

"I'm here to see Talia," I told him, and he nodded, his face distinctly uncomfortable. Great, she must be up to something. Just what I needed to deal with tonight.

"She's right inside."

I opened the door to find the clubhouse maybe half full. Men wearing Nighthawks colors sat around talking, and girls flitted back and forth, fetching beer and giggling. Along one wall I spotted Cord and the other malcontents watching the rest with calculating eyes. A few women wearing leather vests sat with them—their old ladies. I'd been studying them closely and was convinced that Cord and his group wanted Marsh gone as much as the Reapers did. That added urgency to the situation, because sooner or later they'd stop watching and waiting. Then we'd have a civil war on our hands and that'd bring down trouble on all the clubs.

I looked around for Talia, spotting her toward the back of the room. Sitting on another man's lap. Fuck. I knew him—Mike something-or-other, another hangaround. The thought struck me—*another hangaround*—because that's all I could be right now. A fucking hangaround, after nineteen years with the Reapers. Going undercover sucked—I missed my club colors.

Talia glanced toward me and I saw her eyes harden. Great. I was supposed to be out here an hour ago, but I'd eaten dinner with Tinker instead. Now she was going to punish me. Deliberately turning her back on me, she swung a leg over Mike's lap and straddled him, her mouth covering his. She obviously wanted a scene, and I'd have to give it to her or roll over and beg like a pussy.

Heh. Wouldn't that serve her right.

Eyes followed me as I strolled across the room, resigned to playing my part. At least she'd picked a nobody. If I confronted one of the brothers, they'd kill me.

Little cunt.

If shit like this happened back home with a woman I was seeing, we'd have a problem but it wouldn't last for long. No brother would pull that on me, and if another man was stupid enough to touch what was mine, I'd put him in the ground.

In Hallies Falls, things were more complicated.

These men weren't my brothers, and they had no reason to back me up. If she'd chosen one of them, it'd all be over because it'd be me against the whole club. She obviously knew that, so she'd picked out a nobody, forcing my hand. If I told her to fuck off, I'd lose my connection to the club. Even worse, it might be seen as an insult to her brother. I'd watched him enough over the past few weeks to know he was erratic as fuck—what made him laugh one night would lead to him beating a man half to death the next. Sure sign he was using his own product. You take a man who starts out as a sociopath and start to give him meth, things get ugly fast. Now the little bitch would get her scene, which pissed me right off. Probably a good thing—it put me in a fighting mood.

That'd make what had to happen here a lot easier.

I moved across the room toward them, playing my part because Talia needed my jealousy to feed her ego. Marsh stepped out of the hallway in the back, presumably to enjoy the show. I caught his eye, then jerked my chin toward the couple making out. Marsh smirked, but he nodded his head and I knew I was in the clear to take care of business.

Catching Talia's arm, I jerked her off the man's lap. She fell to the floor as I caught him by the front of his shirt and pulled him to his feet.

"You don't touch what's mine," I growled. "Now get the fuck outside and we'll finish it."

He held up his hands.

"No need to fight over a gash."

"That's my sister you're callin' a gash," Marsh said loudly, obviously enjoying himself. "You sayin' she's not worth fighting over?"

I could practically see the thoughts racing through Mike's head as he finally realized just how fucked up the situation was. Man apparently wasn't that bright.

"Get your stupid ass outside," I told him again. "I don't want to make a mess in the clubhouse. That'd be plain rude. You don't want to be rude to the Nighthawk Raiders, do you?"

He blinked, and I realized the dumbass was drunk as fuck. Christ. Talia hadn't taken any chances—Mike was a lamb to the slaughter.

"I'll kick your ass," he slurred, and we started for the door. Voices rose around us, a new energy in the air. Everyone loved a good fight.

Outside there was just a trace of light still in the sky, and the evening air was hotter than it had any right to be. I caught a whiff of smoke and wondered if they'd been stupid enough to start a bonfire or something. There was a burn ban across the whole region. Last summer there'd been huge wildfires and we'd gotten even less rain this year. Combine that with low snowpack and a couple lightning strikes up in the hills, and building a fire was a real, real bad idea. Hopefully even Marsh wasn't that stupid.

Mike stumbled into the parking lot ahead of me as the bikers followed us. He must've been faking me out, because suddenly he turned and tried to sucker punch me. I managed to dodge it, which left him off-balance, opening the way for me to slam my fist into his kidneys. Fucker groaned but kept to his feet, which impressed me.

"Fight, you fucking pussy!" Talia shrieked behind us. Mike lunged and I danced back out of the way, feeling the anger rise. Anger at Talia, anger at Marsh. Hell, even at poor Mike for wasting my time. Some men loved to fight, but I'd never been one of them. Not that I was scared of anything—I'd stood up for my brothers time and again—but destroying a man with my fists was just another job.

Man? Hell. Mike hardly qualified, I decided, catching him in the stomach. Barely old enough to drink legal, and while he had strength and energy, I had experience on my side. Mike crashed to the ground, groaning, and I gave him a kick for good measure. Men shouted all around us, and I realized some of them were taking bets. Fuckwads.

Shooting a glance toward Talia, I caught her licking her lips, mesmerized by the violence. She loved this, having two men fight over her. Fed her ego, made her feel important. Christ, but I hated her.

The thought caught me off guard.

She'd pissed me off and disgusted me, but in that moment I realized it was true—I genuinely hated the bitch. Huh.

Mike lunged for my leg, catching me off-balance while I was distracted. *Fucking moron, keep your mind in the game.* He tackled me as I went down, the annoyance and frustration I'd felt blazing to new life. Fucker wanted a piece of me? I'd give him a goddamn piece.

He tried to pin me to the ground, but I broke free, thanking my high school wrestling coach for that little move. Guess muscle memory never dies. Then I kicked out, catching him and throwing him to the side as I jumped back to my feet. All bets were off now, and I kicked him again, this time in the ribs. I actually heard them breaking—Mikey-boy better hope he hadn't punctured a lung. The kid moaned, rolling to the side.

"You out?" I snarled. He started to nod, then Talia shrieked at him.

"You ever wanna be in this club? Fight like a fuckin' man!"

Jesus. Christ.

Bitch'd get him killed at this rate. Mike tried to push himself back up again, moving painfully slow. He was gonna force me to end it. *Moron.* I caught the front of his shirt, positioning him for one final punch to knock him out. Five seconds later he was on the ground, and this time he wasn't moving.

Raising my head, I stared at Talia.

"You happy now?" I snarled. She giggled, nodding her head. "Then get over here."

She scampered toward me as the men around us laughed, money changing hands. Nobody lifted a finger to help Mike. Guess he was just collateral damage, poor bastard. Grabbing Talia around her biceps, I dragged her toward the corner of the building, because she'd had her fun and now it was time to pay. We passed the corner and I marched her into the darkness.

"Cooper, you were so hot," she said breathlessly. I slammed her against the wall. She dropped a hand down to my dick, massaging me through the denim of my jeans, and I realized I was hard. Adrenaline from the fight, combined with the lingering memory of Tinker's soft smile.

I wrapped a hand around Talia's throat, squeezing just hard enough to hurt her. She laughed, stroking me faster. Woman had no fear and no common sense. Bitch was getting off on it, I swear.

"Time for you to learn some fucking rules," I snarled. "You like to play games, you need to find yourself a different man. I let you get away with it tonight. You pull that shit again, we're done."

Talia's lips opened and she panted, eyelids drooping. I felt her fingers fumbling with my pants and then she was unzipping me, pulling my cock out into the hot night air. I tightened my grip around her throat again and she moaned, her hand pumping me hard and fast.

I closed my eyes and thought of Tinker. Fuck, what I'd give to have her up against a wall like this . . .

"I'll make it up to you," she whispered, her voice hoarse.

Groaning, I lifted one of her legs and wrapped it around my waist, grinding against her. The little skirt she wore rode up until the only thing between us was the fabric of her thong. Jesus. My cock was so hard I thought it might split—apparently the fact that I hated this cunt didn't matter one bit, because my body wanted to fuck her. She choked and I realized I'd started squeezing harder.

Letting her throat go, I dug my fingers into her hair and jerked her head back.

"No more games."

"No more games," she whispered, eyes bright with excitement, and I knew she was lying. Bitch lived to play games.

"Then suck my cock."

She dropped to her knees in an instant, wrapping both hands around my dick as she licked the tip. Talia had many, many faults, but her blow job skills weren't in question, that was for damned sure. She played with me for several minutes, stoking the need that'd been burning through me all evening. First it was good. Then it wasn't enough. Grabbing her hair, I pushed deeper into her mouth and she took it like a pro, opening wide and sucking me down. Her fingers moved to my balls, one hand toying with them while the second massaged directly behind, her firm pressure on the root of my cock almost more than I could bear.

Then she pushed forward, taking me deep into her throat.

Fucking hell.

I closed my eyes, wondering how a woman I hated this much could make me feel so good. I imagined Tinker on her knees like this, and my balls drew up tight, heavy with come. God, I could see it now. Bright red lipstick and those straight-cut bangs hanging over her big eyes. She'd stare up at me and I'd wind her hair around my hands and fuck her mouth forever, just because I could.

Talia moved faster now, and she sent a finger wandering back to my ass. It pushed against the opening then slid inside. Her mouth was hot and wet, her throat closed tight around me as she found the spot that made me gasp. I imagined Tinker again, licking her lips, and my balls exploded into Talia's throat. Over and over again I pumped, shooting her full of my frustration and anger and come until she nearly choked on it.

Finally I let my hands drop and pulled my cock free. Talia stared up at me in coy triumph.

"You'll always come back for that," she said. I shook my head slowly.

"You're good, Talia, but I'm not your bitch. You want a man you can give orders to, find someone else. I meant what I said— you're *mine*, not the other way around. We clear?"

She shrugged, standing slowly. Then she leaned into me, dropping a hand down to squeeze my ass.

"Clear," she said. "Now let's go back inside. I want to see how bad Mike is hurt. You could've killed him, you know."

I could kill you.

"He'll be fine," I snapped. "Hope you enjoyed your moment of glory."

She reached down, cupping my softening cock. "Oh, I enjoyed it. You have no idea. Now buy me a drink—I need to rinse out my mouth."

TINKER

The next couple weeks passed quickly enough. Work was crazy, because not only did I have my regular orders to fill, but I'd gotten a major order from a law firm looking to hire my future ex, Brandon. He was hot shit, of course. I knew this because he told me regularly, but also because people were always trying to lure him into private practice. He wouldn't go—not with the King County Prosecuting Attorney's office up for grabs—but none of that mattered to me. We might be getting a divorce, but I still had a business to run. That's why my part-time shop assistant—Randi—and I were so busy that I closed the tea shop entirely so we could focus on production. This wasn't a particularly big deal, seeing as we never sold anything anyway.

As for Cooper, there wasn't much to tell. Eventually I decided that I'd imagined the tension between us. Not that I could complain about his work ethic—he kept himself busy enough, but whenever we ran into each other, he was only casually friendly. He'd give me a wave or we'd discuss work around the place, but his eyes were distant. Blank.

And of course, *she* was always around. Ugh. I don't know who disgusted me more, myself or Talia. She might be the immature brat, but I was certainly feeling like one. Who gets jealous of some guy they've never even kissed, anyway?

Stalkers and crazy people.

We hadn't entered full-on stalker territory just yet, but sometimes I felt like it was close. I caught myself watching him around the property, unconsciously tracking his schedule so that I could just happen to be around when he was. Pathetic. Lame. But, oh my God, the man was a work of art . . . And when he smiled, it felt like my heart might explode. Well, something definitely wanted to explode. Ha! On the bright side he was getting tons of work done and probably putting in more hours than was fair. For the first time since my mom died, I didn't feel all stressed out about the apartments.

Cooper's repairs weren't the only changes in the building, either.

That weekend a new family had moved into the last vacant unit, and overnight the place had burst with energy because there were four kids.

Yeah, four. In a two-bedroom apartment.

That violated my policy on the number of people per bedroom, but I had a soft spot for the mother, Janelle. We'd gone to school together and she'd gotten pregnant about the same time as my friend Carrie. Her story hadn't ended as well. The father took off right after the baby was born and Janelle's parents kicked her out. She'd drifted from one dead-end job to the next until about ten years ago, when she married a man whose main purpose in life seemed to be drinking and knocking her around.

They'd had three more kids together before she'd gotten up the nerve to move out, and when she'd come to me asking about the empty place, there was no way in hell I'd have said no.

Now I came home every day to find children running wild around our little courtyard, and while it was noisy it was also fantastic. Sure, I got the occasional twinge, the memory of little Tricia bittersweet and full of pain. But when they started building a fort using pallets and scraps from one of my dad's old projects, I didn't have the heart to tell them no.

There was only one downside . . . Janelle's first child, Sadie, was all grown up, and she was part of Talia's little posse. Now the bitch had two reasons to come hang out around my building, and I didn't like that one little bit.

Still, I felt optimistic that Thursday night. I'd made all the special-order caramels and had dipped about half of them. If I finished the rest by tomorrow, I'd be able to take my first weekend totally off in forever. Carrie and I had already booked ourselves into the day spa for manis, pedis, and drinkies.

That's why—despite my inner creeper when it came to Cooper—I was feeling all pleased with myself. Dad was already in bed, and I'd settled onto the porch swing with a book, enjoying the fading light and night air. These days it was too hot to spend much time outside, but the evenings were perfect. Living in the northwest, I had only a month or two each year where it was actually warm enough to sit outside in the dark. I liked to take advantage of them.

The book was good, and I was sucked in deep enough that I didn't even notice when someone started up the porch steps.

"Tinker, you got a minute?" he asked, startling an unattractive squawk out of me. Cooper laughed, and I glared up at him.

"Think you're pretty sneaky, don't you?"

He shrugged, the smile on his face crinkling the edges of his eyes in an impossibly sexy way. Sheesh. Did he do *anything* that wasn't hot? (Okay, I'd watched him kiss Talia the other night and threw up a little in the back of my mouth, so I guess there was that.)

"Sure, it's all my fault," he replied. "I wrote the book, snuck it into your house, and then waited for my moment to scare you."

"You're not helping," I said, trying to stare down my nose at him. Seeing as he was taller than me and also standing up, this was less than effective. "So what's up?"

"I wanted to go over a couple things with you about the building," he said, holding up a little notebook. "Mind if I sit down?"

Sit down? Next to me? Yes, please.

Scooting over, I made room for him, reminding myself that it wasn't stalkerish if he was the one who'd asked to sit there in the first place. Cooper settled on the swing, which was just a little tight for someone his size. That meant his leg was pressing against mine and our shoulders touched. Then his special scent washed over me and I had to hold back a shiver.

"So I noticed some of the upper-floor apartments have water stains on their ceilings," he said. "I talked to the tenants, and apparently the roof started leaking last winter. They talked to your dad about it, but . . . Well, it didn't get fixed. I guess your mom gave them a cut in their rent in exchange for putting up with it, and told them the roof would get repaired this summer."

I frowned.

"I didn't see anything about that in her files," I said, feeling my stomach sink. *How many more little surprises did she leave behind?* "But we were just in survival mode after she passed."

"That's what I figured," he said, twisting to look at me. Our shoulders bumped and he frowned. "This is awkward—do you mind if I put my arm behind you?"

"Um, sure."

He raised it to the back of the swing and for one glorious instant I thought he might actually touch me. Instead he let it rest on the back side of the swing seat. Pisser. I wanted to lean into his body as he held me close. Then he'd pull me in and kiss me and . . . What? Sweep me off into the sunset on his magical winged lion while singing songs about my beauty? That was about as likely as him making a move on me right now.

Stupid reality, fucking up all my fantasies.

"So how bad is it?" I asked, mentally tallying my bank balance. I had some savings, but not a lot. There'd be more once the divorce was final, but despite all my lawyer's calls to Brandon's lawyer, we still hadn't made any progress. The big holdup right now was whether or not to sell the house. He was being a jerk about it because I didn't have enough cash to buy him out. But we'd put in a commercial kitchen in the basement and I'd need it if I moved back to Seattle . . . Brandon kept saying I should sell the apartment building to pay him off—I couldn't begin to wrap my head around the idea. Not only that, it seemed like there was less money in our investments than I remembered. It didn't add up, and we'd been arguing about it for months.

I couldn't decide if there was something fishy about the whole thing or if he was just stalling.

"Well, you'll need a whole new roof in the next few years, there's no help for that," Cooper said, holding out a notebook covered in diagrams and cramped writing, all of which meant nothing to me. "But I can do some basic repairs that should hold for another winter or two. I have the time and I know how to do it, but it's still going to cost. I've run some numbers, and I think we're looking at close to five grand for materials and equipment rental."

I met his gaze, swallowing. It was a lot of money, but we had it in the rental account. Good thing I'd filled that last empty unit, though, because we were barely cash-flowing as it was. I looked back up to find him studying me, our faces so close that I could feel the heat of his breath.

"I can swing that much," I said quietly. "How long do you think it'll take?"

He tilted his head, and I realized he was watching my lips. It felt like there wasn't quite enough air around us. Everything was hot, and I couldn't decide if it was the heat of his body or mine making me so uncomfortable. Licking my lips, I leaned toward him unconsciously.

Cooper swallowed.

"I think about three or four weeks, depending on what else comes up. If you want, I'll start work this weekend."

"Don't you have plans?" I asked, my voice a whisper. He shook his head slowly.

"Nothing," he said, his voice rough. He swallowed and I saw his eyes drift down toward my chest. I'd dressed for the heat in a light tank, the same one I usually wore to bed. It had a little shelf bra built in but it definitely hadn't been designed for maximum coverage. Normally I wouldn't even wear it outside the house. It'd only been the porch, though, and darkness was already falling.

Now my nipples poked through and his breath caught.

"Tinker—"

"Cooper—"

I laughed nervously, then raised my arms, crossing them over my chest. He shook his head, as if trying to wake up.

"I'll charge the materials to your account at the hardware store, if that's all right."

"Of course."

"Tinker, right now things are complicated. Talia—"

Flushing, I pulled away from him, because I didn't need to hear the speech. I'd been repeating it in my head ever since I'd learned they were dating.

"No worries," I said, standing up abruptly. "I need to get inside, check on Dad. Keep me posted on the roof and all that."

Then I scuttled inside the house like a big, fat coward, because the last person on earth I wanted to talk about was stupid Talia.

As for Cooper, I don't know what he did.

Probably went off to boink his girlfriend because she was so much better than me.

Stupid jerkwad.

CHAPTER SIX

TINKER

Cooper spent the weekend working on the roof.

Without a shirt.

By Sunday afternoon I'd decided this constituted cruel and unusual punishment, but that didn't stop me from hanging out in the yard and watering the flower baskets so I could watch him. It'd been a real challenge keeping them alive this year—we'd had the driest summer in memory, with more wildfires sparking in the national forests every day. Fortunately, none of them had come close to human habitation. Yet.

I was almost finished when Cooper climbed down off the roof, put away his tools, and disappeared inside, presumably to shower off the sweat. (Just the thought weakened my knees.) It was a good thing, too. Watching him was very nice, but it probably wasn't particularly healthy, and I definitely didn't want to talk to him any more than I had to. Not when every conversation ended with me tied up in knots from sexual tension while he moseyed off to his girlfriend.

By the time he came back out, I'd settled onto the porch with the glass of wine I traditionally awarded myself every Sunday afternoon, determined not to notice if he happened to reappear. Then he was in front of me and I forgot all about my vow not to notice, because seriously . . . his hair was all wet and hanging around his face as he walked up the porch steps. *Yum.*

"Hey," he said. "How's it going?"

"Fine," I replied, smiling without quite meeting his gaze—this was part of my new plan for dealing with Cooper whenever he got too close. If I looked at his eyes, I might fall right into them and say something stupid, but if I focused on his shoulder I could pretend I was talking to Brandon. This worked, because talking to Brandon was the least sexy activity on earth (outside of actually *having* sex with Brandon, of course).

"Did I do something to piss you off?" he asked bluntly. "Because I thought we were friendly, but all weekend you've been disappearing every time I try to talk to you."

I had, actually, although I hadn't realized I'd been doing it so obviously. (Creeping around and watching someone without talking to them is more complicated than it looks, especially in a town as small as this one.)

"No," I said, startled into meeting his eyes. Ah crap. They were deep and brown and so rich they could've been made of chocolate. *Danger!* "Of course not. I really appreciate all the work you've been doing around here."

"Well, I appreciate the job, not to mention the hospitality," he said, offering a sexy smile. It transformed his face, and my womb quivered. Yeah, you read that right. My womb fucking *quivered*, because there's really no other way to describe what this man did to me. This man who had a girlfriend, a girlfriend I knew all about because his bedroom wall and my bedroom wall were right next to each other. Sometimes his bed thumped against it while they had crazy monkey sex.

"I'm glad you're enjoying your new place," I managed to say.

"I am," he replied. "Although I feel kind of sheepish, since you fixed me dinner and I never paid you back. Too bad I can't cook for shit, but I'm picking up some Chinese tonight instead. Wanna share it with me? You can even bring your dad if you want."

OMG he likes us! my quivering loins shrieked, making an end run around my common sense. *Say yes. Yes!*

"Sure," I said quickly. Probably too quickly. "But my dad's in bed. He wasn't feeling good. I think it's just a cold, but he gets tired easily these days."

"I hope he feels better," Cooper said. "I'll go grab the food. Meet you at my place in about half an hour?"

"See you then."

Never has a half hour flown by so quickly.

I told myself it was because Chinese sounded so good. That I'd had a long work week—the last thing I wanted to do was cook for myself. Not only that, I really needed to hit the grocery store, because there wasn't much left in the house anyway.

My quivering womb called bullshit on this, emphatically pointing out that I hadn't gotten laid for way too long and that it wasn't like he was *married*.

"Come in!" Cooper called when I knocked at his door. I stepped inside hesitantly, looking around to see what he'd done with the place. There wasn't much furniture, and what he did have seemed to be mostly of the thrift shop variety. He walked out of the little galley kitchen toward an old Formica table, which I noted had been set with mismatched plates.

"Guess what I didn't get in the divorce," he said lightly, offering a quirky smile.

"Furniture."

"You nailed it," he said. "But that's okay—the kids need it more than I do, so I left everything with my ex. Want something to drink?"

"Water's good."

I sat down at the table, feeling awkward. My own home was so comfortable, and this just seemed . . . bleak.

"You should get some plants or something."

He laughed, reaching forward to open a steaming container.

"I'd probably kill them," he admitted. "Not really a plant kind of guy. This is mostly just a place to sleep and shower while I start over again."

I frowned, wondering what I'd do when he left. Unrequited lust aside, I had a lot more unfinished projects. "When do you think you'll hit the road again?"

He shrugged.

"Really just depends. I'm figuring things out on the legal front right now. Taking some time for myself. I've done well enough that I'm not too worried about money, at least not for a while, but if I leave the area, my ex might try to pull something, you know?"

"So you're in limbo," I said, spooning some broccoli beef out onto my plate.

"Yeah, you could say that. Watching and waiting."

"I know how that feels, actually. When Mom died last winter, it was sudden. She was always so healthy and strong, and she was only in her sixties. Then I got a phone call that she'd slid off the road one night. It wasn't even a bad accident, but I guess she hit her head exactly wrong and it was all over."

Cooper didn't say anything at first, and I looked up, expecting to see that old familiar look of pity. People never knew what to say, about my mom *or* the baby. There wasn't a hint of pity in his face, though. I couldn't read his expression, but he didn't feel sorry for me, and that was better than I could've hoped for.

"Sorry to hear that," he said quietly. I shrugged.

"It is what it is. I was only planning on staying for a week or two, but then I realized things weren't right with Dad. I can't leave him on his own, but I can't see putting him in a home, either."

"So you moved back to Hallies Falls to take care of him."

How to answer that? I wasn't sure I knew the answer myself.

"I haven't decided yet," I admitted. Cooper raised a brow.

"You already relocated your business and took over the apartment building. What's left to decide?"

He was so matter-of-fact about it that I laughed.

"What?" he asked.

"Everyone dances around, but you just blurt things out, don't you?"

"Call it like I see it."

"I never planned to move back home permanently," I told him. "And the the way I'm doing business right now is completely unsustainable. If I'm going to stay in Hallies Falls, I'll need to put that commercial kitchen in the house—those aren't cheap. The little one down at Mom's store passes Department of Health standards, but it's no good long term. Among other things, it's not big enough for all my equipment."

"That's a big investment," Cooper said, leaning back in his chair.

"Yes," I admitted. "And it means a real commitment to the town, which was never my plan. At the same time, Dad is happy here. He's not a danger to himself, at least not yet. Just confused. I can't imagine taking him away from his home unless there's no other choice—I think he'd be totally lost."

"Tough situation," Cooper said. "But it sounds like you've already made your decision."

I cocked my head, startled. "How's that?"

"You just said you can't imagine taking him away," he replied casually. "And I've seen the way you watch him. You love him and you want to take care of him more than you want to be in Seattle—otherwise you'd have left by now. Looks like you need to sell your old place and move forward."

"But then I'll be trapped here," I said, my voice low. "It's not easy being a single woman in this town. You wouldn't believe how many small-minded assholes live here, and they just love to gossip about me."

Cooper smirked. "So I've heard."

I groaned, closing my eyes.

"So you know about that?"

"I heard you're a cougar who likes to seduce college boys on the weekends," he said, cocking his head at me. "Nobody's actually come out and said it, but I get the impression you also drink their innocent blood to maintain your youth and beauty?"

I leaned my elbows on the table, rubbing my temples, wondering how my life had ever come to this. "There's a perfectly reasonable explanation. It's not flattering, but believe me, I'm not some cougar on the prowl."

Cooper started laughing. Frowning, I flipped him off, which made him laugh louder.

"What's so funny?"

"I know you're not on the prowl," he said. "I live next door to you, Tinker. You're in bed by ten every night and haven't gone on a single date since I moved in. Either you're having a hell of a dry spell or you don't get around nearly as much as they'd like to imagine. So tell me, where does the cougar rep come from?"

"It's really embarrassing," I admitted, pushing my plate to the side.

"The best stories usually are," he said, grinning at me. "Tell me. I'll even bribe you."

He stood and walked over to the fridge, pulling out a giant, fancy cupcake balanced inside a domed plastic container. Carefully removing the cover, he set it in the center of the table.

"That thing's huge," I said, laughing.

"Yeah, women say that to me a lot," he replied, deadpan.

"You're terrible."

"No, the general consensus is that I'm pretty good," Cooper said, allowing his mouth to quirk. "See? That's so lame I'm humiliated and ashamed of myself. Now you have no excuse not to share your story."

I bit my lip, trying not to laugh at him.

"Confession is good for the soul," he prodded.

"Okay," I replied, wondering if I could really go through with it. But he'd hear it all sooner or later anyway. Almost everyone in town knew already. "You have to promise you won't judge me."

"You got it."

"So I left my husband a year and a half ago," I started. "It was a rough time. No need to get into details, but I'd fallen into a slump and just couldn't seem to pick myself up again. Four months ago I got an invitation for a bachelorette party in Olympia for my friend Margarita. She was in high school with me and Carrie, and now she's a professor down at Evergreen State."

I paused, staring at the cupcake. Could I really tell him this?

"And?"

"All right, so Carrie and I drove down together, and a big group of us met up at the hotel for the party. Rented a suite and everything. It was almost like a high school reunion for me, because a lot of the guests were women I grew up with but hadn't seen for years. We all moved away from town a long time ago, all except for Carrie, Heather Brinks—she's Margarita's cousin like ten times removed, but Margarita's mom made us invite her anyway—and Maisy Braeburn, who invited herself along with Heather. They were bitches back then and they're bitches now, and it never occurred to us that they'd actually show their faces. Anyway, that night everyone went dancing, and eventually we landed back at the hotel around three in the morning. Maisy was feeling sick, so she went back to her room while the rest of us gathered in the suite. That's when the strippers showed up."

Cooper smirked. I felt my cheeks start to heat up.

"They did their dancing thing, and we were all laughing and having a great time and there was one who kept hitting on me. Now, he was pretty to look at, but I felt sort of weird perving on him because he was probably twenty-one at most, you know? Barely legal. Not only that, he looked sort of familiar but I couldn't quite place him. Then he invited me to do some body shots off him, and the next thing I knew we were back in one of the bedrooms and he was doing body shots off me and . . . Well, let's just say we got real friendly real fast."

He stared at me, obviously stunned. *Shit, this was a huge mistake. He's judging me and—*

Then Cooper burst out laughing. Not hateful, mean laughter, but genuine amusement.

"Stop it!"

He laughed harder, holding up a hand.

"Calm down," he finally said.

"I can't believe I told you that," I moaned, wondering if I could make a break for the door. I mean, the situation was so awkward already—was it even possible to make it worse?

Cooper shook his head, grinning at me. "So you fucked a stripper—they're people, too, you know. There are uglier crimes."

I groaned, rubbing my temples again. *You started it, now finish it.*

"It gets worse," I admitted. "Maybe half an hour later, the room door bursts open and everyone comes trooping in looking for more booze. Carrie and I had hit a liquor store that afternoon, and the backup stash was in the bedroom, you know? Anyway, here I am buck naked on top of the guy and they're all staring at me. Next thing I know, Heather whips out her phone and starts filming."

Cooper's eyes widened. "You have a sex tape floating around out there?"

"Yesss . . ." I admitted very quietly. "And that's not all."

"Jesus, and I thought it was funny before," he said, shoulders shaking. I glared at him, but there wasn't any judgment in his eyes, just honest laughter. "Hey, I don't care that you have a sex tape. Human beings fuck, despite what some of these gossipy prudes around here want to admit. Why should you be ashamed of it?"

I just shook my head, because obviously Cooper and I had very different definitions of the word "shame."

"Anyway, they're all laughing at me and I'm humiliated and all that. The guy jumps up and tells them to leave. Then all of sudden I hear Maisy's voice, and she is *pissed*—her aunt owns the Hungry Chicken downtown, it's not far from my store. She starts screaming at me and I'm all confused and still drunk and then it suddenly falls together. The guy I slept with? He was her cousin, Jamie. He grew up in Hallies Falls until his folks got divorced and he moved to

Spokane to live with his dad. *I used to babysit him!* Now he's stripping to pay his way through college. I hadn't seen him in years, and let me tell you—he'd grown up a *lot* during that time. None of us even recognized him! Not only that, Heather texted the damned video to half the town. I *still* don't know how many people watched it or who has copies. Guess who isn't welcome at the Hungry Chicken anymore?"

Cooper leaned back in his chair, raising a brow.

"You fucked up."

"Yeah, I fucked up," I agreed, seriously considering crawling under the table. "I had no idea, Cooper. None. I was drunk as hell and he kept coming on to me. Turns out he's had a crush on me since he was just a kid or something. When he saw me at the party he decided to go for it. Maisy wasn't there when he first showed up—she was drunk and puking back in her own room—and the rest of us didn't recognize him. The rest is history. I'm the town whore who seduced the innocent kid I used to babysit. The only good thing is that the Braeburns managed to shut it down *fast*—I mean, people around here know everything, but so far as I can tell nobody uploaded it online or anything, so I guess I have that going for me. Oh, and Maisy was so pissed at Heather that she *still* won't talk to her. The whole thing was beyond crazy."

"What a fucking cunt," Cooper said, shaking his head. "Who does that?"

"Apparently Heather Brinks," I told him, my face on fire. "She's hated me for years. Heather's high school boyfriend dumped her and then asked me to the prom. I thought Carrie was going to kill her that night in Olympia. Even now she practically hisses and spits at her every time they run into each other. My dad was shocked, although I have to give him credit—he never judged me. We decided to ride it out, but now half of Hallies Falls thinks I'm the Whore of Satan. Can you see why I might not want to live here anymore?"

"Yeah, I can see it," Cooper admitted. "But Tinker, if you think about it, you didn't actually do anything wrong. I mean, you probably should've locked the door, but other than that, the kid's a legal adult, right?"

"Of course," I said. "And it wasn't like I hired him to sleep with me. Things just happened . . ."

"And you were drunk," he added. "Was the guy drunk, too?"

"Maybe a little buzzed," I admitted. "But nowhere near as drunk as me."

"So he saw his chance and went for it," he continued, still smiling. "Can't blame him—you've got a bangin' body, Tinker. He knew what he wanted and took it. Not his fault his mom's a bitch. You know, if a guy fucks a stripper for free, everyone thinks he's a stud—why should this be any different? And why do you care what a bunch of small-minded cunts think anyway? Not like you lost any friendships that matter. You can't tell me that Carrie and Darren give a flying fuck about any of this."

It took me a minute to answer, because I was still hung up on the "bangin' body" comment. Then I processed the rest of his words.

"Carrie said she was jealous," I admitted. "Said she'd have done him in a heartbeat if it wasn't for Darren. And I think Darren just enjoyed how pissed off Maisy was. She's been a bitch to all of us for years."

Cooper smiled.

"So there you have it. If it makes you feel better, I've fucked all kinds of strippers. Managed a club for a couple years, actually, and if they play the game right, they make damned good money. And they're real people, just like the rest of us—it's not like you went down on a donkey. Hell, the kid got lucky. Gotta admire that kind of initiative on his part."

I stared at him, trying to wrap my head around what he'd said.

"It really doesn't bother you, does it?" I asked. Cooper shook his head.

"Nope, it really doesn't bother me," he replied, his eyes growing darker. "I'd have done the same damned thing in his place."

Wait. Did I hear that right? *Holy shit!*

"Are you hitting on me?" I asked, unnerved. "Because I know you have a girlfriend. Just because I slept with a stripper doesn't mean I'm a slut."

He caught and held my gaze, dark eyes intense.

"I'm telling the truth," he replied, his words slow and deliberate. "You're smart and sexy and hot as hell, and if I was free I'd be all over that. But you're right, I've got a girlfriend and I'm not looking to break up with her. Doesn't mean I can't appreciate a beautiful woman when I see her. Now, you want to eat that cupcake or not?"

CHAPTER SEVEN

GAGE

"Can you share some of the blanket with me?"

I reached for it as Tinker nodded, eyes glued to the TV. I'd convinced her to stay and watch a movie after dinner, which hadn't been easy. Not sure I'd ever seen anyone turn as red as she did while she was telling her sex tape story.

Have to admit, it caught me off guard.

I'd heard rumors around town about her. Not that I'd paid much attention—backstabbing bitches flapping their mouths had never interested me. Hearing what she'd done, though . . . I was sort of impressed she'd gone for it, and more than a little jealous of the little fuckweasel, because he knew what that tight cunt of hers felt like and I could only imagine.

Damn.

As for judging her, those bitches could eat shit and die. Wasn't like she'd done anything that bad. I'd fucked more strippers than I could count, and considering the crimes I'd pulled in the last few weeks alone, Tinker was a goddamned angel. Even so, I'd known she'd start avoiding me if I let her leave while she felt uncomfortable, so the movie was serving a purpose.

But now I was starting to second-guess my plan.

For one thing, there was a very sexy woman sitting less than six inches from me. I didn't want the blanket because I was cold—I needed cover for my massive boner. I couldn't even focus on the show, because I was too busy watching another movie in my head.

Tinker's sex tape.

She'd been on top. I kept picturing it, only instead of some dumbass kid, she was riding me. Did she sit straight up, or lean over, letting her boobs dangle right over his mouth? That's what I'd want—tits flying just within reach, and my hands on her ass to guide her. I shifted on the couch, hating the fact that I couldn't do jack shit about this growing, aching need.

How long would it take to finish up business with the Nighthawks? Too fucking long.

"I can't believe how late it is," Tinker said, yawning, and I realized the movie had ended. Now she stretched upward, the blanket falling to her waist as her boobs pushed forward.

God, how much should a man be expected to take?

I should've stayed away from her completely—that'd been the plan—but something had snapped when I'd seen her out in the courtyard. Couldn't remember the last time I'd met a woman like Tinker. She was smart and sexy and funny, and she worked damned hard to take care of her family and business. Sure, I wanted to fuck her—you'd have to be gay not to—but I respected her, too.

"I should probably get going," she said, offering me a smile so sweet I wanted to bite her lips. "I like to check on Dad before going to sleep, and I've got to be up early in the morning. I've got to package orders for the courier tomorrow—if they aren't ready by two p.m., I'm screwed."

I considered rolling over on top of her. Pushing her down into the couch cushions, shoving my leg between hers, and showing her what a real man feels like.

"Cooper?" she asked, looking confused. I blinked a couple times, forcing myself to focus on her face.

"I'm going to watch another one," I told her, because I'm a goddamn masochist. "You sure you're ready to head out?"

She frowned, and I could almost read her thoughts. Yes, she should leave. But she wanted me as much as I wanted her. And yeah, I realize that makes me sound like an egotistical ass, but this wasn't my first rodeo. I saw the lust in her eyes, and the way she licked her lips and stared at my mouth. This wasn't a one-way street, not even close.

"I guess I could stay a little longer," she whispered. Christ, she was so sweet and soft. I wanted to bite her even more now. Suck that pouty lower lip into my mouth and shove a finger up her ass.

Break her.

You're one sick fuck.

Why yes. Yes, I am. Thanks for noticing.

I managed to control the urge, catching her hand instead, giving it a friendly squeeze like some kind of pathetic tool. Her fingers tightened on mine, then she pulled away and snuggled back down under the blanket, raising her feet to rest on the coffee table. I grabbed the remote and clicked through the menu.

Tomorrow I'd do my job. I'd fuck Talia and spy on Marsh and look for any kind of weakness that might end this situation, the faster the better. Tonight, though . . . Tonight I'd pretend this wasn't a waste of time.

Goddamn, but my dick hurt.

The next hour was torture.

Tinker sat next to me, all cute and classy and absolutely refusing to make any kind of eye contact. I don't know how she felt, but to me the sexual tension hanging in the air was thick and heavy. I kept thinking about her hand in mine—small, but strong. The hand of someone who knew how to work hard. So far as I knew, Talia had never held down a job, let alone supported herself.

The couch shifted, and I glanced over to find Tinker sliding deeper into the cushions, drawing the blanket up to her chin. Our legs were maybe six inches apart. She shifted again, and then her hand bumped mine under the blanket. She jerked it back quickly, and I caught the hint of a flush on her cheeks. That was another thing I liked about her—her skin was so pale that I could see every hint of arousal.

Grabbing her hand, I pulled it over to rest on my thigh. This was a really bad idea, so I pointedly refused to think it through. Her hand tensed at first, then relaxed into my strength. My cock swelled against the fabric of my jeans, just inches from her fingers—it'd be so easy to push her hand toward it, wrap it around my painfully swollen dick, and just go to town.

Tinker's fingers gave a quick squeeze—almost more of a spasm—and I bit back a groan.

Yeah, okay. Really, *really* bad idea. I should get off the couch and shut this shit down right now, because I couldn't afford to blow things with Talia just yet. Instead I found myself leaning toward Tinker, bumping shoulders.

God.

I'd grown a pussy. No other explanation, because I couldn't figure out why the hell else an adult man would sit holding hands under a damned blanket like a kid. A member of the Reapers MC, who fucked more women in a year than most did in their lives. A man with blood on his hands. Fresh blood.

But Tinker smelled really good.

I'd get up in a minute—no, five minutes. Five more minutes wouldn't matter. Tinker sighed, letting her head fall against my shoulder, and I smelled peaches. Christ, I loved the smell of her hair. If Picnic could see this right now, he'd shit bricks. Of course, considering how far the club had stuck its neck out for his woman, wasn't like he had the right to complain.

Tinker's hand shifted, brushing against my cock. I heard her breath hiss and she jerked her hand away, but that instant of contact was enough to set me on fire, lava boiling through my veins. Enough of this shit—I wanted her, and I'd waited too long already.

I turned, catching the back of her head and pulling her in for a hard kiss, because fuck loyalty.

She stiffened at first, then her lips softened. My tongue slid in and all thought ceased. She tasted like cupcake. Cupcake and caramel and every kind of deliciousness that I wanted to eat. God, what would her pussy taste like? I had a feeling it'd be sweeter than all the rest put together. I thought about all those pretty candies she made, and imagined shoving a piece of caramel up her cunt just so I could suck it back out again.

Jesus, I needed to stop thinking. Right now.

Fumbling with the blanket, I pushed her down onto the couch, shoving a knee between her legs. Fire exploded as my dick met her stomach. I started grinding against her, which made holding the kiss a bit of a contortion, but so fucking worth it. Hell, if kissing her felt this good, what would it be like when—

The front door flew open so hard it cracked the drywall.

I jumped up, shoving Tinker into the couch and reaching for the gun I kept stashed under the couch. I raised it, covering her with my own body, wondering if Marsh had finally figured out who I was. Talia charged in, eyes blazing.

Great. Just fucking great. Exactly the end to the evening I'd hoped for.

"What the hell is going on here?" she demanded. Tinker moaned, and not in pleasure. What a fucking mess. I didn't feel guilty—I owed Talia jack shit—but I'd dragged Tinker into this, and that was a dick move.

Gotta stop thinkin' with your cock.

"I need to get out of here," Tinker said frantically, trying to push me off. I didn't move, holding Talia's eyes. For all I knew, she had a weapon—I'd let Tinker up when I knew it was safe, and not a second earlier.

"Talia, get your ass over there," I said, nodding toward the opposite wall. "Tinker's gonna leave and then we'll have a talk."

"Oh, we're gonna *talk*," she snarled. "Right after I cut your dick off!"

She lunged and I jumped up, catching her before she could reach my landlady. Tinker rolled to the floor, scuttling back and away. Talia tried to knee my balls. I blocked her, grabbing one of her hands and twisting it behind her back. We stood glaring into each other's eyes, hers promising me a slow, painful death.

Right back atcha, sweetheart.

"Let me go, asshole."

"Tinker, get out of here. I'll talk to you later."

Talia lunged forward and caught my chin in her teeth, biting down like a Tasmanian devil. Holy shit. I reached up, locking my hands around her jaw as Tinker screamed. Something hit Talia over the head, and she unlatched abruptly, spinning around to attack Tinker, who was clutching the motorcycle parts manual that she'd used to defend me.

"I can't believe I just did that," she said, eyes wide.

Neither could I, actually.

Talia screeched again, stomping on my foot to break free, determined to punish Tinker. I loved a good catfight as much as the next guy, but this was getting out of hand. Diving for my fake girlfriend, I caught her and swung her up and over my shoulder, hissing and spitting. "Let me *go*!"

Tinker stared at us, chest heaving, eyes wide.

"This was a horrible mistake," she said quickly, and I could see she meant every word. "I'm sorry, Talia. I'll never talk to him again."

"You'll never *talk* again after I cut out your lying tongue, whore!"

"Shut up!" I bellowed, the room going silent. Breathing deep, I took a minute to control my anger. I wanted to throw Talia through the window. Instead I'd have to make peace with the crazy bitch, which meant banging her until she forgot what'd pissed her off in the first place. Hard as my dick was, her snatch wasn't the one it wanted.

And Tinker? At this rate I'd never see her again. *Christ, what the fuck was I thinking?*

"I'm out," Tinker said breathlessly, making for the door.

"That's right, slut. Run away!" Talia hissed. "You may act like a stuck-up bitch, but we all know the truth about you!"

"Shut the fuck up!" I growled, smacking her ass. Wasn't hard enough to really hurt, but definitely hard enough to catch her attention. Considering that she'd clawed up my neck and was doing her damnedest to pull out a chunk of my hair, I didn't feel bad about it at all. Talia lurched, knocking me off-balance. I caught a glimpse of Tinker slipping out the door, pushing past Talia's crony, Sadie, who was lingering in the doorway. Great. Apparently Talia had a spy in the building. Just what I needed, because obviously life wasn't shitty enough already.

"Get the fuck out of here," I snarled at the little rat, and Sadie took off running. I'd have to deal with that one sooner rather than later. Or maybe not, because much as I hated this little game, it wasn't over. Not yet. Everything boiled down to Marsh, and how fast we figured out his secrets.

"Let me go," Talia snarled, slapping at my back again. Instead I carried her into the bedroom, throwing her down with a rattling thump onto the secondhand bed. It knocked the breath out of her and she stilled. *Finally.* I pinned her down before she had a chance to recover, hands high over her head, legs trapped under mine.

Talia narrowed her eyes. I narrowed mine right back, wondering if she had any clue how easy it would be to strangle her. She was alone in an apartment with a very pissed-off biker. A biker one hell of a lot bigger than her. I'd played the pussy for weeks, but now she'd attacked Tinker.

This was a game changer.

"Let me up."

"Not until you calm down," I said, allowing some of the anger to show in my voice. "We're gonna talk this shit out."

"What's to talk about? You were cheating on me!"

And here we go . . .

"We aren't exclusive," I reminded her. "You've been sleeping around the whole time we've been together."

Her eyes widened.

"You knew that?" she whispered. *Jesus Christ.*

"Yeah, the used condoms sort of gave it away. Oh, and the way you were always texting other guys, even when we were together. Don't leave your fuckin' phone on the table while you pee if you want to keep shit like that quiet. Damned thing buzzes every twenty seconds. I only fought with Mike because you set me up to look bad at the clubhouse."

The rage drained out of her eyes, replaced with uncertainty and maybe a hint of fear. Nice. About time, too.

"So you did this to get back at me."

"Not really," I said bluntly. "We aren't a couple. We're just two people who fuck sometimes."

"What if I want more than that?" she asked softly. For an instant I wondered if I'd read her wrong—did she actually care about me? Maybe, I decided. Hell, she looked almost vulnerable. I could use this. Until now she'd had the upper hand in this little arrangement.

Time for a change.

"I just got out of a relationship," I said, the words slow and crisp. "We've been having fun and that's about as far as I want to go with it, at least for now. You want more, try showing me you have more to offer."

Talia seemed to shrivel in on herself. Water pooled in her eyes, and for a second I thought she might cry. Then she pushed out her chin, setting her jaw and glaring up at me.

"I don't want you fucking that bitch Tinker Garrett," she said. "It's her or me. You think you can handle that?"

Took everything I had not to roll my eyes, but I managed to pull it off.

"Like I give a shit about Tinker," I said. "I invited her to dinner because I felt sorry for her."

"You try to screw everyone you feel sorry for?" she asked, her voice hardening.

I shrugged. "We were watching a movie. It got cold so I grabbed some of the blanket and then she went for my cock. I'm only human. But think about it, Talia—Tinker's at least fifteen years older than you and probably a good twenty pounds heavier. You really think I'd pick her over you?"

Fuck yeah, I would. She had curves and class and she didn't throw temper tantrums like a fuckin' two-year-old.

"*Thirty* pounds," Talia sneered, and I knew I had her. God, the woman was so damned full of herself. When this shit ended, the boys back home owed me free beer for a year, I decided—I'd earned it. "You should see her sex tape. It's hilarious—she looks like a fat whale."

I stilled.

"Sex tape?" I asked, playing dumb. Talia laughed.

"Stupid bitch got caught fucking a stripper at a party," she said, eyes dancing. "Someone caught a video of it. I couldn't stop laughing the first time I saw the thing."

"Is it online?"

She shrugged. "I don't know. Probably. There's a billion other ones out there, too, so how would you know unless it went viral? Not that it would—she's nothing special."

The image of Tinker, naked, riding cock, took over my imagination. Would she be totally bare, tits swinging and ass shaking? Or maybe she'd been wearing a skirt, hiking it up and going to town just like that.

"Let me up and I'll show you," Talia said suddenly. "I have it on my phone."

That startled me right out of the fantasy. "What? Why the hell would you have that?"

"I knew she was watching you," she told me, obviously pleased with herself. "Fat bitch doesn't know you're out of her league. Marsh got a copy and I told him to send it. Thought it might be useful. Like I said—it's funny. She looks really stupid and then the guy gets really pissed off. She probably had to pay him and he knew he wouldn't get his money since they got interrupted. Oh, and Maisy Braeburn tried to attack her or something. It's hysterical."

I'd bet my Harley nothing Tinker did could look stupid, although

I wasn't sure I liked the idea of actually seeing her with the guy. Imagining her screwing some random stripper was one thing, but a real person? Not so much. On the other hand, it'd be a chance to look at her naked.

"Okay, show me," I said, rolling off Talia. "Although I still think it's weird you have it."

Talia sat up and reached into her jeans, pulling out her phone. She thumbed it on, then flipped through it, laying back against me as she held up the tiny screen.

The video started with a bunch of women dancing around with a couple of male strippers, obviously drunk off their asses. They were all about Tinker's age. Carrie walked by and looked at the camera, frowning.

"Turn that thing off," she said. "Nobody wants you taking pictures in here."

"What's the matter?" a female voice asked, sounding louder. Had to be the one holding the phone and recording. "Afraid Darren will be pissed?"

Carrie rolled her eyes, then flipped her off casually. Another woman shouted, "I need more tequila!"

The phone swiveled to show a short woman with long, dark hair, deep brown eyes, and a bright red dress so tight it must've been shrink-wrapped around her. On her head was a red veil with two little devil horns, and in one hand she held an empty liquor bottle turned upside down. She frowned at the camera, shaking her head like this was the most tragic event in the history of time.

"So sad . . ." she whimpered.

"There's more in the bedroom," someone said off camera, then the scene shifted abruptly, images rising and falling as its owner walked across the room. I saw flashes of leg and wall and generic hotel door opening, then a whispered, "Holy shit." Suddenly the camera snapped up, zooming in on one very naked Tinker Garrett.

She was straddling a man across a bed, facing the camera as she arched her back, eyes closed and face full of bliss. My cock hardened in an instant, because Jesus fucking Christ. Her tits were amazing—round and natural and bouncing as she rocked her hips across his once, twice, a third time. His hands tightened around her narrow waist and his body clenched, moaning as he came with an agonized groan. Tinker kept moving, reaching down between her legs and I nearly came myself, just from the sight of it.

Goddamn. Cancel Christmas. This was the best spank bank material ever.

"What the fuck? *Tinker?* Jesus, Heather, stop filming!" someone shouted.

That was Carrie's voice. Tinker's eyes flew open, a look of shock and utter horror taking over her face. She screamed, arms coming up and across her chest in a pathetic attempt to cover herself. A hand flashed in front of the phone. The video perspective jerked upward, showing the ceiling, as Carrie snarled, "Heather—I'm serious. Put the fucking phone down."

"What's going on?" Someone else called off camera. The phone suddenly dropped back down to show the couple, who'd just realized they'd been caught. More women's voices rose, and I heard a feminine laugh of pure delight. The red-veiled woman stumbled into the frame, clapping her hands in approval. "Go, Tinker—you kick ass! *Wooohoooo!"*

"Get out!" Tinker yelled, eyes wild and frantic. The man rose upward, wrapping his arms around her body protectively before turning to glare at the women who'd invaded the room.

"Don't worry about it," the red-veiled woman said, flapping her hand at the two of them. "Carry on. I'm just gonna grab some of this . . ." She stopped next to the bed, kneeling down to dig through a brown cardboard box.

"Heather Brinks, I *will* kill you!" Carrie said, her voice full of feral rage. I caught a glimpse of her face as the phone jerked again, this time flying across the room. Miraculously it landed sideways on a chair, still filming. This gave me an excellent view of Tinker's ass, which was just as ripe and juicy looking as I'd imagined. Her hair was wild and tangled, flowing down her back. Would've been perfect if there weren't another man between her legs.

He rolled her over, grabbing the corner of the bedspread and dragging it up and across her body. Then he was on his feet, facing down the gaggle of women staring in from the doorway.

"Get the fuck out of here!" he shouted, and I heard a muffled thump near the phone. A hand reached up, flashing across the screen and then another caught it, jerking it back down.

"Bitch!" Carrie hissed, and there were more thumps. Wow. I couldn't tell for sure, but it sounded like she and Heather were in one hell of a wrestling match. The stripper grabbed the woman with the red veil by one arm, pulling her toward the door.

"Jesus, look at that ass on him," Talia whispered in my ear, her voice admiring. "She's a cow, but he's incredible."

"I've already seen more of him than I ever wanted," I replied. Didn't like him. Didn't like him at all. Tinker had every right to fuck the guy—I couldn't argue with that—but I wasn't a fan. What I really wanted more of was Tinker. And yeah, that probably made me a piece of shit human being, but I'd come to Hallies Falls specifically to fuck my way into a motorcycle club and spy on them. When I'd first gotten here, I'd even helped my club brother, Painter, kill a guy, so it wasn't like I'd started on the side of all things good and true.

"What the hell is going on?" a new woman demanded, pushing her way through the crowd at the door. She was tall, probably mid-thirties and sort of frumpy looking. Big, teased up hair with the claw on the front, straight out of a Whitesnake video. I flinched, my dick softening.

"That's Maisy Braeburn," Talia said, her voice deeply satisfied. "This is the good part."

"Jamie?" Maisy asked suddenly. The stripper's body flinched, but he held his ground. Maisy puffed up visibly with anger, looking exactly like a Thanksgiving turkey as she stalked toward him. A hand grabbed the phone and it went down, going dark, but you could still hear the audio. Must've fallen on the floor. "Jamie Brae-burn, you're going to burn in hell for this!"

Someone started laughing, and then more laughter.

"Get the fuck out, Maisy," he said. "This has nothing to do with you. Nothing to do with—"

The recording ended, but the laughter kept going. Talia was giggling against me, rubbing up and down my chest with one hand, reaching for my cock with the other.

"Told you it was funny," she said in my ear before slithering on top of me. Then she gave a little shimmy, and my confused dick hardened right back up again.

Stupid fucking slut of a cock—according to it, a wet hole was a wet hole.

"I'm gonna think of Jamie's ass while I fuck you," she whispered, nipping at my neck.

"Fuck off," I said, pushing her away. She could picture me as Santa Claus if that's what turned her on, but I needed to maintain some kind of control. Talia rolled to the side, pouting.

"Hey, you're the one who said we weren't in a real relationship," she told me. "So what if I get off on his ass? Either you care or you don't."

Time to lay out the rules, I decided. Otherwise this could get out of control fast.

Who are you kidding? It's been out of control since the beginning, asshole.

"You wanna fuck me, then get your clothes off," I said harshly. Reaching down, I grabbed my dick through my jeans, giving it a tug while I stared her down. Talia's eyes flashed with heat. "But if you wanna fuck him, get out."

"Sorry," she said, her voice quiet and weak, like a little girl's. She did that sometimes. Creeped me right the hell out. My dick softened and I had to bite the inside of my cheek to keep from snarling. Thankfully, it manned back up when she reached down, pushing my hand out of the way and taking over.

"Is this for me or for her?" Talia asked, that little hint of insecurity back in her eyes, and I knew I had her. For whatever reason, she cared about this relationship in some way. I'd just won a twisted, manipulative fuckbuddy lottery. Maybe I wouldn't be

stuck playing club gigolo as long as I'd thought. Good thing, too—
nobody stupider than an unpaid whore, and I'd definitely fallen
into that category by now. Probably shot out IQ points every time
I came inside her.

"Cooper?" Talia asked, using that same little voice as she un-
buttoned my pants.

"All yours, baby," I told her, wishing it weren't true. Then I
closed my eyes as her fingers gripped me tight.

*Suck it up, dickwad. The faster you work your way into the
Nighthawks, the faster you can end this. Your brothers are counting on you.*

Fuckers.

CHAPTER EIGHT

MONDAY MORNING
TINKER

"Well, I'd say I've never been more embarrassed in my life, but that's a big fat lie. Why do I do stupid shit around men?" I moaned to Carrie, the phone clutched between my ear and shoulder. Where the hell were my keys? I dug through the purse, searching for them. Then my fingers found a rough metal edge. *Thank God.* A second later I had the shop door unlocked and open.

"We all do stupid shit, but this is a whole new level," Carrie replied, blunt as ever. "What the hell were you thinking?"

I stepped into the shop, turning the "Closed" sign around automatically.

"My brain shorted out, obviously," I replied. "I know everyone in Hallies Falls already thinks I'm a whore, but until today I've never felt like they were right."

"Don't beat yourself up too much," Carrie said. "Cooper and Talia aren't even exclusive. Darren and I went to Jack's Roadhouse on Friday night and she was there making out with some other guy. The situation is trashy, but it's not like you broke up a marriage or something."

Trashy. Not a word I liked to associate with myself, but it fit the situation just fine.

"Yeah, I hear you," I said, sighing. "And much as I'm enjoying my pity party, I need to pull my shit together and move on. I've got about a million chocolates to package for the courier and Randi just called to say she needs the morning off, so I'm on my own. Guess she had to take one of her little sisters to the doctor or something."

Carrie snorted.

"That girl needs to get the hell out of here. Her mom's just using her for cheap childcare. She had a scholarship to Central, you know."

"Yeah, I know. But it's her choice."

Carrie humphed, obviously itching to say more. Instead, she changed the subject.

"Want me to stop by at lunchtime? I feel like we haven't thoroughly discussed the Cooper situation—we need a full postmortem, don't you think?"

"No, not even a little bit."

"Great. I'll be there at noon. You want your usual sandwich?"

"Can you get a salad instead?" I asked, giving in to the inevitable. "I'm feeling a little pudgy next to Talia the Twig. Not that it matters, but . . . it matters."

"You're not fat, dork. You're lush. You have a great figure—even Darren notices it."

I shuddered.

"That's gross. He's like my brother."

"No shit. Apparently he saw you bending over to grab something at the grocery store a while back and totally checked you out—it's that ass of yours. Guys love it. Anyway, he was perving on you and then you stood up and he realized who it was. Poor baby called me from the parking lot, freaking out. Wouldn't fuck me for two days, just kept muttering about being 'unclean.'"

I laughed, setting my bag down on the counter. Talking to Carrie always made me feel better.

"I think I remember that, actually. Couple months ago. I tried to wave him down but he jetted right past me, wouldn't even look me in the eye. I guess now we know why. You do realize I'll never let him live this down, right?"

"Definitely," she said, sighing happily. "That's why I told you. He's been uppity lately, could use a little harassment. Will you be all right packaging the candy for the courier?"

"Yeah, bigger shipment than usual," I told her. "There's some sort of client-appreciation thing happening at that law firm. They ordered a ton of individual gift boxes. Don't know the full details, don't care. Just know that they pay cash up front."

"Well that's good, I guess," she said. "They trying to suck up to Brandon? I'll bet he hasn't told people about the divorce. He wants you back—you'd be good for his campaign."

"Ha!" I said, giggling. "He'd change his mind if he knew about that sex tape . . . Speaking of, I told Cooper about it."

"What?" she asked, obviously stunned.

"I told Cooper," I repeated. "He's a good listener and it just sort of slipped out. He'd probably hear about it sooner or later anyway. Get this—he seemed to think it was kind of funny."

"Well it *is* kind of funny," she admitted. "I mean, if it wasn't such a time bomb hanging over you, I'd be giving you shit over it every day. I just hope it never goes viral. You don't need that kind of headache."

I walked into the kitchen, setting my purse on one of the counters.

"You know, it was kind of liberating to tell him about it," I admitted. "It sucked, but it's not like it ended my life. It was kind of nice, not feeling like I had something to hide."

"Tinker, you have *nothing* to be ashamed of," she said. "You had sex with a consenting adult in your own hotel room. The asshole in this situation is Heather Brinks, may she rot in hell. Or maybe the bathroom in Walmart. That'd be a good punishment, too."

"You're right, although it doesn't always feel that way," I said, sighing. "Sometimes I wonder if I'll ever feel normal again. Like me, instead of being sad . . ."

"Wish I had an answer," Carrie replied, her voice serious. "Some day there will be a new normal."

"There has to be," I replied, then gave myself a mental shake. "Hey, I need to get going—I have those special orders to fill."

"You sure it won't backfire on you, letting the lawyer dudes assume you and Brandon are together?"

"Well, we're still legally married and own a house and stuff," I said reasonably. "He's the one doing all the arguing and stalling. If he's going to play bullshit games, then why shouldn't I take advantage for the sake of my business?"

"Now, that's what I like to hear," Carrie said, sounding pleased. "Work it. I'll see you in a couple hours. Love and kisses."

"Love and kisses."

Two hours later, I'd packaged up almost half of the pumpkin caramels for my weekly delivery. Randi wasn't back from her appointment yet, which wasn't ideal, but it also wasn't the end of the world. I could package and watch the store at the same time. Wasn't like a ton of people came in here anyway, and anyone showing up on a Monday would be local. *I really should just shut the place down . . .* By eleven I'd entered the zone and almost missed the bell jingling out front when someone came in.

"I'm in the back—be out in a minute!" I shouted, kneeling down to grab a fresh stack of cardboard boxes out of the cabinet under the far counter. Footsteps echoed across the scratched wood of the floor, then I felt someone's presence behind me in the small kitchen. I stood up, smile firmly in place, then froze.

Oh fuck.

Talia Jackson stood staring through the doorway.

Guilt and shame coursed through me, my cheeks heating.

Say something! my conscience hissed. But what? *Sorry I made out with your boyfriend last night, but he kissed me first so maybe you should take it up with him?* Yeah, that'd go over just great.

Cooper's girlfriend gave me a super-creepy smile, hands tucked behind her back as she cocked her head almost flirtatiously.

"Wow, that's a lot of chocolate," she said, nodding toward the stack of trays on my work counter. Each metal tray held close to a hundred candies, and there were six of them. I nodded carefully, senses on full alert. "Whatcha doing?"

"Packaging them up for sale," I said, wondering what her game was. "My courier will be here later this afternoon—he drives them to Seattle and delivers them to all my customers."

"And you make all of those by yourself?" she asked, moving toward me. Her eyes hardened. "Lot of work. Be a shame if something happened to them."

Oh shit.

She stepped forward, face darkening. I backed away, bumping into the stainless steel sink. Talia took another step, stopping right next to the tower of trays. Then she very slowly pulled her hand out from behind her back and raised a long, sharp knife, pointing it at me accusingly. It was one of those big survival knives, the kind that's practically a machete.

"You and I need to talk," she said sweetly.

My heart started hammering, eyes darting, trying to find some way to defend myself. This girl was certifiably insane or close enough that it didn't matter. My hand bumped into an unwashed metal cooking sheet in the sink. If she lunged for me, maybe I could use it as a shield, because apparently my life was turning into a Quentin Tarantino movie. The setting was certainly right—it was just the two of us back here, and I knew for a fact these old brick walls were thick.

Nobody will hear you scream.

"What did you want to talk about?" I asked, trying to sound calm, although I heard the quaver in my voice.

"You want to fuck my man," Talia said, wagging the knife like I was a naughty child. "I've seen how you watch him. I didn't really care at first—you're nothing but a dried-up old hag and he's not interested, so why bother? But you stepped over a line last night and now you're going to pay."

"I'm sorry," I whispered, swallowing. There was something about her eyes—they were intense. Too intense and bright. Not only that, her pupils were really tight. God, was she on drugs?

"Oh, you'll be sorry," she said, casually poking one of the chocolates with her knife. I fumbled for the dirty tray behind me, wrapping my hand around the edge. If she attacked, I'd have one chance to defend myself—I couldn't afford to fuck this up.

"These are very pretty," she continued, nodding toward the chocolates. "And I'm sure they're good. Otherwise your ass wouldn't be so fat. No wonder you don't have a man."

She raised the knife again, then lunged at me. I whipped the cooking tray up in front of my body, banging the hell out of my hand in the process. This was a good thing—the pain sharpened my focus. The knife didn't hit it, though, because she'd faked me out. Talia laughed, raising a brow.

"You think that's gonna stop me? Now listen up, *cunt*, because I have a few rules for you. First thing—you're never stepping into his apartment again," she said. I felt a rush of relief, because this meant she wasn't planning to kill me, at least not yet. "I know he does work for you around the building. From now on, your only communication with him happens in the form of Post-it notes and text messages, got me? We're gonna give it a week or two, and then you're going to fire him and kick his ass out. Better think of some excuse, because if you tell him about me, I'll come back here and slit your fucking throat. That's a promise. Then I'll call my brother and he'll make your body disappear somewhere that they'll never find it. This is your only warning. Got it, bitch?"

I nodded my head quickly.

"I'm leaving now," she said. "But remember—talk to him and I'll slice you. Go into his apartment and I'll slice you. In fact, you so much as fucking blink in his direction, I'll cut out your heart and eat it."

She gave me one last sweet smile, then slowly and deliberately pushed the stacks of trays over. My breath caught as a week's worth of work—nearly six hundred handmade chocolates—crashed, scattering across the floor. Then Talia turned and walked back out through the store, the bells on the door chiming with a friendly jingle. I stood there, stunned, nausea roiling up from my stomach in silence.

Holy shit. Things like this didn't happen to real people—not in my world.

Crossing my arms over my chest, I held myself tight, sliding down onto the floor as my entire body started to shake. Why hadn't I done something to defend myself? I wasn't a weak person. I'd started hunting with my dad when I was six, took down my first buck when I was ten. I'd used a knife just like hers to dress it out. I should've seen it coming, protected myself.

But this was supposed to be my safe place.

Mom's shop was where I'd come after school for hugs and fresh cookies. She'd give me peppermint tea while I did my homework at one of the tables, until Dad came by to pick us up and take us home. Bad things weren't supposed to happen here.

Maybe Brandon was right.

Maybe I should go home to Seattle, where people weren't crazy and I had a real kitchen instead of this cramped little pocket of space. None of the chocolate would be salvageable, not after hitting the floor. I'd have to call my clients, let them know there was a delay. I'd always been reliable—hopefully I wouldn't lose too much business long term. I felt a curl of anger deep inside and decided to focus on it. Anger was strong, and I could use a little strength right now, because seriously . . . what a fucking *bitch!*

Forcing myself up, I took a deep breath and considered my options. I could call the cops, of course—that's what people did in Seattle. But this was Hallies Falls, where the Nighthawk Raiders made their own rules and the cops looked the other way. Everyone joked that they were on the club's payroll, but it wasn't a funny kind of joke.

We all knew it was true.

And it wasn't like I had any evidence that Talia had threatened me, either. Sure, there was chocolate all over the floor, but the only thing that proved was that I was clumsy. At most I'd get a restraining order, and we all know how great paper is in a knife fight.

Carrie. I'd call Carrie.

Reaching for my purse, I dug around for my phone. My fingers landed on the small can of pepper spray I kept in there for self defense. A grim smile twisted my face. Dad had always laughed at it, telling me I'd be just as likely to spray myself as an attacker, but he was wrong—I'd never had a chance to spray it at all. Finding the phone, I dialed Carrie's number.

"What's up?" she asked brightly.

"Think you could take an early lunch?" I asked, my voice shaking. "Something just happened, and I could really use some company."

"Are you all right? You don't sound all right. What's going on?"

"I'm fine," I said, squeezing my eyes shut for a minute. *You will not cry. There's no crying in gourmet chocolate.* "Just come over as soon as you can, okay?"

"I'm going to kill her," Carrie fumed. I'd shut down the store for the day, putting out the "Closed" sign before retreating back into the kitchen to wait. I hadn't wanted to be out in the main shop where people could see me, so instead I put on some water for tea and started cleaning up the giant-ass mess Talia had left behind her. The damage was pretty bad—not only was the candy on the trays toast, but most of the boxes I'd already packaged had gone spilling across the floor, too.

When Carrie arrived, it'd taken all my force of will to walk back through the main shop and open the door.

"I just want to keep it quiet," I told her, pulling a stool up to the worktable.

"No fucking way."

"Hear me out," I insisted, holding up a hand. "Talia Jackson is insane and she hates me. What do you think will happen if we call the cops? They'll take a report and maybe give me a temporary restraining order, which will be worth exactly jack shit when she decides to murder me in my sleep. Oh, and that's assuming they aren't on her brother's payroll. You know how things work around here."

Carrie bit her lip, and I could see she wanted to argue with me, but I was right and we both knew it. The Nighthawk Raiders owned this town. I wasn't sure I wanted to be the test case for how far their influence reached.

"Then we'll tell Darren," she said finally, determined. "He'll protect you."

I shook my head. "Bad idea. He'll go all Iron Man on her ass, and then her brother and those bikers will come after him and suddenly you'll be a widow and your kids will be orphans and . . ."

My breath caught as I felt tears starting to well. *No. No crying*, I reminded myself.

"Calm down," Carrie said quickly. "You raise a good point about Darren—we shouldn't tell him, because he *will* lose his shit and I can't afford to have him murdered until after the girls graduate college. But where does that leave us in terms of options?"

"I'm going to do what she says," I told her flatly. "Not because what she did was okay. It wasn't. And not because I'm scared of her, although I totally am. I'm doing it because she's right, Carrie. What happened last night between me and Cooper was wrong and a huge mistake."

"I know," she said steadily. "But he started it, not you."

"And I could've ended it if I wanted to," I replied, meeting her eyes. "But I didn't. In that moment I didn't care about anyone but myself. I acted like Brandon, and I'm better than that."

"You did *not* act like Brandon," she said, her voice firm. "You can regret last night all you want, and I definitely think it was a mistake . . . But you have a long way to go before you're on Brandon's level. Stop beating yourself up and start focusing on how we're going to fix things."

"Maybe I should just move back to Seattle," I said quietly.

"No."

"Not back with Brandon," I insisted. "But this town . . . You've always loved this place, Carrie, but I never saw myself in Hallies Falls. You know that. The only reason I'm here is my dad."

"Okay, calm down," she said. "You're freaking out, which is fair. Talia is scary as hell. But you can't just up and move to Seattle because one crazy bitch threw a tantrum."

"A crazy bitch with a machete."

"Yeah, that part is troubling," she admitted, and I snorted. "Geez, it's hard to wrap my head around. And talk about bad luck, having her walk in like that. I mean, you've been a fucking saint since—"

"We agreed to never speak of it again," I reminded her, holding up a hand.

She nodded her head, then cocked a brow at me.

"Still can't believe you banged Jamie Braeburn. I was so proud of you, babe! Nothing like getting laid to help you forget a man. And Brandon—"

"Stop," I said, flushing. "We're not rehashing this, and I think we should put the discussion of Cooper on hold, too."

"I agree. But sometimes I wonder . . . Why are all the hot guys crazy?"

"Darren is hot."

"I rest my case. Don't suppose you still want your salad after all that?"

"Maybe I'll just put it in the fridge for later. My stomach is still queasy from the adrenaline. I need to get things cleaned up here, and then I've got to start making more caramels. The deliveries will be late, obviously, but I should be able to get most of this replaced by Wednesday morning if I put in long enough hours. I'll drive it to Seattle that night, then start my deliveries on Thursday. If everything goes well, I can come back and work through the weekend to put out next week's product."

"You're going to kill yourself doing all of that, especially since it's all by hand," Carrie said seriously. "It's not realistic—it's time to put in a real kitchen. Darren can help you with remodeling the basement in your house. You need to make this sustainable, and that can't happen if you're running a tea shop and hand-dipping every single one of those caramels."

I looked at her, wishing she weren't right. I'd managed to hold it together so far, but my back and shoulders ached every night from all the leaning and dipping. My enrobing machine could do it all in an hour or two, easy. It was all ready and waiting for me, back in the basement in Seattle. The tea shop kitchen wasn't big enough to hold it.

"Maybe I should just move Dad to Seattle," I said softly. "Get a property manager for the building and end this. I never planned to stay in Hallies Falls this long."

Carrie reached across the table, squeezing my hand.

"I know things aren't perfect here," she said softly. "And I'm biased, because I want you to stay in town. But before you make a decision like that, really think about your dad. We can all see that he's failing. Nobody knows how long he'll last, but one thing we do know—he's in a house that feels safe and right to him. He's comfortable, he's happy, and he has his routine. He may not always remember that your mom is gone, but he always remembers where he is. He knows where to find a drink, he knows how to walk around the neighborhood. If you take that away from him, he'll lose whatever quality of life he has left."

Her words hit like a punch to the gut.

"I'm scared," I admitted softly. Carrie nodded, her face determined.

"I know," she said. "But we're going to protect you. First thing, we shut down this shop for good, so you can work in peace without worrying about the crazy sneaking up on you again."

I opened my mouth to protest, but Carrie held up a hand, cutting me off. "Your mom loved this place, but it's not a functional business. She never would've expected you to keep it open and you know it."

She was right.

"So, that takes care of the shop," she said. "Now we need to deal with the candy crisis. Should you try to make up for all that lost work here, or should you go to Seattle so you can use the heavy equipment? I hate to even suggest it, but I know you'll get more done in your big kitchen there. Of course, you'll also have to clean everything up first and make sure it's running right. Not only that, you'll have to deal with Brandon. Not that I care if it's inconvenient for him. The fucker's been dragging his feet on the divorce and selling the house, so he can suck it up and share with you for a couple days. The real question is whether you can tolerate him long enough to get the work done."

I considered her suggestion, weighing the pros and cons as dispassionately as I could.

"I should go to Seattle," I finally concluded. "With the equipment there I can replace the lost candy twice as fast. Gives some time for the situation with Talia to cool off, too. I'll have to do something with Dad, though."

"Take him with you."

"What happened to keeping him in the home he loves?"

Carried rolled her eyes.

"You're not supposed to *stay* there, dumbass. You go, you catch up on your work, and then you come back. Bring Randi, too—I'll bet she'd love to get out of the house, and she can do all the packaging. She can also help keep an eye on your dad."

"And the apartment building?"

"Darren will deal with it," she said. "It'll be good to get away from the whole Cooper/Talia situation. He may be hot as hell, but so far as I'm concerned, the man is pond scum. He's got a girlfriend and he's making moves on you, which means he's dog shit in my book. I don't care what the rules of their relationship are—he had no business dragging you into his mess."

"It wasn't like that," I insisted. She raised her brows. "Okay, what he did was pretty shitty. But I shouldn't have gone to his apartment, either. I'm adult enough to own my own mistakes, Carrie. It's not like his relationship with Talia was a secret."

She shrugged.

"Let's agree to disagree. Now, what needs to happen to get your ass to Seattle?"

Looking around, I frowned at the kitchen. The cleanup alone would take hours.

"No, I'll take care of the mess here," she said, apparently reading my mind. "You just grab your supplies and pack some clothes."

I sighed. "I'll need to call Brandon."

"Call and leave a message with his paralegal. Treat him like he treated you, and if it's inconvenient, that's just frosting."

The look on her face was so gleeful that I had to smile.

"Tell me how you really feel."

"Just respecting the no-bullshit clause in our friendship, Tink."

"I know," I said. "That's what I love about you. Well, that and the way you're always bringing me food and booze."

"Priorities, babe. It's all about the priorities."

"Ah crap," I muttered, realizing I had another problem.

"What?"

"There's no way I can carry everything in the convertible," I said, groaning. "What was I thinking, trading in my van for a Mustang?"

Carrie burst out laughing, and I glared at her.

"If I hear the words 'midlife crisis' I'm strangling you."

"You were being impulsive for once in your life, which you deserve," she replied. "Now, ask nicely and I'll loan you my Suburban."

"May I please borrow the great big giant SUV you drive because you're short and compensating?"

"Yup. And I'll even throw in a bottle of wine, just in case Brandon gets handsy. You can break it over a counter and cut him with it."

"Oh, I like that idea. I like that idea a *lot*."

GAGE

"Made a helluva mess," I told Picnic. I sat on my couch, feet up on the coffee table, considering my options.

"Sounds like it."

"You're a ray of fuckin' sunshine, aren't you?"

Picnic laughed, and I could almost see the expression on his face through the phone. "I like to look on the bright side."

"So let's discuss the next step," I said. "I managed to patch things up with Talia. Wasn't easy or fun. Never thought I'd be saying this, but I'm really over the sex. I'm also worried she'll do something crazy to Tinker. Bitch was unhinged."

"You gotta stay the course," he said. "We don't have the information we need yet."

"How much proof do you need?" I asked, feeling frustrated. "The Nighthawk Raiders are fucked, it's obvious. Why can't we just sweep in and take over? They're a support club—not like they have any rights in the situation. We come in, we clean house. Problem solved."

Picnic sighed. "You know it's more complicated than that. It's not just about them. Marsh is working with someone north of the border and we don't know who. We step in now, we've only solved half the problem. His partners will find some other asshole to work with. We need more information so we can shut them down for real."

"I need Tinker safe."

He didn't say anything for long seconds.

"How important is this woman to you?"

"I don't know," I admitted. "I mean, I want to fuck her. Can't stop thinking about it."

"So you want to blow a major operation because you're horny?"

I considered the question, then figured I might as well lay it all out for him.

"No," I said. "I mean, yeah, I wanna fuck her. But it's more than that. There's something about her. I can't quite explain it, but I'm thinkin' about her a lot. Maybe . . . I dunno."

"Never heard you talk like this. Surprises me."

"You and me both."

"Okay. Hang on as long as you can and keep us posted. You're the one with eyes on the situation. If you need backup or something, let me know. We could also extract her. If you're serious about her, I mean."

I considered the suggestion.

"Think I might be."

Picnic gave a short laugh. "This should be entertaining."

"Go fuck yourself."

"I'd rather fuck London," he said. "Hang in there, okay? We've got your back. And remember, pulling her out is still an option if you think she's in real danger. I'll ride over and do it myself. It'll scare the shit out of her, though, so let's not pull the trigger on that unless we're out of options."

"Sounds good," I told him. Then I thought of something. "Pic, can you do me a favor?"

"Possibly."

"You ever hear of a prosecutor named Brandon Graham? He's the director of the King County criminal division."

"Sounds familiar," he said. "I can ask around, see if we've got any intel. Why?"

"Well, technically he's married to Tinker Garrett."

Picnic burst out laughing. "You have got to be fucking kidding me. You can't keep it simple, can you?"

"Just tell me what you find out," I replied, wishing he were here in person so I could flip him off. "I gotta get to work. Should probably make sure Tinker's okay this morning, too. That'll be a fun conversation."

Picnic snorted, and I hung up on his ass. Then I stood slowly, running a hand through my hair. I'd well and truly fucked things up, no question. Still, remembering the feel of her mouth under mine I couldn't quite regret it.

Damn.

Peaches.

I spent the morning working on the roof, keeping an eye out for Tinker. We needed to talk. I could've gone down to her shop, of course, but that felt too much like an ambush—no point in making things worse.

A gray Suburban pulled up around two in the afternoon, and I watched from above as she jumped out and went into the house. Where was the Mustang? Climbing down, I brushed off my brown Carhartts and walked over to the door, ringing the bell. Her dad answered.

"Is Tinker around?" I asked.

"Yes, but she's busy," he said. His eyes were alert today, not confused. "Guess we're going to Seattle for a couple days. She says she needs to use the fancy kitchen there, but I don't like it."

He leaned toward me, his voice low. "I think she's really going so she can see her husband. I just hope she's not planning on getting back together with the asshole. Never liked him."

Fair enough. I didn't like the fucker much, either.

"Look, I really need to talk to her," I said. "It's important. About the building. It'll only take a few minutes—think you can let me in?"

He studied me, then nodded his head. "See if you can talk her out of it."

Stepping back, he made room for me to follow him into the living room, then disappeared into the back of the house to find his daughter. I studied the place while I waited. It was pretty, in an old-fashioned kind of way. Lots of dark trim and furniture with wooden legs. Lamps with beaded shades. Polished hardwood floors. Made me think of the tea shop, like something out of a different time.

Tinker was like that in a way, too, with her retro hair and pinup girl outfits.

"Dad says there's something wrong?" Tinker asked, her voice abrupt. I looked up to find her standing in the archway between the living and dining rooms, arms crossed over her chest. Her face was tight with strain. *You really fucked it up this time, asshole.*

"We need to talk about what happened last night," I told her. Tinker shook her head, offering me a fake-as-hell smile.

"There's nothing to talk about," she said. "So far as I'm concerned it didn't happen. End of story. If you have any issues regarding the building, text me."

"Your dad says you're headed out of town," I countered, walking toward her. She took a step back. *Shouldn't back away from a predator, babe.*

"I've got an extra large order to fill," she said quickly. "I need to use the equipment in my commercial kitchen and the tea shop can't hold it, that's all. No big deal."

I moved closer, herding her toward the wall. "Your dad's worried that you're going back to your ex. He got anything to be worried about?"

Something flashed in her eyes, and she straightened.

"That's none of your damned business," she said, her voice stronger. I liked that, although I didn't like the way she was dodging my question. I'd never been a man to put up with bullshit and this was a load if I'd ever heard it.

Frustrating as hell.

That's probably why I leaned forward, scenting her hair. Peaches, all right. Predictably, my dick hardened, and I wondered if I'd ever be able to walk through a produce section again without getting horny.

It'd be funny if it weren't so fucked up.

"Will you be seeing your ex?"

"Well, he lives in the same house, so it seems likely," she said sharply. "Not that it's any of your business. You work for me, Mr. Romero, and I think we should go ahead and keep that association professional. If you need something, you can text me or Darren. Other than that, there's no reason that you and I should be talking to each other."

There was something ugly in her eyes as she spoke, a hint of fear or disgust. Like I was beneath her. Fuck that. Taking the last step, I pushed my body into hers, cock stiffening as her sweet smell surrounded me. Her hands came up, pushing against my chest, and I caught them, pinning them to the wall on either side of her head.

"You sure you want to take that tone with me?" I asked. Tinker's lips parted, and I remembered her taste. Sweet. Juicy. *Perfect.* She swallowed and her eyes softened. For an instant I thought I had her. Then her chin jutted out.

"I've been bullied enough today. I'm over it. If you don't let me go and walk out of here right now, I'll kick you out on your ass. You can kiss your apartment good-bye, too."

I smiled, because if she wanted to go there, I'd play along.

"That's illegal, sweetheart," I said. "Don't you know your landlord-tenant law? I have a lease. You can't kick me out without a court order.

You really sure you want to explain to a judge about our little arrangement? I wonder what the IRS would think of it . . ."

"Excuse me?" she asked. "You're out of line, asshole, and this isn't about judges and the IRS. *You* kissed *me* last night. While you were dating another woman. That's a dick move."

"You kissed me back," I reminded her. "And the situation with Talia is complicated, but believe me—she's got no fuckin' room to complain. None of that changes the fact that I'm a legal tenant in your building, yet instead of collecting rent, you're having me work under the table. You're not paying any FICA on me, are you? You really want to play the eviction card?"

"Get out," she hissed, and I laughed.

"Not until we talk this through."

She twisted, and I felt her knee jerk upward. I blocked it easily—Tinker might be a hell of a chef, but she wasn't a street fighter. She growled, twisting again, trying to buck me off. Seeing as I held her hands pinned, all it accomplished was bringing her hips into contact with mine.

I breathed deep, trying to hold on to my control as my cock dug into her stomach.

Jesus.

This woman was gonna fuckin' kill me, so why did I want to kiss her so goddamn bad? Kiss her and lay her out across that old-fashioned dining room table, maybe test it to see whether that traditional craftsmanship could stand up to a good bangi—

"Get the fuck out of here!" she said, her voice rising. Great. Now she was panicking, which I'd love to say was a turnoff but it really, really wasn't. It made me feel powerful, and yeah, I know that's fucked up.

I never claimed to be a decent, healthy kind of guy.

That's when I should've let her go, but instead I shoved my hips deeper into Tinker's, breath hissing as her softness cradled my swollen cock. Oh *fuck*. My balls burned, they were so full and ready for her. Jerking her hands up and over her head, I caught both of them in one of mine, freeing the other to dig into her hair.

Tinker stilled, eyes wide.

"You bikers are a bunch of fucking bullies," she whispered, licking her lips nervously. I leaned forward, ready to take what I wanted when the words caught me.

You bikers.

Bikers.

Plural.

Jesus. Fucking. Christ.

My hand tightened in her hair and she squawked, turning pale. *Shit.* I loosened my fingers slightly, enough to hold her without hurting her, then studied her face.

"I'm gonna ask you a question and you *will* answer honestly," I said. "Got it?"

Her eyes narrowed.

"Did something happen to make you run off to Seattle?"

"Yeah, I have a business," she snapped. "Sorry, Cooper, but the whole fucking world doesn't revolve around you and your motorcycle club."

"You talkin' about the Nighthawk Raiders?" I asked carefully, my anger growing. This was about more than a kiss. Had Talia threatened her? Or sent one of Marsh's bullyboys to terrorize my girl?

I'd fucking strangle them with my bare hands.

"Well, we don't have a bunch of Shriners running around town on mopeds scaring the hell out of people, so yeah, I'm talking about the Nighthawks," she said. "I don't want anything to do with you, Cooper. Not. One. Thing. Now, let me go and get the hell out of my house."

They'd done something to her, it was obvious.

Killing rage filled me. Jesus fucking Christ, I'd put those fuckers in the ground. My hands must have tightened again, because Tinker gave a small, pained whimper. I let her go abruptly, stepping back before I did something truly stupid. She lowered her hands, rubbing her wrists. Great. I'd hurt her.

"Tell me what happened," I said.

Tinker glared.

"Here's a little story for you," she said after a long pause. "I was stupid enough to take someone at face value and hire him to work for me. Then I was even stupider, because when he casually invited me over for dinner I said yes, even though I knew he had a vicious skank of a girlfriend. Then he threatened me with the IRS because he's a giant, raging asshole. End of story. Now I'm driving to Seattle to use my cooking equipment. I've made a lot of mistakes this past month, but at least I'm smart enough not to make the same mistakes twice in a row. Get the fuck out of my house."

"You heard her. Time to go."

I spun around to find Tom Garrett standing in the dining room, pointing a shotgun at us. Fucking hell—if he pulled the trigger right now, he'd catch me *and* Tinker. I raised my hands, hoping he hadn't completely lost touch with reality.

"Dad, will you please put down the gun?" Tinker asked, her voice shaking.

"This boy needs to treat you with respect," he said. "It's a good thing your mother isn't home. She wouldn't let him get off this easy. Time for you to walk away, boy. You leave her alone at school, too—if I hear you've been bothering her, I'll come and find you. Got it?"

Well, shit. Guess I had my answer about his state of mind. I glanced at Tinker, whose face had gone white.

"I understand and agree," I told him, backing away from her, because if the old man actually decided to pull that trigger, no reason for both of us to die. "I'm gonna walk to the door, okay?"

"At least he can follow directions," Tom said, shaking his head as I moved across the room, still facing him.

"Daddy, I'm going to come stand next to you, all right?" Tinker asked, her voice shaking. "Then I want you to give me the gun."

She started toward him, smart enough to follow the wall, well out of his line of fire. I kept backing toward the door, holding his gaze the entire time, trying to figure out my next move. I couldn't just walk out of there and leave Tinker alone with him.

Knowing our luck, he'd forget who she was and shoot her.

"Mr. Garrett, I promise I won't bother your daughter anymore,"

I said carefully, trying to look harmless. Not so easy when you're six-three and weigh more than two hundred pounds, but I gave it my best. "Here's the thing . . . I'm not comfortable with Tinker in the same room as the gun. She looks kinda scared to me. Seeing as I'm already at the door, you think you could break that shotgun open so she can relax?"

Tom glanced at Tinker, who'd almost reached him.

"You worried, honey?"

"Daddy, you know how much Mama hates it when you have a loaded gun in the house, especially around me."

He nodded slowly, lowering the weapon.

Thank you, Jesus. Owe you one for that.

"I appreciate it, Dad," she said, glancing toward me. Whatever anger she'd been feeling before, it was gone. Now there was only sadness. I waited as her father broke the gun open, folding the barrel down. Tinker reached for it, slinging it over her arm in a way that told me this wasn't the first time she'd handled a weapon.

Woman was full of surprises.

"You can go now," she said, looking exhausted. I nodded.

Fucking weird day.

CHAPTER NINE

TINKER

I carried the shotgun upstairs with the breech still open, my pulse racing. I'd never seen my father point a weapon at another person before, not in my entire life. How much crazier could this day get? I wanted to sit on the couch and cry or maybe smash something. Unfortunately, I didn't have time to fall apart.

First thing, I needed to make sure every gun in the house was locked up.

Then I needed to track down Cooper before he told anyone what'd happened. I wasn't sure how to handle my father, but I didn't want anyone else stepping in and forcing decisions on us, either. This was family business and I'd be damned if I'd feed the town gossips any more ammunition.

What if Cooper files charges against him?

Maybe I could claim self-defense or something. I mean, there'd been a reason Dad had gone for the shotgun—Cooper had probably assaulted me, at least technically. But by the time Dad pulled the gun on him, there hadn't been any danger. He'd already let me go, and who knew what a judge would do, especially if he heard my father testify.

Dad was proud. I couldn't put him through that.

So, first things first:

1) Lock up guns.
2) Talk to Cooper.
3) Pick up Randi and drive her and my dad to Seattle.
4) Somehow not get killed by Talia when I get back.

I could do this—Team Garrett for the win, and all that good shit.

"Dad, can you start packing for Seattle?" I asked when we reached the top of the stairs. My father frowned, staring pointedly at the gun in my arms.

"Why is that out of the case?" he said, shaking his head. "Your mom will blame me if she sees you with that, Tinker Bell. You know better."

"We were just putting it away," I replied quickly. "She asked us to make sure all the guns were locked up while she was out, remember?"

He seemed confused, then nodded his head.

"Sounds like her."

"Are there any more around the house? Maybe in your room?"

"Yup, I got one in the bedside table," he said. "I'll go get it."

"I'll come with you."

Twenty minutes later all the guns were accounted for. Not that we had a ton of them, but for most of my life Dad had hunted—providing almost all of our meat growing up, actually—so he had several hunting rifles in addition to the shotgun, not to mention the pistol next to his bed. They were all safe and secure in my grandfather's cabinet now, using an old bicycle lock. I'd put the only key on a string around my neck until I figured out somewhere to keep it. Maybe a safe-deposit box?

Exhausted and knowing I still had a ton to do before we could leave town, I headed back downstairs, stopping dead when I saw Cooper in the living room. He was leaning against the back of the couch with his arms crossed and a determined look on his face. Huh. At least he'd been easy to find.

"So . . ." I started, wondering what the hell I should say.

"So?" he asked, raising a brow. "That the best you got?"

Sadly, it was.

"This is awkward," I said softly. "Um, we should probably talk about what just happened."

"Ya think?" he asked, jerking his chin toward the stairs. "Your dad just went from absentminded to dangerous as hell. This is a problem, Tinker."

"Are you going to call the cops?" I asked, feeling sick. Cooper raised a brow.

"Do I look like the kind of guy who goes running to the cops?" he asked, and I wondered if it was a trick question. I mean, he had the criminal-biker look down perfect, but who was I to stereotype? My dad was the one with the gun.

My chest tightened as the full reality of the situation hit.

I'd gone to work this morning and had my life threatened by a crazy woman with a machete, and it wasn't even the most fucked-up thing that'd happened to me so far that day. Suddenly I felt dizzy.

"Breathe," Cooper said, lunging toward me as I started to sway. He caught my arm, pulling me down to the couch. Then we sat down, and he pushed my head between my legs, which helped.

"I can't believe that just happened," I moaned, wondering if a person could splinter from too much . . . too much whatever the hell was wrong with me? Grief? Stress? Just too much, period. "It's so much worse than I ever imagined."

His hand rubbed my back, something I should've discouraged but it felt really good to lean on someone else, even for a few minutes. I still couldn't believe what'd happened. Since when did my father start pulling guns on people?

"What does his doctor say?" Cooper asked, his voice a low rumble that I felt all the way down my spine. Shit, I needed to sit up and move away from him right now, before I did something stupid, like lean in and let him bear some of this endless weight for a while.

Yeah, because having a man fixes everything, right? my brain sniped. *How'd that work out for you and Brandon?*

Apparently I wasn't so good at the whole learning-from-my-mistakes thing because I stayed right there and answered him.

"He hasn't been to the doctor, at least not since Mom died," I admitted.

"Why the hell not?"

"Because he's a stubborn old bastard," I said, forcing myself to sit up and look Cooper in the eye. "Because it didn't really seem that bad, and every time we talked about it he put me off, and I guess I was in denial. This is a big deal, isn't it?"

"Yeah," he said, his face full of pity. Goddamn it, I didn't want his fucking pity. I wanted his—

Um. No. We wouldn't be going there.

"I have medical power of attorney," I said. "I mean, as a backup. I got one for each of them when they did their wills a few years back. I've always known I'd have to force him if he ever needed help—that's the kind of guy he is—but I guess I just kept chickening out."

"Hey," Cooper said. "It is what it is, all right? He took care of you for years, now you take care of him. That's how it works. It's not always easy, but you can do it. You need to start by making a doctor's appointment. Probably shouldn't be leaving him alone anymore, either."

"Fuck," I said. "Fucking fuck *fuck!* And now I'm headed to Seattle. At least Randi's coming with us. Maybe it's for the best—our family doctor here is older than Dad. I think the only reason he still has an office is there's no one to replace him. Guess I'll start making some phone calls."

"Hey," he said. "Come here."

Cooper opened his arms, and I considered for a minute. I knew exactly what I should do—stay away from him and his stabby girlfriend and whatever other baggage he might still have hidden in his *illegally tenanted* apartment. But I was tired. Really tired. Instead I found myself sort of leaning forward and collapsing against him. That's when I noticed my cheeks were wet—I'd started crying without even realizing it.

Then Cooper pulled me into his lap and the tears broke free.

I cried for my dad and my mom and my baby and the fact that things were never, ever going to be the way they should've been. I cried because a crazy lady had threatened me with a knife and because the whole damned town thought I was a whore. Finally, I cried because the first guy I'd liked in ages was probably a criminal—definitely an asshole—except at the moment he was being really, really sweet. There was something so damned unfair about the whole situation.

After what felt like forever, the tears dried up, and I found myself leaning against his shoulder, wondering how I was going to get everything taken care of and still keep my business up and running and—no. I'd had one breakdown already, that was enough. Just because it was all too much for one person to handle didn't change a damned thing, so I'd find a way.

I always did, because Garretts are *tough*.

Dad taught me that, back when he'd been the one taking care of me. Now it was my turn, just like Cooper said. He ran his fingers through my hair gently, and I settled in, feeling better. Nothing like a good cry, I guess.

"Does this mean we can have a truce?" he asked, chest rumbling against my cheek.

"Sure," I said, because once your dad points a shotgun at a guy, it gets harder to justify a grudge.

"Just tell me this—are you really going to Seattle because you need to use your kitchen equipment, or are you running scared from something? Because I can protect you, babe. I promise."

Talia's face popped into my head. Mostly that weird expression she'd worn when she poked her big knife at me. She'd meant every word she'd said, that much I believed.

Cooper was her man.

It didn't matter how sweet he was being right now, I realized, because he had divided loyalties—at the end of the day, a man's gonna side with the woman sucking his dick. This is reality.

"I need the equipment," I said, reminding myself that it wasn't a lie. I really did, seeing as his bitch of a girlfriend ruined a week's worth of work in one tantrum. "Not only that, I need to talk to Brandon and find some kind of specialist to check out my dad."

Cooper stiffened.

"Brandon?" he asked slowly. "You mean, you need to talk to him about finalizing the divorce."

"Tinker, I'm out of shampoo," my dad said from behind us, and I pushed off Cooper's lap abruptly, feeling weirdly guilty. "Other than that, I'm all ready to go. Hey, Cooper. Good to see you."

Wow. He had no memory of threatening Cooper.

None.

Damn.

"We were just going over some stuff for the building before you leave on your trip," Cooper said. Dad smirked.

"I'm old, not stupid," he replied, laughing. A knife twisted in my gut, because Dad was the strong one. He took care of things, and whenever something was really wrong, he fixed it.

This. Sucked.

"Guess you caught us," Cooper replied lightly. "I was just heading out, though. Tinker, you need help loading anything?"

"No, we're fine," I told him. "You can text if anything comes up. Dad, we need to pick up Randi soon, so go throw your stuff in Carrie's Suburban, all right? She's letting me borrow it."

"Sure thing, baby," he said, smiling at me fondly. "It'll be fun, taking a road trip together. Just like when you were a little girl. I know you'll be busy with work, but maybe we can go up the Space Needle while we're there."

"That'd be great, Dad," I said, sighing. "I love you. I hope you know how much."

He gave me a funny look. "Love you too, baby. Forever and ever."

GAGE

Guess I wasn't the only one with a complicated life. I'd started working on the roof again, but my mind was racing. The situation with Tinker's dad wasn't good, but there was definitely more going on here.

Talia. Had to be.

I debated calling Picnic to discuss my options, but decided I needed more information first.

Tinker and her dad pulled out around four that afternoon. Marsh texted me at five, asking if I'd meet him out at the Nighthawks' clubhouse that evening. Apparently he had "business" to discuss, which was a good sign. The sooner we got his shit sorted, the sooner I could end this fucking farce with Talia.

Taking a fast shower, I rode downtown to grab some dinner down at Jack's Roadhouse. I figured I'd grab a burger and collect any available gossip before heading out to the clubhouse. That was the best—and worst—thing about a town like this. People stuck their noses in their neighbors' business.

I'd just passed the old library when a cherry red Mustang jetted past, going in the opposite direction. Then I heard the squeal of tires and the roar of an engine as I watched the driver pull a U-turn, coming right at me. *What the fuck?* She was honking the horn and flashing the lights, obviously trying to flag me down. I realized it was Carrie, Tinker's best friend. They must've swapped vehicles, which explained the SUV she'd been driving.

Pulling over, I swung off the bike and walked over to her, wondering what the hell was going on. Jesus, it'd been only a couple hours—hardly enough time for something else to go wrong.

Carrie ripped open the Mustang's door, marching toward me with fury written all over her face. Seeing as she was about a foot shorter than me and close to a hundred pounds lighter, she came off more like an angry pixie than a true threat, but the rage in her eyes . . . that was definitely full-size.

"You!" she snarled, stepping into my space and poking her finger right into my chest. I stared down at it, wondering whether she had the slightest clue how easy it'd be for me to snap it off. "You've got a lot of fucking nerve, asshole."

"Hard to argue with that," I said casually. "But you're gonna have to narrow it down a little. What'd I do this time?"

"Your girlfriend threatened Tinker with a fucking knife this morning," she snarled. "Said she'd cut her if she didn't stay away from you, and then she destroyed an entire week's work of chocolates. Now Tinker has to go to Seattle and try to make up those orders before she loses all her clients. I don't know what sick games you're playing with Talia Jackson, and I don't care. Tinker's my girl, and I'm gonna protect her. We clear?"

Jesus. I'd suspected Tinker wasn't telling me the whole truth, but hearing it was something else. Sudden, furious rage filled me, because Talia had stepped over the motherfucking line and there was no going back. Something dark must've shown in my expression—Carrie's face faltered, and she took a step back.

"When did this happen?" I snapped out. "Tell me. All of it."

Carrie's eyes flashed with something. Surprise, maybe? Like she thought I'd defend Talia. Fuck that shit—this ended, and it ended *today*.

"Tinker was alone in the shop this morning," she said. "Packaging the shipment for her Seattle delivery. Talia showed up and cornered her in the kitchen. Threatened her with a big fucking knife and destroyed almost all of her product. Now she's got orders she can't fill, which means she'll be working night and day trying to catch up. To pull it off she needs her kitchen in Seattle. That means staying in the same house with her asshole of an ex, who'll probably try to convince her to come back to him. I lost my best friend to that bastard once, but I'm not going to lose her again. I don't know what happened last night and I don't give one flying fuck. This is your fault and you will fix it. Clear?"

Oh, she was clear. So fucking clear my vision narrowed into a red tunnel of rage.

Carrie stepped back, fear flickering across her face. Then it hardened with new resolution, and I knew it didn't matter how much I might scare her—she wasn't going to stand around and watch while her best girl got hurt.

Tinker's friend was one of the good ones.

"Where's your man?" I asked. She glanced away, dodging my gaze.

"He's not part of this."

"Really? Because from what I saw the other night, he's not the type to let his woman do this kind of work. You didn't tell him, did you?"

She glared at me, shaking her head.

"Darren is a *real* man," she said—the implication that I wasn't all too clear. Not the kind of shit I'd usually take, but under the circumstances I couldn't exactly argue with her—I'd played the pussy and fucked up. The fact that I'd done it for the club didn't change the reality that I'd gotten an innocent woman hurt.

A woman I happened to like a little bit too much.

"So you're scared to tell him," I concluded. "Scared he'll come after me with a shotgun."

Lotta that goin' on in this town.

Carrie held my gaze steadily, refusing to answer. If I weren't so pissed, I'd have smiled—Darren was my kind of guy. Needed to keep a closer eye on his wife, though. Carrie might be a firecracker, but confronting me alone had been stupid as hell.

Almost as stupid as Tinker refusing to tell me what'd happened with Talia.

"Next time, tell your man the truth."

"I fight my own fights."

"Fight using the weapons you have. You're lucky. Darren's a strong one, so don't be afraid to ask him for help. When it comes to physical confrontation, you and me aren't equals, and you had no business taking me on alone. But in this case, I happen to agree with you. Tinker doesn't deserve this. I'll make it stop."

She nodded once, turning and stalking toward the Mustang. Then she paused and glanced back at me.

"You're physically stronger than me," she acknowledged, her eyes hard. "And you're friends with a bunch of thugs. I have no doubt they could hurt my husband. Maybe even kill him . . . but there's something you might want to keep in mind. When a motorcycle tangles with an SUV, the SUV always wins. I drive a Suburban, and accidents happen. Tragic, random traffic accidents. Don't think I'll hesitate to run you down like a rabid dog if your girlfriend hurts Tinker."

With that she climbed back into the shiny red car and slammed the door, pulling away with a screech of her tires. I stood staring after her for a few minutes, then pulled out my phone and dialed my president.

"Hey, Pic. Things are unraveling fast," I said, wishing I had something to punch.

"What'd you fuck up now?" he asked.

"Thanks for the vote of support," I snapped. "Work with me, Picnic."

"Okay, lay it out and we'll find a solution."

"Thought I set Talia straight last night, but she went after Tinker this morning," I told him. "Now Tinker's runnin' scared and took off for Seattle with her dad for the week. Oh, and speaking of her dad, he pulled a shotgun on me this afternoon, so that was fun."

Silence.

"You wanna run that by me again?"

"Tinker's dad is losing his mind. Like, literally. He saw me arguin' with her and pulled a gun on us, confused as hell. It was a special moment."

"Why were you arguing with her?" he asked. "Thought we decided to watch and wait."

"Because she's gonna go see her husband in Seattle. You find out anything about him yet?"

"You don't do it halfway, do you?"

I snorted. "No fun in that."

Picnic laughed, startling me. I'd known him most of my life and could usually call his reactions. This time I wasn't so sure . . . Knew one thing, though. Somewhere along the line, protecting Tinker had become a very high priority. How or when this had happened, I had no goddamn idea, but it was the truth.

"You're really serious about this woman."

"Yeah, boss. I'm serious about her, whatever the hell that means," I said. "I'm also frustrated and pissed off. Christ, Pic. You got no idea what bullshit this is. The Nighthawks are a fuckin' joke, I'm banging some bitch who thinks she owns my cock, and the woman I'm falling for is scared shitless of me. We're not making any *progress*, boss. I want to call the operation. There's more than one way to extract information. We should bring in the brothers, take Marsh back to the Armory, and get our fucking questions answered."

"Okay, calm down," Picnic said. "I hear you. Things are obviously changing and we need to adjust our plans."

His words caught me off guard. I didn't know what I'd expected—that he'd get pissed I wasn't focused enough, or something, which was ridiculous. I'd been through hell with this man more than once, and I knew the Reapers brothers would die for me, every last one of them.

"So how do you want to do it?" I asked slowly.

"First up, shut down Talia. Do whatever it takes, got me? You're supposed to be her man and she fucked around on you. Let her know payback's a bitch, and that you're done with her bullshit. You don't want her fuckin' up your living situation—"

I snorted again. "She wanted me to move into one of the trailers out by the clubhouse—can you believe that shit?"

"Yeah, do that and you'll wake up with your throat slit," he replied sourly. "Remind Talia that she's your bitch, not the other way around, and she'll do what she's goddamned told. That means leaving your landlady out of it—she touches Tinker, she'll pay. If that ruins things with Marsh, we'll come in and shut down the Nighthawks early. One call is all it takes, brother. We got your back."

"Good to know."

"Don't relax yet," Picnic said. "Like I said, one call is all it takes, but a lot's been going on while you've been away. Issues that impact the situation. This Friday the Bellingham and Portland chapters are making a two-week run down to Cali. We got some serious shit goin' down with the cartel, which means we don't have a lot of backup locally. If things fall apart on your end, we gotta call the Devil's Jacks out of Portland."

Fucking great. The Jacks might be our allies, but that alliance wasn't the friendliest.

"What about the Silver Bastards?" I asked.

"They'd come, but they're ass-deep, too. Union stuff down at the mine. It's not a good time for them."

"Got it."

And I did.

Picnic was leaving the decision with me—they'd come if I needed them. But that'd require calling in some damned big favors, costing us our advantage in the relationship with the Jacks. Seeing as less than two years ago we'd been in a shooting war with them, this wasn't something to do lightly.

"I'll try to hold things together around here a little longer," I told him, frustrated but resigned. "Don't like it, but I'll do it. Tinker gets hurt for real, though, all bets are off. You got a problem with that, you need to pull me out of here because it's nonnegotiable."

Pic didn't say anything for a minute, then he gave a low chuckle.

"Yeah, have fun with that, brother. On the bright side, I do have some intel on the husband. He's a piece of shit."

"Kinda figured that already," I told him. Picnic laughed again.

"Well he's a dirty piece of shit," Pic continued. "As in, you can pay him money and he'll change how your case is prosecuted. Allegedly. We tried to pay him off a few years back after some trouble with one of the support clubs, but he's also got political aspirations. By the time we got to him the case was too high profile."

"You find out anything about his family?"

"They're well known in Seattle. Supposed to be old money."

"Why does a guy from a family like that need to take bribes?" I asked, thinking.

"No idea," Pic replied, and for once he was dead serious. "Maybe they ran out of money. We'll keep looking. You focus on covering your ass and remember—we *are* here for you. One call is all it takes."

"Thanks," I said.

"Take care, brother," he told me, hanging up. Shoving my phone into my pocket, I climbed back onto my bike, kicking it to life.

Time to put Talia in her place.

Fifteen minutes later I pulled up to her trailer, backing my bike in next to a car I'd seen parked at Tinker's building. Belonged to Sadie's mom.

Great. Now I got to deal with the girl posse, too.

Of course, that might not be a bad thing. Sadie needed to learn a lesson about respecting my fucking privacy. Taking the steps two at a time, I pounded on the door and then shoved it open hard enough to bang back against the wall.

"Everyone but Talia out."

Four sets of glassy eyes blinked at me. They'd been painting their toes, the nail polish fumes so heavy I couldn't believe they hadn't lost consciousness. Fuckin' ridiculous. Talia offered a cloying smile.

"Looks like someone needs to get laid," she announced with a giggle. "They can hang out here, baby. My room's got plenty of privacy."

Baby. I hated it when she called me that. Not just the word, but the way she said it with a breathless little-girl voice. Made me feel like a damned pedophile.

"I said get the fuck out," I repeated, pitching my voice low and hard as I dropped my hand to the hilt of my knife. Suddenly, the girls couldn't stand up fast enough. Thirty seconds later it was just me and Talia. I locked the door behind them, then started walking toward Talia with slow menace.

"What's wrong with you?" she demanded, hands on her hips. "Who the hell do you think you are, coming in here like this?"

"I'm the man who owns your ass," I reminded her. "And usually I'm pretty easygoing. I don't care what games you play, because I like the way you suck my dick. But this morning you fucked up, even though I warned you to stay out of my business. You went in and scared the shit out of my landlady like a jealous, insecure little bitch. Now I gotta worry about losing my place and my job. Did you think for one minute that your snatch is worth losing my apartment?"

Her mouth opened, then closed again, thoughts racing behind her eyes. God, she was transparent—I saw the exact instant she decided to pull her power play.

"You apologize or it's over," she said. "I won't eat shit from you."

"The only one who ate shit today was Tinker Garrett," I said, cracking my knuckles slowly and deliberately. Her eyes widened. *Yeah, you should be afraid, bitch.* "Listen to the words coming out of my mouth, because I won't be repeating myself. Tinker Garrett is nothing to me—we covered this already. Now promise you'll let it go or we're over. Period. Life is too fuckin' short."

Angry eyes narrowed, and for a minute I thought she'd kick me to the curb. God, that'd be a relief in its own fucked up way. Then the facade crumpled and I swear, her eyes started getting red.

"Crying changes nothing."

"I'll leave her alone," she said finally. "But only because I believe you aren't into her. I don't trust her, though. She chases after men like you wouldn't believe. You remember the video—"

Oh, I remembered. Vividly.

"Like I care about a goddamned video?" I asked. "You don't get it, Talia. You're young, you're hot, and you suck my cock like a goddess. You wanna make this work, I'm with you. But I am *not* down with you fuckin' everything that moves and then crawling up my ass just 'cause I got horny when you weren't around."

"So what you really want is an exclusive relationship?" she asked, sounding hopeful. Christ. Time to take another one for the team.

"Not if you're gonna bitch at me twenty-four/seven," I reminded her. "And not if you fuck up my job. You want to give things a try, I'm up for it, but you make another move on Tinker Garrett or pull any more manipulative bullshit like that fight the other night? Yeah, we're over."

"But otherwise, that's what you want?"

Delusional. She didn't even care about the damage she'd done, or who she hurt along the way. *Sound like anyone else you know?* I asked myself, and I didn't like the answer.

Just get through it. Do it for your brothers—they've risked their lives for you, they've served time for you. Now suck it up and do what you have to do.

"Sure," I said, letting a slow smile slide across my face. It was sexy—I knew this, because women fell for it every time. Talia did, too. So fucking predictable. She licked her lips, then reached down to cup one of her tits.

"Why don't you come over here and let me show you exactly how I feel?" she whispered.

"Can't," I said, and while I tried to inject a hint of regret into my voice, it wasn't easy to pull off. "Your brother wants me out at the clubhouse. Said we had something to talk about."

Talia perked up.

"I'll ride with you," she said. "Let me grab my bag."

I wanted to protest, but figured I'd pushed her far enough already. All I had to do was manage the situation for a few more weeks. Then I'd be free.

"I'll be outside waiting."

CHAPTER TEN

Proving once again that women made no sense, Talia was in a great mood by the time we pulled up to the clubhouse.

"Hey, Cooper!" shouted one of the prospects, a kid named Cody. "Good thing you're here. Boss is lookin' for you."

"He knows we're coming," Talia told him. "I already messaged him."

"Well, he said to watch for Cooper, and then send him in as soon as you guys got here. He's waiting for you."

Talia and I walked into the clubhouse, which smelled like weed and burned chemicals. Someone must've gotten their hands on some seriously low-quality meth, which surprised me. You'd think with Marsh's connections, he'd be using better stuff.

Marsh sat toward the back of the room on a couch, hand tapping nervously against the armrest. A young girl sat on his lap. She had a blank, stoned look and while I could see her hand stuck down his pants, there didn't seem to be much action happening. Approaching them, I caught Marsh's eye and waited for him to speak. He pushed the girl off and stood up, blinking at me through bloodshot, dilated eyes, one hand still twitching nervously.

Great. He was tweaking.

"C'mon, Coop," he said, eyes darting toward Talia. "You stay here, baby girl. We got business."

Talia pouted, but turned away toward the bar as I followed Marsh into a pool room. Their chapel. Lining the walls were old leather vests—colors from brothers who'd died—and a few prizes they'd taken off other clubs who'd wandered into the wrong town. Marsh grabbed a couple of pool cues, tossing one to me.

"Let's play a game and talk," he said. "Shut the door."

I did, then watched as he racked the balls. He radiated a wild, nervous energy that could only come from one place. Meth. Fuck, I knew we had to play it out as long as we could, but at the rate he'd been using, things could fall apart fast. Seemed like it was worse every time I saw him.

"Gotta job for you," he said, leaning over to take the first shot. His hand trembled. Fuck. Hopefully he'd be steady enough for me to throw the game plausibly, because I had a feeling Marsh wasn't a gracious loser. The balls broke with a crack, and thankfully he sank two stripes for a good start.

"What's that?" I asked, carefully casual.

"Need someone to haul some cargo," he said, frowning as he lined up another shot, eye twitching. "Someone we can trust. You been hangin' around for a while and you got your own rig. Figured you might be ready for a shot at some money."

His cue skipped as he made his next play, hitting the ball off-center. Scratch. Marsh scowled.

"I'm always interested in money," I said slowly, pretending to weigh the offer. "What's the run?"

"We've got some shit for you to take up through Bellingham," he said. "You'll cross the border there and drop the load in Vancouver—all legal—and then drive across to Penticton to pick up another load. Come back through the border at Oroville, which is the most dangerous part of the trip. From there you'll drive down to the Tri-Cities and deliver it to some friends of ours."

"The path's a little random," I said. If I went through Bellingham the local Reapers could back me up, but the rest of the time I'd be well and truly on my own. "I can think of better ways to do it."

"Not your job to think," Marsh said slowly. "We'll be watching you, so don't fuck it up. Our Canadian partners will be at both drop points, and they'll be in charge of paying and verifying the shipments. It's your job to drop one trailer and pick up another—simple. Any questions?"

"Yeah," I said. "What's my cut?"

Marsh stared at me.

"Standard shipping rates, Coop, payable when you finish and they verify delivery. So far as you're concerned, this is just another job."

There was a trap if I'd ever seen one—only a moron would agree.

"It's my ass on the line," I said, wondering if the risk was worth it. The Reapers needed information, but I'd never be able to tell them what I'd learned if Marsh slit my throat in a fit of paranoid rage. "You treat me right or I'm out. Your sister's hot, but she's not *that* hot."

The man burst out laughing.

"You're a good guy, Coop," he said. "You call it like it is, and you aren't pussy-whipped. Talia's my baby girl and I love her, but business is business. Let's make a deal."

Standing, he walked over and lifted a faded velvet painting of an American eagle off the wall. Behind it was a safe. Marsh opened it, then came back with a stack of bills in a rubber band, handing it over. I flipped through the money, doing a quick count.

"I'll give you this now and another just like it once you finish the deliveries," he said.

"And what's to keep me from taking the money and running?" I asked, quirking a brow. Marsh laughed again.

"Talia says you're fond of your landlady," he replied, rolling his eyes. "Got her panties in a twist about it, and I understand why.

Bitch is hot. I'd love to give her a test ride, and if you don't come back on time, that's exactly what I'll do."

The muscles in my legs stiffened, but I managed to keep the friendly smile on my face.

"Just 'cause I'm horny for some bitch doesn't mean I care about her."

"Yeah, but you probably care about your kids," he said. "So if you're planning to make a run for it, you might want to stop off and pick them up along the way. Otherwise, I'll find them and eat their little hearts for breakfast. We clear?"

"Crystal," I said, my voice hardening. My fingers twitched, itching to kill the bastard. Lucky for Marsh the kids weren't real— otherwise the fucker'd be dead already.

"Perfect. How soon can you get on the road?"

"Tomorrow morning," I said. "Got some shit to clear up around the apartment building. Otherwise it'll look suspicious. Oh, and Marsh?"

"Yeah?"

"Your sister. She tried to fuck with my living situation, and I'm over it. We had words. That gonna be a problem?"

Marsh laughed and shook his head.

"The only man she really cares about is me," he said. "She'd be bored of you already if she hadn't caught you fuckin' around."

"We got an understanding, then?"

"Yeah, we got an understanding. You take care of the cargo, I'll take care of Talia. We all do our jobs, everyone lives happily ever after. Easy. Now let's finish the game."

Took a couple hours to extract myself from the clubhouse that night. Helped that Talia had gotten herself wasted while I was talkin' to Marsh, which meant she and her girls would be partying until the early hours. Seeing as I had a job to do the next day, I'd managed to escape following a quick fuck in the bathroom.

Had to say, all those years managing the strip club and I never fully appreciated what the girls went through in the VIP rooms.

Now? Yeah, let's just say I was developing some empathy.

Grabbing a beer out of the fridge, I cracked open a new phone I'd picked up a few days ago in Omak. Still wasn't sure whether Marsh had decided to trust me, or if it was a setup, but either way, Picnic needed an update.

He answered on the third ring.

"Aw, sugar," he said. "Three calls in one day? You really love me, don't you?"

"Fuck off," I countered. "Got an update for you."

"What's that?"

"Playing the hard line worked. I shut Talia down and Marsh doesn't seem to have a problem with it—all he cares about is money. Get the impression her tantrum is more about hurt pride than anything else. He wants me to run a load up to Vancouver, then bring another load back down through Oroville. Delivery to the Tri-Cities."

"Think it's a setup?"

"Possibly," I said, considering the question. "But my gut tells me no. He's not like us—he's sloppy. No fuckin' way a man in my position should be brought in this early, but he's got prospects that barely know how to ride their bikes. He's stretched thin as hell and it's showing."

"Guess it's decision time, then. You up for moving forward?"

I considered the question. It was a legitimate concern—for all we knew, Marsh wanted me out of the picture. That didn't feel right, though, and I'd learned to trust my gut over the years. "Yeah, I think it's worth the risk. I'll leave tomorrow. You give the boys in Bellingham a heads-up—they can help me go through the load, see what kind of intel we find. The sooner we end this shit the better."

"You got it," he said. "We'll have them meet you at a truck stop in case Jackson puts a GPS on you. Should be easy enough to pull off. If you ever get asked why you stopped, just say you needed to take a shit. Sooner or later we all do."

"This is getting more personal than it needs to be."

Picnic laughed. "Let me know when you leave town. I'll call

Bellingham and make the arrangements. Good job. This run is exactly what we need—access to their network and proof they're stealing from us. And I don't care how fantastic her tits are, don't let Tinker distract you while you're workin'. We've got your back, but we can't ride in the truck with you. Keep your focus on what really matters here, got me? I fuckin' hate funerals."

SEATTLE
TINKER

We pulled up to the house at eight that night. I hadn't been back for six months, and it seemed weird how unchanged everything was. Brandon hadn't really spent much time there while we were married, and apparently he still didn't. Not that the house wasn't in perfect condition—we had a service for that—but it didn't feel lived-in. The whole place was as sterile as our marriage had been.

I got Dad and Randi settled in their rooms before heading downstairs to check out my kitchen. Much as I hated what the rest of the house had come to represent, I loved what I'd created down here. Shining metal counters, giant sink with a built-in drainboard. Beautiful stove top and the enrobing machine. Rolling tray racks.

God, I missed it.

You could just stay here, an insidious voice whispered in my head. *You don't have to go back and face that crazy bitch. Leave it all behind. Your dad's losing his mind anyway. In a few weeks he won't even remember living somewhere else.*

"Tinker?" I spun around to find Brandon. He was tall and svelte, all perfect hair and wearing a suit that had to cost thousands. I knew his family had money, but I'd always thought it looked bad for someone on a deputy prosecutor's salary to wear clothes that flashy. Not that it was my business at this point. The sooner we finalized the divorce, the better.

"Hi, Brandon," I said, offering him a tight smile. "I'll only be here a few days. Shouldn't mess with your life too much."

"I'm not worried about that," he said, walking toward me. "You look good, Tinker. I've missed you. How are you doing?"

"I'm fine," I told him. "I'm only here because I had a batch of caramels go south on me, and I needed to get caught up. Figured it would be good to use the full kitchen for a couple of days."

Brandon pulled a stool over to the center island and sat down.

"Do you have a few minutes?" he asked. "I wanted to talk to you."

Ah, now I was remembering why I didn't want to stay in Seattle. Whole damned town was infested with Brandon.

"You've got five," I said. His eyes hardened and I could see the hint of frustration he tried to hide—Brandon never liked it when people set limits. Guess the house wasn't the only thing that hadn't changed.

"It's been eighteen months," he said in his Very Serious Voice. Juries always fell for it, which I guess I could understand. I used to fall for it, too. Now it just sounded ridiculous. "I think it's time to discuss our separation."

Sighing, I grabbed my own stool and pulled it over, sitting down to face him. "You're right. I talked to my lawyer last week about moving things along faster. He says he still hasn't gotten all the financials from you. What's the holdup?"

Brandon frowned. "That's not really what I meant, Tinker. All along, I've tried to give you space. I understood that you needed time to heal, and then when your mother died . . . well, we went through a series of tragedies, and that's enough to shake any couple. But we've both had time to recover, and I think we need to discuss reconciliation."

"Are you high? No. Just . . . *no*."

"Tinker, you're not even listening to me," he said, his calm mask cracking. "I don't think you understand the situation. The current Prosecuting Attorney is stepping down, and he's going to back me in the next election. It's great news, but our supporters want you as part of the package. It's about family values. You're a beautiful woman who's built a fantastic business centered on the home arts—"

The blood in my head started to pound.

"You've been lying to people about us, haven't you?"

He shrugged. "I've told them about the baby, of course, and then explained about your mother. Everyone understands, but I really need you back in Seattle now. If you don't show your face soon, it could cost me the election."

"You're delusional," I said bluntly. "We're getting a divorce. Things have been crazy and our finances are complicated—or so you keep telling me—but it's been eighteen months. You need to send all the documentation to my attorney so we can move forward. I don't want things to get ugly, but we're over, Brandon. There's nothing to reconcile."

My phone buzzed, and I pulled it out of my pocket, giving it a quick glance. Carrie had texted, wanting to make sure I'd arrived all right. Setting it down on the counter, I looked over at the man I'd wasted ten years of my life on.

"You've had a rough day," he said softly. "I shouldn't have bothered you tonight. Would you be free to have dinner with me tomorrow?"

"No, but my attorney might be."

He laughed, the sound forced. I'd had enough.

"I need to prep," I told him. "You should go back upstairs and let me work."

He opened his mouth to argue, so I decided to ignore him, sliding off my stool and walking over to my storage closet. Hopefully, I still had some boxes in there to replace the ones that'd been damaged. My supply shipment had been delayed, and while I theoretically had enough for the next week, finding more would make life easier. I found an entire flat waiting to be folded. Nice. Randi could work on them tomorrow while I cooked.

Stepping back into the kitchen, I found Brandon still sitting at the work island.

Holding my phone.

"What the hell, Brandon?"

He looked up at me, eyes dark with anger. "Who's Cooper?"

I raised a brow.

"Seriously? You're spying on my phone now?"

"It kept buzzing. I wanted to be sure there wasn't an emergency," he replied, as if what he'd done were perfectly reasonable. He'd always had a gift for that—making it sound like I was the crazy one, not him.

"Hand it over," I snapped, holding out my hand. He dropped the phone into it, and I saw the message that'd flashed across the front.

COOPER: I know about what happened with Talia. Sorry doesn't cut it but at least I can promise it won't happen again. FYI—I have to head out of town for a couple days. Short term job. Call me

Great, because his crazy girlfriend wasn't pissed off enough already. Fucking men, always thinking they knew how to solve everything.

"So who is he?" Brandon demanded, the words clipped. I sat down, stretching my neck, because this was officially the day from hell. What could go wrong next? Maybe a meteor would hit us. That'd simplify things.

"He's my handyman," I said absently. "He moved into the building about a month ago."

"Your handyman?"

"Yeah," I said. "You know, the guy you call when something breaks? He does maintenance around the building. Huge help."

"And who is he, exactly? How do you know you can trust him? I really wish you'd had me do a background check before you—"

What a smug, self-righteous asshole. The anger and frustration and grief and rage I'd suffered over the past year and a half boiled out and I turned on him.

"Shut the fuck up, Brandon," I snarled. "Jesus, how fucking stupid are you? I'm not your wife anymore, and I haven't been for a long time. Our daughter *died* and you didn't even bother to show up. Once you pull something like that, it's all over. You can't argue with me, you can't bully me, you can't do anything, because *we aren't a couple anymore*. You don't exist in my world, got it?"

Brandon gaped at me, and for once he didn't have a damned thing to say. The phone buzzed again, and I looked down to find another message.

COOPER: I need Darrens number

Fucking men. Always making demands.

"Are you cheating on me with him?" Brandon asked, scowling. I blinked at him. Shit, maybe he really *was* high.

"Yes, Brandon," I replied. "I have mad, passionate sex with him every night. Him and all his motorcycle club friends. Until recently I was limiting myself to male strippers, but all that body oil gets messy after a while, don't you think?"

"We're still legally married," he said stiffly, and I burst out laughing.

"Get out."

"Tinker—"

"It's time to leave now," I said. "I'll be here until the end of the week. Don't feel like you need to change your schedule—it's not like I want to see you. And think about those financial papers, because if you don't start cooperating, I might just lose my shit and do something crazy. Now get out of my kitchen."

He opened his mouth to reply. I turned around, opening a drawer to pull out a chef's knife. It wasn't my favorite, but it'd do. Spinning back toward him, I raised it, as if studying the blade.

"I've got a lot to do here, Brandon," I said, testing the blade's sharpness with my finger. "It's been a long day and I'm feeling a little hormonal. Isn't that what you always said about me? That I let my hormones do all the thinking? You wanna find out what they're suggesting I do right now?"

Silence fell between us, his eyes glued to the knife.

"Are you threatening me?" he asked slowly. "Because that's a very serious—"

I slammed the knife down on the island, then offered him my sweetest smile.

"I never make threats."

He stood and slowly backed away, eyes wide. "We aren't finish—"

"Good night, Brandon," I said. "Sleep tight and lock your door, sweetheart."

"You're crazy."

"Oh, you have no idea." I laughed as he walked away, because even if he was right, I didn't care. It'd been a big day, and I'd learned an important lesson.

Talia wasn't the only one who could use a knife.

CHAPTER ELEVEN

GAGE

Tinker texted me Darren's phone number the next morning, along with instructions to contact him—not her—if something went wrong with the building. Whole fuckin' situation pissed me off, but it was probably for the best . . . Until I finished things with Talia, there wasn't much to discuss. I'd figure things with Tinker out later, because Picnic had been right about one thing—I couldn't afford to lose focus on this run. If things fell to shit, I could find myself in prison or even dead.

Strangely, the trip itself was anticlimactic.

I mean, I knew it was supposed to be easy, but Marsh wasn't exactly trustworthy. I reached Bellingham without drama, pulling off for a sandwich at a truck stop while a couple of the local Reapers went through the truck. Most of what they found matched the manifest—scrap metal and recyclables. Well, scrap metal, recyclables, and about four kilos of cocaine. If I'd had any illusions up to that point that Marsh was a criminal mastermind, him sending that much product with an unknown like myself was enough to kill them. So much for his promise that everything would be totally legal.

That was strike one against him.

The drugs were well hidden, I had to give him that. Throw in the fact that my cover was clean as a whistle, and I'd felt perfectly safe crossing the border. The shipment was just another nail in Marsh's grave, though. If he wanted to move product through the Reapers' territory, we expected him to pay the appropriate taxes. Clearly, that wasn't happening.

Strike two.

I off-loaded the stuff in Vancouver, playing my part perfectly. Transportation only, no questions asked. Then I moved on to Penticton, picking up a load of fruit-processing machinery, of all things. I searched it myself before crossing the border back into the States, just in case they were setting me up. If Marsh's people were smuggling something back down, damned if I was able to find it.

Still, I'd managed to meet not one but two sets of his Canadian contacts. That was progress.

Now all that remained was figuring out the Penticton fruit connection—we were still missing a major piece of the puzzle. Either that or Marsh really had gotten into the fruit-processing business, which made no damned sense no matter how you looked at it.

By the time I pulled up to the apartment building on Thursday afternoon, I was tired and hungry and more than a little frustrated to discover that Tinker didn't seem to be home from Seattle yet—the shades were shut on the house and there were no signs of her car. The fact that I'd been hoping to see her like some dumbass kid frustrated me even more, for obvious reasons. The situation with the Nighthawks was a powder keg and the situation with Talia was even worse.

God only knew what fresh hell was ahead of us.

SATURDAY AFTERNOON
TINKER

"Lot of smoke in the air," Dad said, frowning from the passenger seat. I'd managed to finish my production on Thursday and did my deliveries on Friday. Between all of that, I'd somehow found time to meet with my lawyer and make a few phone calls about Dad. We'd be seeing a specialist in a few weeks—one of the best in Seattle. Good thing, too. Dad had been more confused than I'd ever seen him these past couple days. Randi had done a hell of a good job keeping him out of trouble, but it'd been stressful for all of us.

"Wildfires," I said. "It's been a dry summer. Hopefully, the weather will turn and we'll get some rain soon."

"I need a bathroom break," Randi announced from the backseat, sitting up. I glanced in the mirror at her. My nineteen-year-old shop assistant's hair was plastered against the side of her face, and her mascara had smudged across her cheek. She'd fallen asleep not long after we left Seattle. "Where are we?"

"Just outside of Wenatchee," I told her. "There's some makeup wipes in my bag, in the side pocket. We'll stop for gas in a few and you can clean up. You look like a raccoon."

Randi nodded sleepily, and I heard her rummaging through the tote I'd packed for the trip. She'd been a trouper this week—we'd been gone five nights, which was more than she'd signed up for. Between the time she'd spent helping out with Dad and her time working in the kitchen with me, she'd get a real nice check out of this one. I'd probably throw in a bonus, too—I'd have been screwed without her.

"What's with all the smoke?" she asked, her voice still fuzzy.

"Wildfires," Dad told her. He seemed to be tracking now that we'd left the city, something that wasn't lost on me. Hopefully, he'd do better once he was back in his home environment.

"Sheesh," she murmured. "Hope they don't burn too close to any towns."

Spotting a gas station up ahead, I flipped on my turn signal and pulled up to the pumps.

"Hand me my wallet, will you?" I asked Randi. She passed it forward and I dug out my debit card. Dad stayed put in the car as she took off for the convenience store, following the pattern we'd established early on in the trip. I'd pump the gas, then park the car and bring Dad in with me. If things worked out, Randi would be done by then, and she'd help keep an eye on him while I took my own bathroom break. So far the system was working.

How much longer will you let this go on? Brandon's voice whispered in my head. *The man's practically a vegetable.* He'd confronted me again last night, full of fresh arguments now that my lawyer was turning up the heat.

I shook my head, rejecting the thought. Why the hell should I let Brandon's bullshit infect me? He had no idea what Dad was capable of on his home turf. He'd snap right back once we reached the apartment building.

Even if he didn't, he wasn't a fucking vegetable.

No, my soon-to-be ex-husband would do better to suck it up and give my attorney the fucking financial information so we could divide up our assets, because this had dragged out long enough. If I didn't know better, I'd think he had something to hide. That was crazy, though. Brandon's family had more money than God—what did he need with our piddly shared savings accounts, anyway? I slammed the nozzle into the tank hard, feeling pissy. I leaned against the car as the gas started to flow, looking out across the hill. The sky was dim, even though it was only three in the afternoon.

"That's a hell of a lot of smoke," Dad muttered when I climbed back into the SUV. "Just like last summer, when Omak burned. Ugly business."

"Hope it stays far away from us," I replied. "Let's go inside. You want anything to drink?"

"I could use some water and a bathroom break. Can't wait to get home. I love you, baby girl, and I'll always support you, but that husband of yours makes me uncomfortable."

"Daddy, I think you forgot—I'm divorcing Brandon. As soon as possible, actually. With any luck, you'll never have to see him again."

My father's face transformed as a blinding smile took over. Then he was hugging me, squeezing me hard as I laughed, because life is weird.

"Thank God," he said. "Don't like the way he talks to you. And don't think I forgot what he did, either—I may be old and losing my mind, but a father never forgets the man who abandoned his grandchild to die alone."

Ouch.

"I'd rather not talk about that," I reminded him, even though part of me rejoiced, because I wasn't the only one who remembered her. He'd loved her, too, from the first minute I'd told him I was pregnant. Whatever was going on in his head, it wasn't stealing away his love for his family, and I needed that. He was all I had left. "But don't worry—it's definitely over between me and Brandon. And you're right about the way he talks to me, too. I'll never fall for his shit again, I promise."

We found Randi inside the convenience store, staring up at a TV mounted in the corner behind the counter. Aerial shots of massive trees engulfed in flame filled the screen. There weren't a lot of people inside, just one other customer and the clerk, but all eyes were glued to the news.

"As you can see, the fires are growing rapidly," a reporter said, her voice incongruously perky. "Although at this point, officials tell us that it hasn't spread outside the national forest and no buildings are threatened. Even so, they're urging residents and those traveling through the region to be careful. Air quality is extremely low in some areas due to smoke, which poses a serious risk to anyone with asthma or other pulmonary conditions. Additionally, the Washington State Department of Transportation is reporting multiple road closures due to poor visibility."

The screen changed, flashing to a map showing several roads highlighted.

"As you can see, I-90 is closed from Vantage to Ritzville. We're also getting word that while Highway 97 near Chelan remains open, visibility is growing worse and officials are considering a closure there in the near future."

"Isn't that where we're going?" Randi asked, eyes wide. I nodded, frowning.

"Yeah," I said. "We'd better get going—I don't want to get stuck driving all the way around. Creepy, isn't it?"

"Very."

Despite the reporter's warnings, we made it back to Hallies Falls just fine.

I dropped Randi off at her mom's house, and then Dad and I headed for the apartment building. As we pulled up, I saw Cooper's semi was parked out back again—guess he'd finished his job.

Whatever.

I parked on the street in front of the house instead of the parking lot, so it'd be easier to unload the car. Even though I was dead tired, I couldn't help but notice how spectacular the sunset was—guess all that smoke was good for something. Raising my phone, I snapped a picture of the brilliant pinks and reds filling the sky across the valley. That's when I heard the sound of footsteps behind me.

"Fires suck, but the smoke sure as hell paints a pretty picture, doesn't it?" Cooper said, his voice low and rough. It sent a thrill racing through me, one that I pushed down ruthlessly, because nothing had changed. He was still attached to his crazy bitch of a girlfriend.

"It's beautiful," I admitted, refusing to look at him. He stepped closer, and I felt the warmth of his body behind me. *Lean back into him. You know you want to.* I moved forward instead, putting distance between us before turning to look at him.

Mistake.

I'd sort of convinced myself that I'd imagined how sexy he was. I mean, theoretically Brandon was sexy, too, but I had no trouble controlling myself around him. (I'd gotten over the whole smooth, metrosexual thing right around the time he was too busy to show up at the hospital when I needed him most.)

Cooper was the total opposite.

He hadn't shaved since I'd last seen him, and his five-o'clock shadow was moving past stubble into beard territory. Combine that with the dark, slightly curly hair pulled back into a short ponytail, the broad shoulders barely contained by his faded T-shirt, and his black leather boots? Yum. The man was delicious.

Too delicious.

"Heard they closed a few roads because of smoke," he said, eyes studying my face intently. "You have any trouble getting back?"

"No, it was okay," I said, wishing he'd leave me alone. "But I'm tired. Been a long week."

"She won't fuck with you again," he said bluntly. "I'm really sorry about what happened—it wasn't okay, and I made that clear. She won't be around here, and if she gives you any more trouble let me know. I'll take care of it."

Something hardened in his face as he said it, something scary. I shivered, rubbing up and down my arms. Cooper frowned.

"You should go inside," he said.

"I need to finish unloading the car."

"Let me help."

Behind him, I saw Sadie step out of her apartment. Our gazes met, and then she reached for her cell. Fuck's sake, like I needed more drama.

"No," I said firmly. "I think it's best to keep our distance, all things considered."

"I work for you. That'll get complicated if we can't even talk to each other."

He was right. He was also standing way too close to me, especially with Sadie watching every move. *End it. You're a grown-up, so say it like it needs to be said.*

"What happened in your apartment . . . that wasn't okay," I said, catching and holding his gaze. He stared back, and for a minute I thought he might deny it. "Neither was what happened with your girlfriend afterward. I have enough drama in my life—I don't need any more."

"I know," he acknowledged, eyes darkening. My breath caught, and I felt a tendril of heat start to wind up from my stomach. "But it's more complicated than you think."

"You still seeing Talia?" I asked. Cooper looked away, rubbing at his chin as he frowned.

"Doesn't sound complicated at all," I said, my voice growing hard. "And you might do maintenance around here, but that doesn't include unloading my car for me. It also doesn't include socializing. If there's an issue with the building I can text you. If we need to take care of something in person, my dad can come with us. I lost a week's worth of work because I ate dinner with a man who's a dead end. My life is stressful enough already."

Cooper's eyes flared, and he opened his mouth like he wanted to say something. *Tell me you broke up with her.* Instead, he shut it again, scowling as he looked away.

"You're right. I'll leave you alone."

"Thank you," I said, wondering why it hurt so much. Wasn't like I even really knew the guy. Probably never would, and that was for the best. He hung out with the wrong people. Our lives were totally different. There wouldn't be anything between us even if he were free.

You thought you and Brandon were the same kind of people, my heart whispered. *How'd that work out for you?*

Not well.

Turning away from him, I looked across the valley at the sunset again, wishing I'd never met him. He stood behind me for long moments, then I heard the crunch of his footsteps as he walked away.

The next week was tense.

I decided not to reopen Mom's store, because there wasn't any point in it. I never sold anything there anyway and I didn't like the idea of someone like Talia being able to walk in on me. This might've been bad news for my shop assistant, Randi, but she'd done such a great job with my dad while we were in Seattle that I asked if she'd be his caregiver while we tried to figure things out.

"I'd love it," she'd answered, seeming genuinely enthusiastic about the idea. I must've looked surprised, because she'd smiled at me shyly and then said, "I like hanging out with Mr. Garrett. I never met my grandpa and Dad took off when I was still a kid. He treats me like his granddaughter, you know? It feels good."

The words had cut me like a knife to the heart, but I understood. Dad had always wanted to be a grandpa. I'd never forget when I called to tell him and Mom I was pregnant—they were ecstatic. Losing little Tricia devastated all of us, and if having Randi around made him feel good, I couldn't have a problem with that.

As for Cooper, he kept his distance.

It's what I'd wanted, and I appreciated it . . . that didn't mean I wasn't thinking about him at night, or that I didn't watch him while he worked. His eyes burned whenever he saw me, but Talia still came around his apartment regularly. Other times I'd see him on his bike in town with the Nighthawks. They were loud, rude, and expected everyone to stay the hell out of their way.

When I was a kid, I remembered them as being intimidating, but not truly terrifying. They'd had the respect of the community. When I'd come back after my mom had died, I'd noticed that dynamic had changed, but hadn't paid much attention. Now I was really looking, and what I saw was a town full of people who were afraid.

TWO WEEKS LATER

MARGARITA: Im coming home this weekend to see the old people. Moms birthday. We need to go out Friday night or I'll lose my mind.

CARRIE: Works for me!!! You know how much I hate going out ;) Tinker you on board?

ME: hell yes. It's been too long! I can tell you all the latest shit with brandon

CARRIE: OMG he's such a cocktwat! You won't believe what he did Margee!

MARGARITA: What?!?

ME: Ugh. Not only is he ducking around on the financial stuff he's being super weird. I think he's obsessed with my new handyman.

MARGARITA: Huh?

CARRIE: Tinker has a hot new guy to take care of the building and Brandon's all jealous. He thinks they're sleeping together

MARGARITA: Oooo . . . And are you?

ME: NO

CARRIE: NO NO NO. Hes hot but he's got a batshit crazy girlfriend. We can talk this weekend. So glad ur coming home!!!!!

MARGARITA: See you soon! Xx

"This is my song!" Carrie shouted, grabbing my hand and pulling me onto the dance floor. Margarita was right behind us. Jack's Roadhouse wasn't exactly a happening nightclub or anything, but it was the closest we had to nightlife in Hallies Falls. The beer was cheap, the music was loud, and nobody checked ID too closely. Not that I wouldn't mind being mistaken for underage. On the weekends they pushed the tables to the side, creating a dance floor. Usually there was a DJ, but tonight they'd actually brought in a live band.

"Oh my God, is that Joel Riley?" Carrie shouted in my ear during the first set, clutching my shoulders for support. I swayed, blinking at the small stage. There were three guys, a drummer and two guitarists, and sure enough one of them was Joel Riley.

"Wow," I said. "He looks even better than he did in high school." This was truth.

Joel had been a year ahead of us, and I'd spent two full years deeply in love with him. So had Margarita, although her infatuation had faded after he'd invited her to prom our junior year. Specifically, things had fallen apart at the after party, where he'd chugged a bottle of tequila then barfed on the side of his car.

Still, the man looked good now. Damned good.

"Joel!" Margarita shrieked, jumping up and down and waving

wildly. His head turned to us, a broad smile crossing his face. Carrie screeched and jumped up next to her, crashing into me and knocking me over. Big hands caught my waist, pulling me to my feet as the people around us pushed us together.

Cooper.

He stared down at me, eyes dark and hungry. My body recognized him, responding instantly, my common sense safely anesthetized by the vodka I'd been drinking all night. His arms wrapped around me, pulling me into his body as my legs clenched. I wondered what it'd feel like, that hard body pushing deep inside. Then he leaned forward, speaking directly into my ear, his voice rough and sexy. I didn't even register what he said. I was too busy imagining him catching my earlobe between his teeth and sucking on it for a while.

His hold on me tightened. Someone bumped into us, and then he was pulling me off the dance floor in the darkness next to the stage, right behind one of the big speakers.

"Are you all right?" he asked. I nodded, staring at his mouth. For such a big, scary guy he had gorgeous lips. They looked soft, but they'd been hard and strong when he'd kissed me. Hard and strong and demanding, just like I imagined they'd be if he fucked me up against the wall right next to the stage. I leaned forward without thinking, mesmerized. Cooper's hand slid up my spine and then—

"Tinker Garrett?" I looked up to find Joel standing next to us, grinning like a crazy man. Apparently the band had stopped playing somewhere along the line but I hadn't even noticed. I'd been too busy . . . *Holy crap, you nearly kissed Cooper!*

Jerking away from him, I turned to Joel, thankful that he couldn't see me flushing in the dim light. Thank God he'd interrupted us before I'd done something really, really stupid.

"Hey, I haven't seen you in years," I said brightly. "Love the music."

"Thanks," he replied, grinning. "I heard you were back in town. Who's your friend?"

"Cooper Romero," I said. "Cooper, this is Joel Riley. We went to high school together."

"Nice to meet you," Cooper growled, dropping a heavy arm over my shoulders. Joel raised his brows and grinned before holding his hands up in surrender.

"Peace, bro," he said. "I'm not trying to steal your girl. Just hadn't seen her since high school."

"I'm not his girl," I said forcefully, shoving Cooper's hand off my shoulder. Joel raised a brow.

"Cooper, what are you doing?" Talia demanded, pushing between us. She slid her hand through his arm possessively, and I wondered how something as simple as a night out dancing could get so complicated so fast.

"Nothing," Cooper replied shortly, eyes snapping between me and Joel, who took a step closer.

"You wanna grab a beer, Tinker?" he asked me, ignoring the big, pissy biker standing next to us. Cooper's jaw tightened. I turned my back on him and Talia, offering Joel my best smile.

"Sure. I'd love to catch up with you."

"Marsh wants to talk," Talia said to Cooper. Catching Joel's arm, I tugged him toward the bar, leaving Cooper and Talia behind us, because whatever drama might be in Cooper's future, I wanted nothing to do with it.

"Interesting dynamic," Joel said as we found a couple of stools at the far end of the bar. I rolled my eyes.

"You could say that."

"So, is that Cooper guy a factor or not?"

"Definitely not," I told him. "Not even a little bit."

He cocked his head at me, raising a brow. I shrugged and smiled.

"Okay, it's complicated. But he's also trouble and I've got no time or patience for that. We're not in high school anymore and I'm well and truly over relationship drama. What about you? What's going on in your life?"

"Well, I got divorced about three years ago," he said. "Kaci and I got married a couple years after high school and things were good for a long time. Then they weren't. I've got no regrets, though. We had two great kids together—and I wouldn't trade them for anything—but by the time it was over, we both just wanted to move on. She lives in Wenatchee now, and we share custody of the kids. How about you?"

This was always the awkward question.

"I'm mid-divorce, no children," I told him. "I'm living at home with my dad right now. Mom passed earlier this year. Wow, on paper that sort of makes me sound like a loser."

Joel smiled, and I swear—the man really was rather beautiful. Tousled brown hair with a hint of light from the sun, blue eyes. He had a nice build, too. Not as big as Cooper, but he gave off very good vibes.

"You don't look like a loser," he said, taking in my low-cut top and tight pencil skirt. I crossed my legs self-consciously, then felt even more self-conscious because it felt like an obvious ploy to draw attention to them.

But what the hell? I had great legs.

"So what do you do?"

"High school band teacher," he said, grinning at me. "Gigs like this help me keep my sanity on the weekends. You?"

"Gourmet chocolates," I said. "I started out as a private chef, but then I started making caramels and things just sort of took off. Now I have clients all over the region."

"And you do all that from Hallies Falls?"

"Yup," I said, reaching for the drink the bartender had set in front of me. Joel frowned.

"Did you order that?" I paused, confused. "No . . . I didn't."

"And I didn't order mine," he said, eyes narrowing at the beer in front of him. Looking up, I saw Margarita and Carrie across the bar, waving at us maniacally. I sighed.

"I think I should warn you right now—the three of us don't get out very much, and both of them are married. They like to live through me vicariously, which means they're trying to get me drunk and laid tonight. Please ignore them."

Joel's eyes widened, and he burst out laughing.

"Jesus, you don't fuck around, do you?"

I took a delicate sip of my drink and shrugged.

"We're in our late thirties, Joel. This isn't high school and there's something to be said for direct communication. But you should know that just because they want me to have sex doesn't mean that's my goal for the night. I'm planning on having a few drinks, dancing for a while, and then going to bed by myself at the end of the night."

Joel laughed again. "Well, I'm always up for getting laid, but seeing as I'll be spending most of the night playing, maybe we could have a few more drinks between sets and catch up."

"I'd like that."

CHAPTER TWELVE

GAGE

Talia threw her leg over my lap, grinding against me in time to the music. The band wasn't half bad, but that piece of shit Riley hadn't taken his eyes off Tinker all night. I wanted to drag his ass out behind the bar, rip off his dick, and shove it down his throat.

Instead, I got to sit at a table with Marsh while his sister crawled all over me like a perverted monkey. This wouldn't be great under the best of circumstances, but to make things even more fun, Marsh was tweaking again, and paranoid as fuck. He wasn't a full-on meth head, or at least I hadn't thought so when I first arrived. Now I wasn't so sure—not exactly the most comforting of dynamics. Two nights ago he'd lost his shit, and beat the hell out of some kid who'd tripped and spilled his beer at the clubhouse. Nearly killed him.

Tinker was dancing right up to the stage, eye-fucking the guitar player while her girls cheered her on. Christ. He had douche written all over him. She'd be lucky if he offered to bang her in his car, instead of just doing her against a wall out back.

Keep your head in the game.

Grabbing my beer, I chugged it down, then leaned over toward Marsh.

"You got any more work?" I asked. He stared at me, eyelid twitching, and I wondered what the hell was going on in that crazy head of his.

"Why?" he asked. "You made plenty of cash on that last run."

Because I need to finish this fucking farce.

"Not enough," I said shortly. "I'm getting to the point where I'm going to have to start taking jobs again. Whatever you decide is fine, but I've been spendin' a lot of time with the club. Figured I'd talk to you before putting out any more feelers."

He considered the question, then nodded slowly.

"I might have more work for you," he said. "But that means taking things to the next level. You ever consider joinin' a club?"

Why, yes. Yes, I have. Been a Reaper for eighteen years, thanks for asking.

"Not really," I said. Talia leaned over and started sucking on my neck. Hard. Bitch wanted to mark her territory. I'd fucked up back there, talking to Tinker. But Jesus, she'd fallen right next to me. I couldn't just let her get trampled, and once I had my hands on her it wasn't like I was gonna let her go.

"Consider it," he said bluntly. "We're heading down to Ellensburg tomorrow. Big classic car show. You remember a guy named Hands? Disappeared right around the time you started comin' around."

"Huh," I said, tugging at Talia's hair. She felt like a leech attached to my neck.

"I got word from a friend—turns out Hands was an informant for the feds," Marsh said, leaning in close.

"No shit?" I asked, wondering where he'd gotten the information. Hands had been an informant, all right. Now he was a dead informant. Not that I'd killed him personally. Nope, all I'd done was help my brother Painter kidnap him, beat the shit out of him for good measure and then hand him off to the Bellingham Reapers like the garbage he was. Wasn't exactly sure what they'd done with him after that, but my best guess was they'd dumped the body offshore.

Fucking shame, all things considered. I'd had to spend three extra nights in that rat trap of a hotel because of him.

"Yeah," he said. "And I got word that Hands is gonna be at the car show. You wanna be part of this club, now's the time to show your loyalty. You helped us deal with this situation and I see lots of opportunity for you down the road. You with me?"

I opened my mouth to answer, but Talia's hand snaked down between us, cupping my cock through my fly. I pushed her off me, annoyed.

"What the fuck, Coop?" she asked. Marsh burst out laughing.

"Been too long since you had a real man, sis. You forget that not all of us sign over our balls at the door. Stop your bitchin' and go grab us some more beers."

She sneered at him, but she didn't argue. I watched as she walked away, feeling almost sorry for her. Growing up with this jackass couldn't have been easy.

"We'll also be bringing some product down tomorrow," Marsh said. "I've got some associates in the Tri-Cities. You met them before. They've got some other goods to swap with ours. We'll pick them up, deal with Hands, and then enjoy the rest of the day. Some of those street rods aren't half bad, even if they aren't bikes. Always plenty of beer and bitches, too. You'll like it."

Tri-Cities. Interesting.

"These the guys in the fruit business?" I asked. Marsh's eyes narrowed in sudden paranoia. God, I needed to be more careful. This man's temper turned on a dime.

"Any particular reason you're asking questions about my business? You workin' for someone else, Coop? Hands was a fuckin' traitor, and this time tomorrow he'll be dead. I can do the same to you. Make you disappear off the face of the fuckin' earth. Never forget that."

Paranoid much?

"Just curious," I replied mildly. "No big deal, boss."

"Well, watch your fuckin' mouth," he said, hand twitching nervously on the table. He really needed to stop using his own product. Fuckin' death spiral. "Hey, that's Tinker Garrett over there, isn't it?"

I glanced toward the dance floor, pretending I hadn't been watching her from the moment she'd come in. "Sure looks like her."

"You hit that yet?"

Shooting a glance at him, I tried to decide if it was a trick question. "No, I like 'em younger."

"Like my sister."

"Like your sister," I agreed, a bad feeling growing in my gut. Marsh's hand jerked, and for an instant I wondered if he was going for a gun. Then he slammed his hand down on the table hard enough to slosh the drinks, laughter bursting out.

"Gotcha, Coop," he said gleefully. "Christ, that was easy. Talia's big enough to make her own choices. She fucks who she wants and that's got nothin' to do with business. But I find out you've been lying to me about anything? Yeah, I'll fuckin' skin you myself."

Jesus. This guy was a goddamned lunatic.

"Here's your beer," Talia said sweetly, handing each of us a bottle before settling down into my lap. She wrapped her arms around my neck and cuddled into me like a kitten.

"We're goin' down to the car show in Ellensburg tomorrow," Marsh told her, eyes on the dance floor.

"Sounds like fun," she said. "I'll ride with Coop."

Marsh shot me a glance, then shook his head.

"Nope, you follow in the truck with the other girls," he said. "Behind the pack."

She gave a pretty pout as my mind raced. He'd been talking about Hands like he was a traitor, but he'd also threatened me. Throw in the fact that I knew damned well Hands was dead, and I couldn't help but wonder if this was some kind of trap. Had he figured out who I was? Hell, even if he hadn't, crazy fucker got more paranoid every day. This game was getting dangerous.

"Babe, I gotta step outside," I said, pushing Talia off my lap gently as I held up my phone. "It's my mom. She wants me to call back. Probably nothing, but you know how it is."

Nodding at Marsh, I made for the door. The band was on another break between sets, and looking around I saw Carrie and her other friend, but no Tinker.

No sign of the guitar player, either.

Stepping out into the parking lot, I headed away from the building, stabbing the phone with my finger. Picnic answered on the second ring.

"Just a heads-up—Marsh Jackson figured out that our old friend, Hands, was an informant, but he's got no clue he's already dead and gone. Jackson's strung out and unreliable. I can't decide if he had real intel on the situation, or if it was just a lucky guess. Now he tells me we're headin' down to Ellensburg tomorrow. Wants to deliver some goods and hunt down Hands. Thinks he's gonna be there."

Picnic didn't answer for a minute, then said, "You think he's onto you? Because I got no clue why he'd think Hands would be there. Man's gone. Like he never existed."

I considered the question carefully.

"Fuck if I know, but I don't think he's pegged me yet," I finally replied. "But the fucker's paranoid as hell, more than when I first got to town. Every time I see him, he's using more. For all I know he's hallucinating giant pink bunnies hungry for blood."

Picnic snorted.

"Christ, I can't believe such a good club could fall so far," he said. "You need anything from us?"

"No, but keep your phone handy. Is Painter still getting out of jail tomorrow?"

"Yeah," he said. "The old ladies are planning a big party for him. He's head over heels for Melanie, London's girl. She's been in to visit him almost every day. I got a feeling we won't be seeing much of him."

"Never saw that one coming," I said, biting back a laugh. "You think it's the real thing this time?"

"Fuck if I know," Picnic said. "But he better watch himself. London's one hell of a mama bear, and I got the feeling she won't be nice if he hurts her little cub. We'll have church first thing in the morning, though. I'll update everyone, make sure they stay sober enough for action until we get the all clear."

"Appreciate that," I said. "Okay, gotta head back in."

"Hey, Gage?"

"Yeah?"

"Don't think we don't see what you're doing for the club," my president said, his voice dead serious for once. "We won't forget this."

"Just don't forget to stay sober, because I might need you soon," I told him bluntly. "And make sure you're ready to ride. I got a real bad feeling about this one. I know we need more intel and I'll hold out as long as I can, but something's changed. Marsh is on the edge. Nothing would surprise me at this point."

Sitting back and watching as the guitar player eye-fucked Tinker on Friday night was just the beginning of one of the longest, shittiest weekends of my life.

Marsh dragged us all out of the bar around midnight, forcing me to leave Tinker with Joel. The thought of that guitar-playing bastard sinking into her hot, sweet pussy while I sat around with my thumb up my ass was almost more than I could stand.

I considered calling it off.

Considered telling Marsh to fuck himself, then walking across the bar and claiming my woman. I'd have done it, too, if the Reapers had been at full strength to back me up. We had a lot of information already, and if it wasn't quite as much as we'd hoped for, such is life.

Then I forced myself to think about what would happen if I did.

My brothers would be in unfamiliar territory, and with Marsh's hangarounds they'd be outnumbered. Ultimately, I knew the Coeur d'Alene Reapers were tougher than those little fuckweasels. We'd take them in the end, that I knew for a fact.

The real question was how many of us would find ourselves in the morgue along the way. Could I justify risking my brothers' lives over a woman who didn't even know my real name?

The Portland and Bellingham brothers were still down in Cali.

If I made the call, the Coeur d'Alene brothers would come. Period. That's just how it worked in our world. But with that kind of loyalty comes the understanding that a man doesn't make the call unless he's run out of options.

Deal with it, asshole. It is what it is.

It was probably a good thing that Marsh dragged us back to the clubhouse. Guitar Fucker had been buying Tinker drinks all night, sitting next to her between sets.

Touching her.

If he'd tried to stick his tongue down her throat, I wasn't sure I'd be able to hold my shit together. Of course, once we left the bar my imagination took over, and damned if it wasn't already pretty vivid when it came to my curvy landlady. She'd been wearing bright red lipstick. Would it be smeared around his cock by the end of the night?

I'd have to hunt him down and shoot him.

Only reasonable response under the circumstances.

Things got worse when we reached the clubhouse. Not only was I tense as fuck, but I realized that the only men out there were Marsh's people. Cord's faction—the original brothers who didn't like Marsh—hadn't showed their faces all night. Either Marsh hadn't invited them or they were planning something. Either way, the split was coming. Maybe soon.

Part of me thought we should pull them aside, maybe see if we could recruit them to our cause. On the other hand, they were the ones who let the situation get this bad in the first place.

We spent the night drinking and playing cards while Talia and her friends kept sneaking off to do more drugs. Marsh was so tense that he punched one of the prospects when he was stupid enough to win a hand at poker with a bluff. The Nighthawks' president kept muttering about Hands, and how we all needed to look out for traitors.

I swear, his eyes followed me when he said it, too.

At least Talia wasn't giving me too much shit—she was too busy hot railing meth with her girls in the bathroom. Around three that morning, Marsh got a text message that pissed him off enough that he threw a chair, screaming, "Shut the fuck up and play poker, you fucking losers!"

Good times.

Throughout it all, the girls were getting wilder and wilder, several of them doing stripteases on the bar—all under Talia's direction. By four, she decided Sadie should pull a train in the back room, and most of the guys followed her back there while I sat against the wall, nursing a beer that'd long since grown warm.

Shit got real at five, when Marsh pulled out a gun and told us to hand over our cell phones. Said he didn't want us warning the traitor. Didn't like that idea, not one bit. Fortunately, I kept mine locked and clean. I also kept an extra burner hidden in a secret compartment on my bike—along with a spare piece—but that wouldn't do me much good if I couldn't make it out of the building. The other bikers' eyes widened, but we all handed them over because what else were we supposed to do? I honestly didn't think that up until that point, most of the poor dumbasses he'd drawn into his net had a fucking clue how serious this was.

Now they knew.

Around seven that morning, Marsh sent three of the women out for food. Then he spent the next hour pacing and muttering, alternating between staring at his phone and glaring at the rest of us. The whole damned clubhouse was like a pressure cooker, slowly building toward some sort of violent explosion.

I needed some fucking air.

Marsh had assigned a couple of his thugs to watch the front, telling them to stop anyone from leaving—comforting, that—so I headed out back instead, where a six foot fence topped with razor wire surrounded an area about half the size of the clubhouse. In the center were a fire pit and some broken-down picnic tables. Talia had told me they liked to have bonfires out there, but not even the Nighthawks were willing to risk a burn at this point. Smoke from the wildfires filled the air, and it was getting worse every day.

Leaning against the back wall, I closed my eyes, wondering

what Tinker was doing. Had she gone home with Guitar Boy? Fucking hell, I'd gut him. He didn't get to touch her. Nobody did. *Totally rational thoughts, bro.* That's when I heard a soft sob. I followed the sound around the side of the building, where a young woman had curled up against the wall, knees tucked against her chest. She flinched when she saw me. Hair covered her face, and between that and the dim light I couldn't see much of her.

"You all right?" I asked. She nodded, refusing to look at me.

"Yeah, just a rough night," she said, her voice familiar. It was Sadie—the same little bitch who'd ratted me out to Talia at the apartment building. Fuck. She'd gone into a back room with half the club, and now she was here. Not good.

"What happened?" I asked, wondering why I cared. She'd caused me a hell of a lot of trouble. But this didn't sit right—the Reapers were supposed to be controlling our support clubs and she was just a kid.

"Guess," she said, sniffing as she burrowed her head deeper into her arms.

"Things got rough with the boys."

It wasn't a question, and she didn't bother answering.

"You need to leave this club behind," I told her. "Talia's not your friend, Sadie."

Her jaw tightened. "I'm not ashamed of myself."

"Never said you should be. But you're obviously not happy, either. The Nighthawks aren't good for you—none of those men will ever treat you with respect, or make you his old lady. Get out while you still can."

Sadie scooted away from me, still refusing to look up. "I didn't ask for your opinion."

"Sorry to waste your time," I said, running a hand through my hair. Fuck it. So much for doing the right thing. Still, I didn't like leaving her this way. "Let me know if you change your mind. Might be able to help you, okay?"

She didn't answer.

"Hey, Coop! You out here?" a man's voice shouted.

"Yeah," I shouted back, heading around to the door. One of Marsh's newer hangarounds—Rome—stood waiting for me.

"Marsh needs to talk to you," he told me, swallowing and glancing back toward the clubhouse. I raised a brow in silent question. "This isn't right, Cooper. You saw how strung out Marsh is? Now he's saying we all have to stay with him today. I'm supposed to work. I can't afford to lose my job over this."

"Stick close to me," I said. "We'll see what we can figure out."

Rome looked relieved, although I wasn't quite sure why. Not like I had any fuckin' power in this situation. I didn't know much about him, but he was young and I got a decent vibe. Like Sadie, he'd fallen into something way over his head. We headed back inside, where things were getting even more fucked up. Marsh stood in front of the door, arms crossed over his chest, glaring at everyone in the room.

"Nobody leaves," he announced. "Not until I find the traitor."

That didn't have a good ring to it. Rome cleared his throat nervously, and Marsh's eyes snapped to us.

"Cooper was out back," Rome said. "Wasn't trying to sneak off, Marsh. Just getting some air."

Marsh nodded sharply. "We gotta talk, Coop. Chapel. Now."

Then he pulled his semiautomatic out of his shoulder holster, holding it casually as he glanced around the room.

"Nobody leaves. Nobody talks. Do not fuck with me."

He started walking across the room toward the chapel, men jumping out of his way so fast one of them fell over. I followed him into the small room, noting the two brothers at my back. One of them shut the door as Marsh raised the pistol, pointing it at my chest.

"You got somethin' you wanna tell me?"

TINKER

Saturday morning was . . . unpleasant.

That's because I'd drunk more the previous night than I had since—well, since Margarita's bachelorette party. Now I had the hangover from hell, except hell wasn't really a strong enough description. I had the hangover from whatever was worse than hell. Justin Bieber concert?

I blamed Margarita for this.

Devil woman.

Every time we went out together, I got drunk and made a fool of myself. Not that last night hadn't been a lot of fun. The three of us girls had closed the bar down, dancing until our feet hurt, shouting slurred song requests at the band. Joel bought me drinks between every set, and by the end of the night I'd decided to go home with him after all.

Then he'd pulled out some pictures of his kids, including an adorable baby girl not much older than Tricia would've been. Sexy, flirty Tinker dissolved and I ended up telling him all about Tricia's death, ugly crying all over his shirt.

Big turn-on, right?

To his credit, Joel took it in stride, listening to what I had to say without making it into a thing. Then he'd offered me a ride home, walked me up to my door, and gave me a very sweet, very platonic kiss on the forehead.

So much for raging passion.

Now it was the next day, and because God is cruel I'd gotten a rush order from a caterer in Bellevue. This was good news financially but bad in terms of production capacity. Fortunately, Randi agreed to help me, and I recruited Mrs. Webbly to keep an eye on Dad.

Things would be groovy once the fucking Tylenol kicked in.

"I think I'm in love," Randi announced as we started our prep. I blinked at her, wondering what this had to do with making candy. She giggled, the sound grating painfully around the interior of my skull.

This. This is why you shouldn't go out with Carrie and Margarita. Why do you never learn?

"Again?" I asked, hoping desperately she'd get distracted and shut up.

Randi sighed happily, oblivious to my pain.

"His name is Rome, and he's perfect," she said, oblivious to my pain.

"Is he new to Hallies Falls?" I forced myself to ask, reaching for the sugar.

"Yes, I think so," she replied. "I mean, I don't really know for sure. We only talked for a couple minutes, but he wanted my phone number. It was at a party over in Omak last weekend. I didn't hear anything from him, so I figured he was blowing me off, but yesterday afternoon he called and asked me out! We're supposed to see a movie after he gets off work tonight. Do you think he knows that guy who does work around your building? Rome spends a lot of time with the Nighthawks, and I've see Cooper with them, too."

That broke through my mental fog, and I glanced up at her.

"How old is this boy?" I asked, suspicious.

"Well, I wouldn't really call him a *boy*," she said, giggling. "I mean, that's part of what I like about him. He's *been around*, you know?"

My stomach soured.

"No, I don't know. Enlighten me."

"Okay, so he's maybe four years older than me," she told me, sighing happily. She was so sweet and earnest that I threw up a little in the back of my throat, choking as I swallowed it back down. (In all fairness, it was probably hangover related. Still, that much perky, youthful enthusiasm is a lot to swallow first thing in the morning.) "He's got dark brown hair, and he's all tan from riding his bike, you know? He's kind of messy and rough, but he got me a drink and sat next to me at the party. We just hung out and laughed and it was really fantastic. I probably would've kissed him, but my mom called and asked if I could come home. She had to go into work at the hospital and she needed someone to watch the kids."

"Huh," I said, wishing my brain would kick into gear. Usually I felt frustrated with Randi's mom over stuff like this. The woman had a good job, and it didn't seem fair that she constantly guilted her oldest daughter into babysitting. When I'd first hired her, Randi had been planning to go to college at Central. Then she'd come in one morning a few months back and told me she'd decided to take online classes instead.

Bullshit.

I still didn't like her mother very much, but maybe this time it was a good thing she'd dragged her out of the party. I wasn't so sure about an older guy connected to the Nighthawks.

"I think you need to be careful," I said, frowning as I pulled a container of heavy cream out of the cooler. "You don't know any-thing about him, and we've got no idea how dangerous the Night-hawks really are. And yes, I know I hired Cooper, but it's not like I'm dating him. He's just another tenant."

Randi rolled her eyes.

"You don't understand."

Oh, I understood a hell of a lot better than she realized, poor kid. She wasn't the only one stupid enough to fall for a biker's crap.

The sound of someone pounding on the main shop's locked door interrupted us, the string of bells ringing painfully. For an instant I thought it was Talia coming to kill me, then I remembered Carrie and Margarita planned to stop by before Margarita left town. Seeing as I'd caught a ride home with Joel, they were prob-ably dying to hear the details.

Randi peered through the kitchen door.

"It's Carrie and some other lady," she confirmed. "Are you going to be talking to them for a while?"

"Probably," I said, head throbbing.

"Then would you mind if I walked down to the gas station and grabbed something to eat? I didn't get any breakfast this morning."

So much for getting a jump start on filling the orders. Clearly this wasn't my weekend.

"Sure," I told her, giving in to the inevitable. "Take your time. Let them in on your way out."

Looking over my checklist, I considered all I needed to get done that day. Too much. Way too much for a woman with a hangover.

"You look like hell," Carrie said brightly, sticking her head through the doorway. I blinked, because *she* looked fantastic. All perky and happy and obviously full of far more energy than was decent. Margarita stepped past her, holding a cup of coffee out toward me. God, she was even worse—somehow she'd managed to do her hair and full makeup.

"Why aren't you hungover?" I demanded. "I feel like something a cat coughed out."

"Vast quantities of caffeine," Margarita declared. "And vitamin C. You should try it. I'd get an IV if they'd let me. We brought you food, too. Grab a seat."

"I need to work."

"You need to eat," she corrected. "Now sit your ass down. The stove will still be there when you're done, I promise."

She and Carrie had already grabbed stools, pulling them up to the center island. I sat across from them, reaching for one of the wrapped sandwiches. I opened it to find pepperoni, prosciutto, and salami, with a heavy mixture of mayo and mustard oozing out the sides like pus.

"I can't eat this," I said, gagging as I dropped it.

"That's mine," Carrie said, laughing as she handed over another wrapped sandwich. "Yours is a veggie wrap. See? I'm not a total sadist."

Margarita laughed, opening a meatball sub that smelled like death. I took a bite of my wrap, then set it back down. Yeah. Eating wasn't gonna happen. Not yet.

"Too soon?" Carrie asked, her voice sympathetic. I nodded mournfully, which hurt my head. *When the fuck is that Tylenol going to kick in?* "So what happened last night? You and Joel were eye-fucking each other when we left. Please tell me you got laid."

I considered lying to them.

Telling them that I'd dragged him to some cheap hotel, then had wild monkey sex with him. Something involving handcuffs and whipped cream and a fluffy purple boa.

"He showed me pictures of his kids," I told them. "He has a daughter about the same age that Tricia would've been."

Carrie and Margarita shot each other a look.

"And?" Carrie asked.

"I ugly cried like a mental case. Then he took me home and kissed me on the forehead."

They groaned in unison.

"Kiss of death," Margarita said gravely. "You'll never hear from him again."

"Hey, let's not leap to judgment," Carrie objected. "Yes, you cried all over him while you were drunk. Obviously that's a huge turnoff. But you didn't see how he was watching your ass, Tink. You were looking mighty fuckable last night, which means there's still hope. He already put in the effort to comfort you while you were sad—I'll bet he'd be happy to collect his reward. Give him a call."

"I don't have his number."

"Way ahead of you," she said, grinning. "This morning I called Anita Schofner. She lives in Wenatchee these days, works at Bi-Mart. Anyway, Anita is friends with Kirstie Inman, who's friends with Brandy Soza. She's Joel's sister's hairdresser and she just happened to have his phone number."

Margarita and I stared at her, eyes wide.

"What?" she asked, all innocence.

"That's some serious stalker shit," Margarita said slowly, and I had to agree. Sometimes Carrie scared me.

"Yeah, it's a disease," Carrie said seriously. "And not only am I good at stalking people, I'm vindictive as hell. That's why you should always buy me lots of alcohol, so I stay in a good mood. Now, here's the plan. Tinker, you're going to text him later today. Tell him you wanted to apologize for going all sad on him, and that you'd like to take him out to dinner or something."

"If I do that and he figures out how I got the number, he'll probably file for a restraining order," I said. Carrie shrugged.

"You already went all crazy on him last night," she said reasonably. "You've got nothing to lose at this point."

I looked to Margarita, waiting for her to shoot down the ridiculous plan. She shrugged.

"I'm the wrong person to ask. Crazy is what I do, remember? And you need a distraction from your hot handyman. I can see why you want to sleep with him. If I weren't married—"

"Not helping," Carrie said, cutting her off. "So, you'll call and ask him out?"

I considered the situation, then sighed.

"What the hell . . . send me the number."

CHAPTER THIRTEEN

GAGE

I stared at Marsh's gun, a surge of adrenaline roaring through me. No fuckin' way I'd be able to get it away from him before he shot me. Nope. I'd have to bluff my way through this one.

"You got somethin' you wanna tell me?" Marsh asked.

This is it, asshole. If he's onto you, you're dead. Of course, my Reaper brothers would skin him alive—vengeance was kind of our thing—but seeing as I'd be in a grave by then, the thought wasn't much comfort.

Time to roll the dice.

"Yeah, I got somethin' to tell you," I said, offering a grim smile. "I'm considering breaking up with your sister, seeing as she fucks other guys. It's getting old."

Marsh stared at me for long seconds, eyes wild, then he burst into maniacal laughter. I kept myself loose and ready for action, but he was lowering the gun.

"Jesus, you're crazy, Romero," he said, shaking his head. "Usually guys piss themselves like babies when I do that."

Yeah, well, I'm a Reaper, not one of your fuckin' pussy rejects.

"Got nothin' to hide, Marsh," I said, holding my hands out to the side, palms up. "You wanna shoot me, not like I can stop you."

"Sit down," Marsh said, jerking his chin toward a chair. I sat, leaning back like I was totally relaxed and comfortable with the situation. "We've got a traitor. Told you about him already—goes by the name Hands."

I raised a brow.

"Traitor? What did he do?"

"Talked to the feds," he said, leaning toward me, knee jittering. "And maybe the Reapers, too. Playing both sides. He sold us out."

"I get the feds, I guess, but what do the Reapers have to do with anything?" I asked carefully, because what he'd said made no fucking sense at all. Hands was dead, and he sure as hell hadn't been a Reapers spy.

Meth logic.

"Nothing," Marsh said, narrowing his eyes. "They think they run Washington, but this is my territory. Just because the old president was willing to crawl up their asses doesn't mean I will. They sent this Hands fucker to spy on us. I gotta figure out where he is. Can I trust you? Things might get ugly."

Nodding my head, I leaned back in my chair. "I'm here, aren't I?"

Marsh smiled.

"Guess you are," he said. "Just remember—you fuck up, Hands won't be the only bastard I put underground."

Charming.

"Go out there and keep an eye on everyone. I gotta keep lookin' for the spies. Nobody leaves, nobody makes phone calls, nothing. You got me?"

Oh, I got him, all right. Crazy fucker.

"Sure thing, boss."

Things got worse as the morning passed.

I stood watch as Marsh grew more paranoid, calculating ways to take him down. He was close to snapping, and I figured shit might get real any minute now. If it happened, I'd probably be able to get myself away if I slipped out the back, but for some reason I couldn't quite bring myself to abandon the others. I kept thinking about Sadie sitting alone in the dark, hugging her knees to her chest, and Rome worrying about saving his job.

He should be worrying about saving his life.

They had no fuckin' clue what they'd gotten themselves into, and for some reason, I didn't want to see them die today. If it came down to it, I'd do whatever it took to stop Marsh.

Stupid of me, I know.

Talia and the girls she'd taken to pick up food came back around eleven, no food in sight. Guess they'd forgotten. She was full of energy, though, running toward me and jumping up to wrap her legs around my waist.

"We should—"

"Listen up!" Marsh shouted, cutting her off. I lowered her as the bikers and their women came closer, waiting for whatever fresh hell he'd planned. "Last night we learned that Hands—he was a hangaround here for a while—was a spy. He disappeared, but I heard he'll be at the car show down in Ellensburg tonight. We leave in ten minutes. Bitches are with Talia in the truck. Coop, get your ass over here. We gotta talk."

I walked over to him, watching the Nighthawks scrambling to grab their shit.

"What's up?" I asked him.

"Where's your cousin? You know, the blond guy who was with you when you first came to town. What's his name again?"

Painter.

"Levi," I said. "He's had a rough time of it, been busy with shit back home."

"Need you to call him, tell him to meet us in Ellensburg."

Hadn't thought Marsh could still surprise me at this point, but this did the trick.

"Why?"

"I need more backup," he said. "And there's traitors in the club.

I can't trust any of these fuckers. Oh, and by the way . . . I don't fuckin' trust you, either. I'm watchin' all of you. Now, go pick up your phone and give your boy his orders. Jakes! Over here!"

He waved the other biker over, making it clear he was done with me. I headed back to the bar, where a big bear of a guy pulled out the box of phones they'd confiscated earlier so I could call my cousin. I found mine and headed out to the fenced area out back, where I could talk without anyone listening in or sneaking up on me.

Pic answered on the first ring.

"We got some serious shit going down," I told him.

"Talk to me."

"Marsh just ordered everyone onto their bikes. He's paranoid as shit, and he wants my cousin, Levi, to ride over for backup. Been trapped here with him all night like a bunch of fuckin' hostages. Took our phones and everything. Only got mine back so I can call Levi. I've got a spare burner on my bike if they take it from me again. Oh, and get this—he thinks Hands was a federal informant *and* a Reapers spy, and that we'll find him down in Ellensburg."

Silence.

"Don't leave me hangin' boss," I said. "We need a plan."

"Sorry," Pic replied. "Just thinking. Guess you weren't kidding about him falling apart, because that makes no damned sense at all. Okay, we just got out of chapel and everyone's already here at the Armory, so that helps. Just have to call them back in. Here's the thing—Painter's only been out of jail a couple hours. He's facing some serious fuckin' time if they catch him violating his parole again. We could go over in a display of force, just a casual trip to see the show. If you needed us we'd be there and if you didn't, the cover won't be blown."

I thought it over. Marsh was like a stick of lit dynamite, and at this point anything could push him over the edge. God help us all if he picked up a nail in his tire. Even if Painter showed, there were no guarantees. The key was surviving on the ride down—once I got there the club could step in if they had to.

"He doesn't need to come," I told him. "They want to put a

bullet in my brain, that's gonna happen on the way down. For all I know, Marsh is lying about Hands and this is just an ambush. He's made it clear he doesn't trust me for shit. Doesn't trust any of us—man is paranoid and losing it."

"How serious a risk do you think it is?" Pic asked. "More intel won't help anyone if you're riding to your execution. We can end this thing now."

I considered the point, trying to stay detached. Not the easiest thing to do when you're talking about your own death.

"Marsh is scattered," I told him. "Twitching, can't hold his thoughts together very well. I think he's running on pure instinct right now—not calculating. I'm not his primary target."

"Okay then, here's a plan," Pic said. "First up, this is your ass on the line, so you pull the plug if things change. Second, I'll gather the brothers and figure out a plan. If I have to call you, I'll pretend to be Levi until you give me an all clear."

"Thanks. Come in soft . . . Maybe we'll get lucky and he'll back down."

"Yeah, and maybe you'll get a magical kiss from a fairy princess, wake up, and discover this was all a dream."

"I'm flipping you off right now," I said, biting back a smile.

"This is not a surprise. Take care, brother. Remember—we're your family. We'll do whatever it takes, got me?"

"Let's just hope it doesn't come to that."

The next four hours were the longest in my life.

I saw the way Marsh watched when I came back in. Speculative. Calculating. Did he have some bigger plan I didn't know about? As for Talia, she was almost giddy with excitement about the trip, although she didn't like that we'd be traveling separately.

"I don't understand why I can't ride with you," she whined. I shrugged.

"Ask your brother. I'm just followin' orders."

"You guys bring in the traitor, he'll give you a patch," she said, changing subjects abruptly. "Especially if your cousin comes as backup. Did you get hold of him?"

Her casual question startled me, and I stopped so suddenly that she bumped into me. Would've been funny if there weren't a slow burn building in my stomach.

"Marsh told you about that?"

Talia smirked, reaching up with one finger to touch my lips, shushing me. "I know everything, baby. Including the fact that you called me a bitch. But don't worry—he thought it was funny. I think it's funny, too. Thing is, I like fucking you and you're pretty to look at, but don't let it go to your head. If my brother has to choose between us, it's not gonna end well for you."

Then she popped up on her toes, offering me a long, slow kiss.

"Ride safe."

I watched her swagger off toward a Dodge Ram quad cab, where the girls had already gathered in a giggling cluster, a now-calm Sadie among them. Couldn't see any bruises from here, but maybe she'd put on a fuckload of makeup or something. Hard to believe she was the same pitiful creature I'd found crying back behind the building earlier that morning. Weird, fucked-up girl. Of course, you'd have to be to stay friends with Talia.

Minutes later, engines roared to life as Marsh and the others pulled out in formation, leaving me, Rome, and the other hangarounds to suck their fumes. There were many, many things I missed about riding with my club, not the least of which was a decent position in the pack.

Exhaust wasn't the only thing we had to suck down along the way. Half an hour into the trip, a thick cloud of smoke rolled down across the highway, tiny specks of white ash raining down on us. Wildfire in the distance. Then we passed a series of blackened patches of ground along the pavement.

Flames had been through here, and recently.

Creepy as hell.

CHAPTER FOURTEEN

I managed to coordinate with Pic along the way, sending him quick text messages when we stopped for gas. Marsh let me keep the phone because I'd told him I'd left Levi a message, and he'd be getting back to me. He hadn't liked it—that much was obvious—but he'd agreed. I had plenty of time to consider the situation while we rode, which always one of my favorite things about being on the bike. Things were grim, no question, but there were some good signs, too.

For one thing, Marsh hadn't killed me yet.

For another, my club brother, Painter, had already agreed to meet me in Ellensburg. That meant he'd chosen to violate his parole—a huge fuckin' risk. He'd be coming in behind the main Reapers pack and meeting up with me separately. Whatever happened after that, at least I wouldn't be facing it alone.

Along the way there were several times where the smoke was thick enough that I wondered if they'd shut down the highway, but we finally pulled into town around four thirty. It took us a while to find a parking spot for the bikes, because the streets were choked with hot rods. Things felt safer with all the witnesses. No fuckin' way Marsh was planning on taking me out, not here. Not unless he was planning suicide by cop—they were out in force for the event.

We parked the bikes just off the main strip, leaving a prospect to keep an eye on them. Down the street was an old brick bank building—you know, one of those with an engraved date on the cornerstone and arches over all the doors. Marsh led us inside and I froze.

Cop bar.

Not like it was full of guys in uniform, but there were framed pictures of officers on the walls, along with newspaper articles and such. I figured most of the local cops were on duty for the rally, but there was a group of three men watching us, and they didn't strike me as civilians.

Jesus fuck, I had no idea where Marsh was going with this, but he was a fuckin' moron. We were meeting his contacts *here,* of all places? Made no sense, unless it was a setup. This wasn't Hallies Falls and I knew damned well the Ellensburg police department wasn't in the Nighthawks' pocket.

Whatever Marsh planned to do, they'd be on him in a heartbeat.

The bar owners had set up a beer garden using temporary fencing in one of the side streets, and by the time I made it outside Marsh already had a tray of shots in front of him. He downed three in a row while I watched, laughing and groping any girl stupid enough to get close. Looking around, I spotted three uniformed officers on the other side of the fence. Then the guys I suspected very strongly were cops in civvies came out, grabbing a table not far away.

Yeah, this was a fuckin' fishbowl.

I turned away to hide the phone as I unlocked it manually—no fingerprint protection for me, not when the man you're protecting it from wouldn't think twice about cutting a finger off—and sent Picnic a quick message.

ME: Downtown at the Banner Bank Tavern. They have a beer garden on one of the side streets—closed to traffic. Marsh

and his crew are drunk as fuck and he's tweaking. Paranoid.
Got six cops watching us. Worried that Marsh will blow it.

PICNIC: Across the street. Don't want to come over unless we
need to. Think it might set Marsh off?

ME: Hang back for now. Painter anywhere near you yet?

PICNIC: He's behind us, should be here soon.

ME: K

Deleting the messages, I wandered over to the outdoor counter, which was basically a pass-through counter to the inside of the building. I ordered a pitcher and glanced through the chain link while I waited. Sure enough, across the street Pic, Horse, Bam Bam, and Ruger walked along a line of custom choppers, looking them over and talking casually.

"Hey, Cooper!" Sadie said, and I turned to get my first good look at her since last night. Thick, pancake makeup covered a swollen face, and her eyes were glazed. Painkillers, probably. She'd had at least one shiner forming—probably two—and yet here she was, nodding and smiling like nothing had happened. Christ, I hoped it was just an act to get through this fucked up, crazy-ass day. "I hear your cousin is coming! I had so much fun with him last time he was in town . . ."

"Yeah, he said he'd head over. Should be here soon. I'm sure he'll be happy to see you."

Unlikely, considering last time she saw Painter, she spent the night puking on him. Behind her, I noticed one of the cops leaning over, speaking quietly into his shoulder radio.

"Wanna dance?" Sadie asked.

"Not really my thing," I told her, reaching to take a pitcher from the bartender. "Can you grab me some glasses?"

Talia met me halfway, catching my free hand and dragging me toward a table. I nearly dropped the damned pitcher as she shoved me into a chair, then straddled me.

"I am so fucking horny right now," she whispered in my ear, because apparently the situation wasn't ridiculous enough already.

"Levi!" Sadie shouted excitedly, and I looked over to see Painter strolling toward us. His tall frame looked tired and his light blond hair was matted from the ride. I glanced around at the cops, hoping to hell none of them gave him any shit. He so much as coughed in the wrong direction, his ass would go back to prison.

"Good to see you," he said, catching Sadie as she ran over to him. She tried to pull him in for a kiss, but he turned his head, so she caught his cheek instead. "Coop said he'd be here, suggested I come over to join you guys."

"Where have you been?" she asked. "You just disappeared that night."

"Jail," he said shortly, surprising me. Guess he figured the truth was easiest—certainly wouldn't hurt him in Marsh's eyes. "Violated the terms of my parole, so they locked me up to teach me a lesson."

Sadie's eyes widened, and she reached up to rub his chest. "Sounds dangerous."

Poor fucker. He'd risked going back to prison and had left his girl behind all to help me out. I decided I should throw him a lifeline.

"Levi!" I shouted, pushing Talia off my lap. Pulling him in for a hug, I took the opportunity to give him an update. "Shit's ugly. We gotta contain Marsh or he's gonna blow everything."

He nodded, then pulled away, nodding toward Marsh.

"Nice to see you again," he said. "Looks like a good time."

Marsh smiled at him, but there was something ugly in his eyes. I watched as Talia slithered over to him, settling herself across his lap like a little girl.

"Were you really in jail?" she asked Painter, coyly licking the edge of a shot glass.

"Yup," Painter said. "Got out this morning. Parole violation."

"What'd you go down for?"

"Weapons charge."

Marsh frowned. "How long was your sentence?"

"Three years."

"That's too long for a weapons charge," Marsh said, his voice suspicious. One of the brothers stood up, moving to stand behind Painter. I glanced over to see two of the off-duty cops watching us.

"It's complicated," Painter replied shortly. "Let's just say it could've been a hell of a lot worse. Had priors, too."

A waitress came over, looking at us warily. "You guys need anything?"

"We needed something half an hour ago," Talia snapped, glaring at her. Jesus fucking Christ, the woman was crazy. "Where the fuck have you been?"

"I'm real sorry I wasn't over earlier," the waitress said. "We're just slammed. I'm sure we can—"

"We deserve a free round," Talia said, standing up and taking a threatening step toward the poor woman. Everything had to be about her winning. Always. "This is your fault, not ours."

Painter and I shared a glance. We had a bar full of cops, more on the street, and now Talia had decided to pick a fight with a waitress.

Just shoot her. No jury would convict you.

"Baby, let's go dance," I said, reaching for her hand. "I want to feel you up against me."

"I'm busy," she snarled, glaring at the waitress. "Are you going to get us the drinks?"

The poor woman nodded her head, obviously terrified. "Sure, I'll be right back."

"See?" Talia said triumphantly. "It's all about how you talk to them. I'm ready for that dance now."

Grabbing my hand, she dragged me toward the small dance floor. Out of the corner of my eye I saw a big guy wearing a bar T-shirt talking to the cops, pointing toward our group.

Yeah. This wasn't gonna end well.

Painter leaned toward Marsh, probably suggesting we clear out. I watched as Marsh snarled something in reply, then several of the Nighthawks moved in on them, and I had one of those moments of blinding, crystal clarity.

My brother Painter had put his ass on the line to protect me, and unless I pulled off a miracle in the next ten seconds, he'd be going back to jail for violating his parole. There were too many witnesses.

Turned out I didn't even have that long.

Marsh exploded toward him, punching him in the stomach, and his pet Nighthawks pounced like a bunch of rabid dogs. Painter went down as I threw myself into the group. I wasn't the only one. The bouncer and the cops charged into the mess. Then Marsh decided a knife would make the situation better.

Was he *trying* to get arrested?

I grabbed Painter by the arms, determined to get him out of the bar as Marsh launched himself toward the off-duty cops. A spray of bright red blood hit us, and then a body slammed into me, knocking me over.

It was one of the cops.

Jesus fucking Christ.

I watched in horror as a geyser of blood exploded from him, pumping in time with his heartbeat. Motherfucking moron had just *shanked* one of the off-duty cops. *In a cop bar.* That's when Rome appeared—somehow shoving two men almost twice his size out of the way—and slammed a wad of something down over the wound.

"You! Call EMS," Rome ordered the bouncer as a dazed Painter pulled himself to his knees next to me. Talia appeared behind him, slamming a glass pitcher over his head. Then Sadie and the other girls were screaming at her to run as Painter pitched forward. I caught him, dragging him back again as uniformed cops swarmed us.

Everything seemed to slow around me.

The waitress was hiding under a table, head down between her legs. Rome was calmly giving orders, blood spatter coating him as he fought desperately to save the cop's life. Talia and company had found a break in the fence and were slipping through it.

Then uniformed cops surrounded us, and I snapped back into reality. One of them yelled for everyone to lie down on the ground, hands behind their heads. Damned hard to do, considering I had Painter's dead weight to support.

That's probably why they Tased me.

Fucking awesome end to a fucking awesome day.

"Good news, at least for you," the lawyer said. Dobie Coales had been one of the Reapers' attorneys for nearly ten years now, but we'd been friends since grade school. He looked like a big, dumb good ol' boy, which had served us well many times, because the man was fucking brilliant. Couldn't imagine anyone I'd rather have at my side, all things considered.

I'd spent a charming night in the Kittitas County jail, which was always good fun. Now it was Sunday afternoon, and Coales sat facing me across a table, holding a file folder of papers I sincerely hoped included some strategy for saving my ass.

Coales was good.

Very good. If there was a way out of this one, he'd find it for me, although I figured my cover was blown. We hadn't gotten all the information we wanted from Marsh, but I didn't give a shit anymore. All I'd been able to think about last night was Tinker.

Specifically, what the rumor mill was telling her about yesterday's incident.

This wasn't exactly the way I'd wanted to introduce her to club life.

"I take it that means the guy Marsh stabbed is alive?" I asked. That'd been my biggest concern. If he'd killed a cop and I got roped in as an accessory, not even the club would be able to save my ass.

"He'll survive," Coales said. Thank fuck for that. "Not sure how much damage yet, but they haven't said anything about lost limbs or brain injuries."

"He wasn't lookin' so good."

Coales shrugged. "Guess he had a rough night, but he's stable. They don't seem to think his life is in danger at this point. That's the important part."

"How about Painter?" I asked. Coales's face went carefully blank. "Ah fuck. He's going back to prison, isn't he?"

"Probably," the lawyer admitted. "Although we'll do everything we can to fight it. Things went south with the probation department back home while you were in Hallies Falls. His old probation officer is gone. Facing corruption charges."

Dobie said the words blandly, as if he hadn't been the one paying those bribes. Heh.

"Shitty to be him," I replied. "We got any worries there?"

Like, is he gonna testify against your ass for arranging the whole thing?

"Aside from losing our influence? No, I don't think so. It'll take time to rebuild, though. Time Painter doesn't have. Shame, too. Guess his girlfriend is knocked up."

"Wow," I said, leaning back in my chair. *Should've told Marsh to fuck off when he asked for Levi.* "That sucks."

"Won't argue there," he said. "But you can't do anything to help him, so let's stay focused on your situation. We've found some friends in the prosecutor's office locally. Talked to one of them this morning. Seeing as you weren't wearing Nighthawks colors and didn't instigate anything, they're willing to look at you as a bystander who got caught up in something, rather than a conspirator."

"How much did that cost?"

Dobie smiled. "Less than it would cost for a full defense at trial. I'm always looking to save my clients money. Good news is you'll be out on bail later this afternoon. Still need to work through the formalities, of course. Prosecutor won't decide whether or not to charge you you until there's been a full investigation proving your innocence."

"Glad to know our public servants are so thorough."

"Always," Coales said, smirking. "I have to say, in my professional opinion Marsh Jackson is a fucking moron. Not only did he attack an off-duty cop, he had enough meth on him to be charged with intent to distribute. I guess attempted murder wasn't enough. The rest of the club will likely be charged as accessories. The picture we'll be painting to the public is that you're the innocent victim of these terrible drug dealers. Gangs like the Nighthawk Raiders really are a scourge on society."

I snorted.

"Do you stand in front of a mirror and practice saying shit like that with a straight face?"

Coales smirked. "I have no idea what you're talking about. Just remember, all we need is a story plausible enough that they won't suspect we paid off the prosecutors. I'll admit, it's a touchy situation, considering an off-duty cop got hurt, but I really do think we'll be okay. They say that kid—Rome—probably saved the guy's life. He's an EMT, did you know that?"

I raised a brow. "No shit?"

Coales grinned at me.

"Yup," he said. "And he's well enough known and liked in the EMS community that they'd be covering his ass regardless of our influence, and as of now they're lumping you in with him, not Jackson. The prosecutor already has his bad guys—patch-holding bikers carrying drugs. He plays that up for the public, nobody will give you another thought. They have bigger fish."

"And Painter?"

Coales sobered.

"He's being transported back to Kootenai County," he said. "They'll set a hearing, and we expect he'll be sent back down to California to finish out his term. Not a lot we can do about it at this point."

Leaning back, I stared at the wall above his head, considering the situation.

"And you said his girl is pregnant? Melanie?"

"Can't remember her name," he said. "But yes, apparently she told him yesterday. He left her to come over here, and now he's going to prison. At least he's only got a couple years left on the term."

"Yeah, I'm sure that's a great comfort," I said. "What a fuckin' waste. He'd been here maybe five minutes before shit went down."

Coales shrugged.

"It is what it is. Ruger and Horse will be waiting for you outside when you get out, along with your bike. None of the Nighthawks have made bail yet—fucking up a cop is a real good way to find yourself in legal limbo. They'll drag out everything and make it as difficult as possible. We'll also reach out to the bail bonds community and see if we can't complicate their situation. Think Pic plans to use that window of opportunity to clean house up in Hallies Falls. They're expecting you to debrief as soon as you're back in town. Try not to get yourself arrested again in the process, okay?"

"Thanks," I told him. "I have a request, if you can help."

"What's that?"

"You said it'll a take a couple more hours for me to get out?"

"Yes. We have to deal with paperwork and bail and some pissed off cops," he said. "I'm confident it's settled, but we still have to jump through the hoops."

"You think you can arrange for me to share a room with Marsh Jackson for a few minutes before I go?"

Coales raised a brow. "Possibly. But think it through first because you're almost out of here. Why take that risk?"

"Because I owe him," I replied. "And the club owes me, so can you make it happen?"

"It's a lot easier to get my clients out on bail when they aren't picking fights. Something to think about."

"He just tried to murder a cop. Every person in this station is itching to beat him bloody but they can't. Let me do the dirty work for them and everyone wins."

Coales leaned back in the chair, studying me thoughtfully for a minute.

"As your counsel, I need to tell you that this is a bad idea."

"Noted."

"Then I'll see what I can do."

They put me in a holding cell at the far end of the hall—enough distance that the deputy supervising could pretend he hadn't heard anything. According to his uniform, his last name was Graves and he looked nervous, but determined.

"Wait in here," he said under his breath. "Two transfer officers will bring him in. We'll give you about ten minutes, then I'll notice the transfer officers made a mistake and come take you back out again. As far as we're concerned, they got the wrong door and didn't realize you were in there. You can't kill him or cause new damage to his face, and if anyone asks it was self-defense."

I nodded, wondering how much Coales had paid him. Graves might be doing it for free. He certainly had the motivation—law enforcement was a brotherhood, too. Stretching my neck, I paced the cell until I heard footsteps coming down the hallway, more than one set this time. Then the door opened and Marsh Jackson stumbled through, arms and legs chained for transfer. Nice touch, although I felt a little hurt that they thought I'd need the advantage.

"Hey, Marsh," I said. He looked like shit, and not just because he'd sobered up. His nose was swollen, with bruising under both eyes. Probably broken. One of his hands was cut up, too, but beyond that he didn't seem injured. Kind of surprised me—I'd have thought he'd go down fighting, and jacked up like that he'd be tough to take. On the other hand, they were the ones with the Tasers . . .

"Cooper," he growled. He'd had enough time to come down off his high now, but not enough to rest and recover. Marsh Jackson was *not* a happy camper. "You talk to anyone else yet? They kept me in solitary all night. The Nighthawks should've sent a lawyer by now—they'd better have a good fucking excuse."

"Yeah, about that," I said, walking slowly toward him. "There's gonna be a problem."

Marsh's eyes narrowed. "What the fuck? Did you talk to Talia? She'll fix shit, you just have to give her the right orders."

"Nope," I told him, flexing my fingers. "But we got another issue. More important."

"Nothing's more important, you fucking—"

I slammed him into the concrete block wall, one arm across his throat, knocking the breath right out of his body. Then I let him choke out for a few seconds. Wanted to be sure he was paying attention.

"Time to listen up," I said, my voice low. "You fucked up. You stole from the Reapers, and we don't like that. Not even a little bit."

"What?" he asked, rage flickering in his eyes. Wasn't sure he quite understood the situation just yet, but he was pissed.

"My name is Gage. I'm a member of the Reapers MC and we've been watching you for a while. Here's what happens next. First I'm gonna hurt you. I'd like to do more, but that would fuck up step two, which is the part where I walk out of here a free man while you sit and rot. Then I'll go join the rest of my brothers and we'll take back our town. Good story, isn't it? I particularly like the happy ending."

Marsh rattled the chains, glaring at me. "Big bad Reaper, beating up a man who can't fight back. Nice."

Then he spat in my face.

I blinked, offering a slow smile.

"Did Sadie fight back?" I asked softly. "Or was that one unfair, too?"

With that, I brought my knee up hard, slamming it into his crotch. Marsh bellowed in pain and I let him drop, enjoying the sight of him rolling around the floor. I stepped to the side and used the back of my hand to wipe the spit off my face. Then I kicked him in the lower back—kidney shot—and his body arched the other way. They'd said not to cause serious damage, but I wasn't wearing my boots. He should be fine.

Or not.

Either way, I'd be out of here before they figured it out, and Coales could blackmail the guards into keeping their mouths shut. Gotta love the American justice system. I leaned back against the wall, relaxing but still alert in case he recovered. After long minutes, Marsh turned his head toward me, hatred burning deep and hot in his eyes.

Fair enough—the feeling was mutual.

"You'll pay for this," he spat out, blood on his lips. "You. The Nighthawks. All the fucking Reapers and their families. Even the fucking waitresses you tip should be afraid, because if they're connected to you, they're on my list."

I laughed.

"Good luck with that, Jackson."

He spent the next minutes glaring at me, as if he could set me on fire with his eyes if he just tried hard enough. Sadly for him, I didn't burst into flames, so I guess he needed to practice that particular superpower a little bit longer. Then the door opened. Graves stood outside with two more officers—the same ones who'd brought Marsh. He smiled at the sight of Marsh huddled on the floor.

"He attacked me," I said blandly.

"Looks like self-defense," he replied. "We'll find a safer place for you to wait out your processing. Sorry about the mistake."

Half an hour later, I walked out into the parking lot, and despite the fact that I'd spent the night in jail, I felt better than I had in a long time. No more fucking lies, no more eating shit.

Horse and Ruger were right there, just like Coales had promised. Horse was a big fucker, and when he caught me up in a tight hug, he nearly broke a rib.

"Missed you, brother," he said, his voice serious for once. "We were worried about you up there. We're gonna clean house tonight. Pic wants to talk, and then we'll call the Nighthawks who aren't locked up together. Wants a full report on everyone, to see if any of them are worth salvaging."

Together we walked toward my bike.

Fuck, it looked good.

The way it was supposed to. For one thing, they'd put the whips back on, and the custom bell I'd gotten from my dad right before he died. Then Ruger handed me a carefully folded leather vest. My colors, with my road name on the front, and Reapers MC across the back. I pulled it on, savoring the smell of the leather, and for the first time since I'd arrived in Hallies Falls things were right again.

"There's a knife in your saddlebag, and I stashed some extra hardware on the bike for you, too," Ruger said in a low voice.

"Missed wearing this," I said, pulling on my cut. "Missed it a lot. 'Bout fuckin' time I could be me again. Got some business to take care of."

"Yeah, they're waiting for you," Horse said. "Gonna have church at the hotel, get your full report. Then we'll make our move on the clubhouse. One thing we got goin' for us—enough of them got picked up that there's only a few left in town to fight."

"Not sure there'll be much of a fight," I told him. "All of Marsh's people went down to the rally. The club wasn't united and those who stayed behind were already pulling away. Anything could happen, but taking Marsh out of the picture is a game changer."

"That's why we should get going," Horse said. "Boss hates to wait."

"Got someone else I need to see first," I told him, rubbing my chin. "Someone important."

"More important than your club president?" Ruger asked, but I was already throwing a leg over my bike. Tinker Garrett was waiting, and for the first time I wouldn't be hiding who I was. My dick got hard just thinkin' about it.

TINKER

"Something big happened down in Ellensburg yesterday," Carrie said, her voice breathless through the phone. I was sitting on my porch, enjoying my Sunday-afternoon wine. No eye candy this weekend, which was probably a good thing. I hadn't seen Cooper for a few days, and much as I missed watching him work, I knew it was for the best.

On the bright side, I hadn't seen stupid Talia or her machete.

"You know how Cooper's been hanging out with the motorcycle club? Well, they got in some kind of big fight and tore up a bar. Then the cops arrested all of them. Not just the guys in the club, but anyone with them, and Cooper was right in the thick of it!"

"What?" I asked, my stomach churning. Cooper was a big guy, sure. And tough. But he'd never seemed particularly violent to me. I mean, he had the strength, but he was usually so even tempered.

"Cooper got arrested," she repeated slowly.

"You know, anyone can get caught up in a bar fight," I said. "Just because they arrested him doesn't mean—"

"There were drugs," she said, and I heard genuine regret in her voice. "Lots of drugs. Meth, apparently. I guess a bunch of the guys were carrying it."

"Meth?" I whispered.

"Yup," she said. "They aren't saying what'll happen to them, but it's not good. A cop got hurt, too, although I don't know how bad. This might be the end of the club here in Hallies Falls. I wonder if he has drugs in his apartment. You should go check—if he's dealing, you need him out of there. You can't trust a guy just because he's hot and mows the lawn without a shirt."

I sat back in the swing, feeling ill.

"Thanks for telling me," I said slowly, trying to wrap my head around it.

"I'm sorry," she replied. "But it's for the best. If he's a bad guy, it's better to find out now so you can evict his ass. That club has gotten worse and worse."

"I can't evict someone for getting arrested," I told her. "That's illegal."

"It's a month-to-month lease, right? Just give him thirty days' notice and get rid of him. You've got enough on your plate already."

Hmm . . . Maybe I *should* evict him. He'd caused me a lot of trouble and I'd already been avoiding him. God. But the thought of him leaving . . . It hurt—it hurt way more than it should've. I didn't want to think about this.

"I have to go, Carrie," I said, hanging up the phone. It was probably rude, but she'd forgive me. We'd been best friends since we were born, so not like she had a choice. Sitting back in the swing, I looked across the empty porch toward the equally empty sidewalk, wondering why the news about Cooper bothered me so much.

Because deep down inside you're still in lust with him, of course.
Dumbass.

Reaching for my wine bottle, I refilled my glass and considered Carrie's words—Cooper had been arrested for fighting, and possibly for meth. She was right. I needed to get rid of him. This was only common sense. Time to pull on my big-girl panties and accept reality.

Panties . . .

Hadn't been wearing any of those that god-awful night I'd gotten caught with the stripper. And everyone knew it, too—even those who hadn't seen the video heard the details. They felt free to judge me, too, because they thought they knew what'd happened in that room. They didn't. So how the hell did I really know what'd happened down in Ellensburg?

You don't.

Cooper should be innocent until proven guilty. Things didn't sound good, but until I knew the full truth, I needed to give him the benefit of the doubt.

Taking another drink of my wine, I looked up to see someone walking quickly toward the building along the sidewalk, arms hugged tight around her body. Sadie Baxter. Damn. There was something about her . . . she didn't look so good.

"Hi, Sadie," I called out. She startled, looking up at me, and I gasped.

Her eyes were a mess of purple and black and . . . Jesus. Someone had hit her. Looked like she'd tried to cover it with makeup, which was now smeared all over her face. There was dirt, too, and a nasty scratch on her cheek. Setting down my glass carefully, I walked down the steps toward her. She trembled like a baby deer, and my heart hurt. I wanted to demand what the hell had happened to her. Maybe wrap her up in Bubble Wrap and lock her in my basement.

Instead I took a calming breath and smiled.

"Do you remember that time I was babysitting you and we built that giant fort out of pillows and blankets?" I asked.

"Yeah," Sadie said softly, refusing to meet my gaze.

"Do you remember why we did that?"

Sadie's lips tightened as she blinked rapidly.

"Because I was scared of the monsters," she whispered hoarsely. "So we built a castle and then you used the monster potion to kill them all."

"Yeah."

"What was that, anyway? The potion, I mean."

"Aqua Net hair spray," I told her. "I'll bet your mom wanted to kill me for getting it everywhere. But it worked, didn't it?"

She gave me a sad little smile, pushing a chunk of hair back behind her ear. "I guess it did. We were safe in that fort. I loved how you read me stories in there."

It took everything I had not to react, because when she'd pushed back her hair, she'd revealed a nasty cut that'd been hidden along her hairline. Looked like it needed stitches, but the girl was so skittish . . . Couldn't risk scaring her off.

"Sadie, I think maybe you ran into another monster," I said, feeling my nose tingle as water built in my eyes. "I want you to know my house is full of pillows and blankets. We could go inside and build one hell of a castle if you'd like."

The girl smiled sadly, then shook her head.

"Monster spray isn't real, Tinker. I gotta go now."

With that, she turned and started walking away.

"Sadie!" I called after her. She stopped, looking back.

"Let me take you to the hospital."

"I'm fine," she said. "And I don't need you interfering in my life. I'm not a little girl anymore."

"Okay," I said, thinking about her as a little girl. She'd been such a beautiful child. "Just answer me one thing—was it the motorcycle club that did this to you?"

She turned away without speaking.

Guess I had my answer.

GAGE

"You're actually serious about going to see this woman before we take care of the Nighthawks?" Ruger asked, cocking an eyebrow. We'd stopped at a gas station about halfway to Hallies Falls.

"Yeah," I said, sliding my card into the gas pump. "Thought we covered this already."

"We did. I just didn't believe you."

"Why not?"

"Well, there's the fact that I've never seen you fuck the same woman twice," he said.

"That's not true," Horse chimed in. "There was that dancer in Vegas. He spent a whole weekend with her."

"Did you know her real name?" Ruger asked me.

"No."

"Doesn't count," Ruger declared. "So what's up with this Tinker bitch? She have a magic pussy?"

"None of your fucking business."

Horse paused to look me over.

"He hasn't fucked her yet," he announced.

"We aren't discussing this."

"Damn, you're right," Ruger said, nodding sagely. "I get it. Sometimes you just want one so goddamned bad and you can't have her. Messes with your head. But this is club business. Priorities, bro."

"What would be more important to you—dealing with the Nighthawks or taking care of your old lady, Sophie?" I asked him.

"Trick question," Ruger replied. "If there was a problem with Soph, nobody'd expect me to be on this run."

"Yeah, well what if Tinker is my Sophie?"

Both men stared at me, speechless. I took a moment to savor the silence, because it sure as shit wouldn't last long with Horse around. Fucker never knew when to shut his mouth.

"You shittin' me?" he finally asked.

"No," I admitted. "I mean, it's early days. Haven't gotten to spend much time with her, and through it all I've been stuck with that crazy cunt Talia. But there's something there. Feels real to me. I'm not gonna walk away until I know what it is."

Crossing my arms over my chest, I waited for the shit to fall. I figured it would come on two levels—first about the club, because it was always about the club. There was also the mandatory torment about me turning into a pussy.

Instead Horse shrugged.

"I knew with Marie," he said. "I mean, I didn't know that she'd be my old lady, but I knew she was different. Wanted her, and not just under me. Never really saw you with a woman of your own, but if you're into that and she's the right woman, you'd be a fuckin' moron not to give it a shot."

"What he said, only smarter," Ruger chimed in. "Fill in the blanks. I think you better call Pic, though. He's expecting you to come straight to the hotel."

"That's it?" I asked, wary as hell.

"What else do you want?" Horse asked. "You need love poetry, go write it yourself."

"You're letting me off too easy."

"You're too pathetic to abuse right now," Ruger said. "And if it's like it was with me and Soph, you're gonna be useless until you figure it out anyway. Now call the boss. If we're changing plans, he needs to know."

I nodded and finished gassing up the bike. Then I grabbed my phone and wandered off behind the station to give Pic a call.

"I'm gonna head over to Tinker's first when we hit town," I told him. "Gotta explain shit to her. It's important."

"You've been holding off for weeks," he pointed out reasonably. "You sure it can't wait one more night? We've got BB watching the house, just in case things go bad. She's safe enough, but it's tense here—we gotta get this resolved before Marsh makes bail."

"I need to talk to her. I've been in Hallies Falls long enough to know how it works—Tinker's probably heard ten different stories about me landing in jail, each one worse than the next. It's not just about seeing her. I've got damage control to do."

"How long do you think it'll take?" Pic asked. "Because I get it. I really do. And as your brother I want you to be able to take care of your business. But remember—you went through everything so we could take these fuckers down, and now's the time to do it. Don't throw away what you've accomplished before we finish it off."

"Don't lecture me about doing my duty," I snapped. "Last I

checked, you were back home partying and getting laid while I ate Marsh Jackson's shit. You owe me this."

He didn't respond for a minute. Probably pissed him off, but I didn't regret my words. If I couldn't be straight with my brother, then he wasn't really my brother.

"Someone's panties are in a twist," he finally commented.

"Someone spent the night in jail while his woman got fed a load of shit."

"Okay. Do what you gotta do."

"That's it?" I asked for the second time in ten minutes. Something was wrong here. Fucked up and wrong. My brothers were being nice, and that wasn't really our way.

Pic snorted.

"Yeah, that's it," he said. "It's obvious your mind is made up. Not gonna hold a gun to your head. Then I might have to shoot you, and blood's a real bitch to get out of leather. Just don't make it too long—maybe an hour or so? We really do need you out here, Gage," he added, his voice growing more serious. "We have to go in tonight, and we can't go in blind. But you're right—you've made a hell of a sacrifice and I respect it. We all do."

Thank fuck for that.

"I won't take more time than I need to," I told him. "But the more people who get to her, the harder this is gonna be. And it wasn't like it was gonna be easy under the best of circumstances."

"Well, that's definitely the truth," he said. "I've got one question for you, though—have you showered?"

"What do you think?"

"Okay, so you probably smell bad. Got any bruising? You feeling calm and laid-back?"

"Yeah, they gave me a spa card as a parting gift when I got out. So fuckin' relaxed I can hardly stay awake. Where are you going with this, boss?"

"Don't scare her," he said seriously. "I know you want to do damage control. But sometimes when you go in too fast, you make things worse. Think it through, brother."

"All due respect, fuck off."

"Fine, do it your way. Good luck with that."

I hung up—because fuck him—and walked back over to Horse and Ruger.

"When we get to Hallies Falls, you guys can head to the hotel. I'll be joining you about an hour later. Pic knows the plan."

"Okay," Horse said. "You want me to come with you? Watch your back? There's still Nighthawks that didn't get arrested. We haven't figured out what to do with them yet."

"I can take care of myself. We'll keep BB on Tinker, though, just until we know where Talia is. Got any idea what's up with her?"

"They didn't arrest any of the girls," Ruger said, shrugging. "They all ran off after the fight. Nobody's seen them since."

"All the more reason to catch her before she hears more shit."

CHAPTER FIFTEEN

By the time I pulled up to Tinker's house, it was dark. BB—one of our prospects—was just cruising by to check on her. I nodded to him as I rode past, glancing up at the house. The light was on in Tinker's room, and I saw a flash of movement in the window.

Excellent.

Nobody answered when I rang the bell the first time. The night air was warm, the smell of flowers and distant smoke hanging in the air. I nearly tripped over an empty glass of wine abandoned on the porch.

That was her Sunday ritual.

She'd sit out there every week, drinking wine, laughing, and whispering secrets with her friend Carrie. Driving me slowly fucking crazy with lust, watching me with those eyes and licking those lips and pretending there wasn't a damned nuclear bomb hanging between us. Even after she'd started avoiding me, she hadn't given up her Sundays.

I made sure she always got a show, too.

Lots of work that needed doing around that building of hers, and damned if I didn't take off my shirt every time she was out there. My cock twitched, thinking about her ass in those cute little shorts she loved so much. Not to mention the way she'd tasted . . .

Soon she'd be under me.

Raw need burned through me, building with every mile like a wildfire, and for the very first time I wondered if Pic had been right about holding off—I wasn't feeling kind and gentle and loving.

I needed to fuck.

I needed to fuck *tonight*.

And yeah, it would probably scare the shit out of her, and no, at this point I just didn't care, because she was right inside and no door was strong enough to keep me away from her. Not now that I was so close. Punching the bell again, I wondered if I'd have to kick the door in.

Then I heard the lock scrape open.

"Sorry," she said, opening the door. "I was upstairs and . . ."

Her voice trailed off as I looked her over, not bothering to hide the need burning me alive. She wore this long, flowing silky robe thing that'd been tied tight around her waist, and her hair was up in a ponytail that'd be perfect for holding tight while I fucked her from behind.

My balls tightened, and I swallowed, staring at her nipples. That thin fabric was doing exactly jack to hide how hard they'd gotten.

"It's a little late," she said slowly.

"Time to talk, Tinker," I replied, knowing I probably sounded like a fucking caveman and not giving one single shit. I pushed through the door, catching her arm and jerking her to the side so I could lock us in. Peaches. There it was. Now I just needed to figure out if her cunt tasted that way, too.

Only one way to find out.

My cock surged at the thought. Slowly, deliberately counting my steps to maintain control, I walked across the room toward a dark wooden table along the wall. *Hold it together. Don't scare her. Fuck her and make her scream.*

Jesus, couldn't decide what I wanted.

All of it.

"What's going on?" she asked, and I heard fear in her voice. Christ, that just made me want her more. I liked the idea of hunting her, chasing her down like a doe, then banging her hard while she screamed for mercy. Those nipples were like rocks . . . She wanted me just as bad as I wanted her. Was she wet already? I could practically smell it on her.

The throbbing in my dick matched the pounding in my head.

Keep it together, moron.

Reaching back, I pulled my gun out of the back of my jeans, setting it down carefully. Then I unbuckled my belt, whipping it through the loops to free the scabbard holding my knife.

"Cooper, I think—" she started to say, but I cut her off. Couldn't take one more damned minute of her calling me by that fucking name.

"Gage."

I set the hunting knife beside the gun, carefully coiling my belt up next to them. Pic might've been right, I realized. My control was slipping. She needed a slow, careful explanation. I needed my cock buried deep in her cunt. One of these would be happening soon, and it probably wasn't the smart one.

"Gage?" she asked hesitantly.

"My name is Gage," I confirmed, turning and stalking toward her. Goddamn, her cheeks were all flushed. I saw fear and excitement in her eyes, and those beautiful tits of her swayed up with every breath, taunting me. The view was outstanding. At some point I should probably figure out where she kept her bras, then take my knife to each and every one of them. Those tits were works of art and they deserved better than to be covered.

"Your name is Gage?" she asked, clearly confused as hell.

Fair enough, what with all the lies I'd told her.

"Yeah, the name was fake," I told her bluntly. I took another step forward, backing her against the front door. "All of it was fake. Lot of shit's gone down in the last two days. Things have changed, so it's time for us to talk."

I let my body push into hers, flattening her boobs against my chest. Christ, that felt good. Felt even better as my cock dug into her stomach. Felt *right*, the same way it felt when I'd put my colors back on. Right in a way that resonated to my bones, and any doubts I might've had about the situation were gone in an instant. I should lock her up, make her my prisoner until she acknowledged once and for all who she belonged to. Maybe even tattoo my name across that ass of hers.

That way any fucker stupid enough to try and get into her pants would know the name of his murderer.

My hand tightened on her throat for an instant—Jesus, the power I had over her in that moment. So sweet it hurt. Then I slid my hand up into her hair, digging deep until the band holding it popped. Tinker's eyes were wild, and I deliberately ground my hips into her, ass clenching as I imagined thrusting deep and hard.

"There's a lot of ground to cover, so I'm gonna give you the short version for now," I said, catching and holding her gaze prisoner, sure as I held her body. "I haven't been free since I got here. Now I am, which means I'm taking what's mine."

Tinker swallowed. My cock hurt. Blood pounded through me, and I decided what she really needed was something bigger to swallow. Christ.

"What do you mean, you're taking . . . ?" she asked, her voice thready and strained.

"I'm taking *you*," I said, nudging her legs apart with one knee. Now I felt her heat, and my hips swiveled again, starting a slow rhythm, mimicking what I'd be doing to her soon. Leaning down, I rubbed my nose slowly along her cheekbone. "You're mine now."

Tinker stiffened, and I tightened my hand in her hair. She needed to know who was boss. That I was in charge.

That I'd take care of her.

She swallowed again and I groaned, hips surging against her. This was better and worse than I'd imagined, because I was supposed to explain but I couldn't think. Maybe I should just fuck her and explain later. Maybe I'd be able to think by then. Kicking her legs wider, I angled my pelvis into hers, pinning her hard against the door, starting a slow grind that simultaneously hurt and felt better than anything I'd ever experienced before in my life.

Tinker gasped, and I knew I'd won. She might be pissed as hell later, but right now the woman wanted me as much as I wanted her. That was a damned good thing, because by the time she knew the whole truth, she'd probably come after me with her daddy's shotgun.

I closed my eyes for an instant, trying to slow down. Remember what I'd come here to tell her. Shitty to be me, because my brain had ceased to function. Now it was all about my cock pushing against her pussy and the feel of her heat through the layers of clothing between us.

"A lot's gone down, but right now the critical information is that you belong to me," I told her, my voice rough. "You're my property. You don't understand what that means, and that's okay. I'll teach you. But when you look back at this moment, I want you to remember there was a before I claimed you and an after. Now it's after. You got me?"

She didn't—I read the confusion in her face, and if I'd been a decent man I'd have let her go. Then she swallowed again, and all I could think about was shoving my dick down her throat. My pulse pounded as my slow grind grew more ragged. I had no fucking idea how I'd managed to keep my hands off her this long, but those days were done.

I'd lost my self-control and I wouldn't be getting it back.

"What about your girlfriend?" Tinker asked suddenly, eyes narrowing. There was a spark of jealousy there, and savage triumph roared through me. She didn't like me fucking Talia. This was good. Sure, we'd probably have a few fights over it, but the best part of fighting is the makeup sex.

"First, Talia has never been my girlfriend—that bitch is nothing," I told her. Tinker frowned skeptically. I reached down, catching one of her legs and lifting it to wrap around my waist. Now my cock hit her pussy at a new angle, and if we'd been naked I'd have already been inside her. "My club sent me here to study the Night-hawks, and she was the easiest way to get inside. Fucking her was like fucking a praying mantis. She's gone, or she will be soon. Either way, I'm done with her."

Tinker shook her head, raising her hands to push against my chest. Like she had a shot in hell of getting away. I caught her hands, pinning them over her head, because I was in charge here, not her. Then I leaned forward, our lips so close I felt the heat coming off her.

"I've been watching you twitch that ass of yours for too long," I whispered. "You sit out on that pretty little porch of yours with your friend. You pretend you aren't scoping me out, but you are. You've wanted it bad for a long time, and now you're gonna get it."

Covering her mouth, I thrust my tongue in deep, taking her as my hips attacked hers. She tasted better than I remembered, all hot and sweet and soft, and if I didn't get inside in the next five seconds, it might kill me.

Making that happen would require pulling away long enough to shove that robe of hers out of the way. This sucked, because I wasn't sure I could do it. The thought of pulling away for even an instant was almost more than I could handle. Then her tongue started tangling with mine as her leg tightened around me. *Jesus.* So hot. The kiss grew more frantic.

My hand caught her ass, pulling her into my body.

Tinker bit my tongue.

Hard.

I jerked back as we stared each other down, chests heaving. Then she spoke.

"Asshole. You lied to me."

CHAPTER SIXTEEN

TINKER

Cooper's face—no *Gage's* face—was flushed and his eyes were hard with need. My head was spinning and my body was screaming, because the lust I'd had for him before was nothing compared to this. When I felt his hard cock push between my legs, I wanted him inside me so bad that I could hardly think.

It'd be so easy.

Just let him do it, I whispered to myself. *Let him take you and make you feel good. You've suffered so much, been alone for so long. You deserve this.*

Maybe I did deserve it, but first I deserved some fucking answers.

"You *lied* to me," I repeated, forcing myself to retake control, each breath a triumph of focus.

"Yeah, I lied to you," he repeated, the words cold, almost indifferent. This wasn't the man I'd laughed over dinner with. Not even close. He was harder, and there wasn't a hint of any real emotion in his eyes. Lust? Definitely. He wanted me as bad as I wanted him, of that I had no doubt. But this wasn't the Cooper I'd come to know over the past few weeks. This wasn't the man who'd helped repair my building or who'd made me feel better about the fact that I'd been stupid enough to get caught on video screwing a stripper.

He definitely wasn't the same man who'd followed Talia around like a puppy when she crooked her finger. He was right about one thing—he'd lied, and not just with his words. Every interaction we'd ever had was fake.

"Let my hands go," I said, my voice cold.

"Or what?" he taunted softly.

I didn't answer, just stared him down. He cocked his head, giving me a twisted smile that could've been a sneer, but he let them go. Slowly. As if making it clear that it was his choice, not mine. Reminding me that he still held me fully pinned and there wasn't a damned thing I could do to stop him.

"Who are you?" I asked, the hard pressure between my legs sending waves of need and desire through me. But I wasn't some little girl to be manipulated by lust.

"Told you—my name is Gage. I'm with the Reapers motorcycle club, and I'll be the man fucking you from now on."

Raising my hands, I pushed slowly and steadily against his chest, making it clear I wanted him to let me go. He didn't. Instead I felt his fingers tighten possessively around my ass.

"We aren't doing this," I said, even though my body disagreed. Strongly. "I don't know who the hell you are, and I don't fuck strangers."

"You fucked a strange stripper at a bachelorette party," he said, narrowing his eyes. "Remember?"

My breath caught, pain punching through me.

"Are you seriously slut-shaming me?" I whispered. Gage's jaw tightened, and then he shook his head tightly, frowning.

"This isn't going right," he said, a flicker of frustration crossing his face.

"What gave it away?" I said, my voice low and smooth, with a hint of ice. "Here's something you should know about me, *Gage*. Sometimes I get beat. Sometimes I lose and life doesn't turn out the way I planned. Sometimes I even feel weak and collapse for a while, but here's the reality . . . I will never, ever give up and I will never give in."

My hands came up fast and I jabbed him in the throat with both thumbs, targeting the soft, central hollow right above the sternum. It caught him hard, and he reared back with a grunt. Taking advantage, I used his body as leverage, shoving to the side with so much force that I fell on the floor, then scuttled back across to the door. I shivered, both from adrenaline and sudden loss of his heat, wrapping my arms around my body. Despite everything, I was still turned on, which was seriously fucked up. It wasn't right, feeling this much lust and anger at the same time.

"Did you really think you could lie to me about everything and expect me to just take it?" I asked, pushing to my feet. He frowned, taking a step back, eyes glittering with a mixture of lust and frustration.

"I wasn't thinking at all," he said, eyes darkening. "I spent the last twenty-four hours in a jail cell, fucking helpless while the whole town was calling you and telling you stories about me."

A bitter smile twisted my lips.

"Half the town doesn't even talk to me," I pointed out. "Remember the whole slut-shaming thing?"

"Fuck them," he said, the words surprisingly harsh. "Fuck all of them. You're better than the rest put together, Tinker, and you're sure as shit better than me. But remember how much they love to spew shit when you hear the rumors about this weekend. Rumors about me, and what's going to happen next. There are big changes ahead for the Nighthawks."

I swallowed, wanting him and hating him at the same time.

"You're part of the Reapers MC," I said slowly. Gage nodded.

"You've heard of them?"

"My husband was a prosecutor," I reminded him gently. "I've heard plenty about your club and other clubs like it. And I know what kinds of things you're responsible for."

Gage shook his head.

"You don't know my club," he said softly. "But you will. They're

here in town because things got out of hand with the Nighthawks—
we both know it's true. I came here to see for myself and found
them terrorizing everyone. Now we're going to fix it. Then I'll introduce you to my brothers and their families and you'll see what
we're really about."

"I have no interest in your friends, let alone their *families*," I
snarled the word, turning it ugly. "Especially if they're all as fucked
up as you."

Gage shook his head slowly, eyes hardening. "Hate me all you
want, but don't judge people you've never even met. My Reaper
brothers are real, just as real as you and Darren and Carrie. They
have wives. Children. We're *people*, Tinker, not stereotypes. We
live life on our own terms, but you're a fucking hypocrite if you fall
for all the shit people say about us, especially people like your ex.
That's bullshit, the same kind of bullshit they've thrown at you
because of that stupid fucking sex tape."

"You can't compare this to that—you got arrested for drugs!"

"No, Tinker, I *didn't*," Gage said. "Everyone who got arrested
for drugs is still in jail. I don't fucking use meth, and there wasn't
a trace of it on me, either. Guess your sources were wrong about
that, hmmm? Wonder what else they got wrong? Maybe you should
ask first instead of making assumptions."

I took a deep breath, shuddering with relief. I hadn't even realized how Carrie's phone call had scared me.

"So you weren't selling drugs out of my apartment building?"

Gage caught my eyes, holding my gaze.

"No, Tinker. I wasn't selling drugs out of your building. I
wasn't selling drugs at all. I was mostly fixing your roof and un-
clogging your toilets and trying to figure out what to do about this
incredible, sexy, irresistible woman who came into my life at exactly the wrong time, because I couldn't get her out of my brain.
Give me a chance, Tinker. I dare you. Meet my brothers. Meet their
families. But keep your mind open. Otherwise you're just as bad as
Maisy and Heather. They've held that tape over you like you're
some kind of whore who deserves to be punished for being human.

But you aren't a whore and the truth is never that black and white. Get to know me, get to know my brothers. My *family*. Give them a chance."

I considered his words, and something hit me. Before I'd been caught on that tape, I'd have felt perfectly justified in judging him. He'd lied to me, and there was no excuse for that. Except it sounded like maybe he did have a reason. I thought about Sadie and her bruising. About the fact that she'd refused to go to the police, and that if she had, Marsh might have punished her for it.

Cooper hadn't lied about one thing—something had gone terribly wrong in Hallies Falls, and it needed fixing.

Try it. Try opening your mind. See what happens.

"So that means I'll meet your sons?" I asked, stomach twisting. He was right—I didn't know what'd happened, and I didn't know this new version of Cooper. I tried to imagine him as a parent—had tried to imagine it all along—but I'd never been able to picture it. The thought of this scary man having children was almost beyond me.

Gage didn't answer immediately. I studied him, growing nervous. There was more—I could sense it. See it in his face.

"I don't have any children," he admitted.

Raising a hand to my stomach, I thought about Tricia.

"You don't have kids?" I asked, stunned. "You lied about being a father to me? Why would you lie about *that*, of all things? What does that have to do with a motorcycle club?"

He sighed. "I lied about everything, Tinker. I created the man I needed to be, for my club. But then I met you and that's fucked everything up worse."

I knew he was still talking, but my brain was shutting down. Jesus, and I'd thought the first lie hurt . . . but this. Treating the idea of having sons—living children—like it didn't matter, I couldn't wrap my head around that. I'd wanted my baby more than anything. I'd give my life to have her back, and this Gage person used imaginary kids as a *prop* in his little motorcycle spy game.

I couldn't do this.

"Get out," I said, clutching my stomach tighter, picturing her precious little face. It'd looked like she was sleeping. A man with sad eyes and a camera had come into my hospital room that afternoon. He'd taken a portrait of me holding her, and then she was gone forever.

Tricia hadn't been a lie.

"We need to talk," he insisted.

"Get out," I hissed, something breaking deep inside my soul. I wanted him *out*, and I wanted him out *now*.

He shook his head. "We're gonna work through this."

"Get out of my house!" I shouted at him, slamming against his chest with both hands as hard as I could, really putting my body into it. In that instant I hated him. Hated him with all the black rage I held coiled inside and *he wouldn't get the fuck out of my way!* Grabbing his shoulder, I tried to knee him like I'd learned in self-defense class. He blocked me at the last minute, catching me and wrapping me tight in his arms, holding me prisoner.

"Settle down," he muttered. I bit his shoulder. Not playfully. I dug my teeth in deep and hard, and if it hadn't been for his leather vest, I'd have drawn blood. "Jesus, fuck! *Stop it!*"

I bucked against him, and while his arms tightened around me I had the advantage, because I didn't give a shit. I didn't give a shit about hurting him and I didn't give a shit about hurting myself.

I just wanted him to leave before I shattered into a thousand pieces.

"Stop," he grunted. Loosening my teeth from his shoulder, I went for his neck instead. He wasn't expecting that, and when I dug in he shouted in a way that let me know I'd hurt him, and hurt him good. *Finally.* Suddenly his arms dropped as he shoved me away, one hand clutching his neck, blood oozing between his fingers. It happened so fast that I fell back on my butt, slamming into the wooden floor. Pain washed through me, but the anger numbed it. Gage backed away, glaring at me. Ignoring him, I jumped to my feet and lunged for the sideboard where he'd coiled his belt.

Coiled his belt and set down his gun.

Grabbing it, I flicked off the safety and pulled back the slide, loading a shell. Then I pointed it straight at the lying son of a bitch.

"It's time for you to get out of my house," I said, and this time the words were steady and strong. He studied me warily, one hand firm against his bleeding neck.

"You know, my club president didn't think you'd take this very well," he said, his voice casual. I blinked, confused.

"What the hell are you talking about?"

"Picnic—he's my club president. He thought you might be pissed off about me lying to you," he said. "Guess he was right."

"Are we having the same conversation?" I asked, raising the gun higher. *What the hell?* I had the gun. He was supposed to do what I said, not get all chatty. "Because I feel like maybe you don't realize what's happening here. If you don't leave my house I'm going to shoot you."

"Yeah, he was right," Gage said thoughtfully. "This was a mistake. And I'll go. But not until you put that down."

"I am not putting down the fucking gun!"

"Okay, keep the gun for now," he said, sighing. "But could you toss me the belt? This probably won't be my only fight tonight, and I don't want my pants falling down during a critical moment."

"Do you realize *that your life is in danger*?" I demanded, my voice growing hysterical. "What's wrong with you? Your belt doesn't matter!"

He took a step toward me, frowning. "But it's my favorite."

My hands started to shake. The gun was heavy, but it wasn't just that. He wasn't leaving, and all of a sudden I realized that I might actually have to shoot him.

I didn't want to shoot him.

I didn't want to shoot *anyone*. I was the kind of girl who made chocolates and watered flowers and occasionally got drunk on red wine while sitting on my porch swing. Girls like that don't shoot men in their living rooms.

"Please go," I whispered, and he smiled softly, taking another step in my direction. Now we were maybe four feet apart. His eyes held mine prisoner and he cocked his head, holding up both hands in surrender.

"Give me the belt. I'll let you keep the gun."

My hands shook more, and I reached back blindly, feeling for the belt. I wanted him gone. I needed to think about things. This was all so crazy, and while I wasn't totally certain how or why I'd found myself holding a gun on him in my living room, the situation needed to end.

Holy cats, how had my life come to this?

Wrapping my hand around the belt, I held it out to him and whispered, "You need to leave."

He reached toward it, holding my eyes the whole time. Then my hand was flying to the side as he knocked the weapon out of my grip. Suddenly I was down on the floor, both arms pinned high over my head as his large, heavy body covered mine. He kicked my legs open, settling between them, trapping me completely.

How had that happened?

Everything was horrible, and it just kept getting worse. I bucked against him again, and then to my disgust I felt tears building in my eyes. I hated crying. There were too many feelings rushing through me all at once and I couldn't control them all, and now he was on top of me again. I could feel his cock hardening against me. Everything was happening too fast. I wiggled, trying to escape, and he gave a low groan. My heart was about to explode from shock and he was turned on like some kind of sick animal.

How was this my reality?

"Just do it," I said, sniffling.

He stilled. "Do what?"

"Rape me or whatever. Just get it over with."

Gage was off me in an instant, backing away. "Jesus Christ, who do you think I am?"

I sat up slowly, wiping my eyes with the heels of my hands. Then I looked at him and shook my head.

"I have no fucking idea," I whispered, and it was the absolute truth. I didn't know him and I never had. "Please leave. I just want you to leave."

Gage stared me down, then nodded, his face shaken.

"I'll leave for now," he said. "But it's not over. We're not over."

"It's over for tonight."

He nodded, grabbing his belt and the gun that had skidded across the floor. I flinched as he stepped toward the sideboard, but all he did was pick up his knife. Then he walked toward the front door, turning once to look back at me."

"This isn't how I planned this, Tinker," he said softly. "I'm sorry. We'll talk tomorrow."

GAGE

Moron.

I was a fucking moron. Pic had warned me not to talk to her, and the bastard had been right. Again. Why that asshole always had to be right I didn't know, but it was damned annoying.

When she'd looked up at me and said to go ahead and rape her, something had died inside me. Don't think I'd ever hated myself quite so much in my entire life as I had in that instant.

One thing did have me puzzled, though. Why the hell—out of all the lies I'd told her—had it been the kid thing that freaked her out? I got that lying sucked and everyone hates feeling like a sucker, but I'd expected her to fixate on me fucking Talia, not that.

Guess I'd just add it to the list of shit I needed to deal with next time I saw her.

List was getting damned long.

My Reaper brothers had gathered at the same cheap-ass hotel I'd stayed in when I first got to town. I counted twenty-six bikes in the lot, and it looked like they'd called in the cavalry because several had Devil's Jacks markings. Fucking shame it'd come to this, but I didn't see how we'd had much choice. With Marsh and his boys still in jail, we'd never get a better chance to make our move.

Pic stood waiting for me out in the parking lot, along with Horse, Ruger, Bam Bam, and several others. I parked my bike, and he walked over to meet me, catching my hand before pulling me in for a tight hug.

"Glad to have you back, brother," he said. "Everything go okay with your girl?"

And now for the fun part—I hated admitting when he was right.

"No."

"You wanna talk about it?"

"Never wanted to talk about anything less," I said shortly, and he laughed.

"Believe it or not, I understand. Everyone's waiting. It's a little crowded inside, but we're ready for you to brief us on the situation."

I followed him into one of the end units, the others filing in behind us. More and more came, filling the room wall to wall.

"Glad to have you back, bro," Bam Bam said, slapping my back. Others followed, and I was surprised that even the Devil's Jacks took a minute to welcome me. Hadn't realized until that moment just how much I'd missed being around my people. My family.

"So, here we are," Pic said, calling the meeting to order. "You all know what Gage has been through these past weeks."

"Saw the picture of the bitch you had to bang," Hunter said. "Sounds like it was rough."

Laughs, which I chose to ignore, echoed around the room.

"Pretty sure she has teeth lining her cunt," I told them. "Believe me, Talia Jackson is a scary woman—don't let the tight ass fool you. The real issue here is her brother, Marsh. We've all suspected for a long time now that the Reapers weren't getting their cut from the cross-border traffic, and I've seen it for myself. Even if they were, though, it wouldn't matter. The Nighthawks are falling apart as a club. Dysfunctional as hell. If they were paying, we'd still have to step in at this point, because the whole situation's a fucking time bomb. Not only that, the club's out of control. Marsh brought in nothing but useless pieces of shit and now we have to somehow salvage the situation or we'll lose control of the territory."

Hunter's face turned serious.

"How'd that happen?" he asked.

"Most of the leadership and the old guard went down in a raid, all at the same time," Picnic said. "Most of them are still serving time. Marsh stepped into the power vacuum. We probably should've shut it down then, but we had no idea how toxic he was at that point, and they were holding up their end of the bargain."

"There are a few who've gotten out since then," I added. "Four of them—Cord seems to be their leader. Wish I could tell you more, but they wouldn't give me the time of day, given that I'm one of Marsh's scabs, at least in their eyes."

"And none of them went down this weekend?" Hunter asked.

"Nope," I said. "I haven't seen any of them since earlier in the week. They didn't go out with us on Friday night and missed his little rampage. He kept us all in the clubhouse that night, asking questions and looking for traitors. Full-on paranoia. I don't know where they are, but they weren't with him."

"They're out at the clubhouse right now," Picnic said. "Waiting to talk to us about what happened. Cord got in touch as soon as he heard the news. Sounds to me like they want to fix things, make it right. You think that's possible?"

I considered the question carefully, weighing our options.

"Tough call," I finally admitted. "If I knew Cord better, I'd have a better answer for you. I don't think that he's an enemy to the Reapers. I think he was outnumbered, so he waited for his moment. There's still a lot of brothers on the inside, brothers who are good men. They're the real Nighthawks, not Marsh and his crew."

"So we let him step in?" Pic asked.

"I can't answer that," I said. "I wish I had a sense of the man personally, but I don't. All I know is he hates Marsh."

"He was a strong brother in the past," Bam Bam said. "I've ridden with him a few times. Kept his shit tight, not the kind to talk much, but I'd have him at my back in a fight. Impossible situation, when your own president doesn't do what's right. I mean, he rats out Marsh, he's betraying his own brother. He doesn't, he's betrayed the Reapers. If it were me, I'd probably watch and wait, too."

"Good point," Pic acknowledged. "Anyone else here want to speak for him or the others?"

"Pipes is a good man," Ruger said. "He's the Nighthawk who stood with Painter and Puck down in California while they were in prison. Still down there, and they'll be sending Painter back to join him once his parole's revoked. Painter told me that Cord was one of the few who made to effort to visit Pipes. We make peace with Cord, that could save Painter's life on the inside."

"That's reason enough right there," I said. "We have any contact with the other Nighthawks inside?"

"Some," Pic said. "But Cord would have more. If we can salvage something of the situation, that's for the best. Otherwise it leaves us with another power vacuum in the middle of the state. Then we'd have to move men into the area."

"You'll need to move someone into the area no matter what," Hunter said, frowning. "Just because you're giving him a shot doesn't mean we can trust him."

"I'll stay," I told them. The men around me stirred, although I saw Horse grinning. Smug fucker.

"You've already given up a lot," Bam Bam said. "You sure you want to do that?"

"It works for me," I said, although I'd be damned if I'd discuss the whole Tinker situation with such a large audience.

"What if we patched them over?" Ruger asked suddenly.

"The Nighthawks?" Hunter asked. "Have you lost your mind?"

"Not all of them," Ruger said. "But we know Pipes is solid—he put his life on the line more than once for Painter on the inside. And Cord is solid with him. Until Marsh took over, we never had problem with them, and they aren't Marsh's people. What we have here is a good support club that got infected by a cancer. Cut out the cancer, we get the club back."

"But to patch them over as Reapers?" Horse asked, skeptical. "That seems a little much."

"Not right away," Ruger said. "But we could give them a chance to redeem themselves, and take it from there. Make them provisional. It's not a case of patching over the whole club—it's shutting down the bad club and patching over the members worth saving. Could send a powerful message to any other support club in the area. Stay loyal and you'll be rewarded. And despite this shit with Marsh, the bulk of the brothers stayed loyal. They're just stuck in prison. Remember, not one of the fuckers testified against his brothers or the Reapers."

"It could work," Pic said slowly. "I mean, it's different, but . . . I need to talk to Shade about this. It's a bigger decision than we can make right here. You guys clear out, get ready for tonight while I talk to him. Regardless of what he says, we need to get out to the clubhouse and meet with the Nighthawks. Otherwise we'll look weak."

Men started to leave, and I stood to join them, but Pic motioned at me to stay. I locked the door behind the brothers as he picked up his phone.

"Shade, it's Pic," he said. "I'm putting you on speaker—want you to hear what's been going on from Gage, who's in the room with me."

"Gage, I've been hearing about your work," Shade said. He hadn't been our national president for that long, but in that time he'd more than earned my respect. "Pic told me what happened in Ellensburg yesterday. Sorry to hear that Painter's in so much trouble. Hate it when a brother goes back inside."

"He's a good man," I said, and it was true. For years, Painter had seemed less like a brother and more like a dumbass kid, but he'd pulled through for all of us in the end. "Fucking sucks."

"Coales will do everything he can," he said. "And that goes for you, too. I hear you're probably out of the woods on your charges."

"Not yet, but it sounds like I will be."

"Glad to hear it. Now, what's the assessment with the Nighthawks?"

"Most of them are shit," Picnic said. "At least, most of those on

the outside. We know the originals—the men in prison long term—
are good. So are a few who are still on the outside. Cord, for one.
He was down to see Pipes in California when Painter and Pipes
were on the inside together. Source of our information in the first
place. Gage hasn't had much chance to talk to him because the
entire time he's been here, he very carefully made himself out to be
Marsh's bitch. Cord and his boys have no respect for Marsh and
his people, so they ignored Gage."

"Guess that's in his favor," Shade said. "So tell me what you're
thinking."

"So, it goes without saying that we have to get rid of the Nighthawks who were with Marsh," Pic said. "The new ones and the
traitors. That won't be hard because they're nothing—not real
brothers at all. Just a collection of losers and followers who didn't
even prospect for real. But it does leave us in an interesting position
in terms of men like Cord, not to mention the original brothers
who are serving longer prison terms. We can't let a club that's betrayed us survive, but we also can't leave a power vacuum. Not
only that, there's a lot of good men who call themselves Nighthawks who have nothing to do with this. Tough situation."

"True enough," Shade said. "You have any suggestions?"

"I want to kick out the crap and then patch the good men in as
Reapers," Picnic said. Shade didn't answer for a minute.

"Your solution to them betraying us is bringing them into our
club?" he asked. "Wanna run that by me again?"

"Okay, I know it sounds crazy," Pic said. "But think it through—
we got good men. Strong brothers. They held this territory for
twenty years and the partnership worked. Then a big group of them
went down and not one testified against us or each other. Marsh
Jackson snuck in and took over while they were helpless, and if anything, we should have been covering their asses. Instead we allowed
it to happen. That's on us, Shade."

I stared at my president, impressed. This was all in.

"I can see that," Shade said slowly. "But you can't seriously think I'll authorize the creation of a new Reapers charter over the phone. Doesn't work that way, bro. We both know this."

Picnic laughed.

"No, I get that," he said. "But when we go in, we can hold it up as a possibility. Tell the existing brothers—the ones who have kept the faith—that the Nighthawks as they exist right now are done. Then hold this out to them as a compromise. We want them here, we're going to work with them, and then if things come together, there will be a reward."

"Gage, what's your thought on this?" Shade asked. "You're the one who's been on the ground. What's your sense of the situation?"

"I don't know Cord well," I said. "But my gut tells me he's a solid guy, if for no other reason than he never fell for Marsh's shit. They were on the brink of civil war already. Cord and his faction weren't around on Friday, and for all I know they were planning to make a move against Marsh this weekend. I think it's worth giving it a shot. Especially since it could have long-term consequences for our boy Painter, who's headed back down to prison in Cali. Pipes— the Nighthawk brother on the inside—he's one of our only allies there. We burn all the Nighthawks, we're burning Painter, too."

"Okay, so walk me through it," Shade said. "Assuming we do this, I'd have to talk to all the presidents and go through the process—we all know this. But I'm willing to hold it out as a possibility if you've got a solid plan."

"First, the timing is good," Picnic said. "Marsh and his boys are all still locked up. We don't have full information on their situation, but it sounds like they found enough product on them to get them for intent to distribute. That means we don't have to worry about them getting out again for a while. If we go in strong now, we clean out the clubhouse and get rid of anyone who answers to Marsh. They're gone. Period. Then we reorganize with Cord and his brothers to start over."

"I'd stay in town," Gage said. "Oversee everything. Make me nomad."

"Big step," Shade said. "You sure you're up for it?"

"He's got a girl here," Pic said. "Pussy-whipped."

Shade snorted. "For real, Gage? You want us to make a whole new Reapers chapter just so you can get—"

Pic burst out laughing. "Okay, that was unfair. It wasn't his idea, actually. But he did meet a woman and wouldn't mind some time here in town. That suits the club's needs, so it works on our end. Do we have your support?"

"Yeah," Shade said slowly. "We can try it, although it'll boil down to a vote by all the presidents. But I can see this working. Keep me posted on the details. So long as Gage is there keeping an eye on things, I think it's okay. You serious about this woman?"

"Maybe," I said. "Better question might be whether she's serious about me. Right now she's a little pissed off. Apparently women don't like it when you lie to them about who you are, and then fuck another bitch under their nose for weeks at a time. I don't know how hookers do it—thought I'd lose my fuckin' mind, and that's the truth."

Shade laughed.

"No, I'd imagine not," he said. "This is why I don't have an old lady. Too much work."

"Fuck off," Pic said. "You got no idea what you're missing."

That was my cue to call him pussy-whipped or something, but for the first time in a very long time, I didn't feel like giving one of my brothers shit for keeping a woman around. Instead I had a feeling he was right. There was something there—something good—and I'd been missing out.

With any luck, I wouldn't be missing out for much longer.

CHAPTER SEVENTEEN

TINKER

"You're fucking kidding me," Carrie said over the phone.

"I'm not," I whispered, feeling sick to my stomach. "I can't believe he played me like this. Nothing about him was real. Nothing! Why do I keep falling for guys who are liars and assholes?"

"Okay, yes—he's a liar and an asshole," she said. "But don't beat yourself up too much. Brandon is evil, and you spent a decade of your life with him. Cooper—"

"His name is Gage."

"Whatever. Gage is just a sexy asshole who got you a little hot and bothered. This isn't a federal crime, although I'd like to throw out my vote for eviction one more time. If he lied on his paperwork, that has to be a good enough reason to get rid of him."

"I can't think about that right now," I said. "God. He's fixing the roof, Carrie. How am I going to get the roof fixed if I kick him out? And I'm supposed to take Dad to Seattle this week for his doctor's appointment. My lawyer wants to talk, too. He thinks that maybe Brandon is pulling some kind of bullshit on the financials.

Until now I haven't pressed him for real, so we thought it was just stalling. But something may be really wrong there."

"Stop," she ordered. "Just stop for a second and take a deep breath, all right?"

Closing my eyes, I tried to do what she said, counting to ten while I inhaled. Slowly I let the air back out again, then repeated the process.

"How's that?" she asked.

"Better," I admitted. "I feel less like my heart is going to explode in my chest. I can't believe he lied to me about having children."

"He told you a lot of lies," she agreed. "And it sounds like he's full of shit on every level. But I think you should consider one thing—and I am not saying this to defend him, all right?"

"All right. What?"

"He doesn't know you lost a baby," she said softly. "And while I absolutely think he's an asshole who deserves to have his intestines pecked out by buzzards, he didn't set out to hurt you when he lied about having a family."

"That doesn't mean I'm forgiving him," I said, my tone dark. Carrie laughed, and it wasn't a nice laugh. More of an evil-queen laugh, with a side of maniacal genius.

"Oh no," she said. "There's no forgiving him. But he isn't worth getting hung up on, either. How about this—I'm slammed with work during the day tomorrow, so why don't you come over for dinner? We can laugh and talk and maybe throw darts at a picture of him."

"I don't have a picture of him."

"No worries. I took one when he was working without his shirt the other day. Through the window."

"That's creepy."

"Yeah, I know," she admitted. "We've covered my stalkerishness before, so let's keep moving here. We'll throw darts at the picture and curse all men. It'll be fun."

"We don't need to curse Darren."

"Not unless he pisses me off between now and then," she said brightly. "But if he does, all bets are off. So, dinner?"

"How about you come here," I said. "I don't want to leave Dad alone. You can bring Darren and the girls."

"Twist my arm," she replied. "You're a way better cook than me. But the girls probably won't come. They're far too fabulous and adult to have dinner with us old people. I think they've got something planned with their friends. Just as well—they'd probably get creeped out watching us throw darts at a picture."

"You're the best friend ever, you know that, right?"

"Pretty much," she said. "And I promise you—we'll get through this. He caught you at a vulnerable time, but this guy is not a big deal. You'll bounce right back."

"And you promise this?"

"Money-back guarantee, baby. I got your back."

GAGE

It was a tense ride out to the clubhouse.

The Nighthawks knew we were in town—they had to know. You couldn't bring that many bikes into a place as small as Hallies Falls without people noticing, and the arrests down in Ellensburg the day before just added to the gossip.

A fresh wildfire had broken out that day, and while it was more than fifty miles away, even more smoke filled the air and tiny white ashes had started falling on everything. I'd never seen a summer like this for fires. If we'd been on a TV show, I'd have taken it for a sign that they were going to ambush and kill us all—it'd be a good show, too.

Seeing as we weren't on TV, I'd be just as happy without the ambush.

Pulling up to the clubhouse, I spotted eight bikes. Not bad odds. Cord's faction had four, and the others might be prospects or hang-arounds friendly to his cause. Or not. What the hell did I know, anyway? Cody—one of the prospects, and not a particularly promising one—watched over them, his face paling as we pulled up, backing our bikes into line carefully.

Picnic strode toward him, followed closely by Hunter, and I watched Cody swallow.

"Prospect?" Pic asked, looking him over. "Gage, you know this one?"

I joined them, studying the kid.

"He's one of Marsh's," I said. "Bought his first bike a few weeks ago."

Pic sighed, running a hand through his hair.

"Kid, you have no fucking idea what you've gotten yourself into here," he said, and his voice wasn't unkind. "Here's the best offer you'll get tonight—hand over your colors, get on your bike, and leave. Your president and his friends are locked up and they're gonna stay that way for a while. The club you signed up for isn't going to exist anymore after tonight, and you aren't ready to prospect anyway. Learn to ride your bike, grow up a little, and give it another shot in a few years. We won't hold this against you."

Cody had never struck me as one of the brightest, although he seemed like a decent-enough kid. Now I could practically see the hamster running frantically on the wheel in his head, desperate for escape.

Get on the bike, kid. Get out of here.

"I'm not giving up my colors, sir," he said, and while his voice trembled, he didn't blink. "I've been told to stay out here and watch these bikes, and that's what I'm gonna do. You'll have to take them off me."

Jesus. Christ.

"You've been watching *Sons of Anarchy*, haven't you?" Pic asked, sighing heavily. Cody swallowed, then nodded. "Fucking show. Whole damned world thinks they're Jax Teller. Pat him down and bring him inside."

In an instant, Horse and Ruger had him up against the wall, checking him for weapons. I watched as they pulled off one small pocket knife, and I do mean small. Little red Swiss Army, with the tweezer and toothpick.

Pic and Hunter shot me incredulous looks, and I shrugged. Wasn't like I hadn't warned them.

The club had fallen to shit.

Pic nodded at me to lead the way into the clubhouse itself. Always fun being point, but it made sense, seeing as the men inside already knew me. I pushed the door open to find Cord and four others waiting for us. Cord took in my newly restored colors in one quick glance, and if he was surprised he kept it to himself. Pic and Hunter followed me in, as others surrounded the building.

"Welcome," Cord said, nodding toward Picnic. "I'm Cord. We've met before—rally a few years back. I'm more familiar with Rance, the Bellingham president. Been expecting a visit for a while now."

"Rance is busy," Pic said shortly. "Asked me to come in his place. This is Hunter. He's president of the Devil's Jacks, out of Portland. I'm assuming you've guessed why we're here?"

"Marsh Jackson ran this club into the ground, didn't pay his tax, and now you're here to figure out what went wrong."

Cord had never struck me as stupid, and I guess my instincts hadn't been entirely off.

"I'm Gage," I said, meeting his gaze head-on.

"Nice colors," he said, the faintest hint of a sneer in his voice. "Funny. Last time I saw you, you weren't wearing them. Wasn't aware the Reapers were afraid to wear their own colors in Washington State."

"Needed to find out what was happening here in town," Pic said, his voice casual. "We heard the club was too easy to penetrate. Figured we'd investigate for ourselves, and damned if it wasn't."

Cord's mouth tightened, and a tense silence fell between us.

"Let's just admit that none of this went down the normal way," Hunter broke in, nodding toward Cord. "Call it what it is—we know you reached out through Pipes. He talked to our men on the inside, and the Reapers responded. They wanted to see what was happening, they saw, and now we're here talking to you because we know you're solid men. Men who can be trusted. Let's find a way to resolve this issue and move forward."

"And you've got a stake in this because . . . ?" Cord asked, sarcasm in his voice.

"The old man is my father-in-law," Hunter replied, nodding toward Pic. "He gets pissy, she gets pissy. Then I get no head. It's a serious issue, bro. We gotta make this right."

"Pussy-whipped?" Cord asked, cocking a brow.

Hunter shrugged. "Priorities. It is what it is. Can we sit and talk this through? Nobody here wants to fight today. The Nighthawks had a problem. The problem's in jail now, which means it's time to regroup."

Cord nodded slowly.

"That's the truth," he admitted. "You guys want a drink?"

"After," Pic said. "We should talk first. Why don't you start by introducing your brothers to all of us?"

"This is Wanker, Charlie Boy, and Tamarack," he said, nodding to the three men wearing full colors next to him. "Those two are Cody and Fuckwit. They're Marsh's prospects. Guess Cody missed the excitement because he had the stomach flu, and I gotta admit, Fuckwit's growing on all of us. I think he might be all right."

"Your boy Cody seems to be taking things very seriously," Pic told him. "When we pulled up outside, we told him to get out while he still could. Refused to hand over his colors."

Cord looked surprised, glancing at Cody sharply.

"Huh."

Cody stood blank faced, although I saw a tremble in his hands. Damn, the kid really wanted this.

"Okay, prospects outside," Pic said. "You watch the bikes with some of our brothers to keep you company. Think things over—you leave tonight, it's no harm, no foul, no judgment. The grown-ups are going to talk now. Where's your chapel?"

We let Cord lead the way to the meeting room, followed by me, Pic, Hunter, Ruger, Bam Bam, and one of Hunter's brothers named Taz. Pic took the president's chair without objection from Cord. Made sense—the Reapers were over the Nighthawks. Always had been, always would be. They owed us their respect regardless of the circumstances.

"Here's how I see it," Pic started out. "There's essentially been two clubs in this town, the old Nighthawks and the new Nighthawks. The old Nighthawks were our allies, and you're their leader. Sound about right?"

"That's a fair assessment," Cord said, his face like stone. "Most of my real brothers are in prison, serving hard time. You should know all about that—your boys might be with them right now if we hadn't kept our mouths shut when the cops swept us up."

"Respect," Pic said, nodding his head. "And those are your real brothers. Marsh and his boys pulled a hostile takeover while you were locked up, which put you in a hell of a spot. Sound about right?"

"Exactly what happened," Cord said, and for an instant his cool mask slipped, and I saw just how exhausted he must be. "I got paroled and found my club turned upside down. Fucked up shit."

"You could've come and talked to us."

"Wasn't my place," he said. "Marsh was the president, elected following the bylaws. You think we're some bitch club that comes running to Daddy for help when things get tough? We'd have taken care of business, sooner or later."

"You never voted for him?" I asked. Cord shook his head.

"Nope, I was still inside at the time. But I understand how it happened—he was the only strong one who hadn't been picked up in the raid. The rest of us were out of the picture—some of those brothers won't see freedom for another ten years. We couldn't afford not to have a strong leader, and the Reapers approved it."

"That's true," Pic acknowledged. "Wish Rance was here— Bellingham is in charge of this area, not Coeur d'Alene. He knows the situation better than me. Say we all agree to share the fault. Next question is, how do we move on from here?"

"You should know we're not letting Marsh come back," Cord said, sharing a determined look with his brothers. "We already voted on it—either he goes or we're turning in our colors. This isn't the club I joined, and while I love my brothers in prison, we can't let Marsh destroy everything we've worked to build. If need be, I'll start a new club. With or without your blessing."

The words hung heavy in the room, because we all knew what that meant.

War. He had to know it wouldn't end well for them.

"You talk to your boys on the inside?" Hunter asked. "What do they think?"

"If the Nighthawks fall, they'll be open game," Cord said. "That's why we want to keep our alliances strong for their safety. Marsh is a time bomb, and I'm not sure the brothers I have left—the real brothers—are strong enough on our own. We'd like to find a solution that doesn't end with all of us dead."

"What if we offered you a compromise?" Pic asked slowly. Cord studied him.

"I'm listening."

"Marsh and his people are out of the game. They're dead to us. They show their faces, cause trouble, you name it, you have our permission to make them go away. We'll back you up. But we agree with you about the Nighthawks. The club has fallen apart, and we can't allow that kind of weakness in our territory. Not only that, the name is tainted—you openly rebelled. There are other clubs that might follow if we let you get away with it. It's over. We're shutting you down."

Cord's jaw tightened.

"And our men inside?" he asked. "Our alliance with the Reapers is keeping them alive—you've got men inside, too. We stand strong together, our brothers are more likely to make it out alive."

Pic nodded, then leaned forward, his voice intense.

"We're prepared to patch you over into the Reapers."

Cord raised a brow, and Tamarack crossed his arms. The man was huge, like a bear, and when I caught his eye I half expected him to growl at me.

"Are you serious?" Cord asked slowly.

"Any of this look like a game to you?" Picnic replied. "I talked to our national president already. He's on board. It'll need to be voted on by all the presidents, of course. Some may argue—we all know you've been cutting the Reapers out of our due on the cross-border trade."

"Not us," Cord said. "That's all Marsh. We've been cut out, too."

"We know," I told him. "I've been watching. I realize you don't like how this went down. Not right for a man to come to your town—your club—without his colors. But we needed to understand what was really happening, and now we do. We're well aware that you weren't part of the betrayal. That's why we're fighting for you and your brothers. None of us want to see Hallies Falls lose their club. This lets all the loyal brothers survive with your dignity intact. Not only that, it keeps our alliance strong, which means our boys inside stay safe. Let Marsh take the fall for this one, Cord. Patch over, and we'll build a chapter in Hallies Falls that's worthy of respect."

Cord glanced around the room. Faded leather vests hung on the walls, along with pictures of members long dead.

"And the men who came before us?" he asked, nodding toward the club's insignia. "The original Nighthawks? You expecting us to forget about them?"

"No," Pic said. "So far as we're concerned, the men who betrayed your colors never existed. The rest of you have served with honor, and we never forget our fallen brothers. They'll stay here with our respect when as you move forward as a new chapter. We'll give you a few minutes to discuss it."

He started to stand and the rest of us followed, but Cord spoke, stopping him.

"And if we say no?"

"Then it's over," Pic said bluntly. "We take your colors and shut you down. We can't allow a support club to betray us like this and survive."

Cord nodded slowly. "Not much of a choice, then, is it?"

"Always a choice," Pic said.

"What about the men inside? You gonna let my brothers serving time—the same men who lied to cover your ass—get slaughtered?"

"No," Pic said firmly. "They'll still be under our protection—they've earned that right. But we both know they'll be stronger if they carry the Reaper name. You'd all be probationary members until you prove yourselves, though."

"Of course," Cord said, his voice bitter.

"It is what is it, brother," Hunter said.

"You aren't my brother."

"All the Reapers are my brothers," Hunter said, glancing toward Picnic. "Even my asshole father-in-law. You join the Reapers, you're getting protection from the Devil's Jacks, too. Something to remember."

With that, we walked back out into the main room, leaving the remaining Nighthawks to discuss their situation.

"That went well," Ruger said quietly.

"You think?" I asked.

He shrugged. "Nobody tried to shoot anyone. That's generally a good sign."

"Yeah, I guess if your measure of success is nobody getting shot, we pulled it off."

"Bro, not gettin' shot is one of my top priorities," he replied, flashing me a grin. "Right up there with not gettin' stabbed. It's a continuum."

Pic pulled out his phone, and I figured he'd be calling Shade to give him an update. I decided to step outside, see if the prospects were still there. To my surprise, they were. Cody was polishing Horse's bike while the big biker stood over him, glaring.

"Piece of shit didn't even volunteer," he said, nodding toward the kid. "I had to remind him."

Hell, I was just impressed he hadn't run off.

"They're ready for us," Taz said, sticking his head back out the door. I walked back into the chapel to find Cord and his brothers waiting, their faces serious. Pic nodded toward him respectfully.

"You make your decision?"

"Looks like we're gonna patch over," Cord said. "I won't lie—this feels weird."

"Guess the important question is whether it feels wrong," Pic said quietly. Cord shook his head.

"What happened here—it's nothing to be proud of. A fresh start is for the best."

"Will the brothers in prison be on board?" I asked.

Cord nodded.

"Nobody has been happy with the way things went," he admitted. "Pipes started talking to Painter for a reason. He was scared. We all knew if the Reapers turned on us, the boys inside would die. We can't survive without you."

"Goes both ways," Picnic said. "Painter will be losing his parole. He'll need Pipes at his back, because our coverage down there is minimal at best."

Cord nodded, then look around. "So how is this gonna work?"

"Gage will go nomad," Picnic said. "For now he'll be acting as your president. The situation still needs to be formalized by the rest of the Reapers before you get your colors, but I don't think it'll be a problem. We haven't forgotten who you were before Marsh took over."

"My brother Taz will stay here with Gage," Hunter chimed in, nodding toward the big man standing next to him. "Officially, he'll be nomad, too. Unofficially, he'll serve as sergeant at arms. He's got one job—make sure Gage stays safe. Gage gets hurt, things will escalate in an unpleasant way."

"Happy to be here," Taz said, grinning and cracking his knuckles. "You guys like beer? I could use a beer."

"We might be able to help you out with that," Tamarack said, a smile cracking his face. "But I'm sorry to say there's a serious shortage of pussy. Marsh's crazy sister ran off all the good ones. We'll have to work on rebuilding our stock."

"Anyone seen Talia?" I asked, thinking of Tinker.

"Bitch knew better than to come here without her brother," Cord said. "If she's smart, she already left town."

"Let me know if you find her," I said. "Oh, and for the record? Tinker Garrett's under my protection, which means she's under your protection."

That startled them.

"Seriously?" Cord asked. "Woman's gorgeous, but I hear she likes 'em younger. There's this video—"

I held up a hand.

"Yeah, from now on, nobody talks about the video," I said. "Or Tinker. I hear anything disrespectful, I'll take it very personally. We clear?"

Tamarack nodded.

"She's a solid," he said. "Knew her in school. You could do a lot worse."

"Beer," Picnic said. "We need beer. The rest of this is details."

"What about the prospects?" Cord asked. "Are they Reapers prospects now?"

Pic and I looked at each other.

"Let's give that some thought," I said. "I gotta admit, they're not promising. But they're also both still outside. Neither of them made a run for it."

"We'll deal with them later," Pic said. "It's a lot to run by national. For now we'll consider them extended hangarounds. We can't figure out all this shit in one night. Usually I'd say it's time for a party, but—"

"There may not be many of us, but we're prepared to show hospitality," Cord said, breaking in. "The old ladies had some contingency plans, just in case this didn't end up in hellfire and death."

Pic laughed.

"Might want to call them, then," he said. "Let 'em know you're still alive."

CHAPTER EIGHTEEN

MONDAY AFTERNOON
TINKER

I'd heard Cooper—no, Gage—pull up to the house around three in the morning. Several bikes, actually, and a whole group of men who clomped up the stairs to his place. Not that they went out of their way to be noisy, but leather boots make a lot of noise in an old building.

When I'd left that morning, I managed not to ram my Mustang into his bike on the way to work—mostly because I love my Mustang and didn't want to scratch her up. When I took Dad to see the doctor Seattle and with my attorney, I'd need to look into evicting his ass, I decided. Carrie had been right about that. It was one thing to give him the benefit of the doubt when all I had was gossip. Once a man tells you himself that he's been lying all along, it's a lot harder to feel guilty about tossing him out.

Now it was four in the afternoon, and I'd finished work early so I could pick up the food for dinner with Carrie and Darren. Make that Carrie, Darren, and *Joel*, because apparently Carrie had texted him earlier that day, inviting him to come along just for fun. I think her logic went something like this:

Gage was bad.

Joel wasn't Gage.

Therefore, Joel must be good.

Pushy as hell, all things considered. I'd always hated that about Carrie. Hated it and loved it at the same time, because no matter how weird things might get, I knew I could count on her pushing me to do the right thing. Tonight, though . . . she'd played me to perfection. From the time I was a kid, we'd always had room for an extra chair around the table. My mother would cut off her own hand before turning down an extra guest, and Carrie knew damned well I'd nod and smile when Joel showed up rather than seem inhospitable.

Looked like I'd be having a date tonight whether I wanted it or not, and because life wasn't quite annoying enough, I'd gotten the cart with the wobbly wheel. It also made a horrible squealing noise whenever you turned it, a noise that echoed off the ancient, cracked floor tiles in Gunther's Good Groceries.

It'd needed a remodel back when I was in high school, a remodel it'd never gotten. No wonder people preferred shopping out of town. Unfortunately, I was in a pinch because Dad had taken the steaks I'd set out for dinner and given them to one of the Baxter kids for a game they were playing (don't ask). Now I had company—including a "date" for me—coming over in less than an hour, I needed a shower, and perhaps worst of all, Gunther's was out of decent wine.

Now I was running around the grocery store, trying to find some steaks that would work, something to drink, and some veggies that didn't look like they'd sat on a truck for a week before delivery.

Not the easiest of tasks.

That's probably why I wasn't paying very close attention as I rounded the corner behind the freezer aisle, running my cart smack into Gage himself. Specifically, the corner of the cart caught him in the crotch, and he doubled over with an agonized groan, catching my arm to keep himself upright.

I'd love to say I didn't enjoy the moment, but that would be a lie.

He deserved it. He deserved it *so* much.

"Oh my goodness, I'm so sorry," I said, smirking. His face had flushed dark red and he took a couple deep breaths, then slowly raised his head and met my eyes.

"Great to see you again, too, Tinker."

A vein fluttered in his forehead, and I realized I really had hurt him. Badly. Good. Except now I felt sort of guilty. Probably my mom's fault, I decided. She'd taught me to be a moral person. Bitch.

"Okay, I really am sorry," I said, frowning. "I was in a hurry and I was going too fast."

"Picked up on that," he said, and what I think was supposed to be a smile twisted his face. More of a grimace really.

Ouch.

"Are you okay?"

He stared at me, then shook his head.

"No, feels like my balls are gonna explode, and not in the good way," he said. "I'll go out on a limb here and suggest you're still pissed at me?"

"That would be a fair assessment," I admitted.

There was a definite hint of humor in his face now—still mixed with pain—and I suddenly realized his hand was on my arm. Too close. I could smell his special scent, and that was never a good thing. First came the scent, then came the tinglies, followed quickly by me doing something stupid.

Shit.

I tried to pull away, but he tightened his grip. He was strong. I'd forgotten just how strong he really was.

"Um, do you mind letting me go?" I asked.

"Are you gonna ram my crotch again?"

"No," I managed to say, feeling my cheeks flush. "I mean, you deserved it, but I'm also sorry. It genuinely was an accident."

"I'm sorry, too," he replied, and this time his smile seemed less forced. "But I promise if you stop beating me, I'll take care of Mrs. Webbly's broken toilet."

"She has a broken toilet?" I asked, confused.

"Apparently. She left me four messages about it. Said she talked to your dad but he forgot to mention it. Did you ever set up a doctor's appointment for him?"

"I'm taking him to see the specialist this week."

"Tinker?" a young man asked. A young man with a very familiar voice. Looking up, I saw Jamie Braeburn smiling at me.

That would be Jamie Braeburn, the kid I used to babysit.

My sex tape costar.

Just thinking about it made me feel like a pedophile.

"Jamie," I managed to say, the words squeaking out. I glanced between him and Gage, flushing bright red. Gage's face was carefully blank, and I couldn't tell if that was because he knew who Jamie was or because he had no clue. To the best of my knowledge, the video had never spread beyond the locals, but once something like that exists you never know who might've seen it.

"How are you doing?" Jamie asked, still smiling broadly. I hadn't seen him since our . . . adventure. He looked good. Tall and buff, his skin carefully tanned and his hair perfectly styled just like someone in a motherfucking boy band.

I'm going to burn in hell for what I did.

"Hey, Jamie, I'm Gage," my handyman said, offering his hand for a shake. Jamie took it, glancing between us. His eyes widened, and I realized he'd gotten the wrong idea.

"Gage is my—" I started to clarify, but then a loud voice cut me off. A familiar, hateful voice.

"Get the hell away from my boy," snarled Flora Braeburn. "Haven't you done enough damage already? *Slut!*"

Jamie and Gage stiffened as I slowly swiveled to find Jamie's mother bearing down on us in all of her angry, beehived fury. She was still wearing her pink waitress uniform, face pale beneath her bright red lipstick and the blue eye shadow she put on with a trowel every morning.

"Mom, back off," Jamie said, startling me with how firm his voice was. That was a man's voice, and not a happy one.

"Shut up," she snapped. "Go out to the car and wait for me while I set this hussy straight."

"Sounds like you don't have anything to say that Tinker needs to hear," Gage said firmly. He stepped up behind me, which I have to admit gave me a little thrill. Or it would've if I weren't in the middle of being called a slut by a clown woman in the middle of a grocery store.

"You're just another of her gigolos, aren't you?" Flora hissed. "She uses men and throws them away like tissues. Did you hear what she did to my little boy? Because—"

Jamie stepped between us protectively, facing her down.

Damn.

"I'll leave town this afternoon if you don't shut the fuck up," Jamie said, his voice firm, but I could the restrained anger. "What happened is none of your damned business and I've had about enough."

Then he turned his back on her, facing me as he raised a hand to touch my cheek gently.

"You doing okay?" he asked, eyes full of genuine concern.

"She's fine," Gage said, wrapping his arm around my waist. He pulled me back into his body hard, the gesture sending a very clear message. Something along the lines of him Tarzan, me Jane. Jamie crossed his arms, meeting Gage's gaze.

"Wasn't talking to you," he said.

"Slut!" Flora hissed in the background.

And that was just about enough.

"I'm in a hurry," I announced, reaching down to grab Gage's arm and tug it loose. He didn't budge. Seriously? "Let me go, Gage."

"Take your mother and get her out of this store," Gage said to Jamie, ignoring me. God, he sounded just like Brandon. Giving orders like he had the right. He didn't. *Nobody* did.

"No," I snapped, digging my nails into his wrist. "I can talk for myself, asshole."

"We'll leave just as soon as you let her go," Jamie said, looking so tough and mature that I was starting to remember why I'd gone into that back bedroom with him.

Because you lost your fucking mind, my common sense reminded me firmly.

"This isn't happening," I announced. "Gage, remove your arm or I swear to God, I'll evict your ass tonight."

"That's illegal," he said, but when I dug my fingernails into his skin, he let me go. I reached for my cart, grabbing the handle to push it toward the front of the store, because fuck drama. That's when Flora started shouting.

"You're a whore, Tinker Garrett! Your mother was a whore, too, and you're the kind of trash this town doesn't need. Go back to Seattle."

I stopped the cart.

Be smart, my common sense said. *She's just a crazy old witch who isn't happy unless she's hurting someone.*

Fuck off, I told my common sense, embracing the rage.

"Flora Braeburn, you're the biggest hypocrite that ever lived," I said, my voice strangely calm. "You've had how many husbands?"

"Six," Jamie said helpfully. "Dad was number five. Number six left three years ago—she hasn't been able to find a new one since then."

Flora gasped.

"You spend all day at that diner collecting nasty gossip," I continued. "Well, here's something you should know. Your son is a *consenting adult.* I'm a consenting adult. The only thing we did wrong was sleep together where your intrusive bitch of a niece and her friend decided to spy on us. What kind of family does that to one of their own, I'm not sure, but if you want to be pissed at someone, take it up with Maisy, not me."

"You weren't *sleeping,*" Flora snarled. "Whore."

"You're right," I said, my voice rising as I threw my hands up in the air in the center of the grocery store. "We were *fucking.* Your unattached, adult son *fucked* an unattached, adult woman in a town far away from here at a party that had nothing to do with you. So far as I know that's still legal in the United States, so maybe you should just shut the hell up before you ruin whatever relationship you happen to have with Jamie, because something tells me *he doesn't enjoy having his private business turned into entertain-ment for all of Gunther's Groceries any more than I do!"*

With that I turned again, grabbing my cart and stalking down the aisle toward the checkout counter. Daisy Wasserman—yet an-other woman I'd gone to school with, because, God knows, you wouldn't want to have any fucking privacy—scurried behind the counter as she saw me coming. She'd obviously been taking in the show. In fact, I was pretty sure half the town was currently staring at me, waiting to be sure their afternoon entertainment was well and truly over before they scuttled off like a passel of rats to share the news with the other half.

They could all kiss my ass.

Just go home to Seattle. No sane person would put themselves through this.

Daisy started scanning my items, glancing toward the still-sputtering Flora and then back at me. She'd been a couple years behind me in school, and while we'd never been friends, she'd never been a bitch, either. I wondered if she'd seen my sex tape.

Of course she had.

Everyone had. Talia and Gage probably watched it at night together to laugh at me.

Daisy scanned the last item, pausing before she totaled out the purchase.

"You know," she said carefully. "That may have been the best thing that's ever happened in this store. Flora Braeburn is like a nasty abscess infecting Hallies Falls, and Jamie seems like a decent guy. Do you have any coupons?"

I blinked, startled.

"Excuse me?"

"Do you have any coupons?" she asked again, offering me a sweet smile.

"No," I replied. "But the other thing . . . ?"

"Flora is a big zit that won't pop. Word of this has probably spread halfway to Omak by now, and I suspect the next time you stop by the bar, everyone and their dog will be lining up to buy you a drink. Not that I've ever seen you there, but if I did I'd love to sit and visit for a while. Now, I have this five-dollar-off coupon, and with our double coupon code that makes it ten. That brings your total down to forty-three dollars and sixteen cents."

She smiled at me again. I swiped my card, then hit the payment key, still off-balance.

"Thank you," I finally said.

"You're welcome," Daisy replied, then she gave me a wink. "Now, get out of here before she thinks of a comeback."

Half an hour later, I hopped out of the shower, pulled on fresh clothes, and made the executive decision that it didn't matter how cute Joel was—for once I wouldn't be doing my hair and makeup.

I just didn't have the energy.

Instead I ran downstairs to get dinner started, because this long afternoon from hell still wasn't over. We had guests coming for dinner, and come rain, sleet, or snow, nobody left the Garrett house hungry. I'd just started cubing sweet potatoes to slow roast on the grill when the kitchen door rattled.

"Tinker Garrett, if I hadn't already married that Carrie bitch, I'd be proposing to you right now," Darren declared, pushing into the room and carrying a midsize cardboard box. He set it on the kitchen island, and I stared at it, confused.

"What's that?"

"That's a case of wine," Carrie said, following him in. I stared at her, stunned—sky blue eye shadow smeared her eyelids, and somehow she'd managed to tease her hair up into a beehive. "The girls at the Hungry Chicken diner pooled their tips to buy it for you. Asked me to deliver it. Guess they appreciated your little scene with Flora this afternoon, seeing as how she treats them like shit. Thought I'd dress up in her honor."

She twirled around proudly, and I realized she was dressed entirely in pink. Not quite a copy of Flora's waitress uniform, but it wasn't half bad. I'd have laughed at the joke if I weren't dying a little inside every time I thought about what'd happened.

"How does news spread so damned fast around here?" I asked, running a hand through my still-wet hair. Darren opened a drawer and pulled out a corkscrew, opening one of the bottles as Carrie went for glasses.

"Does it matter?" Carrie asked. "This is your victory wine. You've earned it, babe. Shame we can't share some with Jamie, poor guy. I heard he dragged her home and dumped her off before heading back out of town. Guess he's had enough of her shit."

"Can't blame him," I replied, reaching for the glass Darren held out to me. It wasn't the greatest, but it was alcohol. "Now, tell me that Joel can't make it tonight and I'll be happy."

"He can't make it tonight," Carrie said. That caught my attention, and I whipped my eyes over to her.

"Seriously?"

"Seriously," Darren said. "He's a single dad and his babysitter fell through."

"I said he could bring the kiddo," Carrie added, frowning. "But he likes to keep dating separate from his daughter. How selfish is that?"

Darren and I exchanged a glance.

"Drink," he said, handing his wife a glass. "You're just grumpy because you missed the show earlier."

"True," she admitted. "But I have to say, it's damned unfair, because that's a video the whole town could've enjoyed."

"You're sick," I told her. She shrugged.

"I love Hallies Falls. I've lived here my whole life and I don't want to live anywhere else, but I'm not delusional. It can be a boring place. Nothing like a good drama to liven it up, you know?"

"Fuck off," I told her, and she laughed.

I chugged my wine and flipped them the bird, deciding the evening might not be so bad after all. An hour later I was in such a good mood that when Joel messaged Carrie to tell her he'd found a last-minute sitter and ask if the invitation was still open, I figured why the hell not, and told him to come on over.

GAGE

It was a long day.

We'd spent part of it looking for Talia, who'd gone to ground like the little skunk that she was. If she had any brains at all, she'd pulled a runner and was already in another state. I'd also had to meet with Dobie Coales to discuss my case. He filled me in on what they were doing to jack things up for the Nighthawks. Fortunately, it didn't look like it would take much pressure on our end. You'd think a career criminal would plan things out better, but Marsh had been leaning heavily on the Nighthawks' reputation and existing structure to cover his ass. This hadn't ended well for him and his fake "brothers"—we'd voted on it that afternoon, and now they were out bad. No club would ever take them in again. As for the prospects and hangarounds, we'd figure them out later. I wasn't sure about the others, but Rome had proven himself solid enough.

It would take a couple more days before we let the news go wide. This wasn't a bad thing, because Cord had to let the original brothers in prison know what was happening. Assuming all went well with the vote on the Reapers' side, the Nighthawk Raiders would cease to exist very soon. End of an era, but it was time.

Throughout this, I'd been thinking about Tinker. Specifically, about how much I'd botched talking to her and the best way to try and fix it. I'd known she was pissed off, but when she ran her cart into my crotch I'd briefly lost the ability to think or form words. Then—before I could even catch my breath to smooth things out—things fell to shit when I looked up to find the little creep from the video standing right in front of us.

I'd pictured myself taking his place under Tinker a thousand times. Pictured beating the shit out of him another thousand times, because I really didn't care for the idea of anyone else banging my woman. One thing to see it on a video—hell, I'd hardly noticed him at all, I'd been busy lookin' at her—but in real life he was a problem.

He wanted to do her again, that was obvious.

Saw it in his eyes when he looked at her. He clocked me, too, and it wasn't lost on him that I'd staked a claim. I expected him to back down like a bitch. Instead he stood up for Tinker publicly, and I hated him even more because he had balls. I'd respect that in any other man, but in his case I'd decided to make an exception.

Fuck him.

His cock had been inside her and that made him fair game.

I even gave some serious thought to ambushing him in the parking lot after our little confrontation, but another scene wouldn't exactly win points with Tinker. Then I'd gotten a text from Pic. There was a hangaround out at the clubhouse causing trouble, and they wanted me to be there when they put him in his place. Things would be like that for a while, I realized—crazy and random— until we got the town back under control. Thank fuck I could wear my own colors now, and my brothers had my back.

Now I just needed to find time to fix things with my woman.

When I finally got home that night, it was nearly ten p.m. Still needed to talk to Tinker, and the light was on in her living room, so I figured no time like the present. I climbed up the stairs toward the door, then caught a glimpse of something through the window—Tinker and the asswipe from the bar. Guitar Boy. They were standing next to each other and the fuckwad was just about to kiss her. Jesus, how many men did the woman have chasing after her?

Feeling rage build, I pounded on the door and they jumped apart. Then Tinker was answering it, Guitar Boy behind her.

"Cooper, what the hell?"

"The name is Gage. We need to talk," I said coldly. Shooting a leave-or-I'll-murder-you look at Guitar Boy, I jerked my head toward the door. "You. Get out."

The guy hesitated, taking in my big frame, the Reapers MC cut, and the knife at my belt. Then he reached for his phone, as if checking the time.

"I should probably head out anyway," he said quickly. "The babysitter wants me home before it gets too late."

What a fuckin' pussy.

Tinker had to be thinking the same thing, because the expression on her face was priceless. Startled as hell, and a little disappointed. Hell, it'd be funny if I weren't so pissed off that the asshole had been there in the first place. He brushed past me on his way out, and I stood with Tinker in the doorway, watching as he drove off in a little Toyota Corolla.

"Nice guy," I said slowly. "Love the way he fought for you."

That snapped her out of her thoughts, and she turned on me.

"What are you doing here?" she asked. "I'm sorry I hurt you at the grocery store, but there's nothing else we need to talk about. Certainly not anything this late at night."

I backed her inside, shutting the door behind us as she kept talking.

"In fact, I think it would be a good idea if you found some other kind of living situation."

"Sure," I answered, catching her shoulders and pushing her gently toward the couch. "I can move in anytime you like. Although, I gotta admit, wasn't expecting an invite this soon."

Fire flashed in her eyes.

"You know what I meant," she snapped. I did, but I didn't care because it didn't matter. No way I'd be leaving my apartment unless it was to sleep closer to her, and if she didn't understand that yet, that's what I was here to clarify.

"Sit down," I said as the backs of her knees bumped against the couch. She sat, glaring as I walked over to the windows and carefully lowered the shades. No reason to give the whole town a show.

"Gage, you have to know I can't keep you on as a handyman," she was saying. I walked over to the sideboard and performed the same little ritual I'd done the night before. Gun out, knife off, belt coiled. Her eyes widened as I did this, and her words came faster.

"I understand that you were lying for reasons that probably make sense to you, but I can't have someone living here who—"

"Shut up, Tinker," I said casually, turning back toward her. Her mouth dropped, and then I saw a hint of fire in her eyes.

"Excuse me?" she asked, the words slow and deliberate. If looks could kill, I'd have been gone already.

"Shut up," I said again, grinning at her. Somewhere in the back of my head I knew pissing her off was the last thing I should be doing, but something about it was just so much fun. "First we're gonna talk, and then we're gonna fuck. This time I want you to really listen to what I'm saying and consider it with an open mind. Think you can do that?"

She stared at me, blinking.

"What did you say?"

"You heard me."

"You have no right to be here," she said, narrowing her eyes. "And I don't owe you a damned thing."

"Yeah, well I've done a hell of a lot of work for you over the past few weeks," I pointed out reasonably. "How much is rent on that apartment? Enough to cover all those hours? I put in that time to help you, Tinker."

"You did it so you'd have cover."

"No, I did it because it needed to be done," I said bluntly. "You were in a bad spot and . . . Hell, I don't know, Tinker. It seemed like the thing to do at the time, and seeing as I'm not some kind of charity, I obviously did it for a reason. I haven't figured all that out yet. I do know that I want you, and I'm not the kind of guy to sit back and wait for good things to come to me. These weeks I've spent here have been hell. I think about you every night. I can't remember—"

"Did you think about me while you were screwing your girlfriend?" she asked, her tone snide.

"Yeah, as a matter of fact, I did," I answered, and her mouth dropped. "I probably shouldn't have copped to that, but you don't like being lied to, so here's reality—I do what I have to do for my club.

Sometimes I won't be able to tell you all the details, but I won't lie to you again. You hear that? I will not lie to you again. Period. All I want is for us to start over—you think that's workable?"

I knelt down in front of her, putting my hands on her knees. Tinker met my eyes and we looked at each other. Wished to hell I could see what she was thinking. At least she was listening.

"You're full of shit," she said softly.

I shook my head. "No, this time I'm really not."

"I don't know," she finally said. "Tell me about your motorcycle club. I've heard about them, and what I've heard isn't good. Of course, most of that was from my ex-husband and he's a bit of a douche, so enlighten me."

"Were the Nighthawks around when you were growing up?" I asked. She nodded. "Things have changed since then, right?"

"Yes," she said. "They used to be regular guys who were part of the community. Then a bunch of them got caught up all at once and went to prison, so obviously there was more going on than what we saw on the surface."

"My club—the Reapers—are more like the original Night-hawks," I said. "We're part of our community. We do a lot of chari-table things, we hang out together. We're a family. A big, loud family that has a shitload of fun."

"But you commit crimes together, too," she replied, meeting my gaze steadily. "Brandon prosecuted a major case against a club. I'm not an idiot."

"We're one percenters," I told her. "Do you know what that means?"

"Not a clue."

"It means we don't let the law get in the way of living our lives," I continued. "We ride our bikes, we party. We have a hell of a good time, and we'll do whatever it takes to keep that life. For the most part it has nothing to do with the civilian world—our battles are our own, and you should know that the Reapers are the dominant club in this region. That means we have alliances with smaller clubs like the Nighthawks, but ultimately we call the shots. What the Nighthawks have been doing—harassing the community, that kind of thing—that's what happens when a club falls out of balance. I came here to fix things. Marsh Jackson is going to prison, and so are his boys. It's time to rebuild the club in Hallies Falls, turn it back into what it was when you were growing up."

A sudden pounding on the door startled us, and Tinker sighed.

"God, I swear, if that's Mrs. Webbly . . ."

I snorted. "I told her I'd get to the toilet tomorrow. She has two bathrooms."

"Let me talk to her," Tinker said, pushing my hands off her knees. She stood and had started toward the door when the pounding came a second time, and a man shouted, "Are you okay, Ms. Garrett? This is Tony Allen, with Hallies Falls PD. Can you open the door?"

Fucking hell. Tinker hesitated, then shot me a quick question with her eyes. Did this have anything to do with me? I shook my head in quick denial, following and standing behind her as she opened the door. A young deputy—hardly old enough to shave— looked at us with wide eyes.

"Um, we got a call requesting a welfare check," he said slowly. "A friend of yours called, said he was concerned about a man coming into your home. Can you step outside, Ms. Garrett?"

Oh, that fucker. *That cowardly little fucker.* Guitar Boy hadn't had the nerve to stand up to me so he'd called in the cops for no damned good reason. Just what I needed.

"Of course," she said, following him. I knew the drill here. He'd talk to her separately, make sure I wasn't forcing her to do anything. If she truly wanted to jack me up, now would be her opportunity. I considered that. Tinker was pissed at me—really pissed. She could tell him I'd lied about my identity, not that much would come of it. The club's lawyers could fix anything that needed fixing, and the local cops followed the Nighthawks' lead. Still, I was a little surprised when she finished talking to the guy and came back inside.

"Sorry about that," she said as we watched him walk down the street to his squad car. "I think Joel called them. He was worried you'd hurt me or something."

"Must've been real concerned," I said, crossing my arms and leaning against the doorframe. "He made that phone call just as soon as he got his own ass a safe distance from yours. Sounds like a real winner to me."

She looked up at me. "You know, for a lying asshole you're sort of cute when you're jealous."

"What?" I asked, thrown off-balance.

"You heard me," she replied crisply. "Let's finish talking. I'm tired and want to go to bed. Alone, for the record. The sooner we get this over with, the better."

"You have a way of making a man feel appreciated," I said wryly, and she shrugged as she closed the front door before sitting on one of the wingback chairs in the living room. I settled on the couch, leaning forward with my arms on my knees to pin her down with my stare.

"Okay, so you were busy avoiding admitting that you're part of a criminal organization," she said quietly.

"If that's what you really believe, why didn't you have that cop haul me out of here?"

"Would he have done it?" she asked. "Because most of my life, I've heard that the Nighthawks own the local police. According to my ex-husband, bikers come hand in hand with crime and corruption. What's your side of the story?"

"You know, it's a lot easier to hook up with girls who don't ask so many questions," I muttered, frowning.

"Feel free to hook up with someone else, then," she snapped. I studied her face, then let my eyes slowly slide down her body. Jesus, the woman really was perfect. Cute jeans shorts that cupped her ass just right, another of those halters she loved so much. It was red with big white polka dots, and for once she wasn't wearing any makeup and her hair was loose and tangled.

"You look good like this," I said. She raised a brow.

"Not wearing so much makeup, and the fancy hair," I clarified, taking her in. "Not that I don't love it when you dress the other way—it's hot as hell. But this works, too."

"You're trying to distract me," she whispered. I slid forward off the couch, standing in front of her. Stepping forward just a little too close, my knees bumped hers. Looking down at her from this perspective, it almost seemed like she was about to give me a blow job. Christ, what I wouldn't give for that to be the case. Giving my lips a lick, I reached down, sinking one hand into her sleek hair.

"Are you distracted?" I whispered.

She swallowed.

"Maybe a little," she said. "But I'm not some stupid little girl you can bully or control."

"I don't want to bully or control you," I said slowly. "Although I would very much like to fuck you. Tonight. You want it, too."

Tinker's eyes flickered to the fly on my jeans. It wasn't much, just a quick glance, but I felt the blood start to pool in my cock.

"You're full of shit."

"Yeah," I admitted. "But I was serious about not lying to you again. I did what I had to do, and believe me when I said I didn't enjoy it. If there's something I can't tell you in the future, I'll be straight up about it. And there will be things I can't tell you. That's how club life works."

It took everything I had to hold her head gently, rubbing one thumb slowly up and down her cheek as she considered the words. Part of me wanted to smash her face into my cock, face-fuck her until the tears ran down her cheeks.

Jesus.

There was something wrong with me.

"I'm not the best of men," I said. "But you know what? I've looked into your ex. He's supposed to be one of the good guys, but he isn't. I'm not sure how much you really know about him—"

"Don't bring him into this," she whispered, sighing. I watched as she raised a hand, running one finger delicately down the length of my fly. My dick grew like she had some sort of magical pull on it, which I guess she did. "You're right about one thing."

"What's that?"

She glanced up at me, her eyes assessing. "We *are* going to fuck tonight. But don't think it's because I like you, or that I've forgiven you. Sex isn't always about emotions. A guy who's screwed plenty of strippers should know that, right?"

"Right," I replied slowly, wondering if I'd heard her right.

"So tonight won't be about emotions," she said, her eyes piercing. "And it doesn't mean I'm okay with your lies or that I've forgiven you or anything. Maybe it's just been a long time, and I'd like to get laid. This is my decision and it has nothing to do with you, so don't take it personally."

"I can work with that."

"Oh, and Gage?"

"Yeah?"

"My dad's a sound sleeper, but try not to lose control. No screaming, no matter how good it feels."

I blinked, then nodded my head, wondering if this was some kind of twisted hallucination.

CHAPTER NINETEEN

TINKER

I couldn't believe I'd just said that.

His eyes widened, and I heard his quick intake of breath as I trailed my fingers along the length of his erection. It grew bigger with every stroke, and I thought about how long it'd been since I'd had sex.

Since Jamie.

Wasn't like I had much opportunity in Hallies Falls. Between Dad and the business, I'd been focused on survival. Why shouldn't I give myself a little treat? I worked hard. I'd wanted this guy from the first minute I'd seen him, and while I didn't think I'd ever be able to forgive his lies— *No. Don't follow that thought. This is your night for fun, not thinking.*

Fair enough. I'd spent the last eighteen months of my life thinking and it hadn't exactly gotten me anywhere. Reaching for his zipper, I slid it down slowly, enjoying the way his breath quickened at my touch.

Gage's cock bulged against the thin, dark fabric of his briefs, and I traced the shape of it again with my fingers. He was big—longer than Brandon, but also wider. I found myself smirking, thinking of my ex and his tiny dick.

Fuck him, and fuck everything he stood for.

Brandon would hate me sleeping with a biker.

Wrong as it was, the thought gave me all kinds of satisfaction. Not as much satisfaction as I planned to take from Gage tonight, though. Then I'd kick him out on his lying ass, but for now?

Time to enjoy.

Grabbing the top of his briefs, I tugged them down, exposing his erection. He was cut, the head red and round, the broad glans hard and tight with need. He moaned as I leaned forward, flicking it twice with my tongue before pulling away. His hand tightened in my hair, and for an instant I thought he might hold me there. Then he let me go.

"Dangerous game you're playing," Gage whispered, the sound harsh.

"I'm not playing," I told him, wrapping my hand around his dick and pumping it twice. Hard. "You want more, you better get those pants off."

I watched as his big hands caught the side of his pants, sliding them down to crumple on the floor. I'd seen his bare chest lots of times, but never the rest of him. He didn't disappoint. Thick, muscled thighs. I leaned forward, catching the tip of his cock in my mouth, running my tongue around it like a lollipop as I started to slowly jack the shaft with my hand.

Gage's body shuddered, and I felt a surge of power and arousal at the same time. This big, scary man was at my mercy, and I loved it.

I loved it even more when I caught his ass in my hand and squeezed. Tight, hard muscle. Gage wasn't carrying anything extra—Brandon's gym-honed body had nothing on him. Then his hips surged, pushing farther into my mouth, and I forgot all about Brandon.

GAGE

I'd never seen anything sexier than the bobbing of Tinker's head as she went down on me.

Not that I'd won the war, or even the battle.

She wasn't some young girl I could blow off with easy answers, and I knew we still had a lot of shit to figure out. I'd run fresh out of fucks to give over about that, though, because her lips were wrapped tight around my dick and it was sweet as hell.

Heh.

Guess sex really was different when you cared about the person. I'd never quite believed that until now, but damned if it wasn't true because this was the best blow job I'd ever gotten in my life and then some.

Too good.

Her hand crept between my legs, fondling my balls, and I had the sudden, horrible realization that if she didn't stop soon I'd blow my load. Not my plan—I wanted to come inside her cunt, preferably after she came first.

I told my feet to step away but nothing happened.

Well, fair enough—what kind of fucking idiot backs off from a blow job? *You, because you're playing the long game.* It took everything I had to pull away, but I did it. My fingers still held her head.

"Feels like I've been waiting forever," I told her. "And I'm not a kid. Don't want to blow my wad too fast. Ladies first and all that."

"Hard to argue," she said with a slow smile, rising to face me. Tightening my hand into her hair, I pulled her in for a kiss, tasting myself on her lips. She opened for me and my tongue slid inside. It wasn't our first kiss and I already knew her taste, but I had to admit—I'd been halfway convinced that I'd imagined how good it was.

This wasn't imaginary.

Reaching around with my other arm, I jerked her against me, pressing her hard against the length of my body as the kiss deepened. My cock was a rock against her stomach, urgent and desperate. Guess things weren't going so slow for the first time after all . . .

Letting her hair fall free, I reached down to grab her ass, boosting her into my arms. Tinker's legs wrapped tight around my waist as I laid her down on the couch, grinding into her the whole time.

No more waiting.

No more interruptions and no more lies.

Sliding my hand down between our bodies, I backed off just enough to unzip her shorts. Her panties were wet for me already.

I wanted a taste of that.

Somehow I managed to break off the kiss, sliding off her to kneel beside the couch. An instant later I had her shorts off and her legs draped over my shoulders, right where they belonged. 'Bout fuckin' time I got to see her pussy, considering how much mental energy I'd put into imagining it. She kept it trimmed neatly, but not totally bare, which worked for me just fine.

Good enough to eat, in fact.

Leaning forward, I spread her lips wide with my fingers as my tongue started to explore. She smelled good—*Christ, is there anything better than fresh cunt?*—and tasted even better. I licked her slowly, playing with the tiny nub of her clit.

"That's really good," she gasped, and I felt one of her hands digging into my hair. Guess turnabout was fair play. I sucked her hard for a minute, then licked again as she gasped. Then I did it again, following her cues until her gasps came closer together and I knew she was close.

I wanted to finish it for her, but I couldn't hold out.

Not any longer.

Pulling away, I rubbed her gently with my thumb as I grabbed my jeans to get a condom. Holding her gaze steadily, I ripped the package open with my teeth, pulling the rubber free and then rolling it down the length of my cock. Tinker's cheeks were flushed, and those glorious tits—tits I still hadn't seen, an oversight I planned to take care of just as soon as possible—heaved with every breath.

Grasping her hips, I jerked her to the edge of the couch and pulled her legs over my shoulders again. Then I fit the head of my cock to her opening and slowly started pushing deep inside.

TINKER

He was big.

Bigger than I expected, even though I'd had my mouth wrapped around him earlier. I guess things tighten up inside when you're abstinent long enough, because it felt almost like the first time as he slid deep inside.

And he was *deep*, believe me.

He leaned forward, stretching my legs as he loomed over my body, pinning me down. I had a moment of realization—he was in control now, and there was nothing I could do to stop him.

Fortunately, stopping wasn't on my agenda.

Gage pulled out, then shoved back in again, harder this time. I gasped at the force of him filling me perfectly. I'd been so empty for so long—this was perfect. Reaching down, I rubbed my clit, hovering at the edge of coming. But I wasn't ready to come yet. I wanted more of this delicious tension, this buildup toward an explosion that would only get bigger if I held it off, so I pulled my fingers away.

"No," Gage grunted, catching my eyes and holding them. They were dark with need and desire and something else I couldn't quite read.

Something intense and almost terrifying.

"I want to see you come," he said. "I *need* to see you come. I've been waiting a long time for this, Tinker girl."

"It's not up to you," I whispered, and he smiled, then reached down between us, dark and terrible things written in his eyes.

"It's always up to me, babe. From now on."

I opened my mouth to argue with him, but his thumb found my clit, pushing down on it expertly right as he thrust deep inside, filling me entirely. The tension that'd been hovering right on the edge outward as my back arched. Release hit, hard and fast, carrying me with it as I cried out.

"Perfect," Gage grunted, moving faster inside me. I clenched down on him, lingering waves of pleasure washing through me as

I rode out my orgasm. *So good.* So much better than touching myself. A thousand times better, or maybe a hundred thousand times better.

I'd missed this.

You never had this, a tiny voice whispered in my head, and I had to acknowledge the truth. Brandon couldn't have gotten me off like that if his life depended on it.

"Fuck, but you're gorgeous when you come," he grunted, pounding into me. It was rough and hard—almost animalistic—and with the way he had me folded up I couldn't really even move. Not that it mattered. I was so overwhelmed and full and satisfied that I wanted to purr. Or something. I collapsed back, ready to let him use me for his own enjoyment when he caught me off guard by reaching between us again.

"You need more," he said, sliding his fingers against my clit. "A lot more. All of it. I've been suffocating, waiting for you, and I don't think you've had it any easier, have you?"

How do you respond to that?

I didn't bother, because I was too caught up in the realization that he had every intention of making me come again, and I wasn't about to fight it. Oh, hell no. Not even a little bit, because the man was right. I hadn't had it easy, and damned if I didn't deserve this.

The second time was different.

My body was already sensitized to his, so when he really started pounding into me, things moved faster. He was hard and thick and deep, every movement slickened by my desire as the need started building again. He'd bent me nearly in half, pushing me back against the cushions. Then Gage shifted over me, his movements growing less coordinated.

"I'm close, babe," he said, the words strained. "I want to take you with me again. Think you can help me out a little, here?"

My eyes closed, burned by the intensity I saw in his, and I reached down between us, my fingers tangling with his. I expected him to let me go—focus on his own needs. Instead our hands moved together as I showed him exactly what I wanted. Throughout, he stared down at me intently, sweat beading up along his forehead.

"Not sure I can hold out much longer," he gasped. "You ready?"

"Yeah," I whispered, fingers flying. Suddenly he stiffened, groaning as his entire body clenched tight. The look on his face pushed me over the edge and I came again. This time was different—no less intense, but in a new way. That had been harder, more blunt. This was softer, waves of mixed relief and pleasure sliding through me as we stared into each other's eyes.

Slowly the moment passed, and I started to notice normal things.

For one thing, he'd twisted me up like a pretzel, and my legs were starting to cramp in a serious way. Also, I was sweaty and disgusting, bare-ass naked from the waist down while he still had on his shirt and leathers.

Awkward.

"Hey, I think I should—"

"Don't," Gage said, shaking his head quickly. I frowned.

"Don't what?"

"Don't think," he replied, offering a slow smile. "Just enjoy the moment. We can think about things tomorrow. After I've fucked you a couple more times, because no way we're done for tonight."

I started to shake my head, but he let my legs slide down around his waist, then lifted me up, a feat of strength I couldn't help but appreciate. Then he was carrying me—ass still bare—up the stairs to my room, and I felt less appreciative.

"What are you doing?" I hissed in his ear as we passed my dad's door.

"Taking you to bed," he replied casually. "What did you think we're doing?"

"I didn't invite you to stay the night," I whispered pointedly, hoping he'd keep his damned voice down.

"It was implied," he replied, sounding amused. "Unless you're just using me for sex? You know, it's really unfair to take advantage of—"

"Shut up," I moaned, dropping my head against his shoulder, because he really did smell pretty good and I have to admit, having a big, strong guy carry me up the stairs sort of kicked ass. Even if he was a lying piece of shit. That's why I didn't argue when he dropped me down across my bed—hard and ready to go again—or when he pushed my head down low or even that third time in the middle of the night, when he flipped me over onto my stomach.

Suppose when you decide to end a dry spell, you might as well do it right.

GAGE

I woke up feeling smug as hell.

Took a minute to orient myself, and another to remember all that'd happened. I'd spent the night with Tinker, and a hell of a night it was. She was cuddled up tight right next to me, and I looked down to find her face relaxed in sleep. She looked different like this—no less beautiful, but most of the time she wore armor. The whole makeup/hair thing was sexy as hell and suited her perfectly, but it also gave her a layer of separation from the world. I could appreciate that.

My Reapers colors did the same for me.

Still, it felt good to see the woman behind the mask. She was real and beautiful and just a little bit sweaty and smudged—what more can a man ask for? Tinker sighed, then rolled away from me to flop on her back. Her boobs were still covered by the sheet, and I tugged it down slowly to get a better look in the morning light. Not bad. Not bad at all. Her tits were nice and round. Not huge, but lush, and they flattened gently to the sides in a way that made it clear they were all natural.

I traced a finger between them, sliding it down her stomach, taking the sheet with me. Her stomach was soft, and I leaned over to kiss it when something caught my attention.

A thin, silvery line running up toward her belly button. More than one. They were delicate, tracing across her skin, and a thousand questions burst through me because I knew damned well what those were—almost every woman I'd ever slept with who had kids had at least a few.

Stretch marks.

At some point in her life, Tinker Garrett had given birth.

The same Tinker Garrett who didn't currently have a child. Not a hint of a child. No pictures, no mention, nothing. No clues at all, except for the way she'd lost her shit over the fact that I'd lied about having children.

Balls.

I'd fucked up.

Fucked up bad.

"Hey," she said, her voice soft and fuzzy. She rolled onto her side, stretching unself-consciously, obviously still half asleep. "What—?"

That's the exact second she remembered where she was and what we'd done. Squawking, she reached for the covers and pulled them up, smacking my face in the process. Jesus, this was a bigger clusterfuck than I could've imagined, and it wasn't like it'd been simple before. I needed to get in front of the situation—otherwise she'd bolt on me. Fortunately, I had a huge advantage in this relationship because I weighed twice as much as she did, so I rolled over on top of her, pinning her down against the bed.

"Good morning," I said, kissing her. Tinker twisted her head away, scowling, because of course it couldn't be that easy with her. That was okay—she was worth fighting for, last night had made that more than obvious. We had some business to take care of first, though.

"So tell me," I said slowly. "How come you never mentioned that you had a baby?"

CHAPTER TWENTY

Tinker's face twisted as I asked the question, a mixture of pain and anger running bone deep.

"That's none of your business," she snapped. "Get off me and get out of here. Nothing's changed."

"Except that I fucked you hard all night and it barely took off the edge," I replied, taking the opportunity to push my morning wood against her stomach. "I'd love to give you another round this morning, but we need to talk first. This is why you lost your shit when I lied about having kids, isn't it?"

She blinked rapidly, water pooling in her eyes as she tried to look away. I didn't let her, though, because we needed to work through it. I wasn't sure what'd happened to her, but whatever it was had been bad. Really bad. Every instinct I had told me that if I walked out that door without us resolving this, I'd never see her again.

Not an option.

"Tell me," I whispered, dropping my forehead to hers. "I want to know. I care about you, Tinker. You can trust me."

"I don't even know your fucking name," she said, closing her eyes. "Why the hell would I ever trust you?"

"It's Gagi Alfonso Leon," I said bluntly. "My birthday is October fifteenth and my social security number is 625-54—"

"Shut up," she said, shaking her head, a motion I followed with my own head, refusing to back off. "You're crazy."

"And you're sexy as hell," I replied, taking advantage of the moment to catch her mouth for another quick kiss. "But we're talking. I lied to you about a ton of things, but all you focused on was the children. Now I find your stomach covered in stretch marks. I'm missing something here, and I got a feeling it's something pretty fucking big. Talk to me, Tinker."

"Okay," she said. "But you need to back off. Let me get dressed first. We'll get some coffee and talk about it downstairs."

"You can get dressed, but we'll talk about it up here," I countered. "We head downstairs, next thing I know you'll kick me out. I'm serious—we need to figure this out."

"Why?" she asked, sounding tormented. "We had sex. It was fun, but you told me yourself you've slept around plenty. Do you interrogate everyone you sleep with?"

"Nope, just the ones I'm serious about."

"Right," she said sourly. "And how many girls have you fed that line to?"

"Not a single damned one," I replied, which was the absolute truth. "Despite what went down here, I'm not usually the kind of man to play games. I like sex. I've had sex with a lot of women. Never been too interested in anything serious, and that's worked for me. Then I met you and it felt different, so I'm gonna check that out. I'm smart enough to see we're not gonna get anywhere until we sort this out. Get dressed and we'll talk."

With that, I rolled off her, biting back any comment as she leaned over and grabbed her crumpled shirt for cover. Too little, too late—I'd already seen everything she had to offer.

She disappeared into an attached bathroom that looked like a newer addition to the house. I suspected her dad had put it in for her. Tinker had always been his angel, something I'd learned from talking to the long-term tenants. They all thought she was the shit, and I tended to agree.

None of them had mentioned a baby, though.

Frowning at the thought, I studied her room. It wasn't one of those shrines to the teenage years, thank fuck. She had a queen-size bed—king would be better, but we could deal with that later—and a nice-enough little bedroom set. The walls were covered in paper and while it was girly, it wasn't so bad that it gave me hives. Reminded me of the shop more than anything, and I wondered how she'd decorated her place in Seattle.

Fuck me. Seattle. Her ex lived there. The *prosecutor*. Cocksucker. Had to hate him on two fronts—not only had he hurt Tinker, hypocritical fucker was dirty as hell. Sooner or later we'd figure out all his secrets. Then I'd hold them over his head, make him give Tinker whatever she needed.

Pity.

I'd rather beat the shit out of him, but blackmail was probably cleaner in the long run. I heard the toilet flush, followed by the sink. A minute later Tinker stepped out wearing that long, silky robe of hers. The fabric was so thin that it covered a hell of a lot less than she probably realized, something I wouldn't be pointing out to her anytime soon.

"So," she said, staring at me as I lounged across her bed, arms tucked behind my head. "I thought about it and I don't think we need to talk. My business is my own."

"Your business is mine," I correctly gently.

"How do you figure?"

"I'm pushy like that," I said, sitting up to pat the spot next to me on the bed. "Come have a seat and tell me what happened. I don't know the details, but I know damned well where stretch marks come from. From the way you reacted to my lie—and yeah, I'm an asshole, et cetera, we can talk about that later—the story doesn't end happy. Tell me what happened. I need to know."

She came toward the bed, sitting down at the foot of it, well out of my reach. Then she stared at me, sighing.

"I'll tell you once," she said. "Then we're never talking about it again. Agreed?"

"No," I said, and she frowned.

"What's that supposed to mean?"

"I promised that I'd never lie to you again," I said bluntly. "Seeing as I don't know what you're about to say, I don't see how I can agree to never talk about it again. Maybe we'll *need* to talk about it."

She sighed, then stared at the wall for a minute.

"We could always fuck if you're not ready to talk," I suggested. Tinker flipped me off, then crossed her arms, taking a deep, shuddering breath to steel herself.

"Okay, here goes," she said. "I always wanted a baby. Lots of babies. Brandon wasn't so excited by the thought, but I figured he'd change his mind. He was always about looking good in public, and his mom sure as hell wanted grandchildren. But it never seemed like the right time to start a family. It didn't help that he worked crazy long hours, but I was starting my own business and . . . Well, for a long time I just figured we still had plenty of time. Then I hit thirty and we had a come-to-Jesus talk that ended with me throwing out my birth control. But I didn't get pregnant."

She stopped talking, pulling the robe more tightly around her shoulders, as if it could protect her from whatever came next.

"I'd almost given up when it finally happened," she said, eyes dimming. "I'd been tracking my fertility for years, had gotten all kinds of tests. Brandon would never get tested, though, and my doctor said there could be a thousand reasons . . . Then I got pregnant. It felt like a miracle, and I was so excited. I'd almost given up by then, you know? Anyway, I expected Brandon to be happy, but he really didn't seem to care. He was working really hard on a bunch of cases, and one of them was kind of high profile. He was going after a motorcycle club, actually."

She shot me another look. "Not yours, I don't think."

"No, wasn't the Reapers," I told her, thinking back to what I'd heard. "Smaller club. Seattle. They're under us, but their own group. Kind of like the Nighthawks."

"So getting that case was a big deal," she said. "Huge deal. He was excited to be working on something so big, and he was busy. I was excited for the baby, and while he wasn't really with me, I didn't care. Looking back, I realize we'd been living separate lives for a long time anyway. We shared a house and had sex sometimes, but not that often. Other than that, I think I spent more time talking to his paralegal than to my own husband."

"Sounds like a real prince."

She snorted. "You have no idea. It's worth mentioning that he cheated on me at least once, with another attorney who worked in his office. May have happened more than that, now that I look back. I'd stopped caring at that point."

"Why the hell didn't you leave him?" I asked, confused. "Life's short—why waste it on someone like that?"

She shrugged. "Habit? I don't know. In retrospect, it's crazy, but when you're in the moment . . . I think a part of me hoped that having a baby together would fix things. I don't know. None of it matters, because when I was eight months along I started having trouble. Spotting. Cramps. A lot of that happens late in pregnancy anyway, but one morning the bleeding started and it wouldn't stop. I lost the baby."

I'd half expected something like this. I mean, either she'd lost the kid or had given it up for adoption. I'd known that from the minute I saw the stretch marks. Still, hearing the words made it real.

"I'm really sorry, Tinker."

She blinked rapidly, and I watched as a tear ran down her face. She ignored it, staring straight ahead.

"She was a little girl. I hadn't found out ahead of time. I wanted it to be a surprise. I named her Tricia, after my mom. Brandon was in court that day and he didn't ask for a continuance or anything. He could've, you know. There's no judge on earth who wouldn't have let him go to the hospital, but Brandon didn't care enough about our daughter to be there."

"Fucking asshole."

"Yeah, you could say that," she replied. "But good riddance, you know? He finally showed up at the hospital late that night. After they'd taken her. I got to hold her, and a photographer shot some pictures, but her own father couldn't be bothered. That's when I decided I couldn't be bothered with him any more, either. Threw his rings right at him in the hospital room."

Tears ran down her face openly now. I reached for her, pulling her into my arms. She resisted at first, stiffening against me, but fuck that.

"He's a piece of shit," I told her, rubbing her back as she relaxed into my hold. "Tricia deserved better and so do you. I'm so sorry, baby. So incredibly sorry."

"I wanted her so much," Tinker whispered, starting to sob. Usually crying women freak me out, but this was different. This wasn't some bitch whining about her boyfriend. I'd never had a kid—never even considered it—but I'd seen my brothers with their children. Losing one would destroy them.

"I kicked him out," Tinker continued. "He moved in with his folks or rented something. I don't know. Didn't care. Then I hired a lawyer to take care of the divorce, but things were complicated because we owned a house and a business, and the finances were always impossible to follow. His family has money, but I didn't know how much and never understood how it works. Anyway, he still wants me to give him another chance."

No fucking way.

"You tell him to fuck off?" I asked, bristling.

She pulled back, giving me a small, hard smile. "I've made sure the situation is clear."

"I'll bet you did," I replied, reaching over to catch a piece of hair glued to her cheek with her tears, tucking it back behind her ear. "You want me to kill him for you?"

She gave a short burst of laughter, shaking her head, obviously under the impression that I was joking.

I wasn't. Not even a little.

"No, Carrie and Margarita have claimed that honor," she said. "I really miss her. Tricia, I mean. You wouldn't think you'd miss a child you only got to hold once, but I loved her from the minute I got pregnant. You have no idea how much I loved that girl . . . And now she's gone. I'd give anything to have her back. Then you came along, and made up having a family like it was a joke."

Reaching out, I caught the back of her head, sliding my fingers into her hair as I held her eyes.

"I will never lie to you again," I said slowly. "I was trying to look normal. To fit in. I needed to learn what was happening in town, and that seemed like the best way to do it. If I'd had any clue . . . Well, I wish to hell I could go back in time and change how I did things, but I can't."

She blinked rapidly. "I'm not sure I can live with that. You should probably leave, Gage. I'm . . . I'm not ready for anything real. I'm not sure I'll ever be ready again."

Fuck, I was in over my head here.

Usually I took what I wanted.

Demanded it.

I lived in a hard world, a world where the only way to win was refusing to back down, but Tinker was fragile. More fragile than I could've imagined. She was also stronger, though, too. No wonder the sex tape hadn't destroyed her life. Who gives a damn about a sex tape when your baby is dead?

"I want to kill your ex-husband," I told her, dead serious. She blinked.

"Me, too," she whispered slowly. "But she'd still be gone. That part of my life is over, even if he doesn't realize it. I'm never going back because there's nothing left for me there."

"You don't need to," I replied, rubbing a thumb down along her cheek, wiping away one of her tears. "You have a life here."

"Right," she said bitterly. "Because Hallies Falls is so fucking great. My dad's losing his mind, I'm stuck with an apartment building I can't even take care of, and everyone thinks I'm a slut."

"Jesus, listen to yourself," I said, frustrated that she couldn't see the reality of the situation. "Tinker, a couple of small-minded cunts think you're a slut. Fine. Small-minded cunts are always looking for someone to judge. You're doing a public service by giving them something to talk about. Everyone else in town thinks you're the shit—you should've seen how impressed they were when you took down that bitch in the grocery store. Open your eyes and you'll see it. And yeah, maybe your dad is losing it. He still loves you and you love him, and you have each other. And for fuck's sake, I'm taking care of the apartment building for you so stop worrying already, okay? Why don't you try living in the moment, instead of focusing on everything that's wrong?"

Her eyes narrowed.

"Living in the moment won't bring back my daughter."

"Neither will hating everything on principle."

"I think you should leave."

"I'm not leaving," I said, surprised at how strong the words came out. Hearing her tear herself down like that actively pissed me off. "And I'm not Brandon. I didn't lie to you as a joke. I don't have any kids because I take that shit very seriously. If I brought a child into this world, I'd damned well take care of it. You grew up in a great place, Tinker. Your parents loved you, you have friends, the works. I didn't. Foster care. Dad died in prison and Mom OD'd when I was sixteen. If it wasn't for the Reapers I'd have fallen apart, but they took me in like a lost puppy. I understand what it means not to have parents. I'd *never* do that to a child. Hate me all you want, but don't give me your hate for your ex, too. That's all his and he deserves it."

I closed my mouth, startled by how much I'd said. She cocked her head at me.

"You're right," she said slowly. "You aren't him. But that doesn't mean I've forgotten what you did."

It was a big concession.

"We'll work on it," I said, reaching out to touch her cheek. "Starting tonight. I'm taking you out for dinner."

She snorted. "You mean like a date?"

"Yeah, exactly like a date. We'll talk and get to know each other. Maybe go out to the clubhouse afterward and you can meet some of my brothers from Coeur d'Alene."

"Not sure I'm ready for that."

"There's a party tomorrow night," I said. "A bunch of the old ladies are coming to town."

She frowned. "That seems a little random."

I sighed, shaking my head. "It's complicated. We're making some changes in the club structure. It's about rebuilding relationships, and having the girls here will help with that. Ultimately the club is for the men, but having all the women on board helps with that a lot. We want the local girls to understand what they're part of. Let them bond with the old ladies, you know?"

"Why do you call them old ladies?" she asked, wrinkling her nose.

"Fuck if I know," I admitted. "It's just what they're called. They're our women—our property."

"I'm not sure which part of that offends me more, the old or the property."

"They're both terms of respect," I said firmly. "If a woman's your old lady, it means you trust her. Not just with your life, but with all your brothers' lives, too. Property is the same way—it's about making it clear to everyone that you're under our protection. They fuck with you, the Reapers will make them pay. Women in our world consider it an honor."

"That's bullshit," she said, eyes sparking. Good. She'd seemed so defeated when she'd talked about her daughter, but now she was coming back. Here was the woman who kept fighting—exactly what I wanted to see.

"Only if you consider 'old' an insult," I replied. "You saying that being old is a bad thing? You know, in the Reapers the older guys mentor the younger ones. Out in the regular world, people stick to their own age groups, but in the MC world everyone is together. You might want to reconsider before making a snap judgment."

Tinker narrowed her eyes. "And property?"

I sighed. "I think you need to see it to understand. Give me a chance, okay? Get to know my people and you'll see what I'm talking about. It's different, but it's good. We're a family."

She still looked skeptical, but she nodded her head.

"Okay, I'll try to keep an open mind," she agreed.

"So I'll pick you up at six."

"I didn't say I'd go out with you."

Yeah, she didn't get a choice, although I was smart enough not to say it.

"Six work for you?" I asked. "I'm not him. Give me a chance and I'll show you how much I'm not him."

She sighed, then nodded. "Okay. But I'm not agreeing to anything more than one date, understand? You haven't won."

"We're both gonna win," I replied, then I leaned over and kissed her. Fuck, she tasted even better this morning, which was saying something.

I could get used to this.

TINKER

"You got laid," Carrie accused when she walked into the shop at lunchtime. Randi gasped, then started giggling. I'd gotten another big order, so I'd asked her to come in for a while to help out. Mrs. Webbly had promised to check in on Dad, and while I wasn't totally comfortable with the situation, it was the best I could figure out for now.

I decided to ignore them, focusing on sprinkling salt across the tops of the caramels before the chocolate set up.

"You can pretend you don't hear me, but you do," Carrie continued. "Tinker Garrett's dry spell is officially over!"

Randi giggled harder, then mumbled something about the bathroom as she ducked out of the room. She burst out laughing for real in the distance, the little traitor.

"Jesus, now it'll be all over town," I said, glaring at my best friend.

"It's all over town already," she said, shrugging. "What, you think you have a private life? Nobody has a private life in Hallies Falls, Tinker. Get used to it. The minute Joel Riley called in a welfare check to make sure you weren't being murdered by some big, scary biker I got three text messages and a photo of his motorcycle parked outside your place."

"I should've guessed that, but sometimes I like to pretend that I have an independent, adult existence."

Carrie rolled her eyes. "You love us and you know it. Now, tell me everything. Was he good in the sack? Have you told him to fuck off for lying to you? I'm really torn here . . . On the one hand I hate him with the fiery passion of a thousand suns for what he did, but on the other you got laid. Tough call."

"Welcome to my world," I muttered, taking a quick glance to be sure Randi was still gone. "So here's the scoop. He showed up last night and we had sex and it was incredible. I'm still not quite sure how that happened."

"Do you regret it?"

"Yes and no," I admitted. "I mean, yes, in that I'm sure it was a mistake and he's a horrible person. But it felt really good. *He* was good. As in, the guy has crazy skills when it comes to getting a woman off. Way better than Brandon ever was."

"Better than Jamie?" she asked, leaning forward and licking her lips.

"You're a pervert," I said.

"And? Answer the question."

"Yes, he was better than Jamie. Best I've ever had, actually. Are you happy?"

"Uh-huh," she said, smiling dreamily. "I'm assuming you threw his ass out and then evicted him, right? Doesn't matter how good he is in bed, the man's a liar and a criminal."

"Do you mind if I run home for lunch?" Randi asked, walking back into the kitchen. She was looking down at her phone, frowning.

"Yeah, everything okay?"

"Um, yes," she muttered. "Actually, no. That big wildfire to the west has been growing and they've put Chelan on evacuation alert. My grandparents have a place in the hills, and the fire's gotten close enough that Mom's driving over and helping them pack some stuff up, bring them back home. She wants me to check on the kids."

"Do you want the rest of the day off?" I asked, and she winced.

"I need the money," she admitted. "We got a little behind on rent, and . . . Well, you know how it goes."

Yeah, I did. Her mom had probably lost a bundle at the casino again. Useless bitch.

"You can have the afternoon off, paid," I said, knowing it was stupid because it wasn't like a few hours of vacation pay would make a difference in that situation. She'd been a hard worker, though, and really flexible when I needed her. That deserved some kind of reward. And the fire situation was definitely serious—the smoke choking the air was getting worse every day.

"Really?" she asked, eyes widening. "Thanks, Tinker. I really appreciate it."

"No problem," I replied, watching as she grabbed her purse and bolted for the door, texting frantically.

"That was nice," Carrie commented.

"I'm a nice person."

"Really? Cause I heard you're a dirty . . ."

"You need to get a life."

"I know," she said, sighing. "It's kind of pathetic. How did I get so old?"

"I hear nothing ages a woman like being evil." Finishing the salt, I brushed off my hands and nodded toward the main room. "You ready to eat?"

Carrie held up the bag holding our customary sandwiches.

"Always. You know how much I love food."

We sat down at one of the tables, surrounded by my mother's things. Sooner or later I'd have to pack everything up, figure out what to do with it. Maybe I could auction it off and use the money to help pay for my new kitchen.

Assuming I *wanted* a new kitchen. Was I really planning to stay in Hallies Falls? Some days more than others, but Dad definitely didn't want to leave. Ugh.

"So you didn't answer my question," Carrie said, popping the top open on a Diet Coke. "Did you kick his ass out the door? The correct answer here is 'yes,' just in case you had any questions. I don't care how good he is in the sack, the man is scum."

"No, Brandon's scum," I said, surprising myself. "I'm not saying Gage is a Boy Scout, but Brandon's a thousand times worse."

Carrie stared at me, and for once she didn't have anything to say.

Of course, being Carrie, she recovered fast.

"I don't disagree . . ." she said. "Obviously Brandon is a piece of shit, no question. But that doesn't mean Gage is a good idea. You can't trust the guy, Tinker. He lied to you. He lied to everyone. Getting involved with him is a really bad idea."

I opened my mouth to argue, then closed it because she was right. Getting involved with Gage *was* a really bad idea, and I still wanted to do it. Desperately. My phone rang, "The Imperial March" from *Star Wars* blaring out. What the hell? Glancing down, I saw Brandon's name on the caller ID.

"Did you change Brandon's ringtone to Darth Vader?" I asked Carrie, who was suddenly very interested in rearranging the lettuce on her sandwich.

"Don't answer it," she said, dodging the question. "If he wants to talk to you, he can have his lawyer call your lawyer. That's how civilized people handle shit like this."

I hit the ignore button and leaned back in my chair, staring her down.

"You do realize you're not my mother, right?" I asked. "You aren't actually in charge of my life."

She shrugged, winking at me. My phone chimed as Brandon left a voice mail, then a text came through.

BRANDON: Call me.

Ha. Unlikely.

"I'm going out with Gage tonight," I continued, ignoring the text. "And don't worry—I'm not an idiot. I know he's a liar, but so what? I had fun last night and I want to have some more fun. I don't have to be friends with him to get laid."

"Fuckbuddies don't go on dates," she countered. "If you want a booty call, great. But why complicate it with dinner?"

My phone rang again, the ominous music ringing out through the tea shop again.

"I'm going to answer," I said, frowning. "Maybe it's an emergency. Asshole. I hate him, but we do still own a house together."

Reaching for the phone, I swiped my finger across the screen.

"Yes?"

"Tinker, it's good to hear your voice," Brandon said, using what I liked to think of as his "indulgent father" voice. *What a fucking tool.* "I need to talk to you about your tenant."

Seriously?

"Which tenant would that be?" I asked, although I had a pretty good idea already.

"The biker," he said. "A large group of them got arrested in Ellensburg this weekend. I did some research and learned more about this guy. He was lying about his name, and he's a member of a gang called the Reapers."

Holy crap. Was Brandon *spying* on me?

"This isn't news to me. What's your point?"

"Tinker, you don't need to take that tone with me. In fact—"

"Say what you have to say or shut up," I said flatly. Carrie gave me a thumbs-up across the table. Brandon didn't respond for a second, and I knew I'd caught him off guard.

"You've changed, Tinker."

"I'm not interested in your opinion. Hanging up now."

"He's a criminal," Brandon said quickly. "They all are. You don't understand what these men really are capable of. I'll need to handle the eviction for you. They're very savvy—smarter than you'd think. He'll use the law against you if he can."

"Not interested. Have your lawyer call mine about the divorce."

Turning the phone off, I set it down to find Carrie watching me, respect written all over her face.

"I've never heard you talk to him like that," she said, and I shrugged.

"You don't know everything about me," I countered.

"Yes, I do."

"Last time we were in Seattle, I threatened Brandon with a knife and told him to get the fuck out of my kitchen."

Carrie sat back in her chair so hard it nearly tipped over. Then a slow smile crossed her face. "Okay, you're right. Obviously, I don't know everything."

"Someone mark the date and time," I announced. "Carrie Constantini just admitted she doesn't know everything."

"Fuck you," she said happily. "Damn, Tinker. I'm really impressed. You owned his ass."

"Not yet, but I will," I said. "Once my lawyer gets done with him. And I'm going out on a date tonight with Gage because I want to. I'm not stupid, I haven't forgiven him, and I won't forget what he did. But I think it'll be fun and I deserve a little fun. Oh, and for the record? Joel is a giant pussy. Last night he totally abandoned me to my fate. Ran out of there like a scared little girl when Gage showed up, although I have to give him a little credit for calling in a welfare check with the cops. Although the rumors it caused will just complicate things more."

"Probably," she said gravely, still smirking. "I'm glad you had fun. Just take care of your heart, okay? It took everything I had not to hunt Brandon down and shank him after we lost Tricia. I'm not sure I'd be able to hold back twice."

"No worries. This isn't anything real, believe me. But it's been a crappy year, so why shouldn't I have fun?"

"When you put it like that, I can't think of a damned reason," she admitted. "Go, Tinker!"

CHAPTER TWENTY-ONE

Without Randi I wasn't nearly as productive as I needed to be. Fortunately I had a bit of an out—my dad had an appointment later in the week in Seattle, so I'd be driving him over on Thursday. That'd let me take care of the deliveries on my own.

By five fifteen, I'd finished shutting everything down at the shop, wanting to get home in time to primp a bit before my date started. I was just climbing into the convertible I really needed to sell at some point when I realized that I didn't have anyone to stay with Dad for the night. I'd been planning on asking Randi, and had forgotten about it when she left. *Crap.*

I couldn't go out on a date—I had to stay home and babysit my father.

"This sucks," I muttered as I pulled up to the house, because it did. I might not be under any illusions that Gage was the man of my dreams but that didn't matter. The idea of a no-strings fling had been growing on me all day, and I'd actually been excited to see him again (what can I say—sometimes hormones conquer common sense). Walking into the house, I was so busy feeling sorry for myself that I didn't notice Dad and Mrs. Webbly in the dining room at first. She was laughing and they had music playing. Country, of course. They also had what looked to be a fairly intense round of poker going, based on the carefully arranged piles of chips on the table.

Place looked like a casino.

"You have a good day?" I asked Dad, kissing the top of his head.

"Mary and I had a great time together," he told me. "It's been nice."

"Glad to hear it," I said, glancing toward Mrs. Webbly, who offered me a sweet smile.

"We've had a lovely day," she agreed. "We used to play cards like this a lot, actually. While you were living in Seattle. When your mom passed, we just sort of . . . stopped. Felt good to play again."

"We talked about her a lot," Dad said, smiling fondly. "She always used to cheat."

Mrs. Webbly laughed. "Lord, didn't she? She knew we were on to her, too. She had to know."

"Oh, she knew," he agreed. "Plausible deniability. So long as nobody called her on it, we could all keep having our fun."

They both started laughing again, and I thought about all the hundreds of times we'd sat around this exact table playing cards while I was growing up. The memories were bittersweet, but for the first time they didn't hurt. I missed my mom and I always would, but maybe I was starting to heal.

I hoped so.

"I'll be right back," I told them, heading toward the kitchen. Along the way I pulled out my phone, sending Gage a quick text.

> ME: I can't go out tonight. I know it sounds stupid, but I forgot that I needed someone to watch over my dad.

He responded immediately.

> GAGE: Mary Webbly will stay with him. We already talked. She likes the idea of you getting out

Um . . . That was a little presumptuous. I couldn't decide how I felt about his making arrangements like that. It'd been thoughtful, but pushy, too.

ME: Okay . . . Next time check with me first, okay?
GAGE: Sure. Glad to hear you're planning a next time.

Ah shit.

"No need for language like that," Mrs. Webbly said, coming up behind me.

"Sorry, didn't realize I said that out loud," I told her, feeling as sheepish as if my own grandmother had caught me out. She grinned at me, then held up a glass tumbler, giving it a little shake. Ice cubes rattled inside.

"Need more whiskey," she said. "Your dad had some, too, but not much. He'll fall asleep early, then I'll go home. Unless he's been wandering during the night?"

"No, he hasn't," I said. "Once he's out for the evening, he's out."

"Some things never change," she said, nodding sagely. "Your mother used to complain about that—how he'd snore like a train and sleep so soundly she couldn't wake him up no matter how bad it got."

"Thanks for helping us," I said, feeling suddenly awkward. "I know this isn't your responsibility."

"Bullshit. I've lived here since before you were born. If that doesn't make me family, I don't know what does. I care enough that I want to keep an eye on him for my own peace of mind. When do you see that specialist again?"

"Thursday."

"Good. Be sure and tell the doctor that while he's had trouble keeping up with the building for the last couple years, this mental stuff didn't really start until Tricia died. It was sudden."

I cocked my head at her, surprised. "I'd assumed I hadn't noticed because I was so caught up with my life in Seattle."

Mrs. Webbly shook her head.

"If that's the case, I never saw it," she said firmly.

Huh.

"Okay, I'll make sure I mention it."

"And have fun with your young man," she added. "I like him. I know he wasn't straight up with us at the start, but he had good reasons. I've lived in Hallies Falls my entire life—nearly seventy years. I've seen the Nighthawks rise and then I saw them change. Might not agree with his methods, but it's good that he came here, Tinker. I'm certain of that."

Okay . . .

"I'm going upstairs now," I said firmly, deciding this was enough. At this rate she'd start giving me sex tips next.

"Just be safe," she replied. "You be sure to use—"

"No. Just . . . No."

Her laughter rang out as I ran for the door.

Sometimes retreat is the only option.

I've never been a motorcycle kind of girl, but the sight of Gage pulling up to the curb on his Harley . . . well, let's just say we hadn't even officially started the date and my panties already needed a change. This was dangerous, I realized. *He* was dangerous, and not just because he was part of a motorcycle club. I'd been lusting after him from the minute I first saw him. In some ways, it was the first real thing I'd felt since I'd lost my mom. The first positive thing, at least.

But where could it possibly go?

All I really knew about this guy were the lies he'd told me.

Remember, this is about having fun. You don't need to marry the man. Just the thought soothed me as I watched Gage walk to the porch. Offering Dad and Mrs. Webbly a shaky smile, I stepped outside, feeling like a girl going to a high school dance. How long had it been since I'd had a date?

Since before I'd married Brandon.

"Hey," I called to Gage, waving a hand limply, deciding I didn't care for dating. I'd had sex with this man less than twelve hours ago, yet here we were. Awkward. Pretending to go through some ancient courting ritual when we'd already slept with each other seemed a bit silly.

You just want to get laid again.

(Yeah. I really did.)

I stepped down the stairs, meeting Gage at the bottom. He hooked a hand around the back of my neck, pulling me in for a fast, hot kiss that stopped all those pesky thoughts. Pure heat replaced them, and I leaned into his body, taking in his scent with a relief so intense it's hard to explain. Standing near him felt right. Safe.

You're infatuated, moron, my common sense pointed out. *Your brain isn't working right.*

I told my common sense to fuck off, then wrapped my arms around his neck, deepening the kiss.

"Get a room!" Mrs. Webbly shouted, and I jerked away guiltily. My elderly tenant and father were standing on the porch, watching us with smirks on their faces. Gage laughed, but I groaned.

"They could at least pretend to give us privacy," I muttered.

"That doesn't seem to be the way you do things around here," Gage said, turning me slowly but firmly toward his bike. We walked over to it—their eyes burning into my back—and I wondered why it hadn't occurred to me to dress for a motorcycle ride. (Probably because I wasn't a motorcycle kind of girl. Duh.) Gage handed me a helmet, and I raised a hand to touch my carefully styled hair.

"You know, I never considered that we'd be riding your bike," I admitted. Gage raised a brow, a knowing smile crossing his face.

"You're a hell of a rider, or at least you were last night in bed. You weren't worried about your hair then. Sometimes you gotta let go and enjoy a little, Tinker. Tonight's for fun, okay?"

"Okay," I said, feeling silly and almost shy. "So how does this thing work?"

"You put it on your head," he replied gently, and I rolled my eyes. "Then I'll take you for a ride before we grab some dinner at Jack's."

"You're a smartass."

"You get off on it."

Reaching for the helmet, I shrugged, pretending he wasn't right about that.

Five minutes later we'd pulled away from the house. My arms were wrapped tight around his waist and his butt was cradled in my hips, something that gave me no small pleasure (the vibration of the bike between my legs didn't exactly hurt, either). You'd think that sleeping with him the night before would've taken off the edge. If anything, it'd gotten worse—I *knew* how good Gage was in the sack, and I wanted more.

The sun was still bright, although it was low in the sky. Air rushed by my face as we headed toward the hills and I wondered where he was taking me. Not that I particularly cared. The last year and a half had been hellish, every moment of every day a crisis. Tonight, though . . . tonight I didn't have to accomplish anything.

Tonight I got to relax and enjoy.

After what felt like no time at all, Gage pulled off the highway onto a county road, and I realized where he was taking me. Mala-chi Ridge. Not a bad call—the mountain had an incredible view and lots of places where a couple could spend a few minutes getting to know each other in the privacy of the trees. Just the thought made me grin.

Gage was taking me to a makeout place!

It was cheesy and silly and wonderful all at once, because I hadn't done something this fun in years. By the time we pulled over at the top of the ridge, my entire body hummed with anticipation. Gage must've been feeling the same thing, because as he turned off the big bike's engine, he reached down to catch my hand, pushing it toward the bulge of his pants. I copped a feel and laughed.

My biker tenant wanted me just as bad as I wanted him, no question.

"So your plan is to take me up here and . . . ?"

Gage caught my thigh, giving it a squeeze. "Well, I was thinkin' we could fuck. Sorta wanted to drag you back to my apartment before we left, but I figured this might be better under the circumstances. Not that I care what your dad and Mary Webbly see, but—"

"I care," I said, finishing the sentence. I rubbed his dick slowly, imagining it inside of me. Yum. "It's a strange dynamic, living with your dad at my age. At least he was focused today."

He squeezed my fingers before pulling them away from his package.

"We better get off the bike before I strain something."

"Hey, I was just trying to be friendly."

"Let me grab a blanket, and then you can be friendly on your back."

While Gage had clearly been to Malachi Ridge before, I knew it a hell of a lot better than he did. We'd been coming here since I was a kid, first for picnics with my folks and then with my friends during high school. Carrie had lost her virginity to Darren up here, a night I remembered all too well. They'd subjected me and Margarita to their endless making-out noises in the backseat all evening, so when they finally stumbled off to do the deed, we'd been thrilled to get rid of them.

Since then, I'd always associated the ridge with parties. I'd forgotten how beautiful it was, though. Gage laid out the blanket on a patch of soft grass above rockfall, leaving us with a gorgeous, open view of the valley.

Catching my hand, Gage pulled me in for another of those powerful kisses he was so good at delivering. I melted into him, allowing myself to simply feel as his hand ran down my back, pressing me into his body. His chest was firm with muscle, and the arms holding me were tight and strong. Everything about him radiated sexy man—even his *smell* was sexy. Not that he wore any cologne or anything . . . it was all him.

Male.

His hands grew more urgent, pulling me down with him to the blanket. The soft ache I'd felt between my legs all day roared to life, sending shivers rushing through me. The need grew as he rolled over me, thrusting a knee between mine, separating and opening me for his touch.

After another long kiss, Gage tore his lips away to kiss down my neck. Then his hands were catching the bottom on my shirt, tugging it up and over my head. I had a moment of self-consciousness as he looked down on my breasts and stomach. I knew I looked good in the lacy black bra, but my stomach was still covered with those silvery lines, proof that little Tricia had been real and part of my life, even if it was only for a short time.

Some women called them war wounds.

I'd lost my war.

Then Gage kissed one of them gently, tracing along the line with his tongue until he reached my bra. Mouthing my nipple through the soft satin, he slid a hand down between us, unbuttoning my jeans. I closed my eyes, savoring the sensations running through me. Restless need. Smug satisfaction that I was doing something fun and silly for once. The warmth of the air, the smell of smoke . . .

Opening my eyes, I looked down to find Gage unhooking the front of my bra, which was covered in tiny white specks.

"What is that?" I asked. Gage kissed the underside of my breast.

"What?"

"Those little—"

He sucked my nipple into his mouth, swirling his tongue around it. My eyes closed again as I collapsed into a wilting pile of lust, forgetting all about the specks. I'm not sure how long he played with my breasts after that. Long enough to drive me crazy, until my legs were shifting beneath his, tension coiling tight inside me. This kissing stuff was great but it wasn't what I needed.

Pushing at him, I reached down to slide off my pants. Gage watched appreciatively, a slight smile playing around the corners of his mouth.

"You're in a hurry."

I shot him a look. "You have a condom? If not, I've got some in my bag."

Gage started to laugh. "You come prepared."

I stuck out my tongue at him and he laughed harder.

"Just grab the condom," I said rolling my eyes. "Oh, and get your clothes off. If I'm going to be buck naked under the open sky, the least you can do is join me."

"You're bossy in bed," he said, waggling his brows. "I like it."

"You'll like it more once you're inside me," I countered, reaching down to slide my fingers between my legs. His jaw dropped almost like a cartoon as I started fingering myself. "Ticktock, time is passing, Gage. You don't want me crossing the finish line by myself, do you?"

Just like that, his vest was off and folded, followed by his shirt, which got no such courtesy. Then he was pulling out his wallet, opening it to fish out a condom. He reached down to unlace his boots and I got frustrated.

Pushing to my knees, I caught the front of his pants and pulled him toward me commandingly. Gage grinned as I unbuckled his belt before reaching for his zipper. Seconds later the pants were around his knees, hobbling him. I took advantage of the situation to jerk him down to the ground, swinging a leg over to straddle him.

Gage's eyes darkened and the grin disappeared.

"Jesus, you're perfect," he said, his voice serious. I responded by sliding myself along his dick, slicking him up with the evidence of my desire. The feel of him against my clit—hot and hard as steel, covered with a thin layer of velvet-soft skin . . . it was almost enough to push me over the edge right there.

Damn.

"Condom?" I demanded, cocking a brow at him. Gage handed it over wordlessly. Ripping it open with my teeth, I slid down his body, leaning over to give his cock a quick kiss and nibble before rolling the condom down over it. Until that moment, he'd been letting me take the lead. That ended in an instant as his hands hooked through my armpits, jerking me up and over him. I felt him at my opening, then he shoved up, thrusting hard and deep from below. My head tilted back.

His kisses earlier had been gentle, but there was nothing soft about this. Bracing my hands on his shoulders, I moved against him, matching each of his thrusts with one of my own. Every few seconds I ground myself into him, easing the deep, needy burn in my clit as the tension inside me boiled fast and hard.

"Christ, you should see yourself," Gage grunted. I ignored him, completely focused on the satisfaction that hung just out of reach. I was close—really damned close. His hands tightened around my hips, working me as our movements grew more frantic. Then he arched his pelvis, filling me in a new way, and I flew over the edge with a moan of strangled relief and collapsed across his chest.

Gage didn't miss a beat as he rolled us over, rising on his arms above me, pounding deep as I tried to remember what my name was.

Oh, yeah. Tinker.

Opening my eyes, I looked up to find him staring down at me intently, jaw clenched as he thrust over and over, hammering me as the sweat dripped from his face. Then his movements grew more erratic, lips twisting as a sudden, powerful cry of relief broke free. His cock throbbed within me as he filled the condom, shuddering.

Slowly, Gage lowered himself again, kissing me one last time.

"Not bad," I said, smiling at him. "You should get a damned good tip for that kind of service."

Gage grinned back. "I'll be sure to bring the tip jar next time."

Catching me, he rolled to his side, tucking me into the crook of his arm. The sky had darkened, the sun very low now. The grade of the hill wasn't too steep to be comfortable, but it was definitely steep enough that we didn't have to sit up to watch the sunset.

"Wow, the smoke from the wildfires makes for a hell of a sunset," he said.

"No kidding," I replied, noticing those tiny white flakes again. I watched as one fell on his glistening chest, reaching over to touch it. It smudged, leaving a gray streak.

"Ash," Gage said. "From the fires."

I sighed, thinking of Randi's grandparents. I'd grown up with wildfires—you can't be surrounded by this much national forest without seeing them—but this year was worse than anything I'd ever experienced. I snuggled into him, relaxed and, for once, not stressed out about anything.

Okay, so maybe this wasn't such a bad idea, my common sense murmured. Just don't get cocky and do something stupid, like fall for him.

Gage kissed the top of my head, one hand rubbing up and down my back in soothing strokes as we watched the sun set. The orange lingered on the hills longer than normal, and then it hit me.

That lingering orange wasn't from the sun.

Those were fires.

Big fucking fires.

"You see that?" Gage whispered, and I nodded against his arm. "Fuckin' unreal."

Indeed.

"Randi—my shop girl—her grandparents are evacuating," I told him. "I've never seen it this bad before."

"It's all still up in the hills," he reminded me. "I know it's big, but it's a long way from town. We should be okay."

"I hope so."

"Next time we do something like that, I need to bring sunscreen," I said, shifting uncomfortably in the booth. Gage had taken me to Jack's Roadhouse for dinner. I ordered a burger and fries, because if he couldn't handle women eating for real in front of him, then we'd have a problem.

"Why's that?" he asked.

"Think I burned my boobs up on the mountain," I admitted, giggling. I had a nice buzz going and was feeling way more relaxed than I probably should've . . . but really, what was he going to do to me? We'd already had sex, and it wasn't like I was holding out for a proposal.

Gage snorted, then started coughing because I'd caught him middrink. That set me off, and he pretended to glare at me. It would've been terrifying, too, if he'd managed to keep a straight face.

"So, I wanted to ask you something," he said.

"What's that?" I asked.

"You wanna ride out to the clubhouse after this, meet some of my brothers?"

I frowned, unsure of what to say. "We've had a fun night, but I think—"

"You've got a lot of fucking nerve!" a woman shouted across the bar, and I looked up to see Talia Jackson powering toward us, and she looked pissed.

"Fuck," Gage muttered. "Let me handle this, okay? Don't listen to her."

I watched as Talia pushed her way through the bar, bearing down on us like an enraged harpy. I had a mental image of her with dirty, ratty wings and fire sparking out of her eyes, setting off a very inappropriate round of giggles. In that instant, Talia's eyes met mine, and the giggles dissolved—she wanted me dead, that was clear. It was written all over her face. Remembering her big knife, I swallowed as my buzz disappeared.

It's all fun and games until someone hacks you with a machete.

"You're a fucking whore," Talia hissed as she reached the table and lunged for me. In an instant Gage was between us. He swung her up and over his shoulder, making for the door as she started screaming. "He's a liar! He'll use you and throw you away, but not before he's pimped you out to all his friends, Tinker Garrett! That's what they do! He'll use your business as a front for running drugs, and when you get caught he'll laugh while you go to jail! The Reapers are a bunch of fucking cowards and—"

Gage pushed through the door, and while I could still hear her screeching, the words were garbled. Blinking slowly, I looked around the bar to find half the town staring at me. Then Daisy Wasserman slid into the booth across from me, reaching over to catch my hand, giving it a squeeze.

"You okay, Tinker?" she asked, her face worried. I frowned, trying to decide if I was or not.

"I'm not sure," I admitted. "Did that just happen? Like, for real? Who *does* that?"

Daisy sighed. "Yeah, that was definitely for real. Talia Jackson has to be the trashiest woman I've ever met. Why she and her brother had to pick our little town, I'll never understand. Things were so much better before they got here. You're shaking."

Holding out a hand, I realized she was right. The fingers were trembling like I'd just . . . well, like I'd just been randomly attacked in a bar.

"I want to go home," I said, my face burning. It was like the grocery store all over again—why did things like this keep happening to me? I was a nice person. I baked things and paid my taxes. My credit score was excellent, and yet here we were again. Publicly humiliated.

"You need a ride?" Daisy asked.

"I should probably find Gage," I said, trying to clear my thoughts. From outside I heard Talia screaming at him, and shuddered at the thought of going out there. "No, I changed my mind—I'll have to talk to him later because this is more than I can deal with right now. Can you give me a ride? I don't have a car here, and I'm not really sober enough to drive anyway."

"Sure," Daisy said, smiling reassuringly. "Want me to ask Jack if we can go out through the kitchen? I'm parked back there."

Talia screamed outside, and I heard Gage shouting back at her, like something on a bad reality show.

"That would be great," I said, digging through my bag for some cash. Pulling out three twenties, I set them in the center of the table, then sent Gage a quick text.

ME: Sorry. This is too crazy so I caught a ride home. Let's talk another time, okay? I had a good time but I don't want to be around her. Give me some space and then we can talk

Nice. Very civilized . . . I really liked Gage, but this side of his life didn't work for me. Not even a little bit. I needed some time to think things over.

"Okay, let's go," I said to Daisy. Eyes followed me as we walked toward the kitchen, weighing on me in silent judgment. My phone buzzed, and I glanced down to find a text from Carrie.

CARRIE: WTF?????? You had a fight with Talia at Jacks????

Ugh. Story of my entire childhood—every wall had eyes. Gage was plenty good in the sack, but drama seemed to follow him everywhere. My life was supposed to be a drama-free zone, and his stupid ex-girlfriend was in so much violation it hurt.

Daisy's little car was parked behind the bar in a space marked "Reserved for Jack," and I gave her a quick look. She blushed and shrugged, looking so cute it was almost enough to distract me from the shrieking in the distance.

Almost.

But not quite.

CHAPTER TWENTY-TWO

GAGE

"You fucking asshole!" Talia screeched, and it took all my self-control not to toss her ass into the bushes. Not a good idea, though—not with people watching us. Fucking cunt. I set her down gently enough that she didn't fall, but it wasn't a smooth landing, either.

"Shut the fuck up," I growled at her. "You don't talk to me, you don't talk to Tinker. I'm gonna give you one chance to get your ass out of town, understand?"

Her nostrils flared.

"Nobody uses Talia Jackson," she hissed. "I talked to Marsh. I know what happened, and I swear to God, you'll pay for what you did. All of you will pay!"

"Whatever," I said, turning back toward the bar. With a screech she jumped me from behind, wrapping both arms around my neck, squeezing tight enough that my vision started to blacken. Fucking cunt. I elbowed her and she dropped as I spun to face her.

"Jesus!" someone shouted. "Call the cops!"

Great, exactly what I needed.

"Talia, don't be an idiot," I told her, thankful that I had more than my fair share of experience dealing with female drama from the strip club. "You can't fight me and you have no place here."

"This is my town. Mine. When Marsh gets back—"

"Marsh isn't coming back," I said bluntly, reaching for my wallet. Keeping a close eye on her, I opened it and pulled out five hundred-dollar bills, holding them out to her. "Take the money and leave. You're young—there's no reason this needs to be your life."

She snatched the money out of my hand, baring her teeth. "I'm not some fucking whore you can pay off. I'll make you pay. I'll make both of you pay! That cunt of yours is nothing, you hear me? Nothing. She can't do what I do. She's got a stick up her ass so high that—"

A siren blipped, and we both looked up to see a cop car pulling up to the curb. Talia's eyes widened, and then she took off running. I stared after her, sighing heavily.

Tinker doesn't deserve this.

Fuck.

The same cop I'd seen the night before at Tinker's place got out of the car, looking after Talia as she ran. Then he glanced at me and I shrugged.

"We have a problem here?" he asked, looking over my MC colors nervously. We knew the local police were in bed with the Nighthawks, but I wasn't a hundred percent sure that they knew about the shift of power. I shook my head.

"She's pissed that I'm dating someone new," I said. "Went after my girl inside—Tinker Garrett—and when I hauled her out, she attacked me in the parking lot."

"That's true," someone said, and I looked over to find a gaggle of watchers.

"She went crazy," a woman said, holding up her phone. "I got the whole thing on video if you want to see it."

The cop shot me another look, then walked over to the woman, to take a look at the phone. I heard the faint, tinny sounds of the video as he watched. The recording ended, and he glanced back toward me.

"I'll need to talk to the folks inside, and get a statement from everyone," he said.

"I'm not interested in pressing charges."

"We're not at that point yet," he replied, eyes darting toward the Reapers patches on my vest. "Let's go find Tinker and take it from there."

He gestured for me to precede him into the bar, so I turned and walked back inside, all too aware there was an armed cop at my back. Never a good position. Then I stopped, because Tinker wasn't at the table, just a stack of bills to cover our dinner.

Fuck.

I turned back to the cop and shrugged. "Mind if I check my phone? Looks like Tinker went somewhere."

He gave me an assessing look, then nodded his head. I opened my vest so he could see inside, then slowly reached into the inside pocket to pull out my phone. Sure enough, there was a message from Tinker.

Double fuck.

"She's gone," I said bluntly. "Caught a ride home because of the drama."

The cop sighed, swallowing. "Okay, let me talk to a few witnesses in here and we'll see what they have to say."

"Talia Jackson was being totally crazy," one of the waitresses announced. Several other people nodded in agreement. "She just ran up to them and started screaming. Then she tried to attack Tinker, so this guy hauled her outside before she could hurt anyone."

The cop sighed again, rubbing at his temples. "Okay, and nobody wants to file a complaint or press charges?"

He looked around, but nobody responded.

"All right, I'll swing by Tinker's place to make sure she's okay, seeing as Talia's gone. If Tinker's fine, we'll call it good."

I wanted to trail the cop to Tinker's place, but the last thing I needed was to come off looking like a stalker. Not only that, I wanted to cool down first anyway. She'd asked for time, and hard as it was, I figured I should probably give her some. I decided to ride out to the clubhouse to clear my head, seeing as I really needed to check in with Pic and the boys anyway.

Only took a few minutes to get there. Outside the building I found the usual line of bikes with a prospect out front to keep an eye on them, but these bikes belonged to my brothers from Coeur d'Alene.

"Pic inside?" I asked the prospect. He nodded, and I opened the door to find the men sitting around, laughing and talking. I took in the scene, spotting Picnic, Hunter, and Cord sitting around a table in the back having what looked to be an intense talk. Then Pic spotted me and waved me over.

"How was your date?" he asked, smirking. "Looks like it ended earlier than you planned."

Rolling my eyes, I pulled out a chair and sat down heavily. Pic slid an unopened beer toward me. Popping the top, I took a drink and then set it down. "That cunt Talia showed up at Jack's. Tried to attack Tinker, made a hell of a scene."

Cord raised a brow. "You keep your shit tight?"

"Yeah," I told him. "Got Talia out of there. Gave her some money and suggested she leave town. She talked to Marsh somehow—they're out to get us, no question. Marsh made threats, too."

"Marsh won't be coming back, not for years," Hunter said, leaning forward against the table. "I like that Dobie Coales guy—doesn't blink, doesn't back down. If he says it's covered, I tend to believe him."

"If Marsh gets out somehow, we'll deal with him," Cord added grimly. "Fucker sets foot in this town, we'll put him in the ground. Still can't believe it got to this. We're lucky you didn't take our colors and call it good."

"Nobody wins if we lose good men who've been loyal for years," Pic said. "And the brothers in prison are counting on us. Hindsight is twenty-twenty, but it's not like you voted for him."

"No, he already had the club under control when I finished my term," Cord said, sighing.

Pic turned to me. "So why are you here and not standing outside Tinker's window with a boom box?"

"Because I'm stupid, but I'm not that stupid," I answered, shrugging. "Last time you told me to cool off before going to see her—I didn't and things fell to shit. Even I can learn. I'll go talk to her after I finish here."

"You gonna bring her to the party tomorrow night? London wants to meet her. All the girls do, actually. You'll be providing our entertainment for the evening."

"In that case, I'm definitely not bringing her," I announced, folding my arms and leaning back in my chair. Pic snorted, and I shook my head for emphasis. Then my president frowned.

"Ah fuck," he said. "You win. We'll be good, but for the love of God, bring the woman. Otherwise I'll never hear the end of it. Consider that a direct order from your president, for what it's worth."

Raising my beer, I gave him a little salute, then looked to Hunter.

"You taking good care of our Emmy girl?" I asked. Hunter and Picnic's daughter—Em—had been together for nearly two years now, and while the two men could stand to be in the same room together, I wouldn't have called them close.

"Em's gorgeous, like always," Hunter said, grinning. "I'm a lucky man."

"She pretty wild in the sack?" I asked, shooting a sly glance toward my president.

Pic stiffened. "Shut your fucking mouth. We're not having a conversation about my daughter's sex life. Ever."

Mission accomplished. I took another healthy swallow of beer, then pulled out my phone to see what time it was.

"Think I'll go check on Tinker before it gets too late."

TINKER

GAGE: I'll be at your place in 20 minutes so we can talk
ME: Tomorrow. Too much drama for one night
GAGE: I'm not going away Tinker. We need to deal with this

ME: Too tired. Grumpy. I have to be up early tomorrow anyway.
GAGE: 20 minutes

I dropped the phone on the couch, flopping back to stare at the ceiling. God, but I was sick of pushy men. Suddenly the strains of "The Imperial March" burst out of my phone, and I jumped.

You summoned him with your thoughts, I told myself darkly, reaching for the cell. Sure enough, Brandon was calling me, because I hadn't suffered enough for one night. *Some people die from weird, rare diseases. I'm going to die from a pushy-male overdose.*

"Yes?" I asked, my voice sharp.

"Just listen to me," he said. "Okay?"

I considered the request. "If I give you five minutes, once I hang up you don't call again. Ever. All further communication goes through the lawyers."

"Five minutes," he agreed, although I knew him far too well to believe he actually meant it. Whatever. Worst-case scenario, maybe I could get a restraining order. That'd look just great for his campaign, now wouldn't it? "I've been doing more research on your handyman. Did you know his most recent job was managing a strip club? The place was raided repeatedly, and—"

"He convicted of anything?" I asked.

"He's a gang member," Brandon insisted. "It doesn't matter if he's convicted of anything—we all know he's guilty."

"Huh, I'm not an attorney, but even I'm pretty sure that's not how it works, Brandon. Innocent until proven guilty. Oh, and he already told me about the strip club. Not a huge surprise."

Brandon fell silent for a moment.

"You knew about the strippers?" he asked, obviously shocked. "This isn't like you, Tinker. What's happened to you?"

"Brandon, you don't know me anymore," I said pointedly. "I'm not sure you ever did. Are we done?"

"No," he said quickly. "Don't hang up. Here's the thing—I want to announce soon. It would be so much better if you were here."

"No, it'd be worse, because the last thing you want is me telling all your supporters what a douchebag you are. How much you want to bet those nice people wouldn't be so quick to back you if they knew you'd decided working was more important than your child dying?"

"It wasn't like that—you had a miscarriage. I'm sorry, but women have them all the time."

Did he just actually say that?

"Did you say what I think you said?" I asked sharply. For a man so good at reading juries, he wasn't real bright.

"I'm sorry," he replied quickly. "I didn't mean it. I'm under a lot of pressure and—"

Whatever he said next, I didn't hear it because I'd already cut off the call. I pulled a couch cushion over my lap, hugging it close.

He wasn't going to make me cry again.

Not ever.

No matter how bad it hurt.

I'd survived my marriage, I'd survived losing Tricia, and when my mom passed, I made it through that, too. Brandon didn't get to hurt me—not ever again. I was still sitting there brooding when Gage knocked on the door. Leaning my head back, I stared at the ceiling, wondering if he'd go away if I just ignored him.

No, probably not. He was almost as pushy as Brandon.

Of course, Gage hadn't heartlessly abandoned me on the worst day of my life, so I guess he had that going for him. Biting back a hysterical laugh, I walked over to the door and opened it. Sure enough, a very determined-looking biker stood on my front porch.

"We'll talk outside," I said firmly, determined to stand my ground. When he didn't move out of the way, I ducked under his arm, moving past him to lean against the porch rail.

"I'm sorry about Talia," he said, studying me carefully. "Wish you'd waited for me, though."

"I'd had enough drama," I told him, shrugging, the memory of all those eyes watching me twisting my stomach. "And it's not like we're a couple."

"My dick was inside you three hours ago," he replied, eyes

narrowing. "I don't know what that makes us, but it's fair to say we've moved past landlord and tenant. Usually when I take a girl out, I like to make sure she gets back home again safe. Hard to do when she disappears on me."

"No," I said shortly, making a snap decision.

"No?" he asked.

"Just . . . no," I repeated. "I had fun, but the thing with Talia? That's a deal breaker. I can't have a crazy woman randomly attacking me all the time."

"I gave her money and told her to get out of town," he said, silently acknowledging the point.

"Oh, and I'm sure she'll just go happily, because criminally insane people always listen to reason."

Gage cocked his head. "You trying to start a fight? Because I can think of better ways to work off energy."

"God, are all men so completely clueless?" I mused. "Brandon's on my case tonight, too."

"That fucker's bothering you again?" he asked, freezing. "I'll take care of him."

I snorted. "You know, that's kind of the problem."

"What?"

"You're too much like him."

"What the fuck?" Gage asked, stepping toward me. He caught my shoulders, forcing me to turn toward him. "I am *nothing* like your ex-husband."

"You're both pushy as hell," I snapped back at him. "He's trying to protect me from you, did you know that? He's been investigating you. Says you're a criminal and that your club is a gang. Is that true, Gage? Don't bother answering—you're too good of a liar for me to believe you anyway."

"Stop it," he snarled, pulling me into his body. Then his fingers were in my hair, jerking my head back, forcing me to look at him.

"Stop what?" I asked with a sneer. "Telling the truth? Stop being afraid your crazy-ass girlfriend is going to gut me? Or did you want me to stop thinking for myself and do whatever you say, because I have to admit, I'm over it. If I wanted a man who gives me orders, I'd just go back to Brandon. At least I don't have to worry about him getting arrested all the time."

Gage's dark eyes flashed. His jaw tightened, and for an instant I wondered if I'd gone too far.

"Oh, I wouldn't count on that," he said. "His hands aren't exactly squeaky-clean."

I stilled, his eyes boring through mine as I processed what I'd just heard.

"Excuse me?" I asked.

"You heard what I said."

My thoughts raced as the implications hit me. Those fancy suits of his . . . he always said his family had money, but when we'd first gotten married, he'd only been able to afford a small ring. And the ring was important to him—he liked the idea of his wife wearing a rock. That's why he kept upgrading it.

He'd been calling me, desperate to get back together.

My lawyer couldn't seem to get the financial paperwork from his lawyer.

"Oh shit," I said, eyes widening. "Oh *shit* . . . how long?"

"Years," he replied. "At least, according to my sources. We're still looking into it."

"How is he getting away with it?" I asked, shaking my head slowly. Then I had a new thought. "Wait. What about our house?"

"What about it?"

"Did he pay for it with . . . you know."

"No idea," Gage said. "And no idea how long he's been dirty. All I know is the word's out—Brandon Graham is for sale."

"But he's a crusader," I said, still not quite believing him. "I mean, he's prosecuted motorcycle gangs like yours. He really believes in this stuff. A whole bunch of bikers went to jail—he won. And what about that serial-killer guy? He's a hero, at least that's how they see him in Seattle."

"I said he was dishonest, not stupid," he said. "A man like that with political aspirations? He's not going to throw the big cases.

It's the littler ones. Going soft on a DUI, pleading people out with time served and probation. If he was obvious about it, they'd have caught him by now. Once he announces his campaign they'll be looking closer. He can't afford a loose end like you."

I leaned into him, dropping my forehead against his chest. All of a sudden the pieces fell together, and I felt like a moron—I'd just been too busy building my business to notice.

"I'm an idiot," I said miserably. Gage's hand started rubbing my back slowly as I tried to process everything.

"No, you just don't think like a criminal."

I sighed, then looked back up at him. "And you do?"

Gage held my gaze steadily.

"Remember my promise not to lie?" he asked. I nodded, feeling sick to my stomach. "I've committed crimes. Some of them I'd do again, given the chance. Others I'm ashamed of. But I've never put an innocent man in prison because he wouldn't pay me off."

I swallowed, feeling sick to my stomach.

"Brandon's done that? I mean, it's one thing to let a guilty man go, but to set someone up . . . ?"

"Yeah, seriously," Gage said sadly. "It's happened to men I know, and it happens more than you'd like to think. Bikers are easy targets—we scare juries. Your ex has used that in the past, at least according to my sources. Those high-profile club cases helped put him on the map. I didn't make the connection at first. My brothers put it together for me."

"How long have you known?"

"Not long," he said, wrapping his arms around me, hugging me close. It felt good. Warm. Safe.

"I don't think I'm ever getting married again," I muttered, wishing I could just close my eyes and make it all go away. Travel back in time, go to a different college. Marry some nice guy who sold insurance for a living. "Who'd have thought he could get even worse? I mean, for real—what else is he hiding?"

Gage gave a soft laugh.

"Does it matter?" he asked. "You'll be free of him soon. If your lawyer can't pull it off for you, ours will. He's a fucking shark."

I shivered and he pulled me closer.

His phone gave a chime in his pocket. A loud one. Then it started buzzing.

"You better check that," I said, trying to pull away. "It's late—usually people don't get in touch this late unless it's an emergency."

"Or they're drunk," he said wryly, reaching between us to pull the phone out of his vest pocket. "Ah fuck."

"What's wrong?"

"There's a level-one fire evacuation notice," he said. "For the whole county. Emergency alert system."

"Oh crap," I said, closing my eyes. "Has the fire grown?"

Using his thumb, he typed something on the phone, shaking his head. "No, looks like there's a new one. They're calling it a complex now, because it's so big that the different fires are merging in some areas. They're also asking farmers to get in touch if they have earth-moving equipment."

I shivered.

"They must be running out of firefighters and bulldozers," I said. "I hope Randi's grandparents are okay."

"I'm sure they're fine. They're just evacuating people to be cautious. And a level one isn't that serious—it just means to be aware. You might want to pack a bug-out bag, just to be safe. But even if the fires keep growing, they'll protect the town. It's the farmers and ranchers who need to worry."

He was probably right.

"So are you gonna go to the party with me tomorrow night?" he asked, tugging me close again. I shrugged against him.

"No," I said, but my heart wasn't in it. *He smells too good. It's distracting.*

"Yes, Gage, I'd love to go to the party," he corrected wryly. "Give it a try—it's a much better answer."

"Will Talia be there?" I asked.

"Not even she's that stupid. With any luck she's left town already. If not, she will soon. We'll keep an eye out for her. You're under my protection now."

"Like I was at Jack's?" I asked. "All things considered, I'd prefer not to go through that again—I'm so embarrassed. I'm still thinking about this criminal thing, too. You said your hands aren't clean. What does that mean?"

"You know I can't answer that," he said.

"Do you . . . hurt . . . people?" I asked, swallowing. What I really wanted was to close my eyes and bury them in his chest. Pretend he was a nice guy like Joel.

Except Joel bailed on me when an angry biker showed up at my door.

"Sometimes," he admitted. "But here's something to think about. Nobody lands in my world by accident. We don't go after civilians, it's strictly opt in. Having said that, you fuck with us, we'll fuck you back. Always. You have to be tough to survive, but the rewards are worth it."

"What rewards?" I asked. "Money?"

"Money's nice," he said. "But it's really about riding our bikes. Brotherhood. The Reapers are a family, and if you show up tomorrow you'll see that for yourself. Give it a chance, Tinker."

"I need to think about it. You should probably go."

My brain knew it was for the best, even if my body didn't quite agree. He patted my back, then let me go, stepping away. Our eyes met in the darkness.

"You really want me to go?" he whispered.

I shook my head, then said, "No, but you need to. I should pack a bag. Dad and I are headed to Seattle day after tomorrow anyway, and it seems like a good idea given the evacuation alert."

"Tell me you aren't staying with your ex again."

"No way. Dad has an evaluation with a specialist, and I need to drop off some deliveries. With luck we'll come back the same day, but I figured I'd take enough for us to spend the night if we need to. Hotel room, I promise. And I'll sleep better knowing we're ready to evacuate—I doubt it'll come to that, but better to be safe."

Gage leaned down, giving me a soft, lingering kiss. The low hum of desire that'd been running through me all night flared to life, and I tamped it down firmly.

"Tomorrow night," he said.

"Let me think about it."

"I'll pick you up at six."

A smile tugged at my mouth, despite my better judgment. He smiled back at me.

"Said I wouldn't give up. We'll figure it out, okay?"

"Okay."

"Now, go pack a bag. Just in case. Oh, and if you change your mind and want me to stay over, just text."

Rolling my eyes, I flipped him off and he laughed. So the night was crazy, he'd all but admitted he was a criminal, Brandon was on the take, and there were huge fires in the hills all around us. Strangely enough, at the end, it was still one of the better dates I'd ever had.

Carrie was never, ever going to let me live this one down.

CHAPTER TWENTY-THREE

The next morning I didn't wake up until after eight, a luxury I hadn't had in years, and one I certainly couldn't afford at that point.

"Fuck," I muttered, rubbing the sleep out of my eyes. I'd forgotten to set my alarm, but usually the sun woke me up before it went off anyway. The light in the room was weird, though. Dim and sort of yellowish.

Forcing myself to get up, I wandered over to the window and opened the semitranslucent curtains.

"Well, that sucks," I muttered. The sky was deeply overcast with smoke, giving everything an orange tinge. Very post-apocalyptic. We'd had it happen before during fire seasons, so I knew it wasn't necessarily a big deal. Still, it was a little unsettling, given the evacuation warning.

I grabbed my phone and searched for the county's Facebook page, then sighed with relief. Still just a level one, although it looked like the fires had grown. Reaching for my robe, I pulled it on over my sleep shorts and top, then started down the stairs in search of coffee.

"Morning, sweetheart," Dad said when I walked into the kitchen. He had a piece of toast in front of him, along with the newspaper. Blessedly, he'd also made coffee.

"Morning," I said, giving him a kiss on the head.

"Fires are getting bad," he told me. "They've put out a level-two alert for Lamont. Still forty miles away, though. We should be fine."

"I was thinking you should pack a bag this morning just in case," I replied. "I know they'll protect the town, but we have to go to Seattle tomorrow anyway. Kills two birds with one stone. Oh, and we need to send in your medical history today, too. Let me grab the paperwork. Can you go get your prescriptions?"

"I hate doctors," he said, frowning. "I still don't see why we need to do this. So what if I'm forgetting things? Hate to break it to you, but that's what happens when you get old."

"Humor me," I said tightly. "Maybe there's a medicine that will help."

He snorted, shaking his head, but he shoved the rest of his toast in his mouth and then left the kitchen to get his meds.

The forms were more complicated than I'd realized.

We started working on them at eight thirty, and an hour later we still weren't finished. In addition to the basic history, there'd been a behavioral questionnaire for me to fill out, and one for him to fill out, too. Now we were down to listing his prescriptions, thank God.

"What's this for?" I asked, holding up a bottle.

"Blood pressure," he said. I wrote it down and then reached for another, feeling vaguely guilty that I hadn't gone through these before. He'd always been such a private person about his health, though.

That and you were in denial, my common sense pointed out.

Yeah, you got me on that one.

"Be right back," Dad said. "Need some water."

"Sounds good—grab a glass for me, too," I murmured, reaching for the last bottle. Amitriptyline. I wrote down the name, then rotated it to see the dosage. My mother's name stared up at me accusingly.

Huh.

I thought I'd cleared all her stuff out. Weird. I started to set it down, then noticed something very strange. The date was from just last month.

What the hell?

"Dad!" I shouted.

"Yeah?"

"C'mere. I found this bottle and it doesn't make any sense."

He ambled back into the dining room, setting a glass down in front of me. I held out the little bottle to him, and he frowned.

"Don't worry about that one. That's your mother's."

"It's dated from last month," I said. "If it's Mom's, why are you getting refills? And I don't recognize the pharmacy name, either."

He sighed, then shook his head. "It's embarrassing, Tinker Bell."

"Dad, I'm your daughter—I love you. You never have to be embarrassed in front of me, because we're in this together, okay? But I really need to know what's going on here. It could be important."

He sighed heavily and sat down.

"It's hard to admit," he said. "But your mother . . . well, she was having a rough time that last year. And then when the baby died . . ."

The knife twisted inside just like it always did. Would it ever stop hurting? But I guess in a weird way that would be almost worse—I never wanted to forget Tricia. The pain reminded me that she'd been real. She'd been loved.

"Your mom got depressed, sweetie," he said. "Real depressed. Enough that she needed some medicine, and you know how this town is. She didn't want anyone to know. So she started looking online and found this pharmacy . . . they put her in touch with a doctor somewhere, and he did an exam over the phone. We paid cash for everything, of course, didn't want it going through the insurance."

I frowned. "Okay, that explains the medicine, but why was it filled last month?"

Dad looked away, then swallowed.

"I got real depressed myself after we lost your mom," he said. "So I started taking them. They worked pretty good, so I kept ordering more. Sounds stupid now that I say it out loud, but . . . I'm a man. We aren't supposed to be weak like this."

Of course he'd feel that way.

Reaching over, I gave his hand a squeeze.

"It's okay, Daddy," I said, hoping he believed me. "You're the strongest person I've ever met, and being depressed doesn't change that. But I think we should talk to the doctor about it, get you a legitimate scrip. We can still fill it online so nobody sees it, okay?"

Dad gave me a sad smile, shaking his head. "I'm an old fool. Too proud, I guess."

"Well, Mom liked you," I pointed out. "And she had damned high standards. That's got to count for something. We're almost done here. I texted Randi. She's supposed to get here in about ten minutes. I'll just get this scanned and sent to them, and we'll call it good."

Naturally, the papers got stuck in the scanner.

Piece of shit.

I glared at it, wondering if I could make it work by sheer force of will. Fishing out the jammed paper, I set it up again, hoping it would work this time. I glanced at my phone nervously. At this rate I'd never get everything ready for my deliveries tomorrow. Crap.

And where the hell was Randi, anyway?

The papers started sliding through, so I decided to grab another coffee on general principle. I'd just poured the last of the tepid liquid into my mug and thrust it into the microwave when I heard a knocking on the back door. Wiping my hands off on a kitchen towel, I walked through the pantry-slash-mudroom to the back door, opening it to find Sadie standing outside.

"Hi, Sadie," I said hesitantly, trying not to stare at the livid bruises on her face. Were those fingermarks around her neck? I needed to report this, whether she wanted me to or not. It was so much worse than I'd realized the other night—it'd been dark, or maybe they'd gotten worse with time. Bruises did that sometimes. I'd had no idea.

No wonder I hadn't seen her around. She'd been hiding *this*.

"Hey," she said, eyes darting nervously as she licked chapped lips. "Um, I wanted to tell you thanks. You know, for the other night. I just . . . well, I wanted you to know that I'm not going back. I'm done with that."

"I'm really glad to hear it," I replied slowly. *Invite her in, dumbass.* "Would you like some coffee? I was just about to put on a fresh pot."

"No, that's okay. But there's one other thing I need to tell you," she said, twisting a scraggly strand of hair.

"Yes?" I asked, hoping she wouldn't spook. The girl looked skittish as hell.

"Talia Jackson. She told us that she's got something planned. Something big. Something to make all of you pay. You know, for Marsh?"

I felt a sinking in the pit of my stomach.

"She tried to attack me last night at Jack's," I said. "Do you think that's what she meant?"

Sadie shook her head. "No, I think she was talking about something bigger. I don't know what—she wouldn't tell me. I don't want to be around her anymore. I only went to see her because I'd left some of my stuff at her trailer by accident. She didn't even ask how I was feeling, you know, after . . . this."

She touched one of the bruises, and I winced.

"Have you been to a doctor?"

"Yeah, my mom made me go," she replied. *Thank God for that.*

"How about the cops?"

"No fucking way. You don't call the cops on a motorcycle club. Ever. They'll kill you, Tinker."

The sickening feeling in my stomach got worse as a terrible suspicion filled me. Gage had said his hands weren't clean—what did that mean, exactly? Had he been part of this?

I had to ask her, but I was terrified of the answer.

"Did Gage—was he part of this?"

Sadie's eyes widened, and she shook her head. "No way. I'm so sorry, I should have told you that part first. I just didn't think of it—he was out there that night, but he wasn't anywhere near when this happened. He even offered to help me afterward, but I told him no. I mean, I went into the back with them willingly, you know? It's not like I was raped."

"You're covered in bruises," I pointed out. "They hurt you. How is that not rape?"

"Because I said they could do it," she replied miserably. "Talia thought it would be fun, and I'd already slept with most of them. I don't know what I was thinking. Usually they're pretty good guys, but a couple of them were tweaking, and Marsh was all kinds of fucked up. Wasn't a good night. Talia said it'd be fine if I just took some more oxy, so I sucked it up and kept going."

"That's rape," I said firmly. "I don't care if you consented at the beginning, those are serious injuries."

"It's my own fault," she insisted uncomfortably. "Look, I don't want to talk about this, okay? I need to get back home. Just be careful."

I wanted to tell her something. Make her understand somehow that she needed help. Take her to a crisis center. Something. But she was already walking away, her shoulders stiff and her spine straight. I'd need to do some research, figure out the best way to handle the situation. My phone buzzed, and I reached for it absently, pulling it out to find a new message.

RANDI: I can't come today. Moms freaking about the evacuation warning and packing

Fuck.

There went my chances of getting the orders done today. Squinting, I looked up at the skies again. The smoke was getting worse.

ME: Ok. Keep me posted and stay safe

Walking back into the kitchen, I turned on the TV. It was a Seattle station, but hopefully they'd still have updates. As a reporter spoke, images of giant planes flying through the air and dumping clouds of red powder on the town of Chelan filled the screen. I could see massive flames licking across the tops of the hills beyond the houses.

The governor has called for a state of emergency as the Chelan Complex fires continue to grow. Much of the Okanogan and Methow regions are under evacuation alert, with firefighters around the region flocking to assist as they try to save the town of Chelan. As of yesterday, the fires were nearly twenty-five percent under control, but flare-ups during the night led to officials reducing that to less than five percent. No reports yet on how many buildings have been burned. We've been told that they won't be able to make a full assessment until the fires die down.

Wow. That was scary as hell. The newscaster continued:

Just a reminder—as of right now, the Chelan area is under full level-three evacuation, which means leave your home immediately. Don't take the time to pack or prepare first, because there isn't time. We're being told that in some areas, emergency services may not be able to respond within an evacuation area if you choose not to leave, so we're urging you—if a full, level-three evacuation is called for your area, you need to leave immediately. Fire danger is real and imminent. A level-two notice means evacuation could happen at any time, so if you get a level-two notice, start packing the car and be ready to leave. Level one means you should be aware, but that evacuation is not imminent.

"Hey."

I looked to find Gage standing in the kitchen doorway, frowning. "It's getting worse."

"Yeah, it is," I said. "I think I might cancel Dad's appointment in Seattle tomorrow. We'd have to drive right through where they're evacuating. Not sure I'm up for that. I'll still send them the paperwork, but I don't think travel is a good idea."

"We're canceling the party, too," he said, walking over to pull me into his arms. His smell surrounded me, and I thought again about poor Sadie. "Nobody likes the idea of the women driving over through this. Visibility is shit and they're shutting down highways all over the state."

"Gage, did you know that the Nighthawks hurt Sadie Baxter?" I asked. He sighed, sounding tired.

"Yeah," he admitted. "She went into the back of the clubhouse with a bunch of them, and then I found her outside later, crying. I offered to help her, but she didn't want anything to do with me. Haven't seen her since I got out of jail."

"She's covered in bruises. Did you hear her screaming or anything?"

He shook his head. "No—and I'd have noticed. She went back of her own free will, although I think Talia pressured her. It was a bad night. Marsh was out of control toward the end there. Drugged up, paranoid, and crazy as fuck. I told her to stay away from them, but some women . . . you can't make a woman respect herself. Sometimes it takes something really bad for them to leave the life. Maybe this will be enough to convince her."

Settling into his arms, I sighed. "I don't like your world very much."

"Tinker, look at me."

Tilting my head, I caught his gaze.

"That's not my world," he said firmly. "There are bikers who beat their women, no question. I'm not one of them, and we don't tolerate that shit at our clubhouse, either. If a woman wants to pull a train, fine. Some of the guys are into that. I don't much care for sloppy seconds, but whatever. We don't rape and beat little girls, though. There's a reason I came to town, and it was because Marsh and his men were out of control. The only Nighthawks left are the ones who weren't there that night, got me?"

A weight lifted off my chest.

"She told me Talia and Marsh are planning some kind of revenge," I told him. Gage snorted.

"No surprise there," he said. I frowned.

"No, she sounded really worried. You need to be careful."

"Babe, look at me." I did, meeting his gaze head on. "Marsh is in jail and he's not going to be getting out for a long time. Probably years. Neither will the men who were with him. Talia can scream and rage all she wants, but my whole club is in town, and they're watching for her. If she shows her face, we'll get her. If she's smart, she left already. I gave her some money last night. With luck, she's already used it. Either way, we'll deal with her."

"You promise?" I asked.

"Yes," he said firmly. "Now give me a kiss."

I did, leaning into him, letting myself enjoy the full body contact. He nipped and sucked at my lips, then his hands were down and around my butt, gripping it as he pulled me into his erection.

We spent a couple minutes making out, until my legs started shifting restlessly from need. It was a good thing, this breaking of the dry spell. Gage started walking me back into the pantry-slash-mudroom, kicking the kitchen door shut behind him, leaving us alone in the tiny room. Then his arms gripped my upper legs firmly, lifting me up until they wrapped around his waist.

"This is a bad idea," I whispered as he started kissing my neck, working his way down. "That door doesn't even lock."

"Who cares?"

He rocked into me, rubbing my most sensitive place, and I decided if he didn't care, I didn't, either. It wasn't like Dad thought I was a virgin, that was for damned sure. Then Gage jerked up my shirt and pulled down my bra to suck in a nipple, and all thought ceased. My handyman was dry humping me against the wall of my pantry and it was outstanding. All I wanted was him inside me, the sooner the better.

"Fuck," he groaned, pulling away. He set me down, ripping open my shorts and shoving them down around my ankles. Then he turned me around, pushing me forward as my hands hit the wall. I heard the sound of his zipper and the tear of foil. His cock found my opening and he filled me with one thrust, bottoming out almost painfully.

"God, that's good," I muttered as his hands tightened around my waist, bracing me for his hammering hips. It was good—really good. Different than what we'd done before, yet exactly what I needed. Desire flooded me, spiraling up fast and hard like a wildfire, and then I flashed over, the orgasm hitting me suddenly and without warning. I spasmed around him, moaning. Gage's fingers dug into my flesh so deep I knew he'd leave marks, but I didn't care.

I didn't care about anything.

He came a second later, grunting with satisfaction. We stayed like that for long seconds, panting, and then he leaned down over my back, rubbing my stomach gently. That's when his phone rang, and he gave an unsteady laugh.

"Not a bad way to start the day," he said.

"I'll second that," I whispered. It'd all happened so fast that if it weren't for the shorts around my knees I'd have wondered if I'd imagined it. His phone rang again.

"Should probably answer that," he said. "Waiting on a call—all our plans are fucked up because of the fires."

He didn't move to answer, though. Instead he started kneading my breasts, and I sighed happily. We were in our own little world, and whoever was out there could just stay the hell away.

Maybe we could just live in here.

Then his phone started ringing again. Gage pulled away. I heard a rustle as he zipped up his pants before answering. Pulling up my shorts, I hopped awkwardly as I fastened them, trying not to listen but totally curious at the same time.

"Who is this?" Gage asked. I heard a woman's voice but couldn't make out what she was saying. For an instant I felt jealous, then realized how stupid that was. It could be anyone. "I'm hanging up."

Her voice grew louder, talking fast. It sounded familiar.

"Talia, you need to let it go. It's over. All of it. Move away and start over before we have to take action. That's the best you can hope for."

A screech rose from the small speaker, and he glanced at me and jerked his head toward the door in a silent request for privacy.

I'd never wanted to listen in on a phone call more than that one, but I managed to do the polite thing and go back into the kitchen. The TV was still going, this time displaying a satellite map showing smoke plumes that covered half of Washington, northern Idaho, and reached up into Alberta. It looked like the whole region was on fire. Then Dad wandered in, and I was all too aware that my hair was messy and my shirt was still twisted partially around my body. Heat rose high in my cheeks. Thankfully, he didn't seem to notice.

"What's up with all the smoke?" he asked. "Someone burning brush outside?"

"There's wildfires, Dad," I reminded him, wondering how he could be so clear sometimes and so fogged at others. "We've got an evacuation warning."

He frowned. "That's no good. Is there gas in the truck?"

"We don't have a truck anymore, Daddy," I said. "We sold it, remember?"

"Oh, I must've forgotten," he said absently. "Well, that's okay. We can use your mother's car."

No, Mom's car got totaled in the accident.

"Mine's got gas," I said instead, glancing toward the pantry. Then I heard the back door slamming shut, and looked out the window to see Gage striding across the yard, his face grim.

What the hell was that all about?

My phone rang. Carrie.

"Hey, what's up?"

"You heard about Chelan, right?" she asked.

"Yeah. Bad scene."

"I know. The Hallies Falls volunteer firefighters are headed south of town—there's a new flare-up and the forest service doesn't have anyone left to respond. Darren went with them. I just got a call from my aunt. They've just moved her to level two, which means it's time to pack her up and get her out. I'm going to go pick her up and bring her back to our place, but I'm worried about the girls. They're at school. I hate to pull them out if there's no reason, but I'm not comfortable leaving town with him gone, too. Not today."

"I'm on it," I said. "Call and tell them I'll pick them up this afternoon. I've given up on working today. Randi's busy helping out her family and can't stay with Dad anyway. Those Seattle lawyers will just have to wait for their chocolate."

"Thanks, babe," she said, and I could hear her relief. "Keep them safe for me. I'm know I'm just paranoid, but—"

"Go get your aunt. It'll be okay, Carrie. I promise."

GAGE

"If the Reapers want to avoid a war for our pipeline out of Canada, you'll need to go through me," Talia said as Tinker shut the kitchen door behind me, letting me take the call in private. God, I couldn't believe how good that woman felt wrapped tight around me. She might be having her doubts, but I wasn't—we'd make this thing work one way or another. I was determined.

"You and your brother have both been making threats, but now I'm supposed to believe we can do business together? How stupid do you think I am?" I asked, wishing she'd just take the money and get out while she could. Otherwise she'd get herself killed. "You don't get it, do you? It's over. We're onto you and we're not interested in your games. You and your brother have both threatened us."

"It's finally hit me," she said bluntly. "I'm fucked. Marsh is gone and you've taken over the club. That part of my life is over and I need to move on. But five hundred bucks isn't enough. You want the Canadian connection and I have it. All I want is a finder's fee for putting you in touch with them. You let me smooth the way."

"We don't need you to smooth anything."

"They know me," she insisted. "They want to make peace with the Reapers. They know our old operation is over and they don't want you shutting them out of whatever comes next. They just don't know how to make it happen."

"Let me guess, you'll get a finder's fee from them, too?"

"That's my business, not yours. All you have to do is work with me to set it up. Then I'll take my cash and leave. I know when I've lost."

"Not interested."

"Yes, you are," she insisted. "I can make this happen today. Otherwise it could take months, and that's a lot of time and energy wasted. We both know I need money, and this the last card I have to play."

She was right.

Fuck.

"Come to the clubhouse in two hours and we'll talk to you."

"How stupid do you think I am? You want me dead."

"No, I want you gone. Big difference—one is a lot less work for all of us."

"No fucking way. If this happens, it happens in a neutral place where the Canadians can protect me during the meet," she said. "It's not an ambush. Bring as many of your brothers as you want—nobody wants to fight."

"I'll talk to the club. We'll see."

"Call me back soon, okay? It has to be today. They've got product sitting on the U.S. side of the border and nobody to move it."

"Once again, not my problem."

"Just tell them about it, okay?"

"We'll consider it."

Hanging up the phone, I glanced toward the kitchen. I could hear Tinker talking to someone in there. Probably her dad. I'd text her later, once I had a better sense of what the day looked like.

The air outside was thick and heavy. Nasty. Everything looked sort of yellowed and aged, like an old picture. Pulling out a bandanna, I tied it around my nose and mouth, then swung my leg over my bike. As I rode down the street, the prospect assigned to watch over Tinker that day passed me slowly, and I raised one hand in salute.

There were only a few bikes out at the clubhouse when I pulled up, and no one outside. Given the air quality, I couldn't blame them. Nobody should be outside in this shit. I parked, then walked inside to find Picnic, Hunter, and Taz.

"I sent the rest of the Coeur d'Alene brothers home," Pic said when he saw me. "Cord and his men went to join the firefighters— they're calling for volunteers, and I guess things are getting real damned ugly south of town. Horse and Ruger decided to go with them, too. What's your plan for the day? I don't like the look of things outside. London says the smoke's reached all the way to Coeur d'Alene."

"I just got off the phone with Talia Jackson," I told them.

"The bitch who attacked your girl last night?" Taz asked, raising a brow. "I thought you chased her off."

"She says she's got the Canadians waiting to meet with us," I replied.

"Yeah, and I have magic fairies in my wallet," Hunter said. "Who gives a fuck?"

"What does she want?" Pic asked, frowning at Hunter.

"She told me they've got product stashed south of the border that they want to move, but they're scared to do anything with it now that Marsh is gone. They want to make peace with the Reapers."

"They *should* be afraid," Taz muttered. "They've been breaking the rules, and now they're going to pay. Shitty to be them."

"What's her angle?" Pic asked.

"Money," I said. "Tinker tells me she's been making threats— this isn't exactly news—but Talia told me she wants funds to move away. That's probably true, but odds are still good that she's lying. Could be an ambush."

"I agree," Pic said thoughtfully. "Too bad we don't have more men here to deal with it. Say we figured out a way to do a meet—you think you could ID the ones you met up in Penticton, right? Might be worth the risk, assuming we can control the contact."

"Yeah, I'd know them," I said. "But it's a big risk. Although she told me we could bring as many men as we wanted, so if it's an ambush, it's not a traditional one. She's not afraid of us showing up in force."

Hunter and Taz shared a look, and I wondered what they were thinking. I didn't know the Devil's Jacks that well. We were allies now, but a few BBQs together weren't enough to seal a relationship.

"Call her back," Hunter suggested. "Put her on speaker so we can all hear."

Glancing at Pic for confirmation, I hit the callback number, setting the phone down in the center of the table. It rang twice, then Talia answered, her voice husky.

"You there?"

"We're all here," I said. "You have one minute. Talk."

"Give it to me," a man said, his voice muffled in the background. "Is Picnic Hayes there?"

"That would be me," my president said. "What do you want?"

"We want to make amends," the man replied. "We know Marsh Jackson is out of the picture. We don't want to end up like him. Tell us how we can make this right."

"You disrupted our alliances and went behind our backs," Pic said. "Once a snake, always a snake. I don't think we can help you."

"Wait," he said quickly. "Things are changing north of the border. You want us on your side, because if we go under, the southern cartels will take over and then you'll be fighting a war on two fronts. That's bad for all of us. All we want is to talk. Truce."

Pic and Hunter shared a look, and Hunter nodded slowly.

"Okay, we'll talk, but you'll be coming to us, not the other way around. It'll be completely on our terms. Where are you right now?"

There was silence on the other side.

"We're in Crownover," he finally said, naming a small town

about thirty miles north of Hallies Falls. "There's really only one place to meet, though. Bar called Jay's Place."

"Okay, stand by. We'll call with instructions," Pic said, then leaned over and turned off the phone.

"Fuckwits," I muttered. "There's maybe two hundred people in that town. That means they've got least a hundred sets of eyes on them right now, wondering what they're doing there."

Hunter pulled out his phone, searching for something.

"Looks like there's a county dump station about ten miles north of Hallies Falls. We could ride up, position ourselves, then have them come down to meet us. We hang back in the woods near the road. Too many show up or things don't look right, we bail. We could send Taz up a tree with a rifle—he was a sniper, you know."

"Fuck you," Taz replied. "No more trees. Setting up a lookout with a rifle makes sense, though."

"All in favor?" Pic asked. We all four raised our hands, then I pulled out my phone and shot Tinker a quick text.

ME: Got an errand to run. See you later today. Stay safe.

Seconds later the phone buzzed back.

TINKER: You too. I'll be at the house all day. Want to keep close to dad. Also canceling our appointment in Seattle tomorrow. FYI—just because we had crazy monkey sex in the pantry doesn't mean you're my boyfriend.

I grinned, then looked up to find the others smirking at me. "You all suck."

"Not me," Taz pointed out. "You guys might be pussy-whipped, but I'm not. Live free or die."

"Enough," Pic said. "Let's go and get this done."

"Give me a sec," I told them, grabbing my phone. "I want to message BB, make sure he stays close to Tinker. Just in case Talia's playing some fucked up game, you know? I want full coverage."

"You sure a prospect's good enough?" Hunter asked. "Can he be trusted?"

"Yes, he can," Pic replied. "Only reason BB hasn't patched in yet is that he needed a medical leave—family stuff. It's just a formality at this point. I'd trust him to keep Em or London safe."

Hitting send on the message, we stood and left the building, locking the door behind us.

CHAPTER TWENTY-FOUR

TINKER

The level-two evacuation warning came through just after noon.

First there was an emergency alert on my phone, followed seconds later by Carrie's phone call.

"Did you see that Hallies Falls is now level two?" she asked, then continued without waiting for an answer. "Can you go pick up the girls at the high school? I'm freaking out here and they're shutting down the highway."

"On my way," I said, grabbing my keys. "Dad! We have to go to the high school. Carrie's kids need to get picked up."

Dad nodded, although there wasn't much urgency in his face. Damn, he was really checked out today. I opened the door to find Mrs. Webbly standing on the porch, a suitcase clutched tight in one of her hands.

"I saw the evacuation notice," she announced serenely. "Either I'm sticking with you or I need a ride to the police station. I'd prefer to stay with you."

"You'll stay with us," I told her. "We aren't leaving town just yet, but I need to pick up Carrie's girls at the high school. Not sure how we'll all fit in the Mustang, but it's not a good idea to leave you here without a car."

"I appreciate that," she said, patting my hand. "And don't worry, honey. I know this is stressful, but Hallies Falls has been evacuated because of fires four times in my lifetime. The town has never burned, or even come close. I'm not worried, just cautious."

"Let me take that suitcase for you."

She handed it over and I carried it out to the curb, popping the trunk to set it inside next to ours, officially filling the Mustang's storage to capacity. Dad climbed into the backseat, leaving the front for Mrs. Webbly. Then the engine roared to life and we were off to the high school, which was across town.

It made for a surreal trip.

The sky was getting darker as more smoke covered the sun, and the air made my eyes water. Everywhere we saw people loading cars, and most of the businesses had their "Closed" signs up. I couldn't even see across the valley—that's how bad the visibility had gotten.

At least the twins were easy to spot outside the school. They looked just like Carrie, but they had Darren's height. I waved them over and they came running, engulfing me in their hugs.

"Thanks for coming to get us," Rebecca said. Her sister, Anna, nodded in agreement.

"This is super creepy," she added. "Can we stop by the house to grab some of our things?"

"If you go fast," I told them. "But there isn't much room in the trunk. It'll have to be small enough to hold on your lap, and you'll be squeezed in the back with my dad."

"Do you think the town will burn?" Rebecca asked, her voice unsteady.

"It's only level two," I reminded her, trying not to show any of my own nerves. "But we need to be ready."

"I don't want to lose all my stuff," Anna moaned.

"Let's worry about staying safe, all right?" I reminded her. "First thing, I doubt you'll lose anything, but if you did, it's beyond our control. There's nothing you own that's worth dying for."

Her mouth snapped shut, and for a minute I felt guilty, because that was a little harsh. Then the guilt passed, because I had more important things to worry about, like making sure none of us burned up. Mrs. Webbly handled the girls from there, and I have to say, she was brilliant. She talked brightly the entire time, telling them about the other evacuations she'd experienced through the decades.

"The forests have to burn," she reminded us. "If they don't, the new trees can't grow."

It only took the twins ten minutes to throw together their backpacks. We left the elders in the car at Carrie and Darren's house, and while the girls packed, I moved through the house with a lightweight grocery bag, collecting their laptop, the jewelry Carrie'd gotten from her grandmother, and as many family pictures as I could find. Then we headed back to our place, passing the police going door to door as we drove. The girls chattered nervously as Mary Webbly and I shared a look.

I didn't care how many times she'd been evacuated—this was officially scary as hell.

GAGE

The dump station was only ten miles from the clubhouse, but it took us nearly half an hour to reach it because visibility sucked so bad. We pulled off at one point to talk about turning around, but it really was just smoke—all the fires were to the south. If anything, we were riding away from the danger. Still didn't like being so far from Tinker, though.

Should've hung up when Talia called.

Once we pulled into the station—which was less of a "station" and more of a line of Dumpsters in a dirt parking lot—Taz and Hunter scouted for a place to hide the bikes. They found an old forest service access road back in the trees that was perfect. They'd be hidden in the trees, but still easy to access. We'd just gotten everything set up when an emergency alert hit my phone.

Level-two evacuation notice for Hallies Falls.

Fucking hell.

"Talia's just gonna have to wait," I told Pic, holding out the phone. He pulled out his own, looking thoughtful.

"No alert on mine," he said.

"Me neither," Taz added, but Hunter shook his head.

"Came through on mine."

"Coverage is spotty as hell in areas like this at the best of times," Pic concluded. "You have a tower go offline and anything's possible."

"Let me call Tinker, make sure she's all right," I said. "Then we can go."

Dialing her number, I waited for the phone to ring. Instead, I got an error message saying the call couldn't be completed.

"Fuck," I muttered. "Call won't go through. I'll try sending her a text, but I need to get back there. Her and her dad and . . . shit. All she's got to evacuate in is the Mustang. BB's there, but he's on a bike so that's no good. If a level three hits, I can load them in the bunk of the semi, and if that can't make it through the fire, nothing will."

"Yeah, you're right," Pic said. "The rest of this shit can wait. Don't panic, though. Level two isn't good, but it's not a full evacuation order, either."

"It'll come down to the wind," Hunter added, frowning. "Think it's picking up."

As if listening to his words, the massive old-growth pines above us started to sway. I hit Tinker's number and tried to call her again, I got the same error message.

Goddammit.

Maybe a text would get through. Typing out a quick message, I started jogging for my bike.

TINKER

By the time we reached the apartment building, Carrie had called saying the highway was closed, so she'd have to drive around the long way. That meant two hours minimum before she got back to town, assuming those roads managed to stay open. We made plans for the twins to stay with me at my place, agreeing that if the evacuation order came, I'd take them with me.

Mrs. Webbly ushered Dad and the girls inside to eat lunch while I started making rounds of the building. Several of the tenants had decided to leave already. Sadie and her family had just finished packing up, and the rest already had their plans. This was a huge relief, because no matter how tight we squeezed in, no way I'd be getting more people in my car.

We didn't need to leave yet, but we might soon. I'd started back across the courtyard when the phone rang.

Margarita.

"Hey," I said.

"You guys okay?" she asked anxiously.

"For now," I said. "I'm waiting for Carrie to get back—her girls are with me. Smoke is real bad, and some people are already pulling out. We're watching for now. I've packed as much as the car can hold."

"That's good," she said slowly. "Um, I'm going to text you a link. It's to one of the news channels, their live stream. Don't freak, okay? They just announced an interview that's coming, one you'll probably want to see."

"Okay . . ." I answered. "What's going on?"

"Let's just watch and see what happens," she replied, her voice strained. "Then call me back if you need to talk."

Sheesh. *Nothing ominous about that.* She hung up, and seconds later a text came through with a link to a Seattle news station. I touched it, bracing myself as the little loading thingie circled around. Then the video started and I saw a shot of Brandon in front of our house.

He looked very serious as a blonde reporter raised her microphone.

"This is Melissa Swartz, live, with Brandon Graham, who is director of the King County Prosecutor's criminal division. Mr. Graham, can you tell us about your wife and what you know of her situation?"

She turned to him, concern written all over her face. He nodded his head, the portrait of a worried husband.

"Tinker is in Hallies Falls with her father, at their family home," he said. "We're very worried about their safety, of course, because officials have just announced a level-two evacuation warning for the town. I think it's important for all of us to remember that real people are suffering right now, my wife among them. Fortunately, she has a home here in Seattle, so she doesn't risk losing everything. So many of our friends in the area may not be so lucky."

My blood pressure started to rise. Friends? Brandon didn't have any friends here. He'd only come to visit maybe three times in the last ten years, the fucking hypocrite.

"Has it been stressful, seeing this happen? Are you planning to travel to the area?"

Brandon sighed, shaking his head. "The authorities have asked us to stay away. So many roads are closed, and those that are open need to be kept clear for emergency services and those evacuating."

"Have you been in touch with Tinker?" she asked. "Has she described what it's like in the town?"

"We're in close touch," Brandon told her. "I'll admit, as a husband, what I really want to do is go to her. But as a public official, I understand how important it is for all of us to work together. This is a state of emergency, and the residents of King County can help most by offering shelter and raising funds to help those in need. We just hope that Tinker's family home isn't lost. I know it would break her heart. On a less personal note, I want everyone to know—on behalf of law enforcement and the entire legal community—that we'll investigate the causes of these fires, and if they're found to be arson, we won't rest until the perpetrators are found and punished."

Melissa nodded gravely as the feed switched back to the main anchor. I stopped the transmission, then took a deep breath, trying to calm myself. The smoke was heavy enough that I started coughing instead.

How *dare* he?

"That fucking asshole," I muttered, pushing into the kitchen. I scrolled through my contacts, finding Brandon's number and punching it.

"Tinker?" he asked. "Are you all right, sweetheart?"

"You're still right there with the reporter, aren't you?"

"Yes," he said slowly. "We're all so worried about you. Just pack up your dad and come home, all right? I'll feel so much better once you're out of there."

"That's not my home and you're the last man I'd turn to for help," I told him. I heard his hand muffling the phone as he asked the reporter to excuse him.

"This isn't the right time for this, Tinker. Stop being so melo-dramatic."

"If you want to help, send your financial papers to my lawyer," I snapped. "Or is there some kind of problem? How about this— you let me worry about evacuating and you worry whether your documentation can stand up to a forensic audit. I've been hearing some ugly rumors lately. Got anything you want to tell me?"

Silence.

Of course, it was too good to last. Brandon always landed on his feet. "I don't know what you're talking about, but we can deal with that later. I love you. I *need* you. Come home, so we can move forward with our lives."

"How many times do I have to say the same thing before you listen to me?" I asked. "Brandon, there's fires everywhere. People could lose their homes, but all you see is an opportunity for publicity. It's disgusting. *You're* disgusting. And what's this bullshit about bringing people to justice? None of the fires are even *close* to your jurisdiction!"

"Tinker, I don't care about publicity," he replied, his voice paternal. "You think it's all about the campaign, but it's not. It's about wanting you back in my life."

"You really that crazy about me?" I asked. "You want me back? Let me guess, you love me unconditionally and it's all going to be flowers and roses if I come home, right?"

"Things will be different," he insisted, his voice low. "I promise. And of course my love is unconditional. It always has been."

Liar. Time to call him on it.

"Okay, Brandon, I'll make you an offer."

"What?" he asked, his voice eager. "You won't regret this, Tinker. We're the perfect couple—you know it's true."

"Once I get back inside the house, I'm going to upload a sex tape to the internet, and then I'm sending links to everyone I know in Seattle. Including the people at your office," I said, smiling smugly. "It'll make you look terrible and probably ruin your campaign hopes, but that's nothing compared to saving our love, right?"

Brandon didn't answer, and I laughed, savoring the moment.

"You made a sex tape of us?" he finally asked. "Tinker, how could you—?"

"No, you fucking egomaniac, I made a sex tape with someone else. I didn't make it on purpose, but it exists. Right now it's not being spread too far, at least that I know of. I'd prefer it stay that way, but if it takes a video of me fucking a stripper in a hotel room going public to get you off my back, it's worth it. Last chance, Brandon. You want me, tell me to upload and I drive to Seattle. It'll be rough—all your friends and co-workers will see it—but like you said, our love is unconditional, so we'll survive it, won't we?"

I heard a choking noise through the phone and I laughed again, feeling liberated.

"It'll ruin your campaign," I continued, savoring every word. "Destroy your reputation. You'll be a laughingstock and everyone will know you've been lying about our marriage. Or I can keep my mouth shut and you can send the fucking paperwork to my lawyer. What's it gonna be, Brandon? True love forever or a divorce?"

"I . . . I can't believe—Tinker, how could you do that?"

"I'll give you thirty seconds. Then I'm hanging up and hitting the upload button."

"No!" he said. "Okay, you win. My attorney will talk to yours. We'll get the paperwork figured out."

So much for unconditional love.

"Lovely," I replied. "Make sure it's all legit. I'd hate to have any unpleasant truths come out in divorce court. Whatever shit you've been pulling, it will *not* touch me. Tread lightly, Brandon, and don't fuck around."

Then I hung up the phone and walked in through the side door, feeling like I'd lost fifty pounds. Well, probably more like a hundred and seventy—at least, that's what it said on his driver's license. Should've done it a long time ago, because I knew one thing for sure. I really would rather upload that video for everyone on earth to see than go back to his lying ass.

"You okay, honey?" Dad asked, wandering into the kitchen. I smiled at him brightly.

"I'm great," I told him. "Finally figured out how to get Brandon off his ass and move forward on the divorce."

"That sounds promising," he replied, returning my smile. "Never liked that fellow. You think you could come into the living room? There's someone at the door who'd like to talk to you. Says his name is BB. Big guy, wearing a leather vest."

I followed Dad back to the living room, where sure enough, there was a great big guy standing by the door wearing a leather Reapers MC vest. He was built like a teddy bear, all round and soft-looking. His skin was medium dark and his hair was pulled back into a long braid.

"Hi," I said, wondering why he was here. "You must be a friend of Gage's."

"I'm a Reapers prospect, Miz Garrett," he said, his voice very polite. "My name is BB, and I was assigned to keep an eye on you today. I've been cruising by every twenty or thirty minutes, but the smoke is real bad and it's getting harder to breathe out there. I figured it would be better if I came in and introduced myself."

I heard a giggle, looked over to find the twins and Mrs. Webbly watching us from the stairwell.

"What do you mean, keep an eye on me?" I asked slowly, trying to process his words.

"We've had someone watching over you whenever Gage isn't around, ever since the arrests this weekend," he said earnestly. "He's been worried that someone might come and hurt you— mostly likely that Talia chick he was—"

I held up a hand, cutting him off.

"I get the picture," I said, trying to decide how I felt about that. On the one hand, it was the same kind of controlling bullshit that Brandon would pull. On the other, I'd been attacked last night in a public bar by a crazy woman. Having someone around in case she decided to come back wasn't such a bad idea. "So what's your plan?"

"I'd like to stay in here with you," he said. "I haven't heard from Gage or Picnic—he's the president—for an hour now, and they aren't responding to my texts. Until my orders change, it's my job to keep you safe."

I studied him, shaking my head. BB seemed very earnest, but also young. Just what I needed. Another chick to shepherd.

"Have you had lunch?" Mrs. Webbly asked, coming down the stairs. He shook his head, looking sheepish.

Suddenly a massive boom exploded the air, and the entire house shook. We all stared at each other, eyes wide.

"What the hell was that?" Rebecca asked, her voice trembling.

"I don't know," I said as police sirens started to wail. "Some kind of explosion."

"I'm going to look outside," BB said.

"I'm coming with you," I told him, but he shook his head.

"It's my job to keep you safe."

"If whatever *that* was comes for us, we're fucked," I said bluntly. "We'll go together."

He swallowed and nodded, opening the front door. We walked out together to find even more smoke billowing. Visibility made it hard to know for sure what had happened, but there seemed to be a big plume rising north of town.

That's when both our phones went off, and I looked down to find another alert.

Level three—immediate evacuation for all Hallies Falls residents and the surrounding area.

BB and I shared a glance, and then I made for the door. Inside, the girls were freaking out. Mary Webbly shot me a sharp, questioning glance.

"There's been an explosion north of town," I said, wondering what the hell could've caused it. There wasn't much up there—just trees and the Nighthawks' clubhouse. There was a forest fuel depot, but that was to the east. "We have to evacuate. Go to the car. You'll be safe with us, girls."

"What about my dad? He's out there fighting this!" There was a touch of hysteria in Anna's voice.

"Save it," I said, my voice firm. "Your dad is strong and smart. He'll be just fine, but only if he knows that you're safe. Out to the car. *Now*. BB, you'll have to ride your bike—there's no room for you in the Mustang. Just stick close to me and we'll get through this just fine."

I hope.

Grabbing my keys and purse, I herded them out the front door, trying not to panic. Then I stepped through, closing and locking it behind me. Funny, all these months I'd wanted to get the hell out of Hallies Falls, but right now the thought of losing my home was almost more than I could handle.

"Take good care of it, Mama," I whispered, laying my hand against the darkened wood. Hopefully she was up there some-where, listening. A quick glance around the parking lot showed that the rest of the tenants were already gone. Gage's semi was still parked behind the building. Hopefully it was insured. Pulling out my phone, I tried to call him but it wouldn't connect, so I texted him instead.

Then I jogged over to the Mustang and climbed into the driver's seat.

"Everyone ready?"

"Let's go," Mrs. Webbly said. "It'll be good to find some fresh air."

I put the key in the ignition, turning it.

Nothing.

Frowning, I tried again. More nothing.

"Are you fucking kidding me?" I asked, hitting the steering wheel with the heel of my hand. "No fucking way. This can't be happening."

"Looks like you need a new battery," Dad said. "I'll swing by the hardware store later this afternoon, pick one up."

"Not right now, Tom," Mrs. Webbly said. "Tinker, what's our plan B?"

I didn't answer, because I had no damned clue.

GAGE

We were maybe a mile outside Hallies Falls when the explosion hit. One big, massive boom that shook the trees and echoed off the hill, then a fresh plume of smoke rose through the air. Pic waved us over, and we all pulled off to the side of the road.

"Jesus, what do you think that was?" Taz asked, looking grim.

"Nothing good," Pic replied. "I'll reach out to BB. Gage, you call Tinker."

"Way ahead of you, boss," I said, raising the phone to my ear. This time it didn't even give a token ring before the mechanical voice said the call couldn't be completed.

"Fuck," I muttered, then sent her a text instead, hoping it would make it through.

"I can't get BB," Pic said. "He'll be with Tinker, though. It's not far now."

I was already kicking my bike back to life. "No luck on my end, either. I'm heading for her house."

"Right behind you," Pic said.

"We'll be with you," Hunter added. Taz nodded, and I pulled back out onto the highway. We'd already reached the clubhouse, although I wouldn't be stopping there. The smoke started growing thicker, and then I saw flames licking through the trees on the west side of the road.

Fuck.

Heat rolled out in hellish waves, the flames exploding upward, jumping from tree to tree. The seriousness of the situation dawned on me—if one of those fell across the road, we'd be well and truly fucked. Throttling up, I tore down the highway, pulling around a broad turn to find the Nighthawk Raiders' clubhouse completely engulfed in more flame.

Holy. Fucking. Shit.

Fire was everywhere, and with a chunk of the roof covering half the road. That explosion had been the clubhouse.

What the hell had happened here?

Not that it mattered, I realized, slowing the bike to steer around the section of roof. Whatever had caused it, the town was doomed unless there was some kind of miracle. Fire to the south, and now this in the north.

Dodging the debris, we made it past the clubhouse and I sped up again. Less than a mile to town now. A cop car came screaming past us, headed in the opposite direction. I hoped to hell there were firefighters behind him. If there weren't, he'd be smart to turn tail and run.

TINKER

"We have to flag someone down to give us a jump," I said, then glanced back at BB, sitting behind us on his bike. "Unless . . . Can you jump-start a car using a motorcycle?"

"We'll find out," Mrs. Webbly said, her voice grim. I nodded tightly, then climbed out of the car and jogged back to where BB sat waiting for us.

"Car won't start," I said bluntly. "Can we jump it with your motorcycle?"

He frowned as I looked over his bike.

"I don't know," he admitted. "I guess we could try. I have cables in my saddlebag."

"We need to get the hell out of here," I told him, feeling sick. Looking around, I saw another car pulling out of the neighborhood in the distance, but most of the houses seemed to be empty already.

"Let's do it," he said. "I'll pull around front. If it works, start driving and don't stop, no matter what."

Two minutes later the hood was up and the cables were attached. BB turned over the bike. Slipping back behind the driver's seat, I said a little prayer, pushed in the clutch, and turned the key.

Nothing.

"We're so fucked," Anna whispered. I straightened.

"Don't talk like that," I said. "I'm sure the police will do a drive through, probably with a megaphone or something. Not everyone has cell phones to receive the alert. I can hear sirens coming from somewhere—we'll start by calling 911. They'll figure out a ride for us."

I climbed back out of the car as BB disconnected the battery terminals.

"Sorry," he said. "That's a sweet ride, but you're gonna have to leave it behind."

"Shit happens," I muttered, reaching for my phone. Then the sound of motorcycle engines rumbled through the air, and I looked up to see Gage and three bikers turn down the the street. Seconds later they pulled to a stop around us. I was already out of the car, wishing I could scream and hug him, but there wasn't time.

The first words out of his mouth were, "Why the hell haven't you evacuated yet?"

"The car won't start," I said tersely. My phone buzzed, and I looked down to see another emergency warning. Residents of Hallies Falls were to evacuate immediately. Emergency services personnel would not be available to assist those who refused to evacuate. Police would attempt to patrol all streets and warn all residents, but they asked everyone to check on their neighbors and provide them with assistance, particularly the elderly and the infirm.

In other words, get out now or you're on your own.

"Put them in the truck," said an older man wearing Reapers gear.

"That's Picnic—he's my president," Gage said. "And he's right—go get in the truck."

He jerked his head toward the semi.

"Okay," I said, not about to argue. I turned to shout. "Everyone out of the car! We're going in the semi."

"Start warming it up," Picnic said to Gage, then looked to me. "We'll leave as soon as we know you've got a working vehicle. The fire's headed for town fast. Fast. We had to ride through it to get here. There's no fucking time left to waste."

Dad, Mrs. Webbly, and the girls climbed out of the Mustang like clowns pouring out of a circus car. Nobody laughed, though. BB helped Mrs. Webbly across the lawn. I guided everyone around to the passenger side of the big truck. The door swung open and the girls leapt up like young gazelles. Poor Mrs. Webbly couldn't even get her foot up to the step. BB lifted her, all but tossing her into the cab. She crashed into the seat, and for an instant I thought she'd gotten hurt. Then the girls were grabbing her arms, pulling her into the back. My dad followed, and I was up after him, watching as BB ran back to his bike.

That's when I realized the truck hadn't actually started yet.

"Why isn't it working?" I asked Gage.

"Takes a minute for the plugs to heat up," he said. "No worries."

Sure enough, the truck roared to life as he turned the key to the run position. I reached for my seat belt, then he pulled the semi forward and out of the driveway. Picnic, BB, and the others rode off ahead of us, and we were on our way.

The next four hours were unspeakably awful.

According to the radio and the cell alerts we kept getting, the safest evacuation route meant driving east through Loup Loup Pass, which meant everyone would be stuck together on the same two-lane highway, inching slowly away from the fires for the next sixty miles. If another fire broke out blocking the way, we'd be fucked.

"You think this is a good idea?" I asked Gage in a low voice. "I know the road south is closed, but—"

"The road running north is on fire," he said grimly. "And the fires are even worse to the west, so this is the best we've got. Who are the girls?"

I gave a startled laugh. "Sorry, I forgot the introductions. That's Rebecca and Anna, they're Carrie's kids. She's out of town. Shit, girls—have you talked to her?"

"I texted her while we were waiting in your car," Rebecca said. "And again when we started driving. She didn't answer. I'm worried about my dad."

"I'll call her," I said, reaching for my phone. A robotic voice told me it couldn't complete the call as dialed. "Crap. Can't get through."

"Did you get my messages earlier?" Gage asked. "I tried calling, too, but no luck."

"Got nothing from you, but I had no problem talking to Margarita in Olympia," I said. "Guess it's all about where you are and who you're trying to call."

We reached the edge of town, and the truck slowed. I looked out to see a line of cars ahead of us, moving slowly through the smoke. "Wow. I didn't even realize there were that many people in Hallies Falls."

"Me, neither," Anna said, her voice still tight. "Are we going to get stuck here and burn up?"

"No," Gage said firmly.

"What about your friends on their bikes? Will they be safe?"

"They don't have the protection of a cab, but they can go a lot faster than us," he replied. "They're probably driving along the shoulders of the road. Biggest danger is some dumbass in a car hitting them in the smoke."

Suddenly I realized something. "Gage, your motorcycle . . ."

"What about it?" he asked.

"We left it."

He gave me a quick, tense glance. "Of course we did. It's just a bike, Tinker. The world is full of them. You left your car and your house. All I care about at this point is getting you out of here alive."

I gave a short laugh, because of course he was right. My Mustang was down there, too. But it was still nice to know he cared about me more than his bike.

As we climbed slowly up the ridge, I was able to look down to see massive flames tearing through the trees north of my home town. There were also police cruisers moving through the streets, their headlights turned on to cut through the smoke, but I only spotted one fire truck.

"Where do you think the rest of the firefighters are?" I asked Gage as we wound our way along the hillside.

"Probably south of town," he said. "Earlier today they called for volunteers, so things must be even worse down there. The danger seemed to be from the south—nobody saw this coming."

"It feels like the whole world is burning up," Anna said. "Do you think we'll lose our house?"

"All I care about is Mom and Dad," Rebecca told her, sniffling. I glanced back to find her eyes red and scared. "Dad's down in that. Do you think he'll be okay?"

"Your dad is smart and safe," I said, wishing I felt half as calm as I sounded. "He knows you're with me, and he knows you'll stay safe. You have to trust that he and your mom can take care of themselves, because they can. Once we all get away from here we'll find them, and you'll be safe again together. That's all the matters."

The girls nodded, although I couldn't tell if they believed me. I was too busy trying to believe myself.

We'd just reached the top of the ridge when I heard the first airplane engines.

Gage pulled around a curve and suddenly a big jetliner passed by, headed straight for town. And I do mean big—it was big like a plane that carries passengers on cross country flights, and it even had rows of windows along the side. As we watched with wide eyes, it swooped low over Halle's falls, dumping a massive plume of red from its belly.

"What's that?" Rebecca asked, her voice quivering.

"Fire retardant," I said. "They're dropping it over the town to try and save it. They'll coat as much as they can, maybe save some of the buildings."

"I hope they spray our house," Anna whispered.

Yeah. I hoped they sprayed mine, too.

It took us hours to reach Okanogan, and I was terrified every minute of it. Amazingly, Mrs. Webbly and my dad had managed to keep the girls calm. The bunk in the back had been folded into a bench seat, and they put down a small table. Dad was teaching them how to play poker. Mrs. Webbly was teaching them how to cheat.

Fortunately, I got cell service back once we'd cleared the valley, my phone pinging rapid-fire as text after text from Carrie downloaded. The girls' phones were doing the same. I dialed Carrie's number and this time she answered.

"Did you get out okay? Where are the girls?" she demanded.

"They're in Gage's semi with me," I said, turning to see them watching me anxiously. "It's your mom."

"What about Dad?"

"Have you heard from Darren?" I asked.

"Yes, he's fine," she said, her voice strained. "They've got him and the other volunteers doing excavation work—trying to control and stop it. I'm not sure it'll work. I saw the fire jumping the river as we drove away."

"Where are you now?"

"Headed east," she said. "Toward Okanogan. You?"

"Probably on the same road as you," I said, slumping back into the seat. "Thank God for that. You want to talk to the kids?"

"Please," she said. I turned and handed the phone back to them as Rebecca burst into loud tears.

"Ladies, please try to keep it under control," Gage asked, his voice tense. "I'm trying to concentrate. Visibility is shit."

"Sorry," Rebecca apologized, and their voices quieted. I sat and watched as the slowly moving line of vehicles inched forward. After a few minutes, Anna touched my shoulder.

"Mom wants to talk to you again."

I took the phone and held it to my ear, speaking quietly. "Hey, feeling better?"

"Thank you so much," she said, and it sounded like she was crying. "I'll never be able to thank you enough. I think this has been the worst day of my life. I can't believe it all happened so fast."

"How's your aunt?"

"It's been awful," she told me. "We had to evacuate faster than planned, and nothing went right. Aunt Ruby boards horses—there were twelve of them on the farm, but her trailer only carries eight. We managed to load six before the sheriff pulled up and told us to get out while we still could."

I swallowed.

"Oh shit."

"We turned them loose," she said sadly. "Hopefully they'll make it. Farmers up and down the valley are setting their livestock free and hoping for the best."

"So I guess we'll see you in Okanogan?" I asked.

"Yes. I'll get the girls from you, and then we'll figure out what we're going to do."

"Love you," I said.

"Love you, too. Drive safe."

GAGE

We met up with Carrie in the Safeway parking lot in Okanogan.

The twins tackle-hugged her, and then she tackle-hugged Tinker. Everyone seemed to be crying, but I was just relieved we'd made it out of there. Pulling out my phone, I walked around the side of the truck for some privacy, then checked my messages.

There was a text from Pic saying they'd arrived safe, and that they'd be heading out for Coeur d'Alene soon. That one had come through an hour ago. I messaged him back.

> ME: In Okanogan. Grabbing food and then we start for CDA. Please have the girls pull together some things for Tinker her dad and her neighbor lady.

Suddenly someone hit me from behind, arms wrapping tight around my body in a powerful squeeze. My instincts were to slam the attacker against the truck, but somehow I managed to control myself long enough to realize she wasn't a threat.

"Thank you," Carrie sobbed against my back. "Thank you so

much for saving my babies. I was so scared, but I knew Tinker would get them out. And you helped her. I'm so sorry for the way I hated you and thought you were horrible. I don't care who you are. All I care is that my babies are alive and I will never, ever forget what you did today."

For such a tiny little thing she was strong, and it took me a couple seconds to pry her hands free. Then I turned toward her and got a second hug, this one head on. Tinker stood just behind her, tears streaming down her face.

"We made it out," she said, holding my gaze. "Thank you, Gage."

"You'd have made it out without me," I told her. She shrugged.

"I'd like to think so," she said, and she sounded exhausted. "But the fact is, when I needed you, you were there."

"That's what we do," I said simply.

"We?"

"The Reapers," I answered. "When we need each other, we're there. And you're with me, now. Tinker. You never need to be alone again."

Carrie loosened her grip, pulling away. "I think you're hugging the wrong woman."

Tinker smiled, then stepped toward me as I pulled her into my arms. For what might've been the first time in her life, Carrie showed some discretion and walked about around the truck to give us some privacy. I leaned down, smelling her hair.

Smoke this time. No peaches.

"Did all that really happen?" Tinker asked against my chest. "It's like something out of a movie."

"Yeah, I'm pretty sure it happened," I said, although I knew what she meant. The day felt like some strange nightmare, unconnected from reality.

"Now what do we do?" she asked, looking up at me. "Carrie and Darren are heading to stay with relatives in Spokane. If you're driving back to Coeur d'Alene, would you be willing to drop us off there? She doesn't have much room in the car. It's full of stuff from her aunt's place."

"Hell, no," I told her, narrowing my eyes. "You're coming home with me. I already messaged the club—they'll pull together everything you need. You'll stay in Coeur d'Alene at my place until it's safe to go home."

"Are you sure?" she asked. "I mean, I know we've slept together a few times, but—"

Leaning down, I caught her lips in a hard kiss, driving my tongue deep because the woman obviously shouldn't be allowed to talk any more, not if she planned on staying crazy shit like that. The kiss wasn't long enough, not even close, but by the time I pulled back her eyes were dazed and her lips were swollen.

"We're going to Coeur d'Alene," I told her. "And then we'll figure shit out. Got it?"

Tinker nodded, then gave me a slow smile.

"Got it," she whispered, and I kissed her again.

It took an hour to get everyone transferred and settled. Tom and Mary Webbly were both exhausted, so we pulled out the bunk and let them sleep while we went shopping for some food for the road. The store was full of refugees, and everywhere I looked I saw the exhausted faces of people I'd met over the past few weeks. Then we climbed back into the truck and pulled out, Tinker collapsing on the seat next to me, her face drawn and tight even in sleep.

Fuck, I thought, watching as the yellow stripes of the highway disappeared behind us. Driving this thing was like driving a tank.

I was really gonna miss my bike.

Of course, I'd have missed Tinker a hell of a lot more, and there was a Harley dealership in Spokane full of bikes just like mine, and some a whole lot nicer. Reaching over, I touched her hair, running my fingers through it. God, she was beautiful.

Yeah, fuck the bike. All I needed was right here.

CHAPTER TWENTY-FIVE

ONE WEEK LATER
TINKER

I sat outside on Gage's deck, watching as a flock of wild turkeys wandered below me on the hillside. I'd been enchanted the first time I saw them, until I smelled their shit. It was rotten, like something dead. Not only that, cleaning it up was a real bitch. The stuff was so sludgy that you couldn't scoop it, but way too solid to spray off with the hose.

That was one part of north Idaho that I didn't like.

So far it was the only part.

We'd had some incredible things happen over the past week, that was for sure. For one, the Reaper women were really nice. I don't know what I'd expected—probably older versions of Talia or Sadie. But these women formed a strong sisterhood that'd wrapped around me like a welcoming blanket. They'd pounced as soon as we'd pulled in, handing over bags of clean clothing, toiletries, and gift cards to buy anything else we might need. Yes, they were tough and some of them looked a little dangerous. But they were also sweet and smart and funny, and so welcoming it made my heart hurt.

And they loved Gage.

When he'd called the club his family, I hadn't quite understood what he meant. I'd grown up with my mom and dad, and some distant cousins who lived down south in Utah. Every other year we got together for friendly but subdued campouts halfway between the two homes. The Reapers were a loud, outgoing swarm of familial love that'd built a protective a fortress around everyone who belonged to them, and I realized fast that so far as they were concerned, that included me. It also included my dad and Mary Webbly.

Maybe they were really that nice, or maybe natural disasters just bring out the best in people, but either way, I'd never experienced such hospitality in my life.

The north Idaho landscape was beautiful, too, although even this far from home the air was full of smoke. I'd seen the satellite images on TV—it looked like a bomb had hit Washington State. Hellish pictures filled the news, and several young firefighters lost their lives when their truck broke down, the flames overtaking them.

As for Hallies Falls, we knew about half the town had burned, but we didn't know which half. Darren had tried going back to assess the damage, but he got turned back by the state patrol. Even now, more firefighters from around the world were arriving to help, some coming all the way from Australia and New Zealand.

Tomorrow would be a big day.

They'd be opening the town for residents to return and check on their property, although we weren't supposed to stay overnight. After a week of uncertainty, we'd finally learn whether the apartment building still stood.

Whether I had a home.

"You ready?" Gage asked, coming out to sit next to me on the lounger. He lived in a two-bedroom condo above the river, furnished entirely in bachelor. Giant TV, comfy couches, no plants. It was nicer than the apartment I'd given him—a *lot* nicer. I felt kind of sheepish about that.

"For tomorrow, you mean?"

"Yeah," he said, nuzzling my neck.

"I'm scared," I admitted. "Of what we'll find. Or won't find, for that matter. I'm so appreciative, though, to you and your club. For everything. Dad's in heaven, by the way. I know I thought it was a bad idea at the time, but he loves his room at the clubhouse. I'm starting to wonder if there's something going on with him and Mary Webbly. I don't think she's left his side since we pulled into town."

Gage grinned. "There's something. Not sure what to call it, but it's definitely there. I know it hasn't been that long since your mom passed, but—"

"If he's happy, I'm happy," I said, sighing as I leaned back into him. "He'll always love my mother, there's no question of that. But life is short, and she wouldn't want him to be alone. You have to make the most of what you're given, because none of us know how much time we have left."

"That's definitely true," he said. I had just turned my head to kiss him when the phone rang.

"Ignore it," Gage said.

"I can't," I replied, laughing. "I'm waiting on a call from the doctor. In all the confusion we left Dad's medications behind. It's been a challenge, because our family doctor is displaced and the specialist in Seattle won't prescribe without seeing him. At least we had a good record of everything on my email, thanks to all that paperwork. The doctor we saw here was fine renewing most of the scrips, but there was one Dad had been taking that was actually my mother's. Apparently it's fairly specialized, not what they'd usually recommend."

Reaching down, I grabbed the phone and slid my finger across the surface to answer.

"Ms. Garrett?" a woman asked. "This is Brenda Gottlieb. I'm a nurse at Dr. Taylor's practice, and he asked me to follow up about your father's medications."

"Thanks for calling," I said. "What's the story?"

"The drug he'd been taking—amitriptyline. You said your mother was using it for depression."

"That's what Dad told me."

"And you'd been planning to bring him to a specialist in Seattle, to talk about his cognitive function?"

"Yes."

"Dr. Taylor is concerned that the medicine may be related to that," she said. "You see, in a very small percentage of patients—less than one percent, actually—amitriptyline can cause confusion and even memory loss. He'd like you to talk to a local specialist and get your father fully evaluated. You'd said that his mental state got worse after your mother's death, when he started the meds?"

"Yes," I whispered sitting up slowly. "And he's been doing really well this week, even though he hasn't been taking it. Clearer."

"I've got a referral for you to a specialist in Spokane," she told me. "The sooner you get that evaluation done, the better. Dr. Taylor made some calls. They can get him in on Friday at eleven."

"Thank you," I said, feeling dazed.

"You're welcome," she replied. "Watch your dad and see how he's doing. The medication should be mostly out of his system by now, although it varies by person. If he continues to clear up, that's important information his doctor needs to know. It could've been causing a lot of his symptoms."

"Thank you," I repeated as she hung up the phone, stunned. Gage looked at me.

"You okay?" he asked. I nodded slowly.

"I think they just told me that Dad's memory problems might be caused by medication," I said, feeling stunned. "I mean, consider how well he's done since we got here. You'd expect him to be more confused, seeing as we evacuated so fast and nothing is familiar. But he's done really well, even in a strange place."

Gage's eyes widened.

"Damn, that'd be amazing."

"I know. I'm also too scared to hope, but it makes so much sense. According to Mary, he didn't start to fall apart until after Mom died, and that's when he started taking it. It's hard to wrap my head around."

Gage laughed. "He's a tough old bastard, no question. If anyone could pull it off, it'd be Tom."

I turned to hug him, feeling happier than I had in a long time. I still didn't know if I had a home waiting for me in Hallies Falls, but in that moment it didn't matter. I had people who cared about me. Real people. And maybe I wasn't going to lose my dad after all. It felt too good to be true, but it really did explain so much.

"I've got an idea," Gage said as I relaxed in his arms, feeling like a huge weight had been lifted.

"What's that?"

"Let's celebrate."

I raised a brow. "And how do you want to celebrate?"

"Like this," he said, pulling me over him on the lounger, resting my knees on either side of his hips. I wiggled, enjoying the feel of him between my legs, then leaned down to give him a long, slow kiss.

"I like celebrations," I whispered. "I like them a lot."

We left Dad and Mary in Coeur d'Alene early the next morning, taking Gage's pickup truck and pulling a trailer behind us. If there'd been a miracle and the house was still standing, maybe we'd be able to salvage something.

We were ten miles outside of Hallies Falls when I got a text message from Darren, showing a picture of their home. Nothing left but the garage.

"Fuck," I said, holding it out for Gage to see. His mouth tightened. "I wanted to ask him to go look at my place, but I'm scared."

"We'll be there soon enough," Gage said. "Let him focus on his family."

I nodded, looking out the window at the landscape. Poor Carrie—she'd be devastated. *They all got out alive,* I reminded myself. *That's what really matters.* The road to Hallies Falls was like something out of a war movie—scorched and barren, although some of the biggest trees still stood. We'd passed three burned-out farms, and at one point I saw a clump of cows staring at us blankly. Then we crested the hill leading down to town, and my mouth dropped.

You could see a line where the planes had dropped the red fire retardant. That must've been where the firefighters took their stand, I realized. They'd saved what they could and left the rest to burn. Half the town was blackened, buildings no more than skeletons, while the other half looked almost untouched. Well, untouched except for ash and the red stuff. My place should be right on the line between them. Straining, I tried to catch a glimpse of it, but couldn't.

"Damn," Gage said. "Looks rough down there."

I didn't answer, clenching my fists while we cruised down the hill, slowing as we reached the outskirts. On this side there was hardly any damage at all, aside from the filth and ash covering everything. People I'd known my entire life stood outside their homes, some dazed or crying while others worked with grim purpose. We passed the high school—still intact—and then cruised past where the post office used to stand. Now the building that'd stood tall for nearly a hundred years was a blackened shell.

"Rebuilding will be hard," Gage said. I stared ahead, torn between desperation to see my home and absolute terror that I'd find another blackened ruin. As Gage turned down the street I'd grown up on, we passed a burned-out house and then another. After that, though, the houses were still standing, and then I saw it.

My home.

The building was a mess.

Most of it was coated in the reddish-orange fire retardant, and the rest was covered in ash. I'd never seen anything more beautiful in my life.

"They saved it," I breathed, choking up. Gage reached over to squeeze my hand.

"Looks like it."

"Oh shit," I said, laughing nervously. "Look at your bike . . ."

We both stared at the once-proud Harley, now completely caked in reddish gook and filth.

"It's red," he said with a startled laugh. "Huh. I wasn't sure to what to expect, but I'd pictured it either burned up or like normal. Wonder if that shit comes off."

"It was insured, right?"

"Yup," he said, shaking his head slowly. "Your car's in rough shape, too."

I looked past the bike to see my Mustang. Sure enough, it was coated in the same stuff.

"We're lucky," I said, thinking of Darren and Carrie's place. Gage pulled to a stop, and I hopped out, walking slowly across the crusted lawn. The front door was open, which seemed strange. I'd been almost certain I locked it when we left. Then I walked into the living room, looking around.

"Doesn't seem like anything's been damaged."

"Check that out," Gage said. I followed his gaze to see boot prints trailing through the dining room to the kitchen. Following them, I found six empty boxes of caramels on the counter, along with a note written on a paper towel.

The kitchen door was open, and we needed a place to rest for a while. We also ate your caramels and slept in your beds. We've been fighting the fire for nearly twenty-four hours, including four hours soaking the back of your building and the others in the neighborhood to save them. Hope you don't mind.

It was signed Frank and Steve Browning.

"Wow," I said, handing it over to Gage, who raised his brows. "You know who they are?"

"No clue," I said. "Although I'll try to find out. I think I owe them more than caramels."

Gage laughed.

"Yeah, I'd say so."

I sighed. "We got really lucky here."

He looked at me, nodding. "We did."

"Gonna be a lot of work cleaning all this up," I continued.

"You still on the fence about staying in Hallies Falls?" he asked, his voice serious. I shook my head.

"No, I want to be here," I said, and it was the truth. "I didn't realize how much I loved it until I almost lost it. I know it's a small, weird town where everyone gossips . . . but it's also the kind of place where two men will fight night and day to save a stranger's home."

Gage nodded slowly, his face thoughtful.

"You'll need some help fixing things back up," he said.

"You offering?" I asked jokingly, although I couldn't look at him when I said it. What if he said no?

"Maybe," he replied, his face serious. "Not in that apartment, though. I'd like somewhere more comfortable. You know, with space to stretch out. Maybe a house."

"You could stay here with me."

"And your dad?"

I shrugged, because at the end of the day, we were a package deal. "Guess that depends on what they have to say about his medication."

"And whether Mary's ready to give him up," Gage said, cocking a brow. "You know, before all the fires, we were looking at maybe closing down the Nighthawks and starting a Reapers chapter in town. I'd be running the show. Could use an old lady to help me."

Walking over to him, I wrapped my arms around his waist.

"Old?" I asked. "I thought you liked younger women."

"I like *you*," he said, digging his fingers into my hair for a kiss. I was just sinking into it when a sudden, random thought filled my head and I jerked away.

"The car!" I said, eyes wide. Gage cocked a brow.

"What about it?"

"Carrie and Darren's place burned down," I told him, breathless. "But when I picked up the girls, I filled a bag full of their stuff. You know, jewelry and pictures and their laptop. Then I shoved it all in the trunk of the car. I need to check and see if it's still there— maybe they didn't lose everything after all!"

Pulling away from him, I ran out the door like a shot, headed for my Mustang. Then I skidded to a stop, because I had no fucking clue where I'd left the keys. Thinking frantically, I tried to remember those last few, panicked moments when we'd been running for the truck.

Had I left them in the ignition?

Pulling my sleeve up and over my hand, I wiped at the ash and fire retardant covering the window, and peered inside. Sure enough, there they were. Seconds later I had the trunk open, looking down triumphantly to see the bag of Carrie's treasures. Whipping out my phone, I called her.

"Tinker?" she said, sounding defeated and exhausted. "How is your place?"

"I think we're all right," I told her, feeling strangely guilty for my good luck. "Darren sent me the pictures of your house, though."

"It's all gone," she said. "There were a few boxes in the garage, but nothing that really mattered. I know it's silly to be so upset over losing our things—it's just stuff—but right now I feel sick."

"When I took your girls by the house to grab some clothes, I went around with a grocery bag," I told her. "I forgot all about it until now, but I grabbed your laptop and your jewelry, and a bunch of the pictures. It's not much, but you haven't lost everything. It's still here, waiting for you."

Carrie burst into tears.

"Carrie, are you all right?" I asked anxiously. She sniffled a few times, then managed to talk again.

"I'm so happy," she said. "It shouldn't matter so much but it does. The laptop has all our important information—you know, the bank accounts and insurance and stuff—and the thought of losing my grandma's ring . . . I don't even know what to say."

"Don't worry about it," I replied, holding back my own tears. "We're going to get through this. All of us. Together."

"Yes, we are," she said. "I can't believe you did that. How can I ever thank you?"

"Promise that you and Margarita will never take me out again and we'll be even."

Carrie laughed.

"I'm not sure I can keep that promise. But I'll try."

"No you won't."

She laughed again.

"No, you're right. I won't try. But I love you."

"Love you too."

GAGE

An hour later, I stood on the porch, watching as Tinker and Carrie pawed through the Mustang's trunk together, laughing like it'd been a year since they'd seen each other. Guess that made sense—the past week had felt as long as a year. My phone rang, and I pulled it out of my pocket, not recognizing the number. I answered it anyway, figuring it might be one of the brothers on a burner.

"Hey, *Gage*," Talia said. "Have to say, I liked the name Cooper better. Miss me?"

"No," I said shortly.

"See you're back in town," she continued, and I looked around, wondering if the bitch was spying on us right now. "Shame about your girlfriend's building. I was hoping it'd go up with the rest of the them, but we don't always get what we want, do you?

"What's that supposed to mean?"

She giggled. "That next time I'll have to plan better. You can't blame me, though. I've never burned down a town before. There's a learning curve."

I stilled. "What did you just say?"

"That I started the fire," she replied, her voice growing more serious. "You know, when I blew up the clubhouse—you should just be thankful I needed you out of there to set it up. Otherwise you'd have blown up, too, but I couldn't figure out how to pull it off. Burning down the town was a nice bonus, though. Marsh says hi, by the way. He wanted me to pass along a little message."

"And what's that?" I asked, eyes searching the street even as I reached for my gun. Was she out there?

"He said to tell you that if we can't have Hallies Falls, you can't either," she told me. "Oh, and Gage?"

"Yeah?"

"Fuck you."

The phone went dead, and I lowered my hand, slowly sliding it into my pocket. Sociopathic cunt. Tinker turned toward me, smiling so beautifully that it hurt, and right there I made a vow. I'd protect her. Forever. Didn't matter what happened or who I had to kill.

I'd take care of her.

I'd take care of this town, too. Cord and I needed to get together, start making plans to rebuild, because I'd be damned if I'd let them win.

EPILOGUE

NINE MONTHS LATER
HALLIES FALLS
GAGE

"Anyone got an extra pair of gloves?" Cord asked, holding up a torn leather work glove in disgust. We'd been clearing out debris from the old clubhouse for the entire morning, and while we hadn't managed to salvage much, we were making good progress overall. This was important, because nearly fifty Reapers would be pulling into town next weekend to help us put up a new building. Our goal was to raise the clubhouse in four days. Totally doable, provided we did the right prep work in advance.

"I've got some," I told him, mentally adding more work gloves to the supply list. The building hadn't been covered by insurance, but we'd gotten a lot of support from the other chapters. Between their fundraising and our sweat equity, things were looking good. Walking over to my truck, I opened the tool box in the back, digging through as I searched for the gloves. Like everything in Hallies Falls these days, the truck was filthy. No matter how much we cleaned, the soot and ash clung to everything.

There were signs of life though, too.

New grass poked through the barren landscape, and the other

day I'd seen a deer and her fawn carefully picking their way down a hillside. The sound of construction filled the air, and while we'd lost a huge chunk of the population, people were starting to come back and rebuild.

My phone rang, and I pulled off my glove, tucking it under my arm as I answered.

Tinker.

"Hey babe. We're getting good work done here—"

"It's time."

I froze. "What? But I thought we had a couple more weeks?"

"Apparently not," she said, her voice full of excitement. "Meet me at the hospital, okay? And shower first. Carrie's driving me and we're leaving now."

"Okay," I said, feeling almost dizzy. Fuck. It was too early. I still had so much to do, we hadn't even finished painting the back bedroom, and . . . *crap*. This was happening. It was really happening. I had to pull my shit together, and fast. "All right. I'm headed to the house now. Is your dad with you, or should I give him a ride?"

"He's with me," she said, sounding happier than I'd ever heard her. "I can't tell who's more excited, me or him."

"Drive safe," I told her, but she'd already hung up. Then I turned to look at Cord, who'd come to stand next to me, a puzzled expression on his face.

"Everything okay?" he asked. I nodded slowly, trying to think.

"Yeah. The baby's coming."

"Now? But don't you have a couple—?"

"Apparently nobody explained that to the kid," I told him. "Stubborn already. I'm so fucked."

Cord grinned at me, then slapped my back.

"Yeah, you really are."

An hour and a half later I pulled into the Mid-Valley Hospital parking lot. I'd taken the fastest shower on record, but even pushing the upper edges of the speed limit, it still took a while to reach

Omak. The whole thing still felt surreal, but also exciting. Tinker had been sending me updates every five minutes, and I could sense her mix of excitement and nerves.

She'd been waiting for this day her entire life, but she was scared, too. No matter how many times they told her the baby was perfectly healthy, she kept remembering Tricia.

All the ultrasounds looked great, though, which was a good thing. I wasn't sure she could survive losing another child.

Tom Garrett met me in the lobby, leading the way to the maternity wing, smiling broadly the entire time. He was a thousand times better since he'd gotten off the meds. He still had his moments, of course, but we didn't have to worry about him being alone anymore. Not that it was a big problem these days—he and Mary spent almost every minute together. When we'd told them about the baby, Mary had announced he'd be moving in with her to give us space, and that was the end of that.

"How's she doing?" I asked, wiping my hands on my pants. Nervous sweat. Fuck. Kid wasn't even born yet, but this whole father thing had me scared shitless.

"Great," Tom said. "Tinker's in with her. The labor's going fast, especially for a first baby. And I have good news—she said you could be in the labor room if you want. So long as you stay up by her head. Guess she doesn't want you seeing more than you need to."

I swallowed, not sure how I felt about that. Tom laughed, seeing right through me.

"Do it, son," he said. "I was there when Tinker was born. Back in those days they didn't like having the father in the room, but Tricia was stubborn as hell. After an hour of arguing, they wised up and realized they should go ahead and give her what she wanted.

We signed in at the birthing center, which had impressive security. I liked that—meant some freak wouldn't be able to walk off with our little girl. Then they opened the doors and Tom led the way to the birthing suite, and I heard a woman crying out.

"Stay strong, son," Tom said, chuckling. "It's not you who has to do the heavy lifting today."

He knocked on the door, and Janelle Baxter opened it, her face tight with strain.

"Hey, Gage," she said. "Sadie said you could come in, but she'd like you to stay up by her head. There's a sheet, and if you happen to see too much, just don't say anything about it, okay? This is a tough day for her."

"She's a brave young woman," I said, meeting her gaze. "How's she holding up?"

"Good," Janelle responded. "It'll be hard on her, I think we all know that. But it's also the right decision. She isn't having second thoughts."

I swallowed, nodding my head. Tinker and I had discussed the possibility, of course, but neither of use liked thinking about it.

Inside the room, Sadie was on a bed that'd been tilted way up, with a bar hanging over it for her to hold on to. The midwife was sitting on stool between her widespread legs, and Tinker stood next to her, holding her hand. The midwife glanced up.

"Just in time," she said. "This baby's excited to be born—first births usually don't go half this fast."

Sadie was panting, her face utterly focused.

"There's another one coming," she gasped.

"Go ahead and give me a big push," the midwife said. "Her head is just starting to crown. We're getting closer, Sadie girl. You're doing a great job."

"Mom, come hold my other hand," Sadie said, and if she saw me, she didn't give any sign.

I'd been a member of the Reapers MC for a long time, and over the years I'd seen a lot of shit. Brave men, strong men. Men who gave everything for the club. I can tell you with all honesty, though, that I never met any man stronger than Sadie Baxter was that day. I mean, I knew giving birth was hard. But knowing it and seeing it for yourself, well, that's a different thing entirely. I lost track of time as Sadie pushed, shoving our baby into the world inch by inch. Sweat ran down her face, but she clutched hands with her mom and Tinker and she *pushed.*

It wasn't fast and it wasn't easy, but half an hour later our baby girl finally slid out into the midwife's hands.

She came into the world pissed off, which seemed only fair, given how she'd been conceived. We'd never know who fathered her, and I couldn't have cared less. When the midwife lifted that bright red, angry, smelly little miracle up and she screamed at all of us, I knew she'd be a survivor, just like Sadie.

"Do you want to hold her?" the midwife asked Sadie. She nodded, and I saw Tinker flinch. Yes, we'd signed all the papers. Sadie hadn't wavered in her determination to give up her baby through the entire pregnancy, but we'd gone into this knowing it could happen.

"Yes," Sadie whispered, glancing at Tinker. "Just once. I want to hold her once. Then I'll give her to her mother, okay?"

The midwife nodded, her face full of compassion as she pulled Sadie's gown open, laying the infant on her chest. Sadie's arms circled her, and she leaned down, nuzzled the small, damp head covered in a shock of black hair. Tinker stepped back, and I came to stand behind her, wrapping my arms around her waist.

"Would you like us to clear the room?" the midwife asked, and we all held our breath.

Then Sadie shook her head.

"No," she said, looking up at Tinker. "You know I'll always love her. But she's your baby, not mine. I'm not ready . . . No. Just take her now. Before I change my mind."

Tinker moved forward, hesitantly lifting the child into her arms. Leaning over, I took in the tiny nose and small, angry eyes. What a little fireball. I reached down, touching her soft cheek. She smacked at me with one little hand, but when my finger touched her lips she opened them, sucking it in hard.

"She's strong," Tinker whispered.

"Yeah, she is."

"I'd like you to leave now," Sadie said, and I looked over to find her lying back on the bed, head turned away from us. "I don't think I can watch."

"Of course," a nurse said, and she led Tinker out of the room. I followed, touching Janelle's shoulder as I passed. She caught my hand, giving it a squeeze.

"I'll take good care of her," she said. "And you take good care of my grandbaby."

"That's a promise," I said. Then I walked across the hallway to the other room, wondering how the hell a man as bad as me could've gotten so damned lucky.

Tinker looked up as I walked in, a smile wreathing her face.

"I think we should name her Joy," she said. "Because that's how I feel right now."

Joy.

I liked the sound of it.

Liked the sound of it a lot.

TWENTY-TWO YEARS LATER
TINKER

"Are you ready for this?" Gage asked, looking me over as I walked into living room. "You look gorgeous."

I swirled, showing off the dark blue gown I'd chosen. Thankfully, our girl had let me pick my own dress, one that flattered me, which wasn't a surprise. All she'd wanted was a simple wedding surrounded by the people she loved. We'd decorated the courtyard gazebo my father had built, and while I'd lost him nearly ten years ago, whenever I saw it, I felt his presence.

When Joy told us she wanted to get married under it, I swear, I heard him laughing all the way from heaven.

Outside, the guests were already sitting in neat rows of folding chairs, and we'd hired a string quartet to play during the ceremony. I'd considered catering it myself, but Carrie convinced me to hire it out instead. She told me I should be worrying about Joy that day, not food, and as usual she was right.

Now Joy was upstairs, putting the final touches on her makeup. Gage would walk her out through the front door of the house, across the lawn and then up to the gazebo through the narrow aisle we'd created with the chairs. There he'd be giving her away to En-rique Saldivar—quite possibly the bravest young man who'd ever lived, because even when Gage and his Reaper brothers growled at him, he still kept coming around.

They were so in love.

Carrie walked in from the kitchen, looking me over.

"You look good," she said. "But don't let Gage kiss you. That'll ruin your makeup. Sadie is here, along with Janelle. They're in the kitchen. She asked if she could see Joy before she goes out."

Gage raised one scarred brow, a souvenir of a brutal attack he'd survived seventeen years ago, but he didn't comment. It'd been an open adoption. Strained at times, but we'd done our best to give Joy a good life, and part of that had been realizing that Sadie had a role to play, even if she couldn't be her mother.

"I'll go check with her," I said, heading up the stairs.

Joy was in our bedroom, surrounded by her bridesmaids as she twirled, showing off her gown in the standing mirror I kept in the corner.

"Hey Mom," she said happily as I walked in. "I can't believe it! Is it time yet?"

"Almost," I said, smiling. "But I need to talk to you first. Girls, can you give us a minute?"

The gaggle scattered, giddy with excitement. Joy turned to me.

"If you want to talk about sex, Enrique and I have been sleeping together for three years," she said dryly. I rolled my eyes.

"No. I wanted to let you know that Sadie Baxter is downstairs. Along with her mother, Janelle. They were hoping to see you before the wedding. I said I'd ask."

Joy grew thoughtful, and she cocked her head at me. "You know that you're my mother, right?"

"Of course," I said, smiling. "I also know she gave birth to you, and she still loves you. But it's your wedding day and you should get to make your own choices. Just tell me what you want and I'll make it happen."

Joy nodded slowly.

"I think it'd be okay," she said. "But I'd like you to stay in the room. Is that all right?"

"Of course, baby. Whatever you need."

With that, I left to find Carrie waiting for me at the bottom of the stairs.

"Send them up," I told her. Minutes later, Sadie and Janelle climbed up the stairs, meeting me in the hallway. Sadie looked good—she'd really made something of herself over the years. It'd taken a while, but once she got away from Hallies Falls things had started to come together. We'd helped her through college and now she had a good job as an accountant in Wenatchee.

"Thanks for this, Tinker," she said. "I don't want to horn in on your special day, but I really wanted to see her."

I nodded, then knocked on the door.

"Come in!" Joy called, and I pushed it open. Sadie walked in and stopped, staring at the vision that was my daughter.

"You're beautiful," she whispered, her voice trembling.

"Thank you," Joy said, smiling. "It's almost time. Was there something in particular you wanted to talk about, or did you just want to say hello?"

Sadie laughed. "I was hoping you'd let me give you a present. Something old, unless you've already got that covered."

"There's always room for more good luck," Joy replied, and Sadie held out a jewelry box. Joy opened it, pulling out a small pin with a pretty, polished rock on it. It wasn't anything special, and from the look on her face I could tell she was confused. So was I.

"I found that outside the hospital," Sadie said, blinking rapidly. "The day after you were born. It was in the parking lot. I don't think it's worth anything, but I liked it. For a long time I kept it in my pocket. Sort of my way of remembering you. I'd rub it when I was feeling tired or sad, and think about all the amazing things you'd be able to do when you grew up. A few years back I took a jewelry making class and turned it into a pin. I realize it doesn't go with your dress, but it's just small. I was hoping that maybe you'd pin it under your skirts somewhere—just so a little piece of me could be with you when you walk down the aisle. You're not my daughter, but I've never stopped loving you and I never will."

Tears welled up in her eyes, and Joy shot me a look. I nodded, letting her know that it wouldn't bother me.

"Would you like to help me pin it on, Sadie?" Joy asked, and Sadie nodded. Joy lifted her skirts, and Sadie knelt down next to her, fastening it to the petticoat underneath.

Then someone knocked on the door.

"It's time," Carrie said. "They're all waiting for you."

Joy gave me a sudden, panicked look and I laughed.

"You've been sleeping with him for three years," I reminded her, my voice echoing hers earlier. "I think you'll be okay. Now let's get downstairs before your father gets bored and decides to go for a ride or something."

The look on Gage's face as Joy came down the stairs would stay with me for the rest of my life.

He'd seen the dress before, of course—he'd paid for it, after all—but still . . . it was different this time.

"You look beautiful, little girl," he said, holding out his arm for her. "Are you sure you want to marry that kid? I don't think he's good enough for you."

"He's the only man I've ever met who will put up with you," she said sharply. "You better take what you can get or you'll be stuck with me forever."

From the lawn, I heard the music start, and the bridesmaids began lining up.

"Time to get our asses outside," Carrie told me. Usually the mother of the bride would be escorted by an usher or family member, but Carrie had insisted on walking me down herself, and who was I to argue? Together we held hands, offering each other a tight squeeze, and then I gave my husband and daughter one last look.

My perfect family. Today everything changed, but I could handle that. Enrique was a good boy, and she loved him.

Joy winked at me, then glanced toward the window.

"It's time, Mom. They're all waiting. You lead the way."

AUTHOR'S NOTE

When I started writing this book in 2015, Washington State was suffering from the worst fire season in its recorded history. By late June, more than 313 wildfires were already burning across the region. Many of these merged into massive fire complexes, including the Okanogan Complex, the largest single fire in state history. On August 19, three firefighters were killed when their vehicle crashed and was overtaken by the flames. President Obama declared a federal emergency that same week, on August 21.

Around that time, my family had planned a trip to Mount Rainier, to be followed by a visit to the Okanogan and Methow regions to research this book. I remember sitting on the deck of my brother's cabin, writing as small white flakes of ash fell across my keyboard. We didn't have full access to the news, but when my brother called later that night to tell me I should cancel the rest of my trip, I wasn't surprised. The interstate (I-90) was already shut down, as were many state highways. We eventually made our way home by following smaller roads. At times, I could hardly see where I was driving because of all the smoke.

That summer and fall, so much smoke covered eastern Washington and northern Idaho (where I live) that the sky was orange during the day, and you couldn't see the sun. Children had to stay inside, and sporting events were canceled. The smoke reached as far north as Calgary, Alberta, where dangerous levels of ozone and particulates were measured at ground level. These massive plumes covered thousands of square miles.

Closer to the fires, residents were forced to evacuate, and I remember watching as the emergency alerts came out, ratcheting up the levels as the situation grew more critical. Enormous planes (DC-10s) flew low over the town of Chelan, dropping red fire retardant on homes as the people evacuated. Just like Carrie's fictional aunt in *Reaper's Fire*, many rural residents had no choice but to turn their livestock free and hope for the best.

By October, more than a million acres had burned as three thousand firefighters, the Washington State National Guard, and the U.S. Army fought to save homes and lives. Joining them were fire crews from many states. There were even fire managers who came all the way from Australia and New Zealand, including some of those who fought the Black Saturday bushfires. As in the book, the governor also called upon residents to volunteer.

The closest thing I've ever experienced to this event was the eruption of Mount St. Helens, which happened when I was a very small child. I hope I never see anything like it again.

Because I was so deeply impacted by this natural disaster during the writing of *Reaper's Fire*, I made a deliberate decision to adjust the series timeline slightly to accommodate its inclusion. I just couldn't see how a book that took place within the fire zone could be written without including the events of last summer. This change doesn't effect the content, story line, or internal consistency of any individual book, but it did create a slight discrepancy within the larger series timeline. Ultimately, the goal of fiction is to tell a good story, and sometimes that means bending the rules. I hope you enjoyed reading Tinker and Gage's story.

Joanna Wylde is the *New York Times* bestselling author of the Reapers Motorcycle Club novels, including *Reaper's Fall* and *Reaper's Stand*, and the Silver Valley series, including *Silver Bastard*. Visit her online at joannawylde.net, facebook.com/joannawyldebooks, and twitter.com/joannawylde.